CHILDREN OF
LIGHT
AND
SHADOW

RYAN KIRK

OLIVER·HEBER·BOOKS

PUBLISHER'S NOTE: This is a work of fiction. Names, characters, places, and incidents either are the product of the author's imagination or are used fictitiously. Any resemblance to actual persons, living or dead, business establishments, events, or locales is entirely coincidental.

Children of Light and Shadow Copyright 2025 © Ryan Kirk

Cover design by Covers by JV Arts

Published by Oliver-Heber Books

0 9 8 7 6 5 4 3 2 1

PROLOGUE

The man who had come to destroy the city emerged from a perfectly circular hole in the air that closed behind him immediately, as though it knew what was coming and wanted to disappear before the disaster unfolded. The man, who was only wearing the shape of a man out of an overabundance of caution, blinked and shielded his eyes from the glaring spring sun, so much brighter than the skies he'd come from.

In the time between breaths, he thrust out his senses and drank deeply of the information they poured into his spirit. Adani, as they called it here, flowed freely through the land, taking advantage of the channels humanity had both carved and cared for. It ran underneath his feet, danced and echoed through the buildings surrounding him, and burned within the spirits of the humans that walked the streets, still unaware of his presence.

His spirit returned before it warned the adanists of their fate. Servants had walked among the humans for years before the emissary was summoned, and their reports had painted a picture of a society advancing quickly, but completely unprepared for the war bearing down upon them. They lacked the awareness to even guess at the danger approaching.

But the Debru had once thought themselves superior, too, until the resourceful adanists had evolved quickly enough to defeat them.

Superiority was never guaranteed. History taught them all that powers rose and fell. Nothing lasted forever, and no one was invincible.

Thus, the emissary's arrival, scheduled long before the adanists could pose a threat.

Chaos reigned up and down the street. Twenty paces ahead, three children ran freely, passing some sort of leather-wrapped ball between them. To his right, two women discussed the perceived failings of their husbands. Behind him, a merchant carefully balanced a set of plates on one hand while opening the door to his shop with the other. Down an alley cloaked in shadows, a young man squeezed his eyes shut and clapped his hands over his ears to muffle the sounds of the street. His stomach rumbled and his head pounded like a drum, both just rewards for his love of drink. Behind closed doors, a woman slapped her child across the face and called him names, accusing the child of failing to live up to the standards of the father they both knew would never return.

All of this and more crashed against his senses, and he ground his teeth together.

No adanists wandered nearby, despite the number of people around him. Such strength burned just beyond their reach, but none possessed the discipline to stretch out their hands to grasp it, guide it, and change their world. No matter, it made his task all the easier. He'd been in this hell for what felt like an eternity, but no one had noticed him yet. Their petty concerns shrunk the sphere of their awareness down to a small bubble that barely extended beyond their skin.

A pathetic lot, but fortunately for them, he brought mercy.

He raised his hand, not because he needed to, but because he wanted to be noticed, wanted to be recognized by these lesser creatures before completing his task. The sudden motion drew attention from every corner. One boy dropped the ball as the pass intended for him bounced off his chest. The startled merchant dropped his plates, and the sound of them shattering against the street was as close to music to the emissary's ears as anything in this world could be. The women let out a collective yelp.

The emissary basked in the moment, briefer than the beat of a human heart, and then he brought forth his power from the depths of his spirit and clenched his fist. A sphere appeared above his head, a marble of perfect darkness about as large as a human head. It hungered, a negative space eager to swallow all the light and warmth in the world. Like a monster of indescribable size breathing in deep, the sphere pulled everything in the city toward it.

Buildings bent as they cracked like saplings in a storm. People were picked off their feet, granted the gift of flight for a few precious moments before their lives abruptly ended. Everything within hundreds of paces raced toward him, eager to accept the message of salvation he had dutifully carried between the worlds.

Then he opened his hand, and for the briefest of moments, all was still, a silent promise of the world soon to come.

None inside the radius of his attack were sensitive enough to notice, but it wasn't buildings, bodies, and air that he pulled toward him, but the energies of the world itself. The debris that followed was nothing more than a consequence. He collected, added plenty of his considerable strength, focused, and released.

As the blast spread away from his body, he idly wondered if this world had ever seen anything similar. It had a long history, but he suspected the answer was no. Their advances, while sometimes rapid, remained meager. They didn't yet understand the true nature of the powers they dabbled with.

His blast wasn't simply compressed air. It was a fire as hot as those that burned within the stars. As it expanded, it consumed everything it touched. Stone, clay, and flesh vanished, broken down instantly into dust and energy the emissary's attack consumed with an insatiable hunger.

He put the period on his message by closing his fist again. The blast vanished in the blink of an eye, leaving buildings and bodies half destroyed. All that remained of the city, for hundreds of paces in every direction, was a fine layer of dust that slowly settled on the perfectly flat, barren soil.

He allowed himself a small smile. It was not his place to bring peace to this world. In truth, this world wouldn't know peace for a very long time. But for this small fragment of the world, the pain and suffering that walked hand in hand with chaos was over.

He sat down in the center of the destruction and waited. One last task remained, but it was not his place to initiate it.

HE'D BEEN PREPARED to wait, but even he was surprised at how long it took the adanists to discover their courage and fulfill their duty. The wandering clans appeared first, not with their bodies but with their senses, and their adani explored the destruction he'd wrought. He greeted them with open arms. He revealed a glimpse of his power, and their adani fled without a word.

No matter. His message would reach the clans, but it would be carried by the messengers he anointed. A handful of training grounds littered the city, and he'd been careful not to destroy any of them, but it was still two full days before the local adanists attacked. Bound spears of adani fell from the sky, golden light shining brightly beneath the dark clouds that threatened rain.

He wiped the spears away with a thought. None among the gathered adanists had ascended, so there was nothing to fear. They tried again and yet again, and each time, he swept the attacks away. Eventually, they retreated, and he resumed his wait.

He could have gone to them, of course, but that wasn't the

point. True submission was voluntary, and so he waited until they came to him and bent the knee.

It took three more days and two more attacks, but they finally came, as he knew they would. They sent one of their elders, either because they valued her wisdom or because they considered her the most expendable. Regardless, he respected their chosen dignitary. For all she knew, she approached her end, but she walked with a determined stride, her head held high. She would serve him well as his chosen messenger, even if she didn't know it yet.

He gestured for her to sit across from him, and she did. She sat tall, her back straight and her eyes stabbing daggers into his. Her gray hair had started to turn white, and what little adani she possessed flowed smoothly through her body.

"Who are you?" she asked.

"Who I am isn't important. You may refer to me as an emissary, for I represent a power far greater than my own meager gifts."

She didn't press further, accepting the truths he delivered without question. She'd already accepted his dominion, though she would deny it to her dying breath. "What do you want?"

That was the question he'd been waiting for, and he told her, laying out in no small detail all the ways her life was about to change. She argued, protested, and pleaded, but the emissary was unmoved. His arrival was not a negotiation, nor was it the opening strike in a long war. It was a declaration.

This world belonged to him.

They would rebel, especially the wanderers. They always did, at first, but it wouldn't matter. The world was his, and by the time his body turned to mist and he vanished, returning to his own dark skies, the adanist he'd spoken to believed it as well. Before, she'd been nothing special, but now she was first among the converted and she would spread the word.

He was pleased.

1

Bael whooped as the dragon dove into the narrow valley between two mountains. He gripped the dragon's scales tightly and leaned forward so the rush of wind wouldn't pull him from his seat. Shayna wrapped her arms more tightly around his waist and leaned against his back, protecting herself from the blast of cold mountain air.

His whoop was echoed by several friends circling safely high above, and Bael's grin spread across his face as the valley rushed up to meet him. The dragon's heart pounded fiercely, and its adani pulsed the same. He hadn't bothered to remember the dragon's name, for tomorrow he'd fly a different dragon, but he sensed in this one a kindred spirit, a desire to push beyond the boundaries that ruled a daily, mundane existence.

Bael had no time to spare a thought for those who remained among the clouds. The slightest mistake now would see him, the love of his life, and the dragon, broken on the jagged and unforgiving rock below. The dragon shifted slightly as it sensed a crosscurrent of wind, and Bael urged it to push its nose down farther, to dive faster. They'd need every bit of speed at the end of the valley.

The dragon hesitated as its rider demanded it essentially drop out of the sky, but like most beings, it bent to Bael's will and dove faster, wind screaming over outstretched wings. They dropped into the crack faster than a falling stone, and the endless open skies to either side of the dragon's wings vanished, replaced by granite walls that had been old when this dragon had been born. Walls that grew narrower as they fell.

Bael's body plummeted, but his spirit soared, finally released from the endless torment of mere existence. He opened wide the connection with the heart in his core, and the world became more vivid than a dream. He felt every nuance of the wind blasting against his face, saw every crack in the granite, and heard the thump of Shayna's heart as it pounded in time to his.

If it was to be him against the world, the world didn't have a chance.

The walls closed in tight up ahead, and the dragon's first instinct was to rise, but Bael demanded it stay low and fold in its wings. The dragon's spirit argued, but bent, unable to resist the sheer force of Bael's will. It made one last adjustment, then folded its wings tight against its body and surrendered.

They shot through the gap faster than any arrow had ever flown, and even Bael's heart skipped a beat as he surrendered himself to the hands of fate. They were through the first narrows faster than the blink of an eye and the dragon gratefully spread its wings.

Again, Bael forced the creature to dive at a steeper angle. They needed speed. Needed commitment. He'd chosen this line because the only way through was to give everything. Anything less meant either failure or death, both of which carried equal weight in Bael's world. The dragon fought against his demands, but only for a moment.

Up ahead, the canyon narrowed again, this time for a far longer stretch. The dragon made a small adjustment, banking slightly to the left to straighten out their line. Once they hit the last part of the canyon, they wouldn't be able to adjust their flight even a little. Bael asked for a bit more angle, and the dragon obeyed, its regret at this decision now clear. They were moving fast, but Bael worried it wasn't yet fast enough. Their momentum alone had to carry them through the gap.

Then it was too late to change anything, and the dragon folded in its wings once again, and like an arrow launched from a bow, they could do nothing but trust in their aim.

The walls rushed together, like a giant hand squeezing them from both sides. Though they had a pace, or maybe two, on each side, if Bael reached out with his hand the rushing walls would tear his arm off. He couldn't breathe, his body frozen, and he used his heart-aided senses to soak in every fear-drenched moment.

Their angle hadn't been perfect. The wall on Bael's left grew too close, and his eyes grew wide. As soon as the dragon's folded wing brushed against the wall, it would be over. They were also too slow. Without the lift from the wings, they were falling more than flying, and they hadn't collected enough speed when they could.

Just when he was certain his life was over, the end of the valley expanded ahead, the light at the end of a tunnel, and they blasted through. The mountains receded behind them and a wide, forested valley stretched out ahead. The dragon stretched its wings, no longer regretting its choice to follow Bael. It would come, now, whenever he called, just as every adanist who circled above them did.

The sound started in his core, a storm of emotions pushing from where the heart met his body. It rose through his gut and was squeezed into a shout by his ribs. He raised his hands and whooped again, expelling everything with one shout he was sure would be heard around the world.

Shayna squeezed him even tighter, and when he turned, he saw her eyes lit with a familiar desire. He nodded, and she smiled, and he turned back around, glad she had shared this with him when no one else would. He urged the dragon higher into the sky, where his friends waited to congratulate him.

THE SPRING NIGHTS still held the memories of winter's bitter cold, and so Bael had demanded they cut down an entire tree for tonight's fire. The stars swirled overhead, the venison they'd roasted was perfectly done and seasoned to perfection by Lyla, his cup of ale was full, and Shayna was by his side as he listened to the others swapping stories about their adventures. Life was far from perfect, but there were moments that couldn't be improved on, and this was one of them.

It was often like this after he pulled off a feat that he hadn't been sure was possible. There was the excitement and nerves of planning, and the rush that came from actually performing the feat was indescribable. After, though, a calm settled over him, as though he'd spent himself completely and his spirit was exhausted.

It wasn't. If necessary, he could have risen and sparred all night, but the storm that raged constantly in his spirit was calm, and all was well.

He imagined this was what it was like to win a battle, if there were any battles left to fight.

But there weren't. He had only training, hunting, and the fulfillment of all the duties Samora, his grandmother, invented to pretend the wandering clans were busy and had a purpose.

Those around the fire tonight knew the truth. The wandering clans had become a solution to a problem that no longer existed. The cities didn't want them or need them, and though Samora and Elian spoke as though the Debru might return any day, they'd been saying the same since before Bael had been born.

They'd beaten the Debru so badly they'd never return, meaning all of Bael's training meant exactly nothing. He'd given his life to prepare for a fight that would never happen.

His friends felt the same. Not just Wolves, but Bears, Coyotes, and Hounds all joined him tonight. Their bond wasn't of blood or oath, but of understanding. Of seeking. Of finding purpose in a purposeless world. He'd much rather have them by his side than his Wolves, who still looked up to his grandmother as though she could do no wrong.

It wasn't that he didn't respect Samora. She was beyond any doubt one of the most skilled adanists in the world, and someone he often turned to when he couldn't learn a specific technique. But she had no vision for the future.

Or, he supposed, because he was in a good mood, she had once had a vision for the future, but it had already come to pass. Humanity had recovered from the blow the Debru had landed, and that was due, in no small part, to her efforts. But now that they had recovered, she didn't know what came next. They kept to the traditions that had served them well in the past, but there seemed little need for them in this new age.

Shayna squeezed his leg. She knew better than to ask his thoughts, for he'd shared them with her often. "You still with us?"

He appreciated that about her. These days, it seemed too easy to let his thoughts wander away, but she kept him focused, kept him grounded. He put his hand on top of hers. "Still here."

It was rare, he thought, to find someone who didn't merely endure him when his temper took hold, but someone who guided him through his darkest moments, someone who followed him, even down the mouth of a narrow valley at fatal speeds. Every warrior around this fire reminded him how lucky he was, but he'd sacrifice them all if it meant saving Shayna.

"So, what's next?" Lyla asked him from across the fire. "Thinking about diving straight down the throat of a dragon?"

Bael grinned and threw his hands up high. "Who knows what madness will seize me next? I have nothing on my mind except this time together tonight and our hunt tomorrow. I am sure, though, by the time we all gather again in the autumn, I'll have thought of something special."

Drinks were raised into the air, a silent toast made, and then poured down endlessly thirsty throats. As Bael looked around the circle, an idea struck him. This group of friends had grown over the years and now numbered more than a hundred strong. Few commonalities existed between them. Most were about Bael's age, warriors of their respective clans now for close to a decade, but others were older. Many were ascended, but not all. They were tied together not out of duty or obligation, but out of choice, out of the knowledge, burning in their spirits brighter than tonight's bonfire, that they were meant for more. Perhaps the time had come for them to seek "more" out.

He leaned over so he could whisper into Shayna's ear. "Do you think Grandmother would allow us to become our own clan?"

An absurd idea at first glance, and Shayna's eyes widened at the thought. "Is that even possible?"

"There's no rule against it. And if the traditionalists argue, we can always claim we're bringing the Spiders back. I'm not sure how it would be much different than when Grandmother and Grandfather split off from the Bears and reestablished the Wolves. They'd become numerous enough and strong enough to form their own clan again. I look around this circle and I wonder if we've accomplished the same."

Shayna considered the question seriously, revealing a side of herself that few saw firsthand but that Bael appreciated more with every passing day. Many in the clans who followed Bael assumed Shayna was enthralled by him, that she would follow him without question no matter what he decided. And though it may seem that way, nothing was farther from the truth. Yes, she followed him because she believed in him, but that belief was only one part intuition, backed up by three parts reason.

"You should," Shayna decided. "Not only would it be good for the other adanists, it would be good for you to bear the burdens of clan leadership, which you won't get with the Wolves for many years."

As easy as that, Bael had decided, too. If she believed in him, he would, too.

They wandered away from the campfire, eventually, stomachs full and steps unsteady. But instead of returning to their tent, they found a patch of soft grass where they could spread out their clothes and lie together under the stars. True wanderers didn't even need tents, and as he fell asleep that night, Bael was convinced his life was about to change forever.

HE WOKE to the feeling of his core being torn from the inside out, as though some giant bear from the mountains had found him sleeping and dug in deep with its claws. He swung at the air and reached for adani, instincts searching for the enemy, but his fists struck only empty air and adani told him that only Shayna was nearby.

Her eyes flashed open a moment after his as she wrapped her arms around her gut. She groaned through gritted teeth, and Bael couldn't get his legs to listen, as though something had cut the connection between his spirit and his limbs.

As quickly as the sensation struck, it passed and Bael was on his feet looking in all four directions for the source of the attack. The rolling hills they'd made their camp upon were as peaceful as they'd been the night before, the greatest threat the songbirds singing their love songs to their neighbors.

He pulled Shayna to her feet, and with a nod of her head, she let him know that she was unharmed.

"Any idea what that was?" she asked.

He shook his head. The attack hadn't been upon him, but upon his world. The echoes of it still reverberated in his bones.

"Gather everyone," he said. "I think we're at war."

2

Samora was standing in the elder dragon's cave when the attack struck like lightning on a clear day. The intricate web of protective adani that she'd woven throughout the rock absorbed and dampened the worst of the attack, but the adani running through her body was still pulled and pushed like a fallen leaf on a windy day. Bile rose in her throat, but she shoved it down as she leaned against the nearest wall for support. The violence only lasted a moment, but its brevity didn't ease any of the fears that suddenly found fertile soil deep in her spirit. She stumbled toward the cave's entrance, her legs not quite convinced they wanted to obey her commands. She met Aldrick halfway as he ran from the entrance deeper into the cave to find her.

That he had felt it, too, meant the attack had been every bit as strong as she feared. His sensitivity to adani had grown over their decades together, but he'd chosen to never ascend, rightfully certain the process would kill him. "What was that?" he asked.

She wished she had a better answer, but she knew little more than her husband. She shook her head to answer his question, then said, "We need to find the others."

He offered his arm, and she gratefully accepted it. His hair might be gray, but he was still strong, his steps still even. She leaned on him, and he supported her weight without problem, the same as he had since they'd first met.

Elian had asked her once, back when they were younger and more willing to drink their inhibitions away, if she had ever regretted not bonding with someone stronger or more sensitive to adani. The question had been poorly worded, but she'd understood the genuine curiosity behind it. He'd asked a few months after Capricia had ascended, and they'd been speaking of the discoveries Elian's wife was making with her new abilities.

Her brother wasn't concerned about Aldrick's worthiness. Aldrick had done nothing but prove his loyalty and love over the years, and the two men got along well despite their vast differences. It was simply that Elian was delighted to share a part of his life with his partner that had previously been locked away, and now he worried his sister would never share the same wonder.

She'd answered no that day without hesitation, and nothing had changed in all the days since. No one else had dared ask her out loud, but their questioning looks and sideways glances said more than enough. Elian's doubts were shared by many, revealing one of the weaknesses lurking within the hearts of those that wandered.

They defined strength too narrowly. As the physical and spiritual distance between the wandering clans and the cities grew, the clans responded by placing even more status on their manipulation of adani. The youngest generation of adanists, in particular, struggled to understand the tremendous value of Aldrick's gifts and character. They saw only that he hadn't ascended, and that if he tried, the process would likely kill him, and they judged him less than worthy.

She feared she would be relying much on his gifts in the coming days. That manipulation of energies had been unlike the enemies of their past, different even from the Vada they'd defeated so long ago. But she knew that whatever happened, Aldrick would be by her side, protecting her with his life and advising her with his deep wisdom.

Killan, their firstborn, landed in the valley below as they exited the cave and stepped into the light of day. Though Aldrick held the title of leader of the Wolves, it was Killan that led the clan through the day-to-day activities that had come to define the wandering clans. When the heads of the various families had questions or concerns, it was to Killan they turned, and rightfully so.

Killan was a born leader. Not as large as Harald had been, he was still tall and broad-shouldered, built like a warrior the clans would naturally respect. He had the long, lean, and weathered look not uncommon among the wandering clans, proof of the many years he'd spent walking plain, mountain, and forest. He laughed loudly, smiled often, and deliberated slowly, a combination of traits that had won him no small amount of well-deserved honor among the Wolves. Neither Samora nor Aldrick begrudged his unofficial leadership in the least.

He had no welcoming smile on his lips today, no laugh ready to boom across the valley. His mouth was set in a tight line, and he moved with a stiffness jarring to the eye of any ascended adanist.

Samora glanced over at Aldrick, whose sharp eyes caught all the same details hers did. They shared a look that said more than many of their clan's legends.

Killan was a leader, and a great one. But he wasn't meant for war. He was a leader for prosperous and peaceful times, and those times had likely just ended. They met by the dragon.

"Any idea what that was?" Killan asked. He fought hard to keep his voice even, and almost succeeded, but she was his mother, and she'd known him since the day he was born. He couldn't hide his fear, not from her.

"I'm not sure, but we'll find out. Is the rest of the family back at camp?"

Killan shook his head. "Everyone but Bael, but he hadn't traveled far for his hunt, so I'm hoping he'll be there by the time we return."

Killan helped Samora climb on, and she was annoyed how useful she found his assistance. Adani kept her much younger than her age would indicate, but she still didn't move like she had when she was younger. Aldrick and Killan climbed up after her, and with a whisper from Killan's spirit, the dragon took off and carried them west.

No matter how many times she took to the sky, the sensation never failed to fill her with wonder. They drifted between the mountain tops, the dragon banking gently as it danced along the currents of the wind. Killan had grown up with dragons, and he took the gift of flight for granted, but she had grown up practically bonded to the ground, and the ability to soar over it had changed her life almost as much as adani.

The dragon dropped as they approached the camp, coming to a soft landing in the long stretch of grass where the other dragons traveling with her family had set up their temporary nests. Samora saw that the dragons Bael had taken hunting had returned, and as Killan had expected, Bael was waiting for them to land. The men hopped off the dragon, and Bael was there in a flash, kind enough to help her down. He offered his arm to her, and she considered slapping it away.

Bael's motivation wasn't just to help, although she was sure that was some of it, but to claim some imagined piece of status as the adanist Samora leaned on.

Samora took his arm. Whatever his motivation, there was no need to abandon manners. He led her to the central cookfire, where the rest of her family was already gathered. Killan's wife Kaeda was there, a gifted healer who'd trained for years under Samora before ascending, as well as their two children, Bael and

Minetta. Deva, Samora's second child, sat in the circle with Emer, her husband, and their daughter Kerina.

She couldn't look at her family without pausing and giving thanks to whatever destiny had allowed her such blessings. There'd been a time, long ago, when the promise of the heart had been so tempting she'd been willing to leave the physical world behind for good, but how glad was she now that she hadn't? Of all the joys and successes in her life, becoming the matriarch of this family of wanderers and warriors was her greatest achievement by far.

And now the peace that had allowed this family to grow and prosper was threatened. She focused her attention and took her position within the circle. "Has anyone attempted to make contact yet?"

No one answered, but many around the circle shook their heads. She wouldn't have expected anyone to try, but it was good to know they'd chosen wisely.

There was no time to lose. Samora extended her hands, and Killan took one and Deva took the other. Aldrick took a step outside the circle and turned around. He couldn't join his family, but he could guard them as they focused on their gifts. When the circle was complete, she connected with the heart in her core. The others did the same, and adani filled the circle, stronger than any gathering ground.

So much adani made her feel like a child again, when the world was filled more with possibility than with threats. When there hadn't been so much to lose.

She quested out with her spirit, though it wasn't hers alone that made the journey. Like a thread woven tightly together, her family joined her, each powered by the heart that had allowed them to ascend. Eight pairs of eyes were better than one, and this way she'd waste no time having to describe the experience to the others after.

Their adani passed through lands familiar to her from her long years of ranging far and wide, strengthened by a web of hearts she had planted as she traveled. It hopped from heart to heart, racing toward the site of the attack. There was no doubting its direction, and before long, there was no doubting its distance. The attack had happened in the city of Nevan. The first city they'd founded after the war, and the largest by far.

Adani swirled and fell toward the city, rushing toward the gap the attack had created. Samora allowed her spirit to be pulled in, but it slowed as it neared the boundary. There was something happening here she didn't understand, a swirling of adani that had no natural cause she could identify. It caught their interwoven thread and circled it around the destruction, and she had to focus and force her adani to break through the boundary that continued to solidify.

The site of the attack was barren to her senses, not like one of the old Debru circles, but closer to what the deadlands had once felt like, before adani had begun the long process of reclamation. Adani channels still existed, but they were withered and dry, and little adani could push past the circling barrier that formed the boundary.

Neither the boundary nor the withering of the channels stopped Samora's advance. She possessed more than enough adani to push through and find the enemy sitting quietly in the center of the destruction.

It observed her adani, its own spirit flickering quickly over hers before veiling itself once again. The examination was so quick, she almost doubted what her own senses told her, but her spirit felt dirty, as though her enemy had walked through her tent with muddy boots. It brought her to a sudden stop.

She thought she'd been prepared for whatever foe she might face, but that examination was unexpected. The difference between them wasn't just one of power, it was one of skill, a familiarity with the powers of the universe humanity still hadn't come close to reaching. She wasn't the only one who noticed.

"It saw...everything," Deva said. Of her two children, she was the more sensitive, second only in the entire family to Samora.

"Impossible. Not that quickly," Bael argued.

"Deva's right," Samora said, silencing the argument before it broke her focus.

Before she could decide whether to proceed, her enemy unveiled itself completely, revealing to her the full extent of its strength. It reminded her of a bottomless void, a hole in the world that extended forever, but it wasn't empty. Not exactly. Power lurked within, not filling the space like shadow or light, but wrapped upon itself, so tightly it seemed it had no choice but to break.

Not strength as she understood it, but potential.

The potential to destroy the world.

No sooner had the monster unveiled its power than it covered itself, now nearly invisible to Samora's senses.

"Back," she ordered, and though her command was met with resistance, they retreated.

Adani returned to bodies moments later, and they were once again around the circle, all eyes turned to her, waiting for answers she didn't have.

She and Elian had feared this future. On good days, they'd been willing to believe they had defeated the Debru for good, that there was no way for their once-powerful tormentors to return. But as Samora reflected on their battles and studied the few Debru and otsoa that remained after the Vada died, she became increasingly certain the threat to their world wasn't over. The Debru had only been their first enemy, not their last. Shadow, like adani, seemed a force that possessed a will of its own, and she couldn't bring herself to believe it was finished with their world.

Elian had agreed, and they had prepared. Their war had given their children and their children's children a peaceful world, a world in which human dominance extended from one coast of their continent to another. They were glad of this. Proud of this.

The years since the war had been challenging, true, but they were challenges of logistics and cooperation, not a fight for survival against an enemy so much stronger than them.

She'd thought they'd used that time well. Thanks to the dragons' long memories, they'd learned more in months than they'd known in generations, and humanity had flourished under the explosion of knowledge. Unfortunately, that long peace, which she wouldn't have traded for anything, came with a price.

Humanity was stronger now, but the fire in their spirits that had saved them more than forty years ago no longer burned as bright.

They weren't ready for this.

"Why did you pull us back, Grandma?" Bael asked.

"It was far stronger, and had we remained longer, it might have attacked us, too. There was no need to take the risk."

Bael's frustration, never more than barely contained, erupted. "It destroyed nearly a quarter of Nevan! It's our duty to defend what's left."

She noted the way Bael leaned forward, eyes lit with an eagerness she hadn't seen in years. When he'd been younger, he'd been her favorite of the grandchildren, the one more interested in her tales than any of the rest. He could repeat her history by heart, backward and forward, but those stories had twisted his spirit in unexpected ways. He wanted to prove himself; to show the world he was worthy of the legendary blood that ran through his veins.

His dreams of glory had thus far not been realized. He'd never fought a Debru, never strove against the forces of shadow. He trained harder than anyone she knew, waiting for a day that never came.

Now he finally saw an opportunity, and he was ready to jump into action without looking twice. If it was as Samora feared, he'd see battle soon enough. He was strong and competent, if inexperienced, but keeping him focused would no doubt prove difficult.

"For now, we prepare. Killan, summon the entire clan, and have them bring plenty of food and any healing supplies they possess. We'll gather here for the moment while we wait to see how this situation will develop."

Bael wouldn't back down so easily. "We need to fight!"

"The fight will come. For now, you must prepare, because when the moment comes, it'll come quickly. We'll be depending on you," Samora said.

It didn't completely win him over, but it kept him silent for now.

"What about Elian?" Killan asked.

Samora allowed herself a sad smile. There were some things that never changed, no matter how many years passed. Her brother still chased after danger like it owed him a meal.

"He's already on his way," she said.

3

E lian felt the twist in his stomach, as though someone had thrust their hand into his gut and yanked at the heart residing deep in his core. The sensation passed before he had time to panic, so he sipped his tea and wondered what had happened.

"You felt that too?" Capricia asked.

Elian finished his tea and nodded. "Trouble, no doubt."

She snorted softly as she put down her teacup. Their matching set was chipped and worn, an old gift from a village elder, given to them after they had slain a Debru that had been terrorizing the village. Tracking and killing the Debru had barely consumed the morning, but the gift had lasted for decades.

"No need to play the wise but enigmatic old master with me, love. That wasn't mere trouble," Capricia said.

"No, I suppose it wasn't." Elian poured the last cup of tea from the pot while Capricia gathered their things. The tea set, uneaten bread and cheese, and skins of water all returned to her pack. When Elian finished the last of his tea, he handed the cup to her, and it, too, disappeared into the pack. She was ready to move before he was.

"Any idea what it was?" he asked. His senses had improved over the years, but Capricia's were far better. Some of the weaknesses of his childhood lingered long past the transition to adulthood. Long past his own ascension, too.

"Not Debru, I don't think."

Elian wondered if that was good or bad, then decided he wouldn't know until he learned more. He shouldered their pack with ease and called for Arok. The dragon had been out hunting, but Elian guessed he had felt the shift, too, and would be eager to investigate. No matter how old the dragon might be, he held onto his childlike curiosity.

"You almost don't seem surprised," Capricia observed.

Elian wondered at that. After a moment's reflection, he said, "I think I've been waiting for this ever since we defeated the Vada. Samora has often said she didn't believe the Debru were our true enemy, that what we really had to fear was the shadow that corrupted them. That's always stuck with me."

"You think this is what she was worried about?"

"No way to tell until we get closer, right?"

Arok landed and they climbed on. "Sorry to interrupt your hunt, old friend, but I think this will require our attention," Elian said. Arok, as expected, didn't seem to mind. He'd been Elian's friend for over three decades now, a constant companion on his wandering journey.

They hadn't been in the air long when Samora reached out to him. They were always connected now, a fragment of her spirit a presence in the back of his mind, just as a small fragment of his was with her. They didn't see the world through the other's eyes unless they willed it, but they were always linked by adani, a thread that bound them together no matter the distance between them. He welcomed her request, and soon she was speaking in his mind. She skipped over most of what would be considered normal conversation. Through their connection, there was already much she knew.

"How long, do you think, until you're there?" she asked.

"Four days, maybe? Three if I push Arok hard."

Miles passed beneath him before Samora spoke again. "We're going to return to the clan. I'll tell Killan to keep the Wolves at bay until I hear from you."

"What do you know?"

"It doesn't feel like Debru, and I don't think it's some new form, either. It's something else, stronger than we've fought before, but a different kind of strength. I'll be curious what you sense when you get closer."

"So, you don't recommend picking a fight?"

"That feels...unwise."

"What is it doing?"

"Right now? Waiting, although for what, I couldn't guess. Nevan's adanists are gathering, but I don't know what they'll do. None of them can hold a candle to this thing's strength."

"What do you want me to do?" he asked.

Another mile passed as she considered. "Study and learn."

Elian nodded, knowing Samora would feel his assent more than halfway across the continent. "Is this what we've been worried about?"

"I can't say for sure, but I think so. Be careful, will you?"

"I won't make any promises, but I'll try."

He felt her amusement through the connection before she broke it off.

***

FOUR DAYS LATER, Arok landed half a day's walk away from the city. Four days of travel that would have once taken him months, and still he complained it wasn't fast enough. If he lived another few decades, they might find a way to travel even faster, and then he'd complain it took too long even if such a journey only took an afternoon. No matter how good life became, he could always envision it better.

Part of the problem was all that happened while he and Capricia were in the air. Mystery piled upon mystery, and not even Samora's exquisite sensitivity to adani could unravel the knot of questions being tied in Nevan.

The being had arrived, and with its arrival, brought destruction not seen in generations. It endured the answering attacks without retaliation, and then, after a brave adanist went to speak with it, it vanished, leaving no clue as to why it had come.

At least, no clue Samora could discern. Nevan's citizens had been moving in new patterns, but she couldn't untangle what they meant.

Nevan's adanists would know more. Samora had advised extreme caution, something about the event worrying her for reasons she didn't fully understand, so Elian and Capricia left Arok behind early, though the dragon promised he wouldn't wander far. Elian didn't doubt that. Despite his years, Arok was a warrior at heart, and always eager for a fight.

Elian's first glimpse of Nevan made him doubt his senses. He'd felt the attack on the other side of the continent, but from a distance the city looked no different than he would expect. Much had been borrowed from those who had come long before. The tallest buildings were all near the center of the city, their five and six level construction visible from miles away.

Even now, the sight of the buildings stabbing into the sky stirred Elian's spirit. He'd known none of this growing up, but children in the city thought nothing of buildings taller than ancient elms.

Capricia's observation gave voice to Elian's thoughts. "I expected more destruction."

Elian agreed. He'd seen villages destroyed by the Debru, and he'd steeled himself to experience something similar here.

Instead, he didn't see any damage even when they neared the outer neighborhoods.

Elian glanced at Capricia, who pointed southwest and led the way, guided by her adani. He followed after her, growing more confused with every intact and quiet house they passed. None had suffered damage from the attack, but they were almost all empty. They'd passed no exodus of people on their way in, either. "Where is everyone?" he asked.

"Most are toward the city's center, but there are also clusters around Nevan burning incredible amounts of adani. It feels like adanists training," Capricia answered.

Perhaps all was not lost, then. The cities had never respected adani the same way the wandering clans did. It had caused him and Samora no end of strife over the years, but despite their efforts, most citizens didn't want to become adanists, just as many of the villagers Elian and Samora had grown up with hadn't wanted to. The process was too challenging, and it was far easier to survive in the city, far easier to let the wandering clans protect them. Maybe attitudes had changed, thanks to the attack. Maybe they finally understood the danger that being weak invited.

The destruction, when they found it, caught him by surprise. One moment they were walking through a normal neighborhood, the next they stepped into a wasteland. Elian stopped at the edge, carved into stone, wood, and soil with a sharpness no blade could match. The homes to either side of him had been sheared in half, the line separating existence from absence perfectly vertical.

Elian went to the nearest house to examine the edge more carefully. Up close, it was as sharp an edge as it appeared from farther away, but it was the condition of what remained that captured his attention.

There was no damage.

Yes, part of the home was missing, but what remained was in perfect condition. Elian could have destroyed half the house, too, but in so doing, would have damaged what remained as some fraction of his power leaked from the attack.

This was perfect destruction, which annihilated everything it touched, but nothing else.

His hand trembled as he took a step away. A deep breath partially steadied his nerves, but the unease remained. This wasn't just a new level of power. This was something entirely new, a depth of skill he hadn't known existed.

Capricia stepped first into the circle of destruction, and Elian followed after, thrusting his adani into the perfectly even ground. He'd expected the destruction to be as complete below as it was above, so he was surprised when his adani slipped, with some effort, into the adani channels beneath his feet. The channels had suffered when the life above had been destroyed, but they hadn't been destroyed like the homes.

Samora had compared the circle of destruction to the dead-lands, and now Elian better understood the comparison. In time, if life didn't return to the surface above, the adani channels would wither, just as those had. Hopefully, humanity would be able to build again and restore what had been destroyed.

Hopefully.

If he planted trees in the soil today, there was no reason they shouldn't grow, but he couldn't shake the feeling that if he planted them, they would wither the same as the adani channels. Another force reigned here, now, claiming this land as its own. The thought sent a shiver down his spine. The opposite of life wasn't death, but emptiness.

There was no other sign of the attacker. His and Capricia's tracks were the only ones in the fine dust.

"There's another adanist approaching," Capricia warned him.

He looked up, nodded, and ran his eyes over the destruction again. Neither sight nor adani could answer any of the questions that most troubled him, but he hoped the adanist might.

She approached from the same direction they'd come from, as

though she was a hunter tracking them through a human-made forest. Had she lived among the wandering clans she would have been an elder, but the cities didn't rely on elders the way clans did. Long gray hair trailed behind an upright stride. Before Elian could bow in greeting, she waved for them to come closer. "Get out of there," she said.

Elian obeyed, the unease in his gut growing stronger. There was something deeply wrong about this city. He had precious little to go on, but his instincts had always guided him well. The attack hadn't broken Nevan's spirits, but had twisted them out of shape, scarring the survivors in ways that would take years to fully heal, if they ever did. Where was the outpouring of grief? The determined gaze as they stepped into an uncertain future?

The elder stared at them as though they were intruders in her home. "You shouldn't be here," she said.

Capricia, thankfully, maintained a composure Elian rarely possessed. "Sorry if we offended, but we're from the wandering clans. We sensed the attack and rushed here as soon as we could."

"Just the two of you?"

"For now, although there are more waiting to hear from us."

"Tell them to stay away!" the elder snapped.

Capricia took an instinctive step back, and Elian protectively stepped between them. "We came to help."

"And if you want to help, all you can do is march out of here and never come back."

"Why? What happened here?"

"He came and did this with a thought. Our adani meant nothing against him, and neither does yours. It doesn't matter that you both have ascended. His instructions were clear, and we intend to obey them. All children are to learn the methods of manipulating adani, and as soon as it is possible, we're to begin planting groves in the center of the destruction where we can grow hearts."

"Wait. What?" Elian understood each word separately but couldn't piece together what the woman was saying.

"It wants hearts," the elder said.

"And you're going to give them away?" The hearts were the source of their greatest strength. The epitome of an adanist's development. Giving them away barely less terrible than ripping out his physical heart.

The elder gestured to the destruction behind them. "Of course. We have no need for them here, anyway."

Elian squeezed his fists tight.

He'd grown up thinking he lacked any meaningful ability with adani. His first love had chosen the jerk in his village over him, and he'd spent most of his young life retreating against the seemingly inevitable advance of the Debru.

He knew frustration, knew the feeling that the world was against him.

But he'd never given up.

Maybe it was just the way he was raised, or some flaw in his character, but there was no sin worse than quitting, no failure greater than surrendering when the strength to fight remained.

And so, he wanted to punch the elder in the nose, make her so angry that she, too, would fight to the end, instead of giving up the hearts so many had fought and died for. Did she understand what he and Samora had gone through to ascend?

Fortunately, he wasn't a youth any longer. More than six decades of living hadn't extinguished the fire in his belly, but it no longer roared like the bonfire it had been when he fought the Debru. He'd raised children, wandered the world, and seen all too many friends and family buried behind him; their spirits returned to the world.

So he didn't punch the elder in the nose, though he wanted to. Instead, he said, "We can help you fight it."

Her refusal came as quickly as a snake darting through the grass. "There's no point. Despite what you may believe, I understand well the power of ascended adanists, and great as your abilities may be, you can't fight against this. None of us can."

As much as he wanted to argue, when he thought of the damage to the homes, he wondered if she might be right.

"That doesn't mean we simply give up the hearts."

A sad smile played at the corner of the elder's lips. "He knew how the ascended would feel, I think, which was why he set out a second set of rules."

This time, it was Capricia who voiced Elian's thoughts. "What are you talking about?"

"First, there are to be no more new ascended. Those that exist may continue to live out their lives, so long as they make no attempt to interfere with the emissary's plan. Second, the ascended are not to approach any of the established training grounds. Third, once the groves are planted, the ascended are not allowed anywhere near those, either."

It took Elian a moment to shut his open jaw. "And if we refuse?"

"There will be consequences."

"What kind of consequences?"

"He will attack us again."

Elian looked to Capricia for guidance. She said, "We can't allow our hearts to be taken like this. We've fought too hard for them. Let us help you."

The elder had a look that reminded Elian of Warran, when the old man would lecture him on something he believed Elian should have already known. "You don't understand, do you? There is no fight. It was over the moment he set foot on our world. If you break the rules, it won't be you that suffers, but us. You say that you'll fight for the hearts, but who will fight for us?"

Elian stepped closer to the elder. "We can't simply give up."

She met his advance with an icy stare. "Why not? He is not like the Debru. He won't kill us if we obey. All he wants is the hearts, and humanity doesn't need them. The leadership of all the training grounds have met, and we're in agreement. We'll spread the word to the other cities, and we ask that you tell the wandering clans. There is no need for further bloodshed."

Elian stared at the woman. Visions of the long past, never too far from his thoughts, crashed through his mind. Father, standing against the Debru. Harald, sacrificing himself against the Belogs. So many more names and faces, lost so that those that lived could live free from fear.

He'd never imagined they would sacrifice that freedom in less than an eighthday.

It couldn't be real.

He took another step forward. "Take me to your training grounds, so I can speak with the others."

The woman held up a hand in warning. "You still do not understand. If you attempt to travel any farther, we'll have no choice but to defend ourselves. There is no need for any of this, so turn and leave us be."

Red tinged the edges of Elian's vision, and only Capricia's voice pulled him back from the edge. "Elian, let's go. We've learned all that we came to learn."

He dug his fingernails into his palms and forced himself to take deep breaths. Finally, he spun on his heel and walked away from the city, barely holding onto the last of his control.

4

Bael couldn't help but grin as he spotted Arok's familiar wingspan on the horizon. Dragon and rider grew larger, and it was clear Arok was closer than ever to the physical transformation that marked the final stage of a dragon's enormous lifespan. If he knew the dragon at all, though, he knew Arok would resist the change as long as possible. Arok was an elder dragon with a spirit that never grew old or weary. In this, dragon and rider were well matched.

He waited for the massive dragon to land before hurrying forward to greet his great-uncle and aunt. They'd last visited the previous autumn, and he'd wished for his uncle's advice more than once since then. Sometimes, it felt as though Elian and Shayna were the only two that understood him.

Elian greeted him with a tight embrace. "It's great to see you," he said.

"Not as great as it is to see you. It's almost impossible to believe what Grandmother is telling us."

"I hardly believe it myself." His great-uncle's gaze rose to the horizon and stared beyond it, to a future only he could see. "But we'll find a way. We always do."

Bael couldn't tell who Elian was trying to convince, himself or his nephew. Regardless, the lack of certainty in his voice shook Bael's spirit. There was nothing Elian couldn't overcome.

Bael led them through the nest of dragons, hoping to escape the routine question he was sure was coming. Unfortunately, he wasn't fast enough.

"Have you chosen a dragon yet?" Elian asked.

Bael shook his head, which was sometimes enough to put the question to rest, but not today. Elian pressed him harder. "I think it would be good for you to do so."

"Maybe after all this is done, I'll think about it."

Elian stopped and planted his feet, as though preparing for battle. "Maybe you should think about it now."

The tone of his voice brought Bael to a standstill. This was no casual questioning. Elian knew something. He shot his uncle a questioning look.

"Arok told me about your latest stunt. The dragons aren't pleased."

On another day, Bael might have deflected and absorbed Elian's pointed questions patiently, but today they had far more important questions to discuss. "So what?" he snapped.

Elian didn't snap back. He was a patient man until he wasn't. Bael had only seen the fiercer side of him twice, but both times had walked away certain that the legends that circled around Elian were all true. Today, though, he said, "Why do you treat them as you do? They've been our allies for generations and taught us more in a decade than we would have learned in a century."

"And their time is past! They have no more techniques to teach us, and even the youngest ascended adanist could kill them with little more than a thought. They ruled over us once, killing us and causing us to forget our history. My respect is not so easily given."

"Do you truly think so little of them?"

Bael let his silence be answer enough.

Elian looked as though Bael's words had cut him deep. "You're strong, Bael, and passionate, and that's good. But learn some humility. There's more to our relationship with the dragons than just what techniques we can learn, and our greater strength means only that we shoulder the burden of caretakers, not commanders. I hope you learn that before it's too late, because with what's happening now, I think we'll need you soon, and we'll need you to be better than your words have shown you to be."

Had it been anyone else, Bael would have dismissed the words without a second thought. But Elian's words carried weight. Bael bit back his retort and considered Elian's censure as he led the older adanist to the central fire. No flames burned today, but all the Wolves had gathered. Samora and her family represented the majority of the clan elders, but they weren't alone. The Wolves had grown rapidly thanks to Father's leadership, adopting those from the cities who believed they were meant to wander. If Bael sneered at them, it was only when neither they nor Samora could see.

They arrived as a disgrace to all true adanists. Their training was incomplete, and they were weak of both spirit and body. Few lasted more than a few months before tucking tail between their legs and running back to the cities. But if pushed, he would confess that many did stay, and those that did often grew to become trusted friends.

"If it is as Grandmother says, do you think we'll get a flood of adanists from the city?" he asked.

Elian stared into the distance again, then shook his head. "I couldn't say. The ways of human hearts are more mysterious to me than the ways of adani."

"But you know as much about adani as anyone who's ever lived."

Elian gave him a knowing smile. "And yet I spoke true."

Bael didn't always understand his great-uncle, but their time alone had come to an end. They took their places among the other elders, the last to arrive. Elian sat while Bael stood guard. Strong as he was, he had no place among the elders.

Samora wasted no time. "All here know the problems that face us. The only piece of news I would share is that I've searched high and low for any trace of our enemy, but I've found nothing. If it is among us, I don't know how to find it with adani."

Bael grimaced. The attack had been so well planned it seemed certain the enemy had known them intimately. How it had acquired that knowledge remained an open question. Bael had hoped Grandmother would find spies, so he could find them and kill them. Someone needed to pay for the death this emissary had delivered.

The elders accepted the news too calmly, and Bael was glad he faced away from them. He understood their admonitions about acting rashly, but they too often deferred to caution when courage was required.

Elian said, "Even if we can't sense our enemy, we have to assume its warnings aren't simply bluffs. At the least, it's not a risk I'm willing to take. But I refuse to capitulate, so how do we fight back?"

Ball's heart threatened to burst with pride. Elian, at least, could always be depended on to fight.

Grandfather Aldrick was the first to argue. "I think you're jumping ahead of yourself. Perhaps there is some wisdom in withholding our response for a time."

Bael's responsibility was to keep his eyes focused outward to protect the council, but he couldn't help but glance back to judge the elders' expressions. Elian stared hard at Grandfather, silently inviting him to explain.

Grandfather gathered his thoughts, then said, "We know this new enemy possesses knowledge and skills we don't understand. It will take time for Nevan and the other cities to train their adanists to cultivate hearts, as there are few among them who currently possess the ability. If this emissary spoke true, it won't take any action so long as we don't actively interfere. We have time, so there's no need to leap into a course of action we're only going to regret later."

Bael scowled at the horizon. There was that caution he constantly ran into, that uncertainty that held the wandering clans back from being as strong as they could be.

"The longer we allow our enemies to do as they wish, the longer they have to establish themselves. I fear they'll only grow stronger the longer we wait," Elian said.

All eyes turned to Samora, who hadn't yet voiced her opinion. The two men went silent as they waited. Bael held his breath, knowing her words would determine the direction of the clans. She knew it as well, which was why she carefully considered her choice.

She chose the middle path. "Neither of you is wrong. We should not rush headlong into a danger we don't understand, but we can't wait, either. The rules state the emissary doesn't want any ascended approaching the training grounds, but we have many adanists who haven't ascended. They can go to the training grounds to see firsthand how others are reacting to the ultimatums. In that time, I can work with others to search for our enemy. We need to learn more, then strike fast."

Bael swore softly to himself. She spoke as though decisive action waited just past the next bend in the road, but he was no stranger to her tactics. She would delay and delay again, her reasons always beyond reproach, and in the end, they'd have done nothing at all as the world was taken from them.

The council continued for some time, but it was discussion of details and logistics, and no decisions of importance were made. Bael waited until the council had ended and the individual conversations had slowly died. He could have waited longer, as Elian and Capricia had announced they would stay with the

Wolves tonight, but Bael couldn't bring himself to let Elian out of his sight.

As soon as Elian made to leave, Bael was by his side. "Send me," he said.

"You heard your grandmother. We'll send someone who isn't ascended."

"But I'm like you were. I developed the internal use of adani before the external, and other adanists don't notice me unless they're looking. I'll be able to approach the training ground, and my greater sensitivity will grant us even more information than if a younger adanist goes. And if something goes wrong, I'm much more likely to be able to stop something than an adanist who hasn't ascended."

Elian sighed. "Even if I agreed with you, and I'm not sure that I do, I already told Samora I'd abide by her judgment. I won't go back on my word to her."

Bael had hoped for more, but hadn't expected much. He couldn't fault Elian for keeping his word, though, so he nodded and let Elian go on his way.

He looked to the training ground, wondering if a session there would bleed the frustration from his veins, but his attitude didn't seem like a disease exercise would cure. He needed to talk with someone who understood, so he, too, marched toward the camp. Shayna had promised to help with mending worn clothes today, and that group usually preferred one of the camp's quieter corners.

He found Shayna and the others near the camp's northeast corner. They talked among themselves as they worked, and Bael slowed as he approached. Shayna's attention was focused entirely on her work and on her companions, and Bael appreciated the chance to observe his beloved. Her hands, calloused from a life-time of training for combat they might never see, worked the bone needle quickly, closing up the cut on the arm of a tunic. She smiled as the others spoke, the light in her eyes an attractive contrast to her dark hair.

Bael only watched for a moment, then strode into the small clearing where they worked. He was greeted warmly, and he begged leave to steal Shayna, which was of course granted without complaint. She finished the stitching she'd started, then set it aside and joined him. He offered his arm, which she took, and he led them just beyond the outskirts of the camp, where they could speak without fear of being overheard.

"Couldn't go that long without me, could you?" she asked.

Her wit broke through the clouds hanging over his head, and he smiled and shook his head. "Life would be so much easier and richer if you never left my sight."

"You'd regret that wish within a day of it coming true, I think. But truly, I'm surprised to see you. Is the council over so quickly?"

No one knew him better, so it came as no surprise she intuited that which bothered him.

"There was little discussion. The elders are scared, and I'll admit, not without reason. The power that was unleashed in Nevan is like nothing I've felt before, but the elders seem content to sit on their hands and wait to learn more."

Shayna looked as displeased by this news as he felt, but she worked through the implications slowly before speaking her mind. "I don't know that I can fault their caution in this moment, but my fear is that their caution will continue long past the time when action is necessary. The time for the greatest courage is when we face our greatest foes. You would think no one would know that better than Elian and Samora."

It was always a pleasure to talk to Shayna, because in her, he'd found not just a beautiful companion but a kindred soul. They often saw the world as though they were looking at it through the same set of eyes, and she often reminded him that he wasn't alone in his opinions. Not only that, but when they agreed on something of import, it suggested to him that he was on the right path. She was wiser than him, and he always felt more confident in his choices after she approved of them.

"I'll confess that I've never understood those two as well as I wished I did. I don't doubt the stories and legends that have grown up around them, but sometimes, it's hard to match what I've heard in the stories with what I see with my own two eyes. They're heroes, but they don't act like it."

Shayna nodded, and Bael sighed before he continued. "If they don't start acting like heroes soon, I'm afraid I might have to do something. Would I have your support?"

She held him close. "You don't even have to ask."

5

Samora sat in the fields south of the main camp, stretching her adani across the continent. She'd turned her attention first to Nevan but discovered nothing she hadn't already known. The circle of destruction remained, and though nearly a week had passed since the attack, nothing had tried to plant itself in the barren land left behind. Even the seeds of grasses and flowers, blown on the wind, seemed to avoid the area. It had been harder to push her adani through the swirling barrier, and she suspected that before long, the site of the devastation would be hidden from her for good. Beyond the destruction, though, the training grounds were busier than they'd ever been, filled with children learning basic adani manipulation techniques, with a particular emphasis on the healing techniques that eventually led to the creation of a new heart.

No matter how hard she searched, she couldn't find any sign of the enemy, nor could she discern how it had learned so much about humanity. To her senses, there was nothing unusual within the city beyond the devastation of the attack and its aftermath.

She pulled her adani back when she sensed Elian leave the camp and start toward her. Even now, after all these years, he still pulled and twisted adani as he passed. She opened her eyes as he stopped a few paces away and started stretching.

The years had been much kinder to him they had been to Samora. Neither had ever figured out exactly how Karla had manipulated adani into granting her such a long lifespan, but it was clear it had something to do with manipulating the internal flow through their bodies. Elian had seen more than sixty summers, but he looked like a man in the prime of his life. If Samora hadn't known otherwise, she would have guessed him closer to forty than to sixty. Samora knew she didn't look much older than him, but her hair was well on its way to turning gray, and she felt every one of her nearly sixty years every morning when she woke. Elian claimed he didn't feel the same aches and pains she'd grown so used to, and she believed him.

She stood and joined him, stretching out muscles that argued they were perfectly content resting for the remainder of the day. A couple of her joints popped as she touched her toes, and she could practically hear the grin on Elian's face. Unfortunately, his mirth couldn't last long, and his questions were about weightier matters than their aging bodies. "Did you sense anything?"

"Nothing useful. The training grounds are busy, though."

Elian gave a bitter laugh. "Of course they are."

Most days, Samora would have chastised him for being uncharitable, but at that moment, she felt much the same. They'd spent years trying to convince the leadership of the cities that basic adani training should be required for all citizens, but their concerns had been dismissed. The training grounds were open to all who were interested, but not many were interested, and the city leadership couldn't be persuaded to force them. Now, though, it seemed that everyone had suddenly discovered a love for their birthright.

"I suppose if I'm trying to be optimistic, I could say that the benefit of all of this is that more people will wake up to the fact they need to be prepared to fight for everything they've started to take for granted," Elian said.

"Perhaps. I fear we'll be too quick to accept subjugation."

Elian nodded as he twisted from side to side and bounced on his feet. Just watching him made Samora's joints ache. "I worry about that, too. Do you also get the sense this enemy is far cleverer than the Vada?"

Again, their thoughts had been running in parallel. "I do. I've long believed that shadow warped the Debru almost beyond reason. The Vada were complex and rational, and the Belogs weren't exactly foolish, but yes, I fear we're dealing not just with a stronger opponent, but one that's far smarter. If we're not careful, it'll soon control the world with only the one attack."

"It's far easier to gently slide into subjugation than it is to be forced to bow. One small surrender at a time, we willingly give up our freedom, until one day we wake up and realize we're slaves," Elian said.

Samora nodded. "Ready?"

"As I'll ever be. It's been a while."

They took position across from one another, and after studying her for a moment, Elian ignited the heart in his core and leaped forward.

Samora hadn't slacked in her training, and most of her daily opponents were ascended, but fighting Elian always put her on her back foot. She still hadn't fought anyone faster or stronger.

The others all made the same mistake. They tried to control the strength that burned within them. Elian let it consume him, which unleashed the full strength of the heart. He'd also learned tricks to focus the incredible energies, tricks that came far easier to him than to the other ascended.

She embraced the strength of her own heart, and adani flooded her from toe to crown. Her senses sharpened and her mind raced, allowing her to see the blur of muscle that was her brother. His fist came at her face, but she tilted her head to the side and wove half a dozen spheres of adani between them.

Elian spun away, then came in low, attempting to sweep her legs out from under her. She thrust the spheres of adani in front of his sweep.

She felt the flow of adani change in his body, but it was too late for her to react. His leg grew stronger, sheathed in the bright light of adani, and punched through the defense she'd been so confident in. Her spheres cracked and disintegrated as his leg powered through them, but she noticed how his leg slowed before he swept her legs out from under her.

She landed hard on her back, and a moment later Elian stood above her, hand out to help her up. She grabbed it and he hauled her back to her feet.

"I didn't realize you'd improved that technique so much."

Elian grinned. He'd tried it the previous time they'd sparred, last autumn, but hadn't been able to focus adani well enough to break through her defense. "It's been most of what I've been working on. I can punch through shields pretty well now, and the technique can also be used to help me defend. Form a spear and I'll show you."

Samora didn't need to be convinced, but Elian wouldn't let her escape without taking part in a demonstration, so she wove a spear of adani and held it in her right hand.

"Now, stab me. Wherever you'd like."

Samora snorted and shook her head, but knew there would be no dissuading him from this path, so she stabbed at his thigh.

She sensed the movement of adani, even as she stabbed. It circled and coalesced, becoming something hard and unbending, covering the flesh of his leg in some sort of impenetrable armor. No small amount of adani had gone into her spear, though, and for a moment, shield and spear competed, until her spear cracked and unraveled.

She took a step back and nodded appreciatively. Thankfully,

once Elian had ascended, he'd brute-forced a technique that almost looked like a shield, but this technique seemed easier for him and would keep him safer in battle.

Elian grinned from ear to ear, and Samora was reminded of what he was like when he was younger. Though his body had aged, and his wisdom had grown deeper, his spirit was still young, brimming with excitement at the possibilities inherent in living.

She envied that about him but was grateful for it all the same.

They each turned east at the same time, their gazes drawn by the same sensation. A flare of adani rose on a different side of the camp, an ascended pushing themselves to their limit. Elian recognized it as clearly as she did, and his face fell. "I'm worried about him," he said.

"More than usual?"

Elian nodded. "He asked me today, after the council meeting, if I would send him instead of another adanist. He believed he would be able to reach a training ground without being observed."

At her look, he said, "I told him no. His arguments aren't entirely without reason, but I think we decided best at council, and I won't act against the council."

That made the corner of her lips turn up in a smile.

"What?"

"It feels like it wasn't that long ago that all you did was disobey the council's rulings. You're barely the brother I knew."

"Wisdom and experience have that effect." He flashed her a grin, but it couldn't last. "He's spent almost his whole life training for a fight that hasn't happened. I'm worried he'll be too eager to make something happen. You should give him something to do, give him a direction while we figure out how we're going to resist this new invader."

Bael's adani flared again, and Elian grunted softly. "He's so strong, too."

"He tells me he feels like there are new levels of power he hasn't been able to crack yet, but he's sure they exist."

"Do you believe him?"

As if in answer, Bael's adani flared even brighter.

"I think I do," Samora said.

They studied Bael with their senses a while longer, then Samora found the courage to broach the subject she'd been waiting for.

"You need to talk to Elyn," she said.

Elian didn't say anything for a while, pretending like his entire focus was on Bael. Finally, his shoulders slumped. "I know. Doesn't mean I want to, though, and certainly not like this."

"If there's a shortcut to understanding what happened, it lies with her."

"I know. She's been on my mind since you first described what the attack felt like. She hasn't reached out to me, though, and I've been using that as an excuse."

"You could always ask Capricia to talk to her."

Elian shook his head. "They've found a tentative peace between them. I won't shatter that by bringing up the past."

Bael's adani flared again, brighter still than before.

"I think he wants me to train with him," Elian said.

"I'm starting to get that impression, too. You should probably get over there before he throws a tantrum."

Normally, Elian would have smiled at her wit, but his thoughts weren't really with Bael. She wanted to comfort him, to tell him it would all be fine, but she couldn't think of a way to say it that was honest. They all had hard days ahead, but his would be hardest first.

"I'll fly to her in the morning. Do you mind if Capricia stays here while I'm gone?"

"Of course not. You know you two are always welcome."

Elian bowed. "Thanks. I'll return right after, and who knows, maybe I'll even bring my daughter back with me."

6

E lyn woke with a start, eyes shooting wide open as she sat upright in her bed. Her throat was dry, and she swallowed hard. The inside of her throat was raw, as though she'd been screaming through the night. She wiped the sweat from her brow and reached over to the table, grabbing the cup of water she'd set there last night and draining it dry in one gulp. Some water missed her mouth and dribbled down her chin, where it fell to her chest and mixed with the sweat already there.

She squeezed her eyes shut and took a few deep breaths, feeling her ribs loosening around her chest with each repetition. Soon, she felt normal, or as normal as she ever could these days. She stripped off her clothes and threw them with the rest of the wash, then walked out the back door of her house. A stream ran there, and she welcomed its icy bite against her skin as she stepped in.

Elyn waded over to where she'd made herself a small chair out of rocks. She sat down and leaned back, allowing the water to run up and around her neck. She couldn't stay in long. The spring water, fed by glaciers high up in the mountains, was cold, even for her. She finished by dunking her head under the water, enjoying the moment of bliss it provided.

For one brief moment, she felt truly alone and at peace, her rushing thoughts frozen by the cold water. She imagined, as she often did, what it would be like to simply leave her head submerged, at peace forever.

Not today, though. Her breath ran out, and she lifted her head. She stood and walked back to the house, toweling herself off, dressed, and broke her fast.

The fields were ready for planting, and with any luck, she'd finish a fair share of the seeding today. She grabbed a hoe and a wide-brimmed hat, then went to her fields.

The day promised the sort of weather no one could find anything wrong with. The air was warm but not hot, a partly cloudy sky provided periods of both sun and shade, and a constant breeze from the north kept her cool as she used her hoe to carve small valleys in the prepared soil. Off in the distance, snow-capped peaks glistened under the light of the morning sun.

Idyllic as the day was, though, it did nothing to ease the disquiet inside her head. Another night of terrors, leaving only questions and dread behind.

She called him "the visitor," for she could think of no better descriptor for the presence that stalked her in her dreams. It was a creature of darkness and violence, but also one of cold rationality. She didn't doubt its capacity for destruction, but wasn't convinced it meant her harm. It watched, lurked, and studied, giving Elyn the sense that it was waiting.

She dug the corner of the hoe into the soil and dug a fresh furrow, swearing silently at herself. The recurring nature of the nightmares shifted her perspective, made her think they were something more than the deluded wanderings of her mind. Her dreams were no more real than the ghosts her distant neighbors believed haunted her land.

The repetitive nature of her daily labor soon drove the lingering remnants of her nightmares firmly into the realm of memory. The long shaft of the hoe had been worn smooth, and her calloused hands slid up and down the wood as the hoe rose and fell. Half the day passed before she looked up and saw that the field was ready for planting. She laid the hoe down next to a bag of seed and took a long sip from a water skin.

Elyn sensed Father's arrival before she spotted the dragon in the air. She looked up and swallowed hard. She'd known someone would come, and it only made sense it was Father, but the unease she'd felt that morning returned, doubled in strength. Soon she saw the dragon, and the sight brought the barest hint of a smile to her lips. The long wingspan and elongated body meant Father still rode Arok, who continued to fight the transition to elder.

As much as the world changed, humans and dragons remained the same. It would be good to see Arok, at least. She'd ridden him frequently when she was younger, and they'd been close before.

She steeled herself for the encounter, but Arok was flying fast, and she didn't feel ready by the time they landed, considerably far enough away to ensure they didn't damage any of her fields. Father climbed off Arok's back, as nimble as ever, immune to the ravages of age Elyn already felt.

Past frustrations sparked to life in her stomach, and she made little effort to douse them. She remained seated, waiting for Father to pick his way carefully through the fields. He stopped a few paces away from her and bowed.

Father had never been skilled at keeping his emotions off his face, and the dread he felt about this meeting appeared to match her own. But he tried to pretend otherwise, as he always did. "It's good to see you. I'm impressed with how much work you've already completed this spring."

Even now, after all that had passed between them, Elyn's

heart nearly burst with pride at her father's praise. More than forty years behind her, and sometimes she still wondered if she was a child who'd never learned how to grow up. She stamped down the pride before it could reveal itself in her expressions.

"The weather has cooperated nicely, and I've been eager to take advantage of the warmth."

Father nodded, almost responded, then sealed his lips. He looked at her but couldn't hold her gaze for more than a moment, then looked around at her house and her lands. He almost spoke again, no doubt about to compliment her on some small detail he'd noticed, then stopped himself. She didn't care for the niceties of polite conversation, now less than ever, and he knew that. He cleared his throat, then looked down at his feet.

She knew why he was here but kept silent. If he had questions, he could ask them. Otherwise, he could leave.

Instead, he pointed to the bag of seed she sat beside. "It looks like you're ready for planting. Care for a hand?"

Any hands but his, perhaps, but he'd raised her not to be rude, and he was trying to be kind. She nodded and stood, and together they began seeding the field. She rapidly outpaced him, as he placed every seed carefully, an old habit from a time when seed was much harder to come by. Despite his slow pace, she did appreciate the help. Depending on how long his visit lasted, she might get even more planting done than she'd expected.

He finally broke the silence after he finished his second row. "Did you feel the attack several days ago?"

"Everyone sensitive to adani felt it."

He waited, as though expecting her to say more, but when it was clear she wasn't, he asked, "Is there anything you can tell us about it?"

That familiar frustration burst into flame, and she clenched the seed tightly in her hand so she wouldn't throw it at him. "What's that supposed to mean?"

Father wouldn't meet her gaze. Supposedly brave enough to

face a Vada and kill it, but afraid of his own daughter. He searched for the right words, and she wished he would just say what he meant so he could leave, and she could return to her solitude. "Samora said that the only time she'd ever felt anything similar was the day you had your...accident. She thought you might have some insight into what happened that eluded us."

Elyn ground her teeth together, and it was as if she was sixteen again, her body not just filled with adani, but attacked by it, pummeling her as though she were a creature of shadow. She sowed the rest of the seed in her hand with a violent toss. "If it reminded her of *my accident*, why should she think I would know anything she didn't? It was an accident, wasn't it?"

Father's jaw twitched and his nostrils flared, but he kept his hands loose. The anger that sparked in his eyes was extinguished quickly when he looked at his daughter.

Elyn turned away, unable to watch the familiar play of emotions.

Everyone in the family called it "the accident," but they didn't treat her like someone who'd been hurt by a falling rock. They didn't afford her the respect of a victim, even if they'd never reveal their true feelings out loud. She hadn't exiled herself from the family because she hadn't ascended, though she knew that was the story that circulated among the Bears, and likely the Wolves and Scorpions and all the other wandering clans.

Elyn had left because they believed she was at fault, that she was to blame for the spiritual injuries that would haunt her far longer than the spectral nighttime presence had. She'd felt like she couldn't breathe under the constant weight of their judgment, and she'd struck out on her own, trying to find some way she could live a useful life beyond the reach of the wandering clans.

How many times had she hoped that with the passing of years, that silent judgment against her would ease? Even now, decades later, Father's unspoken assumption lurked behind everything he said or did to her. *If she'd only been stronger, if she'd only been better, none of this would have happened.*

"That isn't what I meant," Father said, his voice hurt, as though somehow, he was the wronged party here.

"Then what did you mean?"

Father breathed deeply, then said, "The attack killed a lot of innocent people, and none of us know how such power was summoned. Samora said it reminded her of what she felt on the day you tried to ascend. I'd hoped that maybe you would have been able to sense something we weren't able to, that you'd have some insight that would help us protect others."

She noticed how he'd avoided her question, and she thought he didn't give himself enough credit. He didn't consider himself much of an elder, but he could avoid speaking directly as well as anyone she'd ever met, and that knowledge only served to increase her anger. "Well, I don't."

He took a deep breath, then tried again. "Elyn, if there's anything you sensed, it might make all the difference in the world. We're facing something that's entirely new to us. If there's anything at all, no matter how small, will you tell us? There's a lot of lives at stake. Perhaps all of them."

She turned and glared at him. "I already told you I don't know anything! Why won't you believe me?"

She hated that she sounded like a child, but she hated it more that he refused to take her at her word.

He bit back his retort, though she heard it loud and clear, echoes of the words he'd always thought but never spoken out loud. *Because you're weak, and because you left us, and because you failed where all the rest of us succeeded.*

Instead, he bowed, adopting a sorrow and a humility she didn't believe he actually felt. "I'm sorry. I didn't mean to offend you. It's just that I'm worried, and I'd hoped that you might know something that would guide us through these dark days."

He straightened, and the sorrow on his face came close to

breaking through Elyn's frustration. "You know you're always welcome back. We all miss you."

She knew. He repeated the same offer with every visit, but she couldn't. Not if all that awaited her was the same judgment she'd worked so hard to flee. And what would she do if she returned? She was of more use here, growing the crops that helped support the nearby villages. It was more use than she'd be among the clans, of that, she had no doubt. She shook her head.

Father was hurt, but not surprised, by her rejection.

"I'm sorry," he repeated. "If you don't know anything, then I'll be on my way. I know you prefer your solitude, and I don't want to interrupt it longer than necessary. Is there anything I can do for you before I leave?"

Stay. Listen, truly listen, and try to understand, without your own beliefs getting in the way.

Elyn shook her head. "No. Thank you, though."

Father lingered, no doubt intuiting that his daughter wasn't being completely honest, but not knowing how to break through the wall that had grown between them over two decades of misunderstandings. She'd given him a plausible excuse, though, and so eventually, he bowed one last time.

"I love you, and I miss you."

Elyn gave him a brief nod. "I know."

And she did. She'd never doubted Father's feelings, not even when they were in the midst of their fiercest arguments.

But sometimes, mere love wasn't enough.

Father lingered, not wanting to stay but also not wanting to go. Finally, he nodded and turned away, walking around the fields to return to Arok. Leaving without resolving anything, without trying to understand her. Again.

Elyn shook her head. She was a woman grown, but after a little time with Father, she felt like a child again, her emotions running ahead of her reason. She blew out her frustration. By now, she was used to how the story went.

Arok reached out and invited a connection with adani. It was a generous offer, as she couldn't manipulate the force any longer, which meant the effort would be entirely on his end. She accepted, and suddenly she wasn't alone any longer. Arok's human form always surprised her, his chosen height never matching the length and majesty of his physical body. The top of his head just reached the bottom of her chin, and his short-cut hair didn't add much.

"I've missed you, too," Arok said.

"And I you. How have you been?"

"Good. Elian has roamed far and wide since leaving the leadership of the clans behind, which means I've seen lands dragons haven't laid eyes on for generations. It feels like getting reacquainted with a home after being gone for too long."

"I'm glad to hear it. How much longer do you think you'll be able to hold off the physical transition to elder?"

"I don't know. I'm the first among the dragons to resist for as long as I have, at least according to the memories I have access to."

Father was close to Arok now and almost ready to climb up, so Elyn said, "It's been good to see you. Take care of yourself."

"It's been good to see you, too." Arok hesitated, then added, "His spirit was in turmoil the whole flight here. At one point, I had to ask him to break our connection so I could focus on flying."

She watched Father climb onto Arok's back, but he made no motion to urge the dragon into the air. Now that he was in contact with the dragon, he'd know Arok was speaking with Elyn, though he wouldn't know about what.

"I don't doubt it, but regret alone won't reunite us."

"What will?"

"The day his faith in me returns will be the day I do, too."

Arok gave her a quizzical look but let the matter rest. "You take care of yourself, as well, my young friend."

"And you too."

The illusion of the human form vanished as Arok broke the connection. Father waved as Arok took off, and Elyn returned it halfheartedly. Then she returned to her fields, the life of an adanist behind her forever.

$\mathbf{B}$ ael and Shayna left the Wolves' camp the next morning, hopping on a young dragon as the sun poked its head above the horizon for the first time that day. He'd told Grandmother the night before that he planned on hunting, and she'd raised no objections. The clan didn't need the food immediately, but she no doubt suspected he needed an excuse to fly and wander.

The need for movement was written in the blood of his family. Grandmother had wandered for years, even after Killan's birth, only settling back in with the clans after her curiosity about their land had been satiated. Killan and Aunt Deva had both wandered alone, too, before settling down and starting their respective families. Grandmother wouldn't deny his need to fly, but she'd be furious if she discovered how far the flight would take him.

Connecting with the dragon came easily, and all he needed to do was say, "Take me to Rydal."

The dragon rumbled beneath him, and in his mind's eye, he saw a vision of a city being destroyed, and the dragon's refusal.

"I'm not going to any of the training grounds. I have a close friend there, though, and I'd like to speak with him. He may be able to tell us more of what has happened."

The dragon considered a long while before agreeing. It launched itself into the sky on a wave of adani, and Shayna wrapped her arms tightly around his waist.

As they flew north and east, to the growing city of Rydal, there was little conversation. Despite Elian's warnings earlier, Bael didn't feel any particular desire to make small talk with the dragon, and he and Shayna had already spoken at length about their plan for the day. Bael didn't speak again until Rydal approached and he asked the dragon to land well before they reached the city outskirts. There was no reason to announce his arrival.

He and Shayna both changed into clothes more in line with current city fashions, made of thinner and lighter fabrics that wouldn't have held up long to the rigors of a clan's wandering. Nearly useless, just like those in the city that wore them.

Then they set off on their way. They covered the handful of miles that lay between them and the city in very little time, following the packed dirt road as though they were ordinary travelers plying their trades between the cities.

It was a lie that wouldn't take anyone long to uncover, but their arrival didn't elicit any particular interest in those that even bothered to notice them.

Bael studied the city with undisguised interest. It had been a year or two since he'd bothered to visit one, and everything about them grated on his senses. There were too many people in too little space, and the sounds of vendors, carts, and laborers layered one upon the other until Bael swore he couldn't hear himself think. Most buildings had been constructed with trees from the nearby forest, but a few had tried to incorporate stone.

Whatever the material, the houses didn't move. They were as rooted as trees, as were the people who called them home. For most, Rydal was their whole world, and as far as he was aware, few ever tried to break free.

There was some movement between the cities and the

wandering clans, but the river of people mostly flowed in one direction. Every few months a handful of people from the cities would attempt to join the wandering clans, and almost every time, they returned to cities within months. It was much more common for the wanderers to make their way to the cities.

A wanderer could settle, but very few settlers could wander. Of this, Bael was certain, and it made what Grandmother and Elian had achieved all the more impressive. No one else could have done what they had, for they had started out as mere villagers.

Tempted as he was to wander near one of the training grounds, Shayna had convinced him the night before he'd be a fool to do so, and he turned instead down the street that would lead him to the house of a man he'd once called a friend, one of those wanderers who had chosen to settle instead of remaining true to his heritage. He'd only been here once before, when Hamond had moved into the city, but the route was seared into his memory.

He kept his adani tightly sealed within his body, and he sensed Shayna doing the same. It didn't hide them completely, but an adanist would have to be close to sense them, and so he had little fear that his presence in the city would be discovered.

"How sure are you that he'll help us?" Shayna asked.

It had been one of the many questions on his mind all day. "I don't know. We were close once, but that was years ago, and we didn't separate on the best of terms. I didn't approve of his move to the city."

"Nor should you have. His departure weakened the clan. He was a strong and useful adanist."

Bael nodded, grateful, as always, that Shayna understood both him and the world so well.

"I agree, but I was also harsher than I should have been. There is a time for cutting words and a time for gentleness. I wasn't wise enough to understand the difference, then."

They arrived at a house barely large enough to deserve the title. It was the smallest of the neighboring houses, and from his last visit, Bael knew it was also one of the oldest. Few of the others had stood here when he'd been here last. It was well maintained, though, so it was clear Hamond held onto some of his pride.

Bael went to the door and knocked firmly. The door opened, and Hamond looked out, eyes wide. "What in the name of all that is sacred are you doing here?"

Hamond poked his bearded face out the door, looked up and down the street, then pulled Bael and Shayna in before they could respond. As soon as they were in, he slammed the door shut behind them. "It's a good thing my wife and son are at the market right now."

Hamond had changed since Bael had seen him last. His beard was thicker, as was his stomach. Now that they were so close, Bael couldn't help but sense him, and his former friend's adani was nowhere near as bright as it had once been.

He'd never seen Hamond so scared. Once, when they'd been barely older than children, they'd stumbled upon a rare wild otsoa. Hamond hadn't even hesitated. He'd charged the dark beast with a spear of bound adani over his head, and Bael had believed he'd do the same if they'd stumbled upon an entire squad of Debru.

It was hard to believe the pale, wide-eyed man before them was the same man. If not for the familiar adani, Bael would have wondered if a new spirit had wandered into his old friend's body and made it home.

He couldn't help himself. The sight of his friend, now reduced to this, made him laugh. It sounded harsh to his ears, but this was everything Hamond deserved for abandoning the clans that had raised him to be so much better than this. "It's good to see you, too, old friend."

Wide eyes narrowed to slits, and Hamond stared daggers at

him, and for the first time Bael saw a familiar glimpse of his friend. It was too funny, though, as Hamond couldn't possibly believe he posed any threat at all to either Bael or Shayna. They'd advanced far beyond this adanist's weakness.

"You know the rules!" Hamond hissed, as though he was afraid of being overheard in his own empty house. "No ascended are allowed near the training grounds."

"And I'm only here visiting an old friend. I'm nowhere near a training ground."

"You blind fool! He never said how close was too close. As we speak, the city council is debating whether we should close our borders to the wandering clans for good, to be safe."

The vehemence in Hamond's voice took Bael aback. "How can we keep the cities safe if you don't let us in?"

Hamond looked at Bael as if he was stupid. "You protect us by staying away!"

Bael shook his head. He could argue with Hamond all day, but he'd only end the day tired, frustrated, and without answers. "What's happening in the city? How are you planning to fight?"

"There is no fight. We all felt the attack, and there's nothing we can do against it."

"Not if you're not even going to try."

Hamond stared at him, open mouthed. Then he shook his head and wandered over to a chair in the corner of the room. He ran his hand through his hair, muttering to himself.

"Speak up. I can't hear you," Bael said, his own ire rising.

Hamond looked up. "You really don't understand, do you?"

"What's there to understand? You haven't said anything!"

"You ask me what's happening in Rydal? I'll tell you what: *nothing*. Our training grounds are now full of students learning how to use adani. We've marked out locations for the first groves in the nearby forest, and our healers are teaching their techniques to any individual who displays the necessary sensitivities and skills. But otherwise, our merchants are selling their wares. Our farmers are beginning their plantings. My wife and I are expecting our second child in the late autumn."

Bael needed a moment to digest Hamond's meaning. "You're not planning on resisting? At all?" A nudge from Shayna reminded him he hadn't addressed all Hamond's points. "Oh, and congratulations."

Hamond offered him a wan smile. "Thank you. But I'm trying to get you to understand. Someone came and said they wanted our hearts, and demonstrated they had the power to take them if they wanted. So, we give them our hearts and our lives go on. What does it matter? There's no reason to fight. Which is why you need to leave, now, before my family returns from the market and finds you here. For the sake of the friends we used to be, I won't tell anyone of your visit, but don't you dare return."

Bael started to object, but another touch from Shayna restrained his impulse.

They'd learned what they came to learn.

Bael forced himself to bow toward Hamond. This might be the last time he saw his former friend, and he didn't want to leave the way he had before. "I'm sorry I disturbed the peace you've created for yourself. We'll leave, and if I don't see you again, please know that I wish for you all the best."

Hamond rose and offered a shallow bow in return. "That means the world to me. I'm sorry I can't introduce you to my son, but I'll be sure to tell him all the stories of our childhood." Hamond paused and smiled. "When he's old enough, that is."

Bael opened the door to leave, but before he could step out, a wave of *something* passed through his spirit. Shadow, perhaps? He didn't know. The wandering clans taught about it, but with the Debru and their wicked influence largely purged from the world before he'd been born, he'd rarely personally sensed the force. It made him want to shiver, even though the day was as warm as the springtime sun could make it.

He saw the attack a moment later. A cloud of darkness gathered to the northwest, swirling, gathering more darkness to it. He stared for a moment, dread racing from his toes up his spine, like a spider scurrying up his back that froze everything it touched. Shayna sent out her adani first, and Bael followed a moment later.

The darkness tightened into a sphere hanging above the city, spinning and pulling the shadows closer. Bael's adani was forcefully pulled in, too, as though someone had wrapped invisible rope around it, attached the rope to a dragon, and raced toward the sphere. Had he possessed less adani, he would have feared losing it all, but the heart burning brightly in his core sustained him.

His adani wasn't all that was being pulled. Bael sensed other people, plants, and trees brush against his adani as it all raced toward the void, as though eager to witness what lay in the center.

He stared, watching the pull of shadow with his eyes while experiencing it directly with his adani. It wasn't until he sensed Shayna yanking against the pull that he remembered he should be fighting the shadow, not feeding it his own strength. Before he could join her, though, his adani struck something new and went still.

It felt similar to when he'd joined Grandmother and his family and sought out the emissary, but not the same. Like the emissary, this attacker's spirit was mostly empty, but with incredible potential wrapped deep within. Unlike the emissary, that incredible potential didn't feel much greater than Bael's own.

He could fight this.

The heart in his core burned brightly as the realization hit him like a slap across the face. He snarled and took firm hold of his adani to pull it back.

The attacker never gave him a chance. The pull ceased, and for the briefest of moments, the world felt completely still. Not at peace, but empty, like the core within the attacker. Even though he'd wandered the vast silences of the unoccupied plains, Bael had never felt such emptiness.

Peace wasn't simply an absence of conflict. It wasn't something negative, something that could be achieved by removing and removing until nothing was left. It was harmony and balance, the gentle flow of a stream around rocks, bends, and fallen trees.

The collected power exploded outward, snapped like a bowstring pulled back too far. Bael's adani unraveled, ripped into shreds and destroyed before he could focus it. The violence rippled down the threads that tied adani to his core and struck like a punch to the stomach.

But even as he fell to his knees, Bael looked up to see the sphere of darkness expanding over the city. Too shocked to use adani, he could do nothing but watch as the sphere grew, swallowing buildings, trees, and streets whole.

What terrified him most wasn't what he saw, but what he didn't hear. The destruction was quieter than a moonless night yet was more destructive than a raging wildfire. He heard no crack of stone or timber, no screams of the innocent, no rumble of collapsing buildings. There was only existence and absence, and the edge of the sphere was the surface that separated the two.

He didn't even have time to wonder if he was about to die. The sphere relentlessly expanded until it didn't, and then it vanished, as though the event had been nothing more than the work of his imagination. Only the sharp pain in his core reminded him it had been all too real.

Sounds returned next. Shouts and screams echoed down the streets and alleys as the city realized what had just happened. Nearby families scrambled for protection, not knowing the attack was already over.

How many lives had just been lost? How many years of building had just been destroyed? All in less time than it took to swing a sword.

There was a muffled thump behind him as Hamond stumbled and fell onto his backside. Bael tore his eyes away from where the sphere had been and turned them to his friend. Hamond's face was pale, his eyes wide, face streaked with tears. "That was over the market."

The declaration carved out a void in Bael's spirit, not all that different from what he'd just sensed. It hollowed out his heart and bounced around in the cavernous space, staining everything it touched.

Guilt covered him like filth. It seeped into every pore of his body, made him want to vomit, made him want to lie in the dirt and be trampled on by the survivors.

Hamond shoved himself back, crab-crawled away from Bael. His limbs didn't seem to want to obey, though, and he only made it a pace or two before falling back on his rear. His lower lip trembled, and he pointed directly at Bael, his finger an arrow that pierced Bael straight through the heart.

Bael knew what was coming. He reached out to the man that would never be his friend again, trying desperately to stop what couldn't be stopped.

"It was them!" Hamond croaked, his voice cracking, barely carrying more than a few steps away.

"Hamond, no!" Bael shouted.

His former friend found his voice. "It was them!" he shouted, and this time, it carried down the streets, causing many to turn their way.

Hamond didn't stop. Couldn't stop. He jabbed his finger, deadlier than any bound spear. "They're ascended wanderers, and they came here!"

He repeated his claims, louder, punctuating them by scrambling farther away.

Bael could do nothing but stare as he watched friend become an enemy, as hate overwhelmed their long history. Only when those who listened started to gather did self-preservation overcome surprise. He scrambled to his feet and pulled Shayna up after him. She was trembling, and Bael sensed the chaotic storm of adani within her core that paralyzed her.

"We need to go," he said.

She shivered and nodded, and Bael walked her away from Hamond, away from where the market had once stood, away from the evidence of his colossal mistake.

After twenty paces he looked back, wishing there was a path open to him where he could beg forgiveness from Hamond. But his friend's screams had only grown louder, and the crowd kept adding more bodies.

Bael looked across the faces gathering and knew fear. For the moment, uncertainty restrained them, but like the attacker he'd sensed at the center of the swirling shadow, the crowd contained an incredible potential, and it wouldn't be long until it was unleashed in his direction.

He didn't fear for his life. Even if they numbered in the hundreds, they lacked the strength to harm him. What he feared was the future he saw barreling toward him, a day in which everyone looked upon him with the same hate he saw spreading slowly across the faces of the crowd. He feared it most because there was nothing he could do to stop it, and perhaps because there was nothing he should do to stop it. He deserved all the hate they possessed.

Bael took one last look at Hamond and at the crowd, then guided Shayna around a corner. Breaking line of sight stopped, at least for now, the gloom that had settled over him, and he pulled Shayna after him as they fled from Rydal.

✵ 8 ✵

I mminent disaster or not, the farm wasn't going to care for itself, and Elyn saw no part for herself in any of the drama to come. Two beautiful days followed Father's arrival and departure, but then a storm came in from the west that poured buckets of water over her fields. She welcomed the much-needed moisture, but it would be another day or two before they dried out enough for her to want to finish planting, so she used the opportunity to travel to the nearby villages. She'd put off going for long enough, and she had grain and herbs that would be put to better use there.

Her pack was filled to bursting when she left her front door, heavy enough that she briefly considered using the small hand cart she sometimes pulled to the villages, but the same mud and rain that had driven her from the fields in the first place made that a terrible idea. She'd spend more time getting it unstuck than she would walking. The pack's weight would be good for her, would strengthen her legs and shoulders for the long days in the field.

She'd built her home within walking distance of two small villages, neither of which seemed destined to grow much larger.

Neither were large enough for names. The first she'd visit was the larger of the two, home to perhaps a hundred people. One of the families there served as the center for trade in the region, and another family made frequent trips to Yolen, the nearest large village, where they traded for harder to find goods. The village had a woodworker, a healer, and a smith, which meant it provided Elyn with all she couldn't create on her own. The second village was smaller, barely large enough to be called a village, but Elyn was more welcome there, and she did her best to repay the kindness.

The fields outside the first village were as empty as hers, and she suppressed a brief bout of nerves. Though she'd spent decades here, they still thought of her as a member of the wandering clans and an adanist, two categories of people who historically hadn't given farmers the honor they were due. Too many adanists believed the grain was theirs by right, while the cities paid handsomely for the same. No matter how often Elyn tried to draw a line between her and the wandering clans in the farmer's minds, it never took. Being visited by living legends on dragons somewhat regularly did her no favors, either.

The farmers tolerated her, and they certainly accepted her grain and herbs without complaint, but walking into the village wasn't much different than walking into an ambush. Normally she didn't worry much, as during the day the village was nearly empty, but today they'd all be there, which seemed a recipe for trouble.

She patted the long knife at her hip. She lacked adani, but she'd trained her entire childhood to be a warrior. They'd be fools to give her trouble, but most people, in her experience, were fools from the moment they woke up to the moment they fell asleep, and she suspected they weren't much different in their dreams.

She made her way into the village, which was surprisingly quiet for the spring season, which only put her more on edge. Even with the recent rain, the paths that ran between the buildings should have been busy, or the village square should have been crowded. But no din carried from the square, and unless everyone was hiding within their homes, which adani told her was not true, she knew where they'd be found.

Mezlin's home could barely be called a home, given that its size was large enough to swallow up any three other homes in the village, but Mezlin refused to call it an inn, though his place was where people stayed if they were visiting. His place also carried the most liquor and food, and for the right price, he was more than happy to share both.

If Jaln's store was open, perhaps she'd be lucky. She could drop off the grain and herbs she'd marked for the village, see if Jaln had anything of interest to trade, and escape without anyone being the wiser. Unfortunately, the store's door was closed and latched tight, so she had no choice but to walk a little farther and step into Mezlin's not-inn.

As soon as she stepped through the door, she realized she'd made a mistake. Every head in the room turned her way, and there were a surprisingly large number of heads. Every farmer in the village was here, and more than a few had brought their families. She'd stepped into the room and into the middle of a heated discussion. She looked for Jaln, and he was here, although an entire village of people sat and stood between them, and they looked even less happy to see her than usual.

The sight of so many upset faces left her at a loss for words. Any greeting she could think of made her look like a fool, but Mezlin, ever the host even when he didn't want to be, saved her the trouble. "You heard the news?"

Realization struck like a bolt of lightning on a clear day, and she was more certain than ever she'd made a poor choice coming here today. "No," she lied.

"Thought you'd sense it, what with your adani and all," Mezlin said. There was malice in those words, more than usual, but there would be, if the attack had been associated with adanists.

"I didn't see or hear anything. Did some of you?" Trying once again to remind them that she no longer had any control of adani, something she'd told them time and time again.

Her question was met with blank stares, a room full of people who spoke with one thundering, silent voice. *You are an adanist. Don't pretend otherwise.*

If shouting and screaming would have done her any good, she would have, but her neighbors were beyond reason, and so she gave up trying to convince them otherwise. "What happened?"

So once again they told her about Nevan, although they had far less information than Father. They believed that a rogue group of wandering adanists had been behind the attack, and Elyn wondered how such a theory came to be accepted. When they'd shared all they knew, she turned to show them her pack. "I'm sorry to hear about Nevan, but I'd come to gift Jaln my excess grain and herbs from the winter."

She'd rather trade, but given the looks she was receiving, her best trade was for good favor. The villagers looked to Jaln, who stood and weaved his way through the crowd. "Kind of you to do so. Let's head over to my place and we can take a look."

She'd always liked Jaln, who treated her most like a person and least like a broken adanist. He traded fairly and she couldn't remember him ever saying an unkind word. Still, she noticed the glances he shot her way as they walked toward his store. Finally, she asked, "What?"

"You lied back there, about not knowing what had happened."

Of course he'd noticed. He'd been a trader for as long as she'd known him, and you couldn't be good at trading without being good at people. He was even-tempered, too, so wouldn't have let his emotions cloud his judgment when she entered Mezlin's.

"My father came to me a few days ago to tell me. He thought I might know something the clans didn't."

Jaln's silence was as good as any question, and she said, "No, I didn't know anything. I sensed the attack. It was powerful enough I think everyone with a connection to adani in the world felt it, but that was all I knew. Father told me, though, that it was something new, a foe the clans have never faced before."

With luck, this would trickle from Jaln to the rest of the village. From his lips, they might believe her story, but never from hers.

"Do you know what the clans will do?" Jaln asked as he opened the door to his place.

"I don't think even they know that yet. From what I gather, this enemy is even more powerful than the Vada. The clans are stronger, too, but I got the sense they aren't ready for this."

"And you?" Jaln asked. He took his position behind the counter and gestured to her pack. She let it slide off her shoulders and onto the counter, and then started carefully unloading her excess grain and herbs, reserving some for the other village.

"There's nothing for me to do, Jaln. Nobody here believes me, but I lost the ability to use adani when I was a child. Best to think of me as just a farmer and nothing more."

Jaln's smile was kinder than anything Elyn expected from a villager, and more precious for it. "No one is 'just' anything, but I take your point."

He looked appreciatively at her goods. "Surely you want something for all this. It will be very welcome here."

"Do you have any soap?"

Jaln reached behind the counter and pulled out three bars. "All I have left, but your grain is worth much more."

"I think I have all I need." She packed up her soap and returned the grain and herbs for the other village. "You take care, Jaln. I suspect there are rough times ahead for all of us."

He chuckled at that. "These days, I think I'd get more worried if they weren't. You take care, too. The farmers say there are more predators roaming these parts as of late, so be careful. Wolves and coyotes roaming in places they don't belong."

Elyn assured him she would, then took her leave. Even though her way out of the village took her past Mezlin's place, no one came out to say farewell.

THE OTHER VILLAGE was only a handful of miles from the first, and she reached it without trouble. This village wasn't busy, but it never was, so Elyn thought nothing of it. She made a straight line to the old healer's house, eager, in her own way, to see Petricia again. She knocked and a strong voice that sounded like it came from a much younger woman bade her to enter.

Petricia sat in a chair near the open window, crushing dried herbs and mixing them together with a mortar and pestle. She gestured at the other open chair in the house, and Elyn took out what remained of her grain and herbs and placed them on the woman's chair.

Petricia looked over the gifts and said her thanks, then, "It's been a while."

"Spring's a busy time."

"Suppose so. How goes planting?"

"Slowly but will hopefully be done soon."

"And what do you know about what happened?"

Petricia would have felt Nevan, though not like Elyn had. The older woman had grown her connection to adani but could only use it for minor healings. Those in the wandering clans would barely call her an adanist, though she was the most accomplished one in the area.

Elyn told her all she knew, which wasn't much, but Petricia was grateful both for the information and the herbs. Both would be put to good use here, and Elyn was glad she'd made the trip. The villagers weren't her friends and maybe never would be, but then again, maybe one day they would see her as one of them, and she'd be welcomed.

After some more pleasantries, Elyn took her leave so she would make sure she was back at her farm before dusk, when the predators began to emerge. Petricia gifted her a loaf of bread baked that morning, and Elyn began the journey home.

She was a little more than halfway back to her farm when she sensed trouble, trouble that took the form of humans, and weak ones at that, their adani barely noticeable though they weren't far away. She paused and let her eyes drift over the horizon while she paid particular attention to any warnings her sense of adani provided. No predators wandered the rolling plains here, but a pair of crows circled ahead.

Elyn pulled the knife at her hip out of its sheath. She doubted she would need it, but better to be safe than dead, even in this world.

The broken family she found on the path would have agreed with the sentiment. A mother and son, from the look of it, covered in far more blood than it was healthy to lose. The flesh on the mother's right leg had been torn to ribbons, and her subsequent struggle to drag her child behind her had ensured the cuts would be packed with dirt and mud. Already the burning red of infection ringed the wounds, and it wouldn't be long before it rapidly spread through the body.

For all her wounds, though, the woman was in better condition than her son. He'd been clawed across the chest, and some of his ribs were visible. The abnormal shape of his chest, combined with his labored breathing, indicated either cracked or broken ribs and at least one lung that had already given up the fight.

They were corpses that hadn't died yet, victims of what appeared to be a wolf attack. They could grow mean out here, and farmers whispered that some were descended from otsoa that had somehow managed to breed before the wandering clans had wiped the last of them out. Elyn doubted the story, but didn't doubt the wolves or what they were capable of. She'd seen these same wounds on dead cattle throughout this land.

Elyn's gaze traced the trail they'd left. They'd come from the west, and she couldn't guess where they were heading. After the attack, though, it had probably only been "away."

When Elyn first saw them, they lay together in the grass, their eyes closed. The mother had pulled the son's head onto her lap, and her limp hand rested on his bloody and matted hair, but when she came closer, the mother's eyes fluttered open. "Help," she croaked.

Elyn squatted down beside the mother, rested her hand first on the boy, then on the mother. She couldn't use adani, but she was sensitive enough to feel what it told her even without having to extend it into another. What it told her wasn't much of a surprise, except that the woman was hurt worse than she could see, as she'd missed a single deep cut across her back that had sliced open some organs. Their fate was sealed, but still wasn't easy to share. "I'm sorry, there's nothing I can do."

If she was still an adanist, the wounds would have been an almost trivial matter. It would have taken time, but she'd been an incredible healer, once. She would have had the woman on her feet in less time than it took water to boil.

She took out one of her skins and offered the woman a little water. She accepted it, and with her lips moistened, said, "Help me stand."

"There's no point. The nearest village is several miles away, and neither of you will live that long."

The woman looked like Elyn had stabbed her again, and whatever fight she'd kept burning in her spirit died as she finally acknowledged the truth she'd been running from. She curled around her son and wept, silent tears mixing with the blood pooling beneath the pair.

Elyn looked around again, searching for approaching danger

or inspiration, but found neither. Perhaps with some long poles she could rig some sort of sled, but even with that, the two wouldn't make it halfway to Petricia's, and even if they did somehow survive, this was beyond the older woman's meager skills. It was unbelievable they'd made it this far.

There were any number of questions she could have asked about where they came from, why they were here, and what had happened, but none of it mattered, and the woman had gone someplace else, hugging her son close to her chest and whispering promises she could never keep.

A familiar fury burned in her chest, one that no amount of time had been able to extinguish. Once she could have helped. Once she could have saved them and thought nothing of it. Now, even prolonging her journey by staying by their side would expose her to the same risks that had killed them. Tonight the wolves would return for the meat. No matter how much grain she raised, no matter how many healing herbs she gifted to Petricia, she was useless and unwelcome.

She let her fury burn, knowing that in time, it would fade again until the burning in her chest was bearable. For now, she sat, and she remained sitting, for no one deserved to die alone, and there was nothing more she could do.

The boy died first, not that long after Elyn found them. His adani fled from his body, which became nothing more than a sack of meat and bones. The woman didn't notice, and she continued whispering into his ear. Eventually, her eyes grew heavy, and she leaned back into the grass, holding the corpse close to her, and stopped breathing.

Elyn stood and considered following their trail to wherever they'd been attacked, but she already knew what she'd find at the end, and the sun was going down. She dug her nails into her palms until they stung, then swore at herself and continued her return to her cold and empty home.

9

Elian woke at the gentle insistence of Samora's spirit. The night wasn't yet halfway over, and his first hope was that Bael had returned after today's disaster.

This afternoon's attack hadn't struck them the way the other had, but anyone sensitive to adani had sensed it. Samora had quested out with her adani and found Bael and Shayna, fleeing from Rydal. They'd climbed on a dragon and flown away, but they hadn't returned to camp, and for good reason. Samora wasn't quick to anger, but Bael's poor choice had everyone who saw the fire in her eyes walking the other direction when she approached.

They'd waited all day, and Elian had gone to sleep hoping for their quick return. Despite Bael's deadly foolishness, he was family, and blood forgave, even when the sin was so deep. Unfortunately, his hopes were dashed as soon as he woke up enough to become aware of Samora's mood, which was darker than the night outside.

"Sorry to wake you," she said.

"What's wrong?"

"There's a large group of adanists from Rydal flying our way. Perhaps a couple of dozen."

Elian sat straight up. Capricia awoke to the movement, concern reflected in her gaze, but she understood the distant look in his eyes and waited for him to finish speaking with Samora.

"Do we need to scramble the dragons?" he asked.

He sensed his sister's hesitation; felt the fears she'd never reveal to anyone besides Aldrick. After a moment's pause, she said, "They might have come to start a fight, but I'd hope we could find another way."

Elian understood. "I'll see what I can do. Where are they?"

"Southwest of camp, about a mile away. Burn bright, and I think they'll come to you."

He was already on his feet and getting dressed. "Any ascended?"

"No."

Elian paused, shirt halfway over his head. "Then what are they hoping to accomplish?"

"I don't know, but it's possible they aren't thinking all that clearly at the moment. Hundreds of their friends and family are dead."

"True. I'll have Capricia prepare the camp, just in case."

He sensed Samora's assent, then her distance as she turned her focus in other directions. He let her remain fully connected so she could see through his eyes if she wished. Then he informed Capricia, who had started dressing as soon as he had. She listened intently, understanding her role in an instant. He kissed her quickly before stepping from the tent into the cool night air.

Once he was clear of the camp he connected with the heart in his core, letting it blaze without restriction. He closed his eyes as its familiar warmth flooded his body. The heart wasn't just strength, but peace. Though his body might not look its age, he felt the weight of years his spirit carried. One of the greatest risks of ascending was the subtle but relentless call of the heart, promising eternal rest. On days like today, that promise was as tempting as a cup of cold water to a man who'd just wandered across the deadlands without a water skin.

He turned away from the temptation and towards the adanists who threatened the Wolves. They neared when they sensed him approaching, and Elian's vision, bolstered by adani, had no difficulty spotting them in the dark. Samora's guess had been accurate, as he counted twenty warriors advancing. A few had bound spears held loosely in their hands, but Elian took a small amount of comfort in the fact no one seemed too eager to let loose.

It wouldn't accomplish anything if they did. The gap between an ascended adanist and one who wasn't was as wide as a sea, and those that gathered against him weren't even as strong as he'd been as a young man fighting the Vada. He wondered, briefly, if they considered themselves strong.

One of the warriors stepped forward and bowed.

Elian appreciated the gesture, and hoped it meant they wouldn't need to fight.

She said, "My name is Loreta, leader of the adanists who still live in Rydal."

She stood taller than Elian, and it was clear she took her physical training seriously. She wore a sleeveless tunic that revealed muscular arms. Her pants were loose, but Elian suspected she could snap a kick that would send most people in Rydal skipping down the street.

He noted her careful wording, too. It was as Samora had guessed. Unlike the first attack, this one had killed adanists as well as civilians.

Elian bowed in return. "Elian, former leader of the Bears."

Several of the bound spears unraveled at the sound of his name, and more than a few took a step back, but in their anger, none fled. They possessed courage, or at least enough righteous fury they seemed to possess the trait.

Loreta took another step forward, speaking more loudly than she needed to, putting on a performance for the adanists that followed her. "We know it was Bael of the Wolves who broke the rules the emissary set for us, Bael who brought down the emissary's wrath, and we know he's here. Hand him over to us, so that some semblance of justice can be served."

So that was what they hoped to accomplish. Elian's stomach knotted tight in his core.

"What justice do you hope to serve?"

He knew the answer to the question, for there could only be one answer, but somehow, he hadn't expected this, and he needed time to think.

Loreta's stare left no doubt about her poor assessment of Elian's intelligence. "One life for the hundreds that were lost isn't justice, but it's close enough."

"He's not your enemy. It was the emissary who attacked Rydal."

"Our wishes were clear. Bael ignored them and insulted our sovereignty. Now, hand him over, or there will be trouble."

Elian shrugged. "He's not here."

Loreta ground her teeth together and her nostrils flared. "This is where the Wolves are camped, isn't it?"

"It is, but he didn't return after Rydal. We don't know where he is."

"Then open up your camp and let us search for ourselves."

The other adanists had stepped closer. He hadn't frightened them for long, and they'd come for blood.

But there was only innocent blood here. He imagined these adanists searching the camp, destroying precious food stores and pulling down tents in their hunt for Bael. The wandering clans were proud and had only become more so in the last few decades. There seemed very little chance of a search ending well. "I don't think that's wise," he said.

It was the wrong answer, at least in Loreta's eyes. He had no trouble putting himself in her place, because he'd once been her. She'd had too much taken away from her, and now she needed to take from someone else to ease the pain that would never truly disappear. When he'd lost his father, and then his mother, he'd wanted to lash out, too. And Bael was a worthy target. His actions deserved consequences, but Elian feared what an angry mob would do to the young man.

Yes, Bael deserved a share of her anger, but this emissary deserved far more. But these adanists couldn't hope to touch the emissary, so they shifted all their rage onto Bael.

"Are you going to stop us?" Loreta said.

"I didn't come to fight."

"Then step aside."

"I'm not going to let you start a fight, either. He's not here, and it will be nothing but another disaster if you attempt to search the camp."

Loreta took another step forward, close enough now that she could strike without warning. Elian remained connected to the heart, so he didn't worry, but he felt any chance for peace slipping through his fingers. "Step aside," Loreta repeated.

She had no reason to believe him, and he'd almost run out of ways to convince her.

"We're on the same side."

"Clearly, we're not. Will you step aside?"

"No."

Loreta stared daggers into him, but they were no more effective than her verbal threats. Elian stood tall, hands relaxed at his sides, appearing defenseless. He didn't know Loreta and had no idea how she'd react.

After a tense moment, she stepped back. Hot as the fire of her anger burned, her reason prevailed. They had no way of defeating Elian, and they knew it. They wouldn't attack, not tonight and hopefully not ever. Still, he had to turn away from the look in Loreta's eyes, because it wasn't just anger. It was disappointment and betrayal, a growing certainty he hadn't lived up to her expectations of him.

The brilliance of the emissary's attack hit him with devastating force.

It had killed far less than the dragons had in their massacre hundreds of years ago, but the result might be even more damaging. The dragons carried the weight of countless lives on their massive shoulders, but at least their actions hadn't been rooted in malice, and once it was over, it had never been repeated. The emissary's attack, though, would linger long after the deed itself.

Loreta might have been disappointed, but she wasn't surprised. Elian saw it in the set of her shoulders and in the sudden decisiveness of her next ultimatum

"So be it. If you won't cooperate willingly with the cities, you leave us little choice but to force your hand. Until Bael surrenders to us, there shall be no contact between the cities and the wandering clans. Any member of a wandering clan who comes within five miles of a city will be considered an enemy. All trade, including food and medicine, will be banned immediately, and any merchant who thinks to put profits above community will be tried as a traitor."

She recited the proclamation as though she'd been practicing it on the journey over, and maybe she had. They hadn't come truly expecting a fight. Prepared, maybe, but not expectant. This had been their plan all along.

Her stare fixed him in place. "Do we make ourselves clear?"

Her proclamations wouldn't kill the clans, but it was as much pain as the cities could inflict without going to war. Their response had been aimed straight at what would hurt the clans worst.

"Is there no other way?"

"You don't get to destroy hundreds of lives and then act as peacemaker. We only require Bael. Once justice has been served, we may speak again. Until then, the wandering clans are alone."

A dozen objections danced on the tip of Elian's tongue, but what was the point? Nothing he could say or do would change their minds. Their course had been determined the moment they left Rydal. He bowed deeply, then turned and walked away. They stared at his retreating back for a time, then returned to the dragons that had carried them across the miles.

Samora had been with him the whole time, borrowing his sight. "What do you think?" he asked.

"I'm grateful we avoided violence."

She was avoiding the true point of contention, though. If necessary, the clans would survive, even though they'd likely be reduced. The cities' demands had the possibility of driving a wedge between the clans, too. Elian knew a dozen elders who would call for Bael to turn himself in, and others who wouldn't welcome their clans suffering because of one foolish Wolf. Others would spit on the cities' demands, simply because the demands came from lesser adanists.

"What about Bael?" Elian asked.

She felt his uncertainty as though it were his own, and in this, the two of them weren't far apart. Eventually, she said, "I don't know. I—I can understand why it might be best to track him down and turn him over, but I don't want to see my grandson die. Especially not like that."

Elian agreed but wondered if it would even be possible to save Bael's life.

Because now it wasn't just the city adanists who would be searching for him, but ascended adanists, too, and there'd be no place in the world he could hide.

10

E lyn woke to another set of nightmares, which she washed off in the cold water of the stream running behind her house, the same as she did every morning. She filled her stomach with a pair of fried eggs, then made her way to the northwest corner of her fields. She hadn't visited for several days, and she cursed at the sight.

The wheat was growing well, or at least, it had started growing well, but the growth had stalled, and when she neared the plants, she saw that the first leaves appeared to be painted with narrow bands of orange. She rubbed a leaf between her fingers and swore again. She should have guessed. It had been a cool and humid spring, ideal for the development of stripe rust, and it had set in quickly.

Elyn walked around the field, squatting down at irregular intervals to examine individual stalks of wheat more closely. It had spread through most of the field, and she feared that if left untended, it would spread to other plots of land, too. She reached the edge of her field and put her hands on her hips, staring across the rows and considering her poor options.

If only she had the control of adani granted to the other

members of her family. Aunt Samora could have used adani to heal the wheat, just as she'd used it to begin the restoration of the deadlands and reinvigorate the lands which had suffered under Debru occupation. Elyn had seen her aunt heal enormous swaths of land and sensed how she'd done it. In her youth, when adani had still answered to her will, she'd even healed some land on her own.

Now, any such healing was impossible. Adani flowed all around her, flowed through her, even, but her will couldn't so much as bend a thread. She could sense the sickness in the wheat clearly, could feel how it knotted and broke the healthy flow of adani through the plants. But sensing the sickness wasn't the same as being able to do anything about it. Not only could she not heal, she couldn't destroy, either. Any child of the wandering clans could weave fire and clear this land of the diseased wheat with little more than a thought, but even that option had been taken from her.

The field would have to go. She shook her head and cursed, trying not to think of the long days she'd spent clearing the field of stones and weeds, of the mornings and afternoons of care she'd already given the young wheat. If she didn't pull the plants, she risked the disease spreading to other fields, but she dreaded the time it would take to pull everything, simply to leave the field fallow for the rest of the season.

She cursed her luck and fate, but no amount of swearing or anger could change what needed to be done.

Elyn was so lost in her frustrations, she didn't sense the other presence until well after it had arrived.

It had not come on a dragon, nor had it walked the miles from the nearest village to reach her. Whatever it was, it hadn't been beside her a moment ago, and now it was, as though it had simply appeared like a waking nightmare.

Once the sense of its presence broke through her preoccupation with the field, she startled and twisted to face the invader. It took the form of a human, though it wasn't human. It wasn't even alive, as far as she could tell. No adani flowed through it, which meant by rights it should be dead, but it appeared very much alive.

She'd never sensed anything similar, and its uniqueness captured her attention. Everything affected adani. Whenever a human took a step, adani bent and twisted to maintain a connection between human and world. The changes were subtle, unless one was speaking of the ascended, whose strong connections with adani shifted the flow considerably. This creature, though, didn't interact with adani at all. Adani flowed smoothly beneath its feet, as if what she saw and sensed was nothing more than a figment of her imagination.

Legends said that even the Debru and their shadow had affected adani more.

Her senses registered it not so much as a presence, but as an absence, a void in human form. A form she suspected was little more than a mask. She'd heard the stories of the Vada, how it had transcended physical form and could take whatever shape it pleased. She suspected she was looking at the way it had learned the trick.

The form it had chosen didn't appear threatening. If she hadn't been sensitive to adani and passed it in the nearby village, she wouldn't have thought anything of it. It stood a bit taller than her, with short dark hair and gray eyes that unsettled her if she looked at them too long. A clean long-sleeved tunic hung loosely from its shoulders, but instead of pants it wore what appeared to be a long, dark skirt.

It squatted down and studied the diseased wheat, then turned its gaze toward her, as though judging her worthiness. It stared for a moment, then stood, those not quite human eyes full of sympathy. "You were meant for much more than this, Elyn."

The timbre of its voice was low, and it spoke slowly, as though its words carried an ancient wisdom that deserved careful contemplation. It made her want to listen, to lean forward so she didn't miss a word.

She couldn't explain why, but it felt like some part of her had always known him, like he was a distant relative she'd seen regularly growing up but hadn't seen in years. It didn't seem strange that he knew her name, nor would it have seemed strange if he knew her likes, dislikes, fears and dreams. She didn't question any of it, just as she didn't question who he was.

"You're the one who left a hole in Nevan. The emissary."

He dipped his head once, slowly. "I am the one who carried my master's message, yes."

"What message?"

"That this world is ours now, and the sooner your warriors come to peace with that, the better it will be for all."

"My ancestors fought and died for this land. It's not yours to claim."

The corner of his mouth turned up in a half-smile, and if he had been human, Elyn would have said he was enjoying himself. "Do you think you can stop me?"

She knew she couldn't, and he knew that she knew, so there was no point in blustering.

He continued, as though she had silently answered his question. "I know I can claim this world, for I've done so with many worlds before, and I shall claim many more in the future. You may think your world and your people special, and so many worlds and people think the same, while the truth is that you are no more than a steppingstone to something much larger than you can possibly imagine."

If she was meant to be impressed, the emissary failed badly. Any sense of wonder Elyn had once possessed had died the day she tried to ascend. The sun wasn't even a quarter of the way across the sky yet, and she had a field of diseased wheat to pull. She didn't have time for whatever games this being was interested in playing. "Why are you here?"

He spread his arms out wide and smiled, though there was nothing human in the expression. "I came here for you, of course. Trust me, I have no need of your fields."

"You're here to kill me?"

The thought sparked a pair of hopes within a spirit that had long laid dormant. The first, that someone might finally end her suffering, that someone might take from her what she'd never convinced herself to take on her own. And second, that she would die because she was worth killing, that her life had value beyond the meager harvest she supplied to the nearby village every autumn.

"Not at all. I came all this way to train you."

The words passed through her, at first leaving no impact, too far divorced from her daily reality to mean anything. Then they hit, carrying with them all the old feelings she'd worked so hard to bury. She still wanted to be strong and useful, the craving woven into the very fibers of her spirit. Years she'd given to the mastery of adani, imagining the day when she'd be as useful to the clans has Father had once been. When that dream had been denied, the same desire had pulled her here, where the daily labor hardened her body and the food she raised benefitted the clan, albeit in only a small way.

And somehow this being knew her, knew what she wanted, perhaps even better than Father and Mother. There was no doubt he knew, for she saw his knowing in the depths of his unsettling gaze.

"Why would I join you?"

The emissary shook his head. "I didn't ask for you to join us. I will, but by the time I do, the question will be little more than a formality. I said that I would like to train you."

"Why would I accept training from the being that killed hundreds of humans in an instant?"

It held up two fingers. "First, because I can promise you the strength that adani has denied you, the strength you spent so many years chasing. Strength that would give you the power to change the world as you see fit. To be more useful than a mere farmer."

His knowledge was too much. "How can you know that?"

"We've been here for a long time, Elyn. We're not like the Debru, who merely expected their paltry mastery of shadow to be sufficient to retake the world they'd once sacrificed. Our aims are grander, our methods more subtle but far more effective. We've studied everyone who might be a threat, anyone who might shape the course of this world's future."

Once again, it was as though the being had wandered in and dumped dry grass over the flickering flame of her spirit, but more than a decade of crushed hopes allowed her to douse it within the space of a heartbeat. "You haven't been looking very closely if you think I matter."

"To the contrary, I'd say we're the only ones who've studied you closely enough. You have tremendous potential. The most of anyone we've found on this world. The only mistake you made was pursuing adani."

"Instead of shadow?"

"Shadow is nothing. A blasphemy we were grateful to see wiped out. I promise you more."

She should turn it away, she knew, but she couldn't deny her pounding heart. "And what, exactly, do you promise?"

He shrugged. "The force has no name on this world, but it is the other half of the pair of forces that seek dominion over this universe. Adani, as you call it, is a weaker manifestation of one, and my strength is the fully formed manifestation of the other."

"Destruction and death."

He shook its head. "You think too simply, although it is no fault of your own. Thanks to the dragons, this world hasn't progressed as far as it should have. You associate shadow with destruction and death, but tell me, isn't the same true of adani?"

"What?"

"Think of the varied uses your wandering clans have put adani to. Yes, they've used it to heal, to save lives and lands that were on the brink of death. But haven't they also used it to destroy? Don't most in the clans seek to master adani so that they may form weapons and kill their opponents? Weren't you just standing here, thinking about how useful adani would be in destroying this field?"

The emissary might as well have come and forcibly yanked her head around, forcing her to see a perspective she'd never considered before.

He continued. "You and the clans associate adani with light and life, and though your philosophy is pointing in almost the right direction, you're blinded by your assumptions. Adani can heal, certainly, but it can also destroy. The same is true of the other force."

Elyn's stunned mind could barely follow the emissary from one revelation to the next. "What?" she repeated

He took a step closer, and she wasn't scared. He held out its hand. "May I?"

As though in a trance, she extended her hand and took his. The emissary's hand was warm and gentle, lacking the callouses that years of farming had formed on her own hand. It turned her hand over, so her palm faced up, then placed a finger from its left hand on her palm. "I can heal as well as destroy."

He did—something—she didn't have the words or experience to recognize. For the briefest of moments, it felt as though her hand had been emptied of bone, tendon, blood, muscle, and adani, and then it wasn't empty anymore, but full.

Of adani.

Flowing smoothly through channels that had long been knotted beyond repair.

She wanted to ask him how, but the words couldn't make it past her throat. He let go of her hand and she almost cried out, needing so much more.

"I told you there were two reasons you would train with me. The first was the strength you've sought your entire life. The second is that I can heal the damage that adani has wrought in your body. Both reasons are promises I make to you."

"Why should I believe your promises?"

"Why should I lie?"

"The same reason anyone has to lie. You have something to gain."

"My ultimate goal is to have you as an ally. Lying gains me nothing."

Again, that hope that her life, after all these years, might have meaning. Weighed against the fact that the offer came from *him*, the being that had so little regard for life or freedom. The words hurt to say, but she said them anyway. "If you teach me, I'll only use the strength you grant me to fight you."

The being's smile never faltered, as though he'd expected the conversation to eventually reach this point, and he was pleased that it had. "If so, you're welcome to try."

"Are you so confident in your strength?"

"I'm confident in my knowledge. You believe you want to fight me now, but once you understand this world like I do, you'll see that I was right all along."

He stood there, waiting for her answer, and some part of her was sure that the emissary would gladly wait for as long as her decision took. He already knew her answer. Had known the answer before he had even revealed himself.

She hated that he was right, but he was right. She gave him the slightest nod of her head. "When do we begin?"

His smile widened, just a fraction.

"Right now."

11

Bael didn't know where to go, but he knew the one direction he couldn't travel, and it was the direction he wanted to travel most of all, toward home. Home wasn't the camp, a collection of tents that made him feel safer than the stone walls of the Scorpion villages far to the northwest, but the people. Father and Mother, who supported him no matter how foolish he acted. His many friends in the clan. But now, more than ever, he craved the company of those who had fought the Vada. Those who understood the violence Bael was sure approached over the horizon.

He swore at himself. Would any of them even meet with him? Grandmother would find him no matter where he landed. Would she send Elian after him, and if so, to what end? To bring him back? Or something worse?

Every time he glanced back, he expected to see all the dragons and adanists of Rydal in pursuit. But all he saw were the looks they had given him as he fled. He saw their looks when he stared forward and when he closed his eyes. If he ever slept again, he was sure the stares would follow him into his dreams.

They would never forget, and they would never forgive.

"Where are we going?" Shayna asked.

Bael swallowed hard and gripped the scales of the dragon tighter. He'd dragged her into this, but he didn't know how to save her. He didn't know how to save anyone, but for her, he could at least act like he did. He pointed to a plateau a few miles away. "We're going to land there and rest for a bit."

He felt her nod against his back, reassured by the certainty he projected. The dragon agreed and began a slow descent, and a new panic seized Bael. What if the dragon didn't want to stay? It was under no obligation to provide him transport, and he had no particular relationship with it. He couldn't think of a single dragon that would risk itself for him.

The dragon landed and dispelled the worry by rubbing its belly deep into the grass. Bael and Shayna slipped off, and they walked together to the edge of the rise. Bael glanced back to ensure the dragon wasn't preparing for a sudden departure, then allowed himself to enjoy the vista. An ocean of rolling grasslands stretched out before him, and he knew that if he flew across them, they'd eventually lead him to the sea. Beyond that, no one knew what existed.

How long would it take Samora to find him, now that he had landed? He wasn't sure, but he didn't want to risk staying too long.

Shayna leaned in and wrapped herself around his right arm. "What are we going to do?"

His jaw tightened. It shouldn't be "we," but "you." He was a fool to have asked her to join him, and a fool not to send her away now. But what good would it do? She'd been seen with him, and the clan certainly already knew she was involved.

He wouldn't lie to her. They could hunt him to the ends of the world, but they couldn't make him sacrifice his honesty. "I don't know. I don't think we can go back home."

"If not there, where?"

He couldn't bring himself to tell her the truth, that not only could they not go home today, he wasn't sure they could ever go home again. That by choosing to join him this morning, she might have joined herself to him for the rest of their days.

Maybe.

He wouldn't give up so easily. The wandering clans wouldn't simply sacrifice him. That wasn't their way, not to the cities.

But he had done wrong, dreadful wrong, albeit unintentionally. Those people were dead because of him, and no explanation would clear the stain of their blood from his spirit. Sentencing him to death was well within their rights, and certainly possible.

"I'm not sure. If they want to find us, there's no place in the world we can hide from Grandmother."

"Then doesn't it make the most sense for us to return? If we can't run, why bother?"

Her reasoning tempted him, giving him an excuse to return home. But he shook his head. "If we return, we condemn the wandering clans by association. This way, if they need to sacrifice us, they can."

They couldn't return to the wandering clans, nor could they run from them. What remained?

He searched his mind and memories for answers, but none came.

Despite the thoughts running circles in his head, he sensed the presence as soon as it arrived. He spun, connecting to the heart in his core as he sensed the same power he'd felt in Nevan, when he'd joined his adani to his grandmother's and searched the ruin of the city. He lashed out without a second thought, binding half a dozen small darts of adani, each filled with enough energy to bring down any of the largest buildings in any of the cities. They shot toward the emissary, leaving lines of golden light trailing behind them.

The emissary did—something—it wasn't any shield Bael recognized, but it served the purpose all the same. His darts struck the barrier and vanished without so much as a whisper of complaint. The barrier didn't unravel the adani, as legends said

97

shadow had, nor did it meet force with force. But one moment his darts were there, the next, they weren't, their energy simply subtracted from the world.

Lack of knowledge didn't stop Bael from following his first attack with a blinding blizzard of golden spears. The separate bindings lacked the strength of the darts, but taken together, they possessed the force to wipe out an army of Debru. Spears swirled and struck at the emissary from all directions, and for each that struck, Bael bound two more and sent them on their way, unleashing a crescendo of destruction to make the world shake.

Except no destruction followed in the wake of his efforts. The boundary surrounded the emissary like an enormous bowl flipped upside down and placed above him, and it ate the spears as eagerly as it had the darts. Bael braced for the powerful waves of force that would pass over him as his attacks landed, but the grass between him and emissary only bowed for the early evening breeze.

No matter. He'd closed the distance between him and the emissary, and now he had two short bound swords in hand. Ascension wasn't simply a matter of mastering the external manipulation of adani. Elian had taught them that in the battle against the Vada. Adani coursed through Bael's limbs, looped and focused, using techniques that had only improved since Elian had first used them.

In the blink of an eye, Bael stood just outside the barrier, and he swung with all his considerable strength. He couldn't see the barrier, could only sense it as an emptiness against his senses, a vague disturbance with fuzzy boundaries, but he knew the instant his first sword struck. The golden blade slowed as a shock traveled up his arm. Not of impact, but of two forces meeting and warring. Adani filled his limbs while the emissary's barrier tried to hollow them out. But Bael didn't fight with his adani alone. He had his, that of the heart, and his connection to the web of life beneath his feet. Too much for even the emissary.

The forces warred like two armies viciously fighting over the same terrain, but despite the emissary's skill, adani was simply too much. Its barrier shattered, and Bael's sword continued its deadly trajectory.

The emissary reacted like a trained and ascended warrior. Its eyes went wide with surprise, but it leaned back, and the sword meant to cut through its neck only scratched it across the throat. The bloodless creature's wound didn't leak any vital fluid. Darkness swirled beneath the creature's body-shaped mask, and the wound healed moments after Bael dealt it, but it didn't matter.

The emissary could be hurt, which meant that it could die, which was all Bael needed to know. He lashed out again, but the emissary shifted, moving faster than Bael had believed it was possible for a creature to move, faster even than a dragon in a full dive. The emissary used no weapon, but thrust its fist into Bael's stomach, so far Bael wouldn't have been surprised if the emissary could open its fist and grab his spine.

The blow drove the air from his lungs, and he could do nothing but wrap his arms around his torso and stumble like a drunk after a night of celebration. His dual swords vanished; the focus required to maintain the binding a thing of the distant past.

The emissary didn't continue its attack. It stepped back, out of the range of any sudden strikes Bael might care to launch, then said, "I didn't come to fight."

It sounded offended, as though coming to a world and destroying large parts of a city should have earned it a warm welcome. Bael lacked the breath, though, to point out the errors in the emissary's thinking.

"I came because you are a unique talent, Bael, and as matters stand, you have nowhere left to run. The cities demand your head in repayment for the suffering you delivered to them, and the wandering clans will lack necessary food and supplies until they turn you over. Fortunately for you, there is still a place for you by my side."

Bael would have laughed, but the sound that rose from his battered lungs was closer to a cough. He tried to reject the offer, but he had yet to find a full breath, so the emissary was able to continue without interruption.

"We've been watching you for many years, Bael, and I can promise you that the only way you'll live the life you've wanted is to become a part of what we're building."

He finally sucked in enough air to respond. "You don't know what I want."

"Nonsense. You want what every true warrior wants: strength and the opportunities to test that strength against others. You've been a dutiful child of the clans, spending your whole life training, but until these last few days, you've had nothing to train for. No hunt challenges you. There were no enemies left to fight. You've trained and studied, pushing your mind, body, and spirit to their limits, but for what? You haven't had anyone to fight the entire time you've been alive."

"You're standing right in front of me," Bael said.

"But I don't consider myself your enemy."

"Then don't fight back, and we'll both be done with this conversation."

"You would attempt to kill the only being walking this world who can give you what you want? I promise you strength and worthy adversaries, and you dismiss it so easily?"

Bael had his breath back, but he didn't attack. Why didn't he attack?

The emissary kept talking, his words worming deeper into Bael's skull. "You're upset because of Nevan and Rydal, but why? In Nevan, I didn't kill any adanists. Only those who had never trained to make use of the wonderful gifts offered to them. Grieve their loss if you feel it's necessary, but the message they sent the wandering clans is the most useful thing they'd done with their lives. Rydal was regrettable, but was only done because you and the other ascended adanists needed to be reminded how serious I am. There need not be any further bloodshed. I require hearts, not lives."

Bael needed to strike, not listen to this creature, who twisted truth like it was a cord that could be knotted over and over again. But how?

A story came to him, the one Elian told when he spoke of his fight against the Vada, a creature that could change its shape like this one. How everything was illusion, but the creature still had a core, something essential that could be pierced and destroyed. Bael needed to find it, and he quested with his senses.

If the creature noticed, it didn't care. It kept talking, dumping lies and half-truths upon Bael, as though convincing Bael was simply a matter of saying enough.

"Join us, Bael. We are the path that leads to everything you've ever wanted."

Bael focused only on adani. If he listened too long to the creature, he might begin to believe. For the creature was right. Not about everything, but enough that its words pulled at Bael's heart, filled him with a longing he'd denied for too long.

"You wouldn't even be the first in your family to join me," the emissary said.

That was almost enough to pull Bael completely away from his search, to surrender to the emissary's temptations.

But then he found what he thought was the creature's core, and it wasn't nearly as strange or unfamiliar as he'd expected. In fact, he knew it all too well.

"Bael?" The creature finally realized it had lost his attention.

For a moment, he wavered, unable to deny the temptation of the creature's promises.

But no, he still knew right from wrong, and the creature was becoming suspicious of his silence. He looped adani tightly through his limbs, pushing muscles and his focus to his limit, then asking for just a little more. He leaped forward before the technique was complete, knowing there would only be one chance, and that surprise was everything.

The bound sword formed in his hand as the emissary's eyes went wide. Within the illusion that was its body, the core shifted, moving far away from where the creature thought he would strike. The emissary stepped backward, fast but not quite fast enough.

Bael tracked the core and cut, his entire spirit contained in one strike. The bound sword cut deep, flowing through the illusion as though it was nothing but smoke, but finished just short of the core.

He swore, but before he could cut again, the emissary was gone, and Bael, Shayna, and the dragon were alone upon the endless grasslands once again.

12

No one had thrown a bound spear yet, though Samora worried it wouldn't be long. That adanists were up in arms wasn't hard to believe. She'd seen the storm coming long before it had crested the horizon and raced toward them, as soon as the adanists from Rydal had delivered their ultimatum. She hadn't expected it to strike with the intensity of a late summer storm, strengthened by the heat and humidity of long-held grudges and deeply held beliefs.

Marcin, an ascended adanist and leader of the recently reformed Hawks, heralded the storm. A smaller and slighter man, he would be easy to underestimate if one wasn't connected to adani. He was young to be a leader, but still older than Elian had been when he'd inherited the mantle of the Bears after Harald's death. Normally soft-spoken and considered, today he paced the inside of the council circle as though preparing for battle. To him, the decisions before them were hardly decisions at all, the path forward wide and gentle, and his belief in his rightness was bone deep and unshakeable.

"Why are we even arguing?" he demanded to know. He gestured to where Samora and Elian stood together. "I respect them as much as anyone, but even they don't question Bael's guilt. They wish only to put their families above the rest of us, and though I understand, Bael is no more deserving of special treatment than anyone else."

Samora and Elian didn't stand alone, a fact obvious to Samora's senses as adani crashed and twisted through the spirits of the gathered adanists. Marcin sought to cast her and her brother as mere leaders, but only the younger generation could shift their views of history so completely. Everyone else was old enough to have trained and ascended directly under either her or Elian and knew them not just as stories, but as teachers.

Still, Marcin spoke convincingly, and there were those that believed him. Even Samora didn't know exactly where she belonged. Marcin grouped her with Elian, and understandably so, but her own views were more nuanced.

Marcin said, "The only choice is to find Bael and deliver him to Rydal. Not only does it best support the wandering clans, but it's also the right decision."

She missed the certainty of youth, which she attributed to a blind optimism that the world could be better and the lack of experience to realize that progress, when it happened at all, was a jittering affair that sometimes crawled and sometimes leaped. Their fight against the Vada had driven her and Elian to new heights, and their renewed relationship with the dragons had unlocked many of the advancements of humanity's past. Those twin victories had spread across the land, and were still spreading, leading many to feel that progress was somehow straightforward, a constant aspect of life.

They didn't look deeper. Didn't see that their advancement had largely stalled years ago. The evidence was here, in this circle, for anyone who cared to look. Every single warrior here had ascended, thanks to the techniques she and Elian had developed and refined.

But none had surpassed them.

And that was the most glaring flaw in Marcin's argument, the scope of which he couldn't even begin to fathom. Acquiescing to Rydal's demands, submitting to the emissary's rule, meant giving up any further hope of advancement. It wasn't the immediate death of war, but the slow death of decay.

Elian stepped forward. "You're wrong, Marcin. Bael is close to our hearts, yes, but so are all of you. I'd fight for any adanist who found themselves in Bael's situation. He made a mistake, yes, but we know Bael. There was no malicious intent, and he would suffer mightily if we turned him over to Rydal."

Marcin faced Elian directly, and the adani in the circle focused as adanists prepared for a fight. "How can it be that you don't see? This isn't just Bael's fate that we're discussing, but all of ours. It's about food and supplies, about being able to allow new adanists to ascend, and about keeping all of humanity together. You'd sacrifice everything for the sake of one."

Samora weighed the reactions she sensed around the circle. If the decision before them was one of feelings and loyalty, she had no doubt Elian would carry the day. But the leaders viewed today's choice as defining the future of the clans, and they were trying to separate themselves from their age-old loyalties. Perhaps only half were successful, but Marcin made a compelling argument, mostly because she wasn't sure it was wrong.

Elian had no retort to Marcin's damning accusation, because again, Marcin was right. Elian would fight for anyone in this circle, would sacrifice everything for anyone in this circle. It was in his blood, and it made him a leader most would follow without question, but the weakness in his outlook meant that he couldn't weigh the choice with anything approaching rationality. He'd fight to the bitter end, and it would be a bitter end unless she stepped in.

She stepped inside the circle, drawing every eye to her. Once, long ago, such attention would have left her in pieces on the ground, but now she hardly noticed. Karla would barely recognize the woman she'd become.

Or maybe she'd foreseen all this long ago, before anyone else.

"I'd like to speak to my brother alone, and we've already stood here for some time, and many of you have traveled far to be here. Let's break for a quick meal and resolve this after."

Marcin wanted to object, for he sensed the tide of the battle turning in his favor, but Samora let him study her, and he was sharp enough to observe how she leaned. He bowed, recognizing the offer of peace when he saw it. With his agreement, Samora's proposal was accepted, and the circle broke into small groups.

Hopefully, no one stabbed one another over stew.

ELIAN GROUND his teeth together as he listened to her in the privacy found far outside the boundary of the camp. "He's your grandson!"

She didn't dignify the observation with a response. If he thought so little of her, there was nothing in her power she could do to change his attitude.

He exhaled sharply through his nose. "I won't sacrifice him like this."

"It will take time to find him, especially if he's smart. Who knows what we might work out in the time he's gone?"

"If we give him up, we're giving up our spirit."

"It buys us time, allows us to repair relations with the cities, and gives us the space to make the best decisions."

Elian paced, reminding her of Marcin's performance in the circle not that long ago. She had no doubts his mind raced even faster than his footsteps, but she was equally certain where he'd end up. He was her brother, and in this, he was as unchanging as a mountain.

Pulling him aside hadn't been about changing his mind. It had been about them having this argument privately, where they could say all that needed saying.

He stopped and faced her, his decision made. "I can't join you in this, and I'll suggest that no Bears join you, either."

It was no less than she expected, but the sudden rift between them hurt all the same, as though the emissary had torn part of a limb from her body.

What else was there to say? Through their connection he could feel her emotion, just as she could sense his determination to overcome all the rules the emissary attempted to bind them with. She just couldn't let it end like this, couldn't let him go without offering him something to keep them from dividing completely.

"I won't help any more than necessary with the hunt. He's clever enough to avoid anyone hunting him for a long time. We'll figure something else out before it's too late."

THE CIRCLE RECONVENED, and she sensed the difference the meal had made. Turbulent adani had calmed, and a look around the circle revealed more calm and considered faces. Samora stepped forward to begin the council.

"After discussion with my brother, I've decided that the wandering clans should aid in the search for Bael, with the intent of turning him over to Rydal's council as soon as he's found."

Her announcement didn't stir the commotion she expected, but then, she and Elian hadn't wandered out of sight, and anyone with eyes to see would have noted the heated nature of their discussion. Elian's own stance was easy to predict, which made the conclusion inescapable.

"Is it decided, then?" Marcin asked. "That the clans will find Bael and convince him, through any means necessary, to submit himself to the cities' judgment?"

RYAN KIRK

Elian stepped into the circle. "The Bears will have no part of this. We will not actively stand against the council's judgment, but we will not offer aid, either."

"And if he comes to you?" Marcin challenged.

"He will be welcomed, but not protected."

Marcin seemed to recognize it was the most he could ask for, and he accepted the peace that was offered. The council debated the details for a time, and Samora told them of the last she'd sensed him, the day before, far away towards the coast. Hopefully, by now he'd be far in another direction.

The council disbanded, with several of the leaders wandering towards dragons who would return them to their clans. Marcin spoke briefly with Elian, but Samora couldn't tell if it was to reassure her brother or to ensure he didn't have some more devious resistance planned to the council's decision. Regardless, they seemed to part on peaceable terms.

Her own spirit enjoyed no such peace. She had as much as voted to execute her own grandson, and when she returned to the Wolves, she'd have a fight with Killan their descendants would be telling stories about. Her choice was the correct one, but it still stained her spirit and reminded her of the times she'd seen the Debru world, covered in shadow.

She reassured herself that at the very least, she'd bought them time. The hunt for Bael would take months, if not longer. The Wolves had raised him well, and despite his flaws, he was among their best.

Time, she reassured herself. She'd bought them time, and with that time, they could make a plan.

13

After a morning spent fighting a battle in the council he didn't know how to win and an afternoon spent with his clan explaining what had happened and what their options were, Elian was more than ready to sit down around a fire and eat with his family. The Bears had flown in to join the Wolves at their camp, and Elian appreciated having his entire family close by. Hadena, his second daughter, and her family had cooked a meal of roast venison, carrots, and potatoes, and she'd always had a gift around the fire, able to turn mundane meals into feasts fit for the kings of legend.

Everyone was there, and Elian sat in the grass next to Capricia. "How'd it go?" she asked.

"About as well as can be expected. None of the families are interested in switching clans, but there are a few who don't like the fact that we're not fully obeying the council's decision. Probably told them too many stories of clan dysfunction growing up, but they don't like we're going our own way."

Hadena, the most level-headed, asked, "What if he does come to us? Will that be a problem?"

"I don't know, but I'm not going to worry about it. I don't think he'll be visiting for a very long time."

Harald, his youngest, stared at his food as though he might find answers buried within. When his son had been born, Elian had wanted to honor his former mentor by naming him Harald, a naming Kati had blessed before she passed away. Part of him had hoped some of Harald's spirit would live on in the boy, but that had proven a hope too great. Harald had ascended, but was timid by nature, a man who preferred quiet contemplation over action. He was a wise child, and Elian loved him dearly, but he would never be a warrior. "I fear that by giving in to the emissary now, it will only be emboldened to demand more, later."

"You're right to worry," Elian said. "If you give an aggressor any ground, they'll push for more."

Hadena asked, "If you're not going to join the hunt for Bael, what are you going to do, Father?"

Elian chewed on a piece of venison as he considered. "We need to find a way to push back against the emissary, but I don't know how we learn more about the force it wields. It would be easier if we could visit the cities again, but Bael proved the emissary is keeping a close eye on us. We'll have to find another way. I'm hoping your aunt will have some suggestions tomorrow."

Elian wasn't sure if it was the lateness of the hour, or if the fire had already burned low, but the darkness around his family felt darker than usual, the gloom harder to pierce. If only he could burn bright enough to always keep the darkness away.

"Will we ever see Bael again?" Melena, Harald's youngest child, asked.

"I don't know, but if we do, I don't think it's going to be for a long time."

It was at that moment a new arrival landed among the dragons, and two visitors slipped off, one whose adani Elian would recognize anywhere. He swore.

Melena looked at Elian, all innocence and smiles, as she said, "Because I think he's here now."

———

ELIAN BURNED the heart in his core and ran toward the new arrivals, but even his speed wasn't enough to overcome the advantage of distance. The Bears were camped farthest away from the dragon's nest, and by the time he arrived, Bael was already surrounded by Wolves who'd formed a half-circle that prevented him from advancing.

Bael burned bright, clearly connected to his heart, but he had his hands in the air and made no sudden movement. Fortunately, he didn't look surprised by the reception, but the sight of adanists pointing spears at other adanists caused Elian's spirits to sink.

They'd worked too hard for too long to be divided so easily. But Elian didn't know how to keep them together. Once, they'd had a common foe in the Debru, but now they couldn't decide if the true enemy was other adanists or the emissary.

Bael kept his hands in the air, making every effort to appear as harmless as an ascended adanist could, even as warriors from his own clan tightened the noose around him. He ignored the advance and fixed his gaze on Elian. "I fought the emissary. It's not invincible."

The leader of the guards, Lieran, glanced between Elian and Bael. Lieran was ascended and a member of the Wolves' council, and had actually trained under Samora, if Elian's memory served. He was loyal to the clan, through and through, and the clan, through Samora, had made their will clear, but it put him in a difficult position. How did one capture an ascended adanist? Bael was second to none in his generation.

Except that Elian saw an opportunity to avoid a fight, and he took it. "It's good to see you, Bael. Please, join me. It sounds like we have much to talk about."

Lieran shot Elian a sharp look, but Elian leaped ahead of his protest. "I'll take him to my sister. You can escort us if you want."

Lieran accepted the compromise, and the entire group made their way deeper into the Wolves' camp.

By the time they reached the center of the camp, all of Samora's family was gathered. Samora had sensed Bael the same as Elian, but she trusted her brother to deliver him safely and had summoned everyone. Killan and his wife Kaeda sat next to Samora and Aldrick, and Emer and Deva sat across the fire. Bael's younger sister Minetta was present, but Kerina, Emer and Deva's little girl, was absent, likely dreaming sweet dreams in their tent.

Elian had halfway expected to find a handful of the Wolves' elders present, too, but Samora hadn't summoned them. Elian felt as though he'd swallowed a stone, because it likely meant Samora had no plans to contradict anything she'd decided in the council meeting.

Bael was greeted with kisses and embraces from his family. Killan was a private man, who kept his feelings more closely guarded than the dragons used to guard their history, but a lone tear trickled down his cheek as he embraced his firstborn son. The others were freer with their feelings, but Elian noted Bael's stiffness and awkwardness, as though he wasn't quite sure he believed in his warm welcome.

Lieran and the other guards, who'd formed a wide perimeter around the fire, were evidence enough that not all was as it seemed.

Poor Minetta was almost in tears as she held tight to her older brother. She, perhaps more than any of Samora's children or grandchildren, had captured Elian's heart. She was kind and gentle, so much so Elian often feared she wasn't meant to live the life of a wandering adanist. Minetta continued holding onto Bael's arm, even as he took a seat around the fire.

At Samora's bidding, he told his story, from his decision to visit Rydal to his meeting and fight with the emissary. The family listened without interruption, and Elian was proud to notice that Bael didn't avoid any of the blame that was rightfully his. He kept his telling brief, but he ended with a revelation. "When I fought the emissary, I sensed the source of its power. It's the void we discover in ourselves when we progress to the point of ascension. We fill that void with a heart, but the emissary does something very different. I can't say what, but it's the same power we have."

Elian was still trying to digest the fact, swallowing it like a piece of overdone beef, when Samora asked, "Can you defeat it?"

Elian knew the answer as soon as Bael hesitated, and fortunately, he was honest enough to admit it, too. "I don't think so. It knows, now, that we can hurt it, and it knows, too, that we can sense the core of its power as it shifts within its form. I don't have any surprises left, and if we were to fight again, I'm certain it would be able to protect itself from anything I might try. But if we all fought it together, we might still have a chance."

Samora looked as though she'd stopped listening as soon as Bael had admitted that he couldn't defeat the emissary, her thoughts running in another direction.

Bael sensed it, too. "What is it, Grandmother?"

"Rydal and the other cities have demanded that you be turned over to them. They've cut off the wandering clans from all contact, food, and supplies, until their demand is met."

"Oh," Bael said. Not surprised, exactly, for he was clever, but maybe surprised at the lengths the cities would go to for his head. But also an understanding, instantly knowing the bind the wandering clans found themselves in, and instinctively guessing what had been decided in his absence. Elian watched his great-nephew's heart break, betrayed both by the clan he'd sworn to give his life to protect and by his own flesh and blood.

Whatever joy and relief the family had felt at Bael's return, whatever warmth they'd shared as they'd embraced him and listened to his tale, was gone.

Elian, morbidly curious, wanted to connect with his sister, to sense, without the intermediary of facial expressions, how she felt. She'd set this trap for herself, so confident it wouldn't snap closed on her own leg. But now it had, less than a day after she'd set it. Now, instead of time to think and plan, she had a stark choice before her, neither of which she wanted.

Bael, for his part, held his head high. He'd always been able to take a punch, to suffer defeat and keep swinging, but he'd never been hit like this before. The cuts that sliced deepest came not from the swords of enemies, but from the daggers of friends and family, dripping with a poison that seeped slowly into the spirit.

Samora started to speak, but the words couldn't quite escape her lips. She swallowed, stared at the ground like she so often had when she was a girl, when she hadn't possessed the courage to meet anyone's gaze. She tried again, seeking some sort of path through the maze of traps that remained. "We can wait a day or two before we turn you over to Rydal. Perhaps, in that time, we can come up with a plan."

Elian drew in a deep, shuddering breath, as a fragment of Samora's emotions washed over him. They weren't even fully connected, so whatever sorrow he'd just experienced was but a fraction of hers. Her emotions mixed with his, for she'd bound herself with her word, thinking she wouldn't have to keep it anytime soon.

This was one of the reasons why he hadn't acquiesced at the council, because if he had, tonight he'd become a liar, too. In this, he respected Samora, for he didn't think he'd possess the same dedication to keeping his word.

Bael nodded, maybe not accepting his fate, but not arguing

against it, either. Even now, his greatest concern was for another. "What about Shayna? She's innocent of all this, and only came along because I asked her to."

"They didn't say anything about her," Samora said, "so she's safe to stay."

"Good," Bael said, as though the whole matter was settled.

Minetta's cry pierced the night. "Grandmother! You can't let them kill Bael. He didn't even hurt anyone!"

Samora stared at the ground and wilted like a flower at the end of its life, silence her only answer against Minetta's wails.

HE DIDN'T STAY MUCH LONGER. Samora understood his feelings as well as he understood hers, and she no doubt sensed that his decision had already been made. Better not to stay, so that she could deny knowledge when they interrogated her. Many knew they shared a unique bond, but few understood how deep the bond went. She'd be safe from retribution, if she chose to be.

Capricia was the first to greet him, and she understood his intent as well as Samora, though she needed only a glance. She took his arm, and they walked together toward the Bears' camp. "Tonight?"

"Can't risk waiting longer. I'll need your help."

She shrugged, as though she had already known and that it was silly he even ask. "Am I staying or coming with you?"

There was the answer he wanted to give and the one that was right, and he couldn't decide between the two, so she decided for him. "I should stay here. This will be like throwing Hadena into the fire, and she hasn't been leader of the Bears for long enough to weather this storm without help."

"Hopefully, she emerges even stronger than she is now. I'm sorry to leave you."

"As long as you do everything you can to come back to me."

"You know I will."

By the time they reached their camp, Elian wasn't sure if he was supporting her or if she was supporting him. After all these years, he wasn't even sure he could tell the difference. Chance had brought them together, but they'd worked hard to build a love that had lasted through the rebuilding of humanity and the demands of raising a family. He didn't fear his own death nearly as much as he did being separated from her without possibility of return.

Hadena and Harald both waited at the campfire, and Elian wished Elyn was with them. Hadena and her sister had always been close, and that bond would have served them well in the coming days.

"They're going through with it," he announced.

"And what will you do?" Hadena asked, even though she knew the answer already.

Elian gave a half smile and a shrug, so Hadena wouldn't have to lie when asked if her father had told her what he was about to do. "Will you be alright?"

She considered for a moment, then nodded, and that was that. Elian was proud of his children, even Elyn, though she didn't believe him when he told her so. They'd grown up strong and competent and what more could a father ask for?

"And you, Harald?" Elian asked.

Harald nodded, too.

"Good. Take care of one another, especially in the days to come. They'll be hard."

He said his farewells, such as they were, and left them to their own planning. He had a bag to pack and a wife to give a proper farewell to.

14

Elyn was a child again, sneaking out from the camp when her parents had told her not to. It was that same heady mix of excitement and fear of being caught that had so enticed her to break the rules when she was younger. She'd thought she was long past the age of such foolish decisions, but perhaps she'd only been waiting for the right opportunity. She didn't delude herself into believing the emissary's noble proclamations regarding her intent, for she'd made peace with the truth long ago.

Weakness was a curse, and she'd do nearly anything to be strong. Anything to be useful.

All her life, she'd been surrounded by the strongest humans in the world, her father a living legend, and though he'd never once told her he expected anything less from her, she'd known it in her bones since she was young. The surprise, in her mind, wasn't that she had failed. It was that anyone in her family had succeeded.

And now, a new adventure, one so far removed from the dreams her father had once had for her it was almost funny. What would he say, she wondered, when she was as strong as him, or maybe even stronger? Would he welcome her with open arms, or would he turn his back on her, proving once and for all it had never been about her strength, but about her?

She flew through the sky on the back of the emissary, who'd left on another mission and then returned once her pack was full, and her house put in order for her leaving. He'd shifted, before her eyes, into the shape of a sleek, dark dragon, and when the transformation was complete, spoke to her as though he were still a man. "Let us go, then."

She'd climbed on without question, wondering why a being that could disappear and reappear at will would carry her like a dragon, when he said, "We must travel to visit another of my allies in this land. The technique I use to travel would kill you, but there are those under me who must use another method, which will be suitable for you."

Useful information, that, and given without hesitation. A sign of trust, or of strength?

Either way, the emissary shifted itself for her, carried her across the land, which was more than anyone had done for her in a decade. She imagined everyone in the wandering clans was searching for him, and he hid in the sky, in open view of anyone who might look up.

It wasn't like riding a dragon, connected by threads of adani. She sensed the tendrils of power running through his body, noted the core which he protected deep in his chest, the spirit that made him an individual. She noted, too, that his core felt familiar, though it took her some time to place it.

"You were once like us," she said.

"No, but the void manifests the same among all. It is no surprise you would think us the same."

He said no more on the matter, and it wasn't long after he descended, landing in a valley that might as well have been in the middle of nowhere. She'd seen no villages, no fields, and no camps as they approached. She climbed off the dragon, who transformed back into the emissary she'd first met.

"I thought there would be someone here."

"Soon. They've been summoned, but the journey is a long one for them. We try not to use many techniques that will reveal our presence to the adanists of this world."

A head appeared over the rise soon after, followed quickly by the rest of a long, lithe body. It ran toward them, eating up the distance in effortless strides. He was tall and darkened by long days in the sun, but he smiled easily and seemed none the worse for wear despite whatever distance he'd just run. He bowed deeply to the emissary, and she sensed something pass between them, a thought she couldn't catch.

The visitor stretched out his hand, and Elyn narrowed her eyes. He looked human, and she thought she sensed some small amount of adani from him, but he was wrong somehow, though even under a close examination she couldn't say how.

A hole opened in the air, a dark oval large enough to step through, its edges sharp enough to cut the wings from a fly. The emissary gestured for her to step through first.

She saw nothing on the other side. The portal was blacker than night, and every sense in her body screamed danger. She'd be a fool to step through.

But why not? If the emissary wanted her dead, all he had to do was snap his fingers. She didn't trust him, but she trusted in that. She'd already taken the first steps, and all the ones that came after were much easier.

Elyn stepped through the portal and left her world behind.

———

SHE STEPPED onto a world both familiar and strange. A jagged, broken mountain range stretched pierced the blood-red sky in the distance, with miles of dead ground between her and the nearest peak. A soft swishing of fabric behind her told her that the emissary had followed her through the hole.

She glanced back, over the emissary's shoulder. There'd been no feeling of transportation or transformation. She looked down at her palms, the callouses and lines of her hands etched in familiar patterns. Nothing but a single step, and she'd landed on another world.

She tried to remember the stories Samora had once told, the visions of a dying world. "Is this the home of the Debru?"

The emissary stood by her side. "No. That world is long gone, now, and the Debru are no more. They needed to win your planet to survive, so their defeat at your hands was total."

More information Samora would have fought hard to obtain, given freely. Her parents had worked long and hard to prevent another invasion that would never come.

"So where are we?"

"Another world, one that is very important to my master."

"Is this what my world is to become?"

"Not if all goes as planned."

Elyn took in the vast stretches of deadlands and wondered if it wasn't too late to turn back. "Because this is hardly a compelling vision of the future, if you think I'll join you."

The emissary gave her a slight smile. "I think you'll come to appreciate it, in time, but you're not ready to understand why, not yet. You still cling to life, because that's all anyone has ever taught you, and you've never had the wisdom to look beyond the lies of your world. Fortunately, I want you to live, and I want your world to live, and so there is no conflict between you and I."

Elyn frowned. "You talk about plans, and about wanting my world to live, yet you've brought nothing but destruction since you arrived."

"In time, I shall tell you more, if it seems right to do so, but today is all about you and your choice."

"And what is my choice?"

"Today it's to decide whether or not you wish to be healed. After that, your choice will be whether to join us or not, to become an emissary and become the leader of humanity's next generation, as your father was for the generations previous."

In a day full of surprises, this last one was the greatest of all. "Me?"

"You're the best choice without doubt. You understand the wandering clans, but you aren't a part of them. Both city and clan will listen to your wisdom, especially when you have the strength they all respect so much. But your years as a farmer also means that you understand the land and how to nurture it. On top of all that, your natural sensitivity to adani means you'll need little help to keep a watchful eye over the entire world. It's almost as though you were born for this."

Born for this.

The words echoed in her head, and she hated the pull they had over her. Once, she'd hoped to lead the Bears, lead all the wandering clans the way Father had, and now the opportunity was being offered to her again, long after she'd given up all hope.

"What happens now?" she asked.

"I must carry you up there," the emissary said, pointing to one of the jagged peaks. "There, we will heal you, and once you're healed, we will begin your training."

"Then let's get going."

ELYN HOPPED off the emissary's back for the second time that day, and again he transformed into the man she knew him best as. He'd flown her straight up to nearly the top of a peak, landing in a small clearing barely large enough for his wings.

Nothing about the clearing was natural. It had been carved as a perfect circle, its sheer walls twice as tall as she was and more than sufficient for blocking the high winds that called this elevation home. A stone platform, about as high as her waist, dominated the center of the clearing. It had clearly been designed to fit one person.

It was the chains and manacles that gave that away.

She shivered, and not because of the elevation. She was used to being on her own, far away from help, but it was only then she realized just how far away from help she was.

The emissary's voice was as soothing as always. "Do not fear."

"Easy enough to say. What's that for?"

"For you, if you choose healing."

"I've never been to a healing that required chains."

"And you've never been healed like this before."

She didn't have a quick reply to that.

The emissary walked over to the platform and ran his hands softly along the surface, as though fondly remembering a scene from his past. He pulled himself out of his memory and faced her. "I will not lie to you and tell you this will be painless. The damage the heart did to your body is widespread, and it will be just as painful to undo as it was to endure the first time. Maybe worse now, as your body has lived with the wounds for so many years."

Her knees quivered. When she wasn't dreaming of darkness, she had nightmares about that day, nearly twenty years after the accident. She'd not known true pain until that day, and despite all the long days she'd endured since, she'd never felt true pain since.

"Not only that, but the healing will take many efforts. I can heal you, of that I'm certain, but it may be days of suffering."

"You're a terrible emissary."

"I'm an excellent emissary, because I bring truth to worlds that are more comfortable with lies. I will do all I can to minimize your suffering but healing you will be the most painful experience you've ever endured. All I can promise you is that once it's over, you'll never have to suffer again."

"And the chains?"

"To restrain you. In the grips of such pain, there's no telling what you would do to yourself otherwise."

Elyn took a step back from the platform. "And if I decide I don't want to be healed?"

"Then I'll summon another doorway and take you home, and you'll never see or hear from me again. An emissary must be willing."

Elyn looked to the platform, to the emissary, and to the blood-red sky above, then swore to herself. She only played at being difficult. She'd made her choice back in the field when he'd healed her hand.

Pain was no stranger.

She forced her legs to carry her forward and she sat on the platform. The emissary nodded and moved quickly, before she could let her fear show. She stretched out her hands and feet, and the manacles went on tightly around wrists and ankles, securing her to the platform. The emissary placed a folded cloth beneath her head as a pillow, then held up a stick wrapped in leather. "Bite down on this, please."

She did, and the emissary put his hand on her shoulder. It was warm, and it spread warmth through her body. He looked down at her, waiting for a final confirmation.

She breathed in deeply and nodded, and she felt the void in her body, and emptiness not even the all-consuming power of adani could touch, a hole nothing could fill.

The emissary hadn't lied. It was like no pain she'd ever experienced before.

Elyn screamed like she did on that day.

15

B ael kept his chin high and his eyes forward as he returned to the tent that wouldn't be his for much longer. Lieran led the adanists that encircled him, surrounded him like he was the greatest threat to the clans since the Vada. He'd looked up to them as a child, and still did, even as they looked down on him.

Shayna gripped his right hand tightly, her palm slick with sweat. As he walked with her, he imagined them walking on any of the many moonlit journeys they'd taken beyond the boundaries of the camp, talking about everything and nothing. He'd imagined a far different future for them, one with a whole horde of children.

It didn't look likely now, but he couldn't let himself think about that, not in front of her.

He was grateful more trouble hadn't fallen on her head. Rydal's fingers pointed to him alone, and he wasn't sure why. Perhaps the cities felt that they could only demand the life of one ascended adanist from the wandering clans. Maybe Hamond, in one undeserved act of mercy and friendship, had only named Bael as the culprit. Regardless of the reason, none in the clans seemed eager to sacrifice her as well as him. They were torn enough about his fate, and leaving her out of the mess seemed an unspoken compromise with the factions that didn't want to surrender Bael to the cities.

Regardless of the reasons, he said thanks to whatever forces looked over them. He deserved the blame, and she deserved better.

They reached his tent and stopped. Lieran had already made himself clear: Bael wasn't to have visitors overnight. Shayna could visit him again in the morning, though a part of Bael hoped that she wouldn't. She would have the harder task of the two of them, for she would have to find a way to move on. She was a warrior, though, and in time, she would.

He tried to memorize the softness of her lips as they kissed, hold on to the feeling of her arms around him, so that he could recall it in the trials to come.

"Don't give up hope. And don't stop believing in yourself," she said as they parted.

"It's the belief in myself that caused this."

She held him close. "Acknowledge the mistake. Learn from it. But please, don't lose your spirit. Anything but that."

His throat tightened, and he feared it was already too late, but he nodded. If she asked, he would try.

"I'll come to you in the morning," she promised.

He nodded, the words getting caught in his throat. They needed to be said, though, for who knew if he'd have another chance? "I will always love you, no matter what."

She gave him half a smile. "I'll hold you to that. I love you, too."

He could have stood there half the night, his arms around her, but Lieran cleared his throat, and they separated. They said their farewells, and Bael watched Shayna until the other tents hid her from view.

"No trouble tonight, right?" Lieran asked.

"Not from me, no." Bael reassured him.

Lieran still left two guards outside his tent, promising them relief sometime in the night, but Bael went into his tent and tied the flap shut behind him. As soon as he was safely out of sight, his legs gave out and he stumbled to the ground. His breath came in short, ragged gasps. He lay down and stared at the ceiling of his tent.

He waited for his heart to stop pounding in his chest, then sat up. Grandmother would have told him to meditate, but any form of focus would have been impossible to find. His body shook, and when he looked at his hands, they trembled. He squeezed his them into fists and held them tight against his chest as he rocked back and forth.

Thank adani the emissary had appeared as suddenly as it had, giving him no time to realize how foolish he'd been for attacking. He chuckled as he trembled. Grandmother had always spoken of the importance of thinking clearly during a fight, but if he'd been thinking clearly, he probably would have wetted his pants. He'd been all instinct and reaction.

Since then, he'd been nothing more than a liar. At first, for Shayna's sake, then, once they returned to the clan, for every Bear that saw him. They needed to see strength, especially for what was coming. It was a lie, but a necessary one.

What the clans really needed, though, was wisdom, and in that area, he was sadly lacking. He hadn't destroyed Rydal, but if not for him, hundreds would still be alive. He was a fool. Greater than a fool, perhaps, for so many had tried to warn him. He'd heard, but not listened. And if he'd been wrong about Rydal, what else had he been wrong about?

He was used to being right. To being certain. Now both had been taken from him, soon to be followed by his very life.

How could he maintain his spirit when he'd seen firsthand, so clearly, what came of his confidence?

Bael lost track of time. He rocked and he trembled, and he held his knees close to his chest and tried to think about anything besides the emissary's dark gaze or the fact that he was going to be put to death soon in Rydal. He tried and he failed.

The stirring of adani, softer than a whisper, finally pulled him from the endless looping of thoughts. He frowned as he tried to sense the bindings, but they moved too quickly and were too weak. Among so many ascended adanists, it was a wonder he had sensed them at all. They unraveled near the front of his tent, so gently he wondered if he'd just imagined it.

Footsteps raced around his tent, but Bael didn't sense any adanist. The rustle of cloth and a soft grunt was all he heard, and though his adani told him all was well, he rose from his sitting position, untied the flaps, and glanced out at his guards.

He found them in Elian's arms, looking for all the world like enormous babies that had fallen asleep on his great-uncle's shoulders. Elian dropped into a squat and laid them down as gently as it was possible to lay down a pair of unconscious, full-grown men.

Bael's frown deepened, but his tired mind refused to interpret what was happening. "Why can't I sense you?" he whispered, as though afraid he might wake the guards up.

Elian looked up and grinned, and though he was an elder, he looked much more like a mischievous child than the legendary leader of the clans. "*That's* your first question?"

Before Bael could respond, Elian rose and pushed him back into his tent. "Pack your things, and quick. We need to leave."

Bael just stared at Elian, jaw hanging partway open.

"Now," Elian said.

Bael shook his head. "I'm not supposed to leave."

Elian stepped forward and placed his hands on Bael's shoulder, forcing Bael to look at him. "I am aware. We can have a long discussion later, but now we need to move. I'm not going to let you die. The clans will have need of you, even if they don't recognize it yet."

There was no real decision. Bael never weighed his options

and chose carefully. All he knew was that Elian was here and would protect him. He'd trained under Elian, too, so following his orders was as simple as throwing on an old pair of training clothes. He didn't think, couldn't allow himself to think.

Elian led him through the quiet camp, then out to where Arok waited. Only once they were climbing aboard the dragon's back did Bael think about Shayna, and asked Elian if she could come with them.

"It's better for her and for us if she doesn't," Elian said.

Bael accepted this as he'd accepted everything Elian had said or done that night, and before he was even aware they'd taken off, they were in the air and far away from the Wolves' camp. Elian said nothing, and the cold air and newfound distance from his troubles slowly cleared the fog from his thoughts.

He leaned closer so he could speak without shouting. "What are you doing?"

"Saving your life."

"At the cost of your own?"

Elian shook his head. "There will be trouble, of course, but they won't seek my life."

"We can't run from the clans forever."

"No, but we can run long enough to learn how to fight the emissary, and once we've killed it, the cities and the clans will be able to cooperate again."

Bael shivered, then pointed down. "Can we land?"

Elian glanced back, then nodded. The dragon took them down gently and they landed on one of the tallest rises among a pack of rolling hills. Grasses swaying in the wind reflected the dull silver reflection of the moon. They slipped off the dragon, and Bael faced the man he'd always looked up to.

"You can't do this," he said.

"I already have."

"You should take me back, then, before this has consequences you haven't considered."

"I won't take you back to be murdered by a city."

Bael shook his head, cast his gaze to the moon, then looked back at Elian. "You weren't there. You didn't see their faces. Even if we defeat the emissary, they won't forget, and they won't forgive. You're acting like this is no more than a problem between clans that can be easily solved, but it can't. They see us as the enemy now."

"If that's true, then there's even less reason to turn you over to them."

"You're missing the point. Giving me to them is the only way there's a chance forward. I'm grateful beyond words you'd be willing to do this for me, but maybe this is what should happen. Maybe this is how I can save the most lives. I'm guilty, even if I didn't kill them with my own hands."

Elian weighed his words, but after a moment, hung his head, defeated like Bael had never seen before. His answer, when it came, was barely loud enough to hear. "I can't."

"Why not?"

"Because I won't sacrifice you."

"If you don't, many more will likely die."

"But they aren't family!" Elian shouted.

The outburst silenced Bael, and he saw the way Elian wrestled with his choice, like a predator biting at resilient prey. "What was your plan?"

"That you and I would study and train together, to find some way to defeat the emissary. You say you came close, which means that together, we're certain to."

Bael hated to dash Elian's hopes, but it would be wrong to lead him on. Truth cut deep, but it healed faster than a festering lie. "It was a lucky chance. It thought me cowed, and if it had announced itself more clearly, I might have been. Its power is far beyond ours, and as near as I could tell, it's invulnerable to external manipulations of adani. It won't let any of us get close again, and the fact it can vanish whenever it wants eliminates any chance of us trapping it. I came close, but I failed, and there won't be another chance."

"I refuse to believe that."

Bael shrugged. Elian could believe whatever he wanted, but reality wouldn't change.

The grasses swayed and the moon crawled toward the western horizon, and the two men stood across from one another, their fates uncertain.

"So?" Bael asked.

Elian didn't answer for a long moment, but then he straightened, and a fire returned to his eyes. "Let me tell you what I believe. I believe that the emissary sought you out because you are one of the best of us. It sought you out because it fears what you might accomplish. If you really want to save lives, the way to do it isn't by sacrificing yourself to Rydal. They're hurt and they're scared, and perhaps you're right, that the only way they'll forgive the clans is if we hand you over. But the clans don't need forgiveness. Our role is to fight and protect, and if you sacrifice yourself, it'll be that much harder. I believe the emissary tried to recruit you because we need you. Join me, and we'll find out why the emissary is scared."

Elian wasn't right. Bael knew, now, that he wasn't as special as he thought he was. That against a superior opponent, he was little better than a coward.

But Elian was so certain, and Elian was no fool. Of that, Bael was certain. Elian was wrong, but Bael didn't want to die, no matter how much he deserved death. He feared Elian's refusal to compromise would kill them all, but he bowed in agreement, and his future was as good as decided.

16

K illan found Samora early the next morning, as she was returning from the healing tent. Her firstborn looked as though he barely believed the news. "Is it true?"

"It is."

Killan was normally a man who controlled his reactions well, but relief was written on every line of his face. Had they been around the council fire, it would have raised suspicion among the other elders that Killan had a hand in Bael's dramatic escape.

Apparently, he worried the same about her. "Did you help Uncle?"

Samora shook her head, though it wasn't, perhaps, the entire truth. She'd taught Capricia the weave she'd used to deliver nightroot powder to the guards. She'd developed it years ago but had never found a good use for it. The idea to use a weave to carry the powder was genius, and if Samora was disgruntled about anything, it was that Capricia hadn't shared it with her earlier. But that wasn't what Killan had asked, and to that, Samora could honestly say that she'd had nothing to do with Elian's decision.

She'd known, of course, before Elian had put his plan into motion. He couldn't keep a secret so big from her.

"Did you know he was going to do it?"

She glanced at him, disappointed he'd asked the question, but he was thinking only as a father, and not as an elder.

"I did. It was clear as soon as the council made their decision."

Killan bowed deeply to her. "On behalf of both Kaeda and I, thank you."

She lifted his head up. There were enough curious eyes on them, although she suspected it wouldn't be long before the full truth was known by all. She'd wondered, maybe, if she might wipe her hands clean of the escape, but the longer she considered it, the less likely it seemed.

No matter. What was done was done, and only the path forward mattered.

"Bael and Elian will be safe. We have larger problems to deal with here, and we need you focused on the clan."

Samora hated this. Hated having to deny her son the proper time to grieve, deny him the time to come to terms with the idea he might not see his son again, and if they were to meet, it might be as enemies. But she needed him, now more than ever.

Killan needed a moment, but he mastered himself and stood tall. "What do you need me to do?"

"It's not about what I need. It's about what the clan is going to need, and that's someone who shows them the way forward. That won't be me or Aldrick, but it might be you."

The expression that passed over Killan's face made her think of when he'd been a child, and she'd asked him a question he couldn't possibly know the answer to. Fortunately, as an adult, he wasn't above asking for help. "But I don't know the way forward."

"Do you want war with the cities?"

"Of course not."

"And you clearly don't want to hand over Bael, so where does that leave you?"

He looked lost, but only for a moment. Elian had been the one that taught him that often in life, when it appears there are only two choices, it was best to make a third. "It means the clans need to learn how to make do without the cities, at least for a time."

Samora nodded. "It will be a hard transition for the younger warriors, but perhaps a good one. The hardship will teach them to be more self-reliant. Lean on the other elders, for they're well familiar with what will be needed."

"You speak as though you won't be around."

"I have no immediate plans to leave, but who knows if I'll be able to stay? They'll all be suspicious of me, and if they ask me to track down Bael and Elian, I'm not sure what I'll do."

Killan looked around the camp. "How did it come to this so quickly?"

"This enemy knows us well. Better, I think, than the Debru ever did, and they were once human. They found a weakness and hit it hard, and now it will be up to us to make sure nothing breaks."

Killan nodded, then embraced her again. He whispered into her ear. "I love you, and no matter what happens, I'll always support you."

"I love you, too, no matter what you have to do to lead the clan."

AFTER SPEAKING WITH KILLAN, she hurried through the camp until she found Aldrick. "I need to step outside the camp for a bit. Care to join me?"

His eyes narrowed. "You almost never ask me to join you. Why now?"

"I might attract some attention, and I'd prefer to remain undisturbed, if I could."

"Is this the sort of guard duty that might put me at risk of throwing up my breakfast?"

"Very possibly."

"Fantastic," he grumbled, but he rose to his feet with just a hint of a smile on his face. He'd never say it, and had certainly never said it in the four decades they'd been bonded, but he appreciated the chaos she brought to his otherwise orderly life.

They made it through and beyond the camp with surprisingly little difficulty, but it was early morning yet. Samora was certain it would be a full day, and she grew tired even thinking about it. But those problems could be set aside for a bit.

Something she'd said to Killan sparked a question she needed to answer. The emissary knew them well—too well, really. Which meant observation over the course of months, if not years. And Bael's transgression had been punished nearly instantaneously. How did the emissary know?

Two possibilities. First, the emissary could use its power the way she used adani, an imperfect tool that could sense events from great distances. But she didn't think so. Or at least, she didn't think that was the emissary's primary tool. The destruction in Rydal hadn't felt the same, and if she was prone to betting, she would have bet it wasn't the emissary's personal work. It had help. People—or beings masked as people—helping it watch over the world.

Could she find them?

She certainly hadn't before they'd struck, but now that she was almost certain they were there...

They walked until Samora's senses weren't pulled so strongly by the wandering clans, about half a mile. She positioned Aldrick between her and the camp, then went on another couple hundred paces. Then she reached into a pocket and pulled out a small pouch filled with hearts, these from the cave where she'd trained with the elder dragon.

She sat down and planted four around her, creating her own small gathering ground. Combined with the heart in her own core, she possessed more than enough adani for today's search. She connected first with the heart in her core, then extended and joined her adani to that of the gathering ground.

In the distance, she sensed Aldrick's stomach churn, and she silently apologized. She saw little point in subtlety today.

She thrust her adani into the world, as though stabbing it with a spear of awareness. It reached down until it struck the rich web of adani that stretched across the land, and then she directed it toward Rydal. If the emissary had servants, one was certainly there.

Her adani hopped from heart to heart, strengthened by each of the gathering grounds she and the other wandering clans had planted across the decades. Thanks to their efforts, by the time her spirit reached Rydal, it was as if she stood just outside the city.

At first glance, Rydal barely seemed any different than normal. The streets and homes were filled with people bustling about their day, busy with whatever tasks consumed the days of the city dwellers. She pushed adani into the circle of destruction near the center of the city, but it was no different than the one in Nevan, and there was nobody there.

She searched for some sense of that void that had so cleanly destroyed two cities, hoping it would be easier to sense in a city full of adani, a darkness in a sea of light. That sea of light shifted and moved, as alive as the actual sea Samora had once visited, but nothing in the beautiful cacophony of spirit so much as hinted at the presence of a servant of the emissary.

She trusted her logic and still believed the emissary had a scout of some sort within Rydal, but even so, she couldn't find it.

She didn't dwell upon the failure, but instead turned the direction of her adani from Rydal to Nevan. The city, the first built in this age, was twice as large as Rydal, with nearly three times as many spirits rushing to and fro. The sum total of all that energy was far greater than a gathering ground, and in better times, when less was at stake, Samora had allowed her spirit to float among them, to be pushed and pulled like waves upon a distant shore.

She searched for anything that might pledge allegiance to the emissary, but as in Rydal, nothing caught her attention. The hole in the center of the city, the blow that had driven the wedge right through the heart of humanity, was now impossible to penetrate with adani. She sensed how busy the training grounds had become, filled with young men and women training to become adanists.

She lingered there a moment. What would Elian say, knowing how little it took to gather so many new recruits? He'd never stoop to the emissary's methods, but there was no denying its effectiveness. She grunted softly. Even though they were training, they weren't making much progress. Their instructors would be busy for a long time, making adanists out of children who'd had no desire before.

From Nevan, she extended her search to a handful of villages chosen at random, but even with fewer spirits to sort through, she couldn't find any trace of the emissary's servants.

Movement much closer to her brought her attention closer to where she sat. Aldrick burned bright, his way of telling her that her attention was needed here. She brought her adani back, and as she did, she sensed the presences making their way from the camp to her impromptu gathering ground.

They were moving quickly, then.

She scooped the hearts up from where she'd buried them and stood, brushing the dirt from her bottom. She calmed the storm in her core, and the heart's adani slowly faded from her body. It got harder to let go every time, and she still remembered the offer the heart had once made to her, to let her spirit flee from her body and join it in eternity.

She'd had so much less to live for then, though. Now she had children and grandchildren, blood that she would do anything to protect. Tempting as the heart's offer was, especially as her body slowly aged and the world fell back into conflict, she no longer wanted to leave any of it behind.

The approaching delegation was led by Killan, and though Samora dreaded the argument they were about to have, she was glad he retained the position of leader. The clan would be better off with him guiding them. She walked forward until she stood beside Aldrick, and the two of them waited together.

Killan, Lieran, and a handful of other warriors stopped a few paces away. Her son spoke without hesitation. "We felt your search from the camp. Are you looking for Elian and Bael?"

"They haven't landed yet, so I don't know which direction they went. I was searching for any of the emissary's servants."

"Are you mad?" Lieran exclaimed. "After what has just happened to Rydal, you would test the emissary again?"

"Not test. The emissary never spoke about using adani to search through the cities, so I deemed it safe."

"Bael deemed it safe when he rode right into one! Is your whole family incapable of following a rule?"

Killan held out a hand to calm Lieran's outburst. "Did you find them?"

"I did not. Either they are able to hide themselves from adani, or the emissary has trained humans to use its power."

Lieran snorted, making his point without saying a word. She'd risked them all and had nothing to show in return.

Thankfully, she'd raised Killan to think more deeply, and he weighed her words. "Both are troubling, but the idea the emissary has been here and successfully recruited and trained human allies without us noticing is truly terrifying."

Lieran didn't seem troubled by the same, and though Samora

had known Lieran since he was a child and didn't believe the thought for a moment, she wondered if he was a traitor, if his focus on hunting down Bael and Elian had a purpose greater than the safety of the wandering clan. She refused to believe it was true, but she could see how it might be and cursed the emissary for even putting the thought in her mind.

Lieran waited until he was sure Killan had nothing more to say, then sprung his trap. "The elders have decided that Bael should face Rydal's elders for the crime he committed against the city, and that Elian must speak before our elders before having any contact with the Wolves. It is expected that you and Aldrick will do all that's in your power to ensure the will of the elders is carried out."

His words cut deep, but they were cuts she had expected. She hadn't been prepared for the looks he gave her, though, as though she was an enemy to be watched. Some of his first training had come from her, and he'd ascended under her close supervision.

None of which seemed to matter today.

She swallowed her objections, which Lieran wouldn't listen to, anyway, and bowed toward the delegation. They left, satisfied, focused more on hunting their own than the enemy that had divided them.

17

Say one thing about the emissary, but he spoke truly, and his medicine was a cure more physically painful than the weakness it sought to treat. Fragments of his spirit wandered through her body, explored even as the pain drove her beyond consciousness. She would wake later, and he would offer her food and water whose origin Elyn couldn't begin to guess, and then she would sleep again, and when she awoke, stronger than before, they would slip the chains on and return her to a painful oblivion.

The first time, she'd almost begged for mercy. It was one thing to expect the pain, but another to experience it, and her whole body had shivered uncontrollably when the emissary had appeared and asked her if she was willing to continue. She'd cried as she nodded, cried like she hadn't since she was a child whose dreams had been stolen from her. She'd still been shaking when they returned to the platform, and she'd needed his assistance to simply walk.

Every time she awoke, he asked her permission to continue.

She'd wondered at that, at first, until she realized the stakes weren't the same as when he'd asked before beginning the healing. That time, she'd believed him when he said that he would return her home. Now he made no such promises. He didn't ask for permission because he cared about her consent, for that had already been given. He asked for permission to test her spirit, to ensure she would willingly bear the suffering for the power he offered. She wondered what would happen if, upon waking, she told him she could take no more.

She suspected he would grant her an eternal rest from her suffering.

The first time had been the only time there had been any real doubt. Her entire right arm had felt as though it had been on fire, her flesh and muscle burning and crisping like a thick cut of beef meant for a feast. And for what? Yes, adani flowed through her hand and wrist, partway up her arm, freely, a sensation she hadn't felt for decades, but the change was so little, and for the first time she understood how much suffering her healing would bring.

She'd learned something new about herself, though, discovered a strength in her spirit she hadn't known had existed before.

She'd once convinced herself that exiling herself from the clan and starting life anew as a farmer had been the true test of her soul. That she possessed the strength to leave everything behind and to devote her life to the back-breaking work of tending a land for the benefit of the warriors who wanted nothing to do with her, and to do it all without a word of complaint.

Her current trials made her question how much she'd been deceiving herself.

It helped that the healing neared its conclusion. Adani flowed smoothly through her arms, legs, and head, and the last few sessions had been crawling ever closer to her core, where the mangled heart resided. Thanks to the emissary, she felt in better health than she had in decades, but she wouldn't be healed until he reached the core.

They walked together toward the platform, under a blood-red sky that never seemed to shift, as though this world knew no day or night. She'd asked, once, why this was, but his explanation, about the spin of the world as it traveled through space, made little sense to her, so she simply accepted it as a feature of this world.

"You're able to endure much more healing than when we started. It's possible, though I'll make no promises, that this will be your final healing," the emissary said.

The comment might have once set her heart racing, but today she only nodded. It wasn't that she looked forward to the pain of healing, but that she'd come to understand that pain and suffering were just experiences, with no greater or less value than pleasure and contentment. She climbed onto the platform and helped the emissary attach the manacles which kept her in place. Then she bit down on the leather-wrapped stick, the third or fourth she'd used throughout the healing, and the emissary rested his hand on her chest. She nodded, and he began.

The pain no longer froze her thoughts or consumed the entirety of her attention, so even as it struck, she was able to keep her senses focused on the process, learning even as her body was made whole again. The emissary's technique was as simple as it was impossible for any adanist Elyn had ever met. The day she'd tried to ascend, everything had gone wrong. She still didn't know if it was because she'd lost control over the process or if she hadn't been ready in the first place. Either way, instead of strengthening her body, the heart had overflowed within her, and the currents of adani had whipped and snapped, knotting themselves within her, too tight for even Samora to unravel.

The emissary didn't bother unraveling the knots. Instead, his void technique sought out each of the hundreds of knots scattered throughout her body, and when it found them, it cut them into shreds. He was, in essence, carving out small parts of her body, which explained the burning across her limbs and the needles of pure ice she endured.

The most surprising part of the healing happened next, after the void had removed one of the knots. Elyn could sense how the healing could be used as an attack, how the use of void spheres could permanently destroy the flow of adani in a body, but the emissary was too careful for that. He used tiny amounts of void, but had such control it removed the void completely from her body when he was done, allowing her own adani to race in and heal what had been broken.

Elyn bit down hard as the healing began. She could sense the void moving through her body, a pinpoint of darkness that floated through her muscles, organs, and bones as though they were nothing more than clouds in the sky. It only became real when it found one of the knots, tied so tightly most healers in the clans couldn't even sense them. Then the void grew and became solid, and everything within it simply vanished.

She'd sensed the destruction of Nevan from the safety of her home, but now she understood it intimately, for it had happened hundreds of times within her own flesh. Her breath caught as part of her lungs disappeared and the air which she took for granted suddenly became the most valuable resource in her world.

Then her adani was there, warm and gentle as a summer breeze, knitting together her lungs and guiding her adani channels back into place. The hole in her lungs healed and she sucked air in through her nose, just in time for another hole in her lungs to appear.

Then there was only the heart left, forever a part of her, a constant reminder of her failure and impotence.

"This will hurt," he said. "A lot. Even for you."

She nodded, and that was all he needed.

The nature of an ascended heart was a mystery to the wandering clans. Did it retain its physical form as it embedded itself in the body of its host, or did it become pure adani, untethered from physical constraints? None of the ascended had died yet, so they hadn't yet opened up a body to find out.

Samora believed that the heart became both, a belief Elyn had never quite been able to wrap her mind around. It was something both physical and energetic, yet entirely neither, as though it existed in a state between the two.

At the moment, it felt very physical. The emissary shaped void in his hand, hard to see because of the angle and the darkness of the sky, but something between a spear and a needle, a narrow tube with a pointed end. The emissary took a deep breath, as though uncertain for the first time since the healing began and brought the spear down.

Elyn didn't have time to react. The void pierced her flesh, dissolving everything it touched as it burrowed toward her core. She gasped. She'd thought she'd come to understand pain, but the war that erupted above her navel made her previous experiences pale in comparison.

The emissary's needle was cold as ice, but everything it touched burned hotter than fire, and when the needle met heart, Elyn's entire body went rigid with white-hot pain, as though a dragon had breathed fire directly into her gut and her insides were bubbling and erupting like the volcanoes far to the south of her farm. She strained against the chains, but not for long, because strength fled from her body, seeking more peaceful pastures.

The needle dug deeper yet, freezing and burning everything it touched, and then it touched the very center of her core.

The emissary might as well have reached in with both hands and torn her insides apart, as she felt her very being pulled out by the needle. A flash of bright light blinded her, and she screamed around the stick in her mouth until the back of her throat was raw.

The darkness that followed the light couldn't come quickly enough.

SHE SWAM in a sea of memories, glimpses of lives she'd left behind. The pride on Father's face when she revealed how she'd learned to loop adani through her limbs, just like he did. Learning how to prepare venison with Mother. How she'd cried the first time she'd killed a hare with an adani spear. The view of the world from the skies, riding on a dragon's back. Sneaking away from camp to trade kisses with the only boy who had the courage to pretend he wasn't scared of Father.

Her own pride, as Samora, Father, and Mother all decided she'd learned enough and grown strong enough to ascend, the youngest by far.

And of course, the nightmare of every day since. The day she'd realized no one would ever look at her the way they once had, followed immediately after by the realization she'd rather not be looked at ever again than endure their mixture of pity and judgment.

The emissary spoke with another, and Samora thought he spoke of a hunt, but the vision darkened and she was in her fields again, able to sense the life all around her but not be part of it.

She woke in a cave with all the comforts of home. Blankets had been piled high on top of her, and a small fire burned nearby, heating the cave and casting warm shades of color against the stone. A teapot steamed through its spout, and a simple cup with a chip on its edge waited to accept the tea. She laid still for a while, feeling every day of her more than four decades of life in every bone and muscle of her body.

Her hand slowly traveled down her stomach, to where the void needle had pierced her skin, but she couldn't feel so much as a scar. The heart was gone, though. She held her hand tightly to her stomach and bit back tears. Strange, that she should feel so empty after the curse that had plagued her was removed. She sat up, and it was if she had never sat up before, the muscles in her stomach and back complaining about the effort. A groan escaped her sealed lips.

The emissary appeared at the entrance to the cave as she sipped slowly at her tea. "You're awake earlier than I expected."

He carried cooked meats on a wooden plate, and Elyn's mouth watered at the smell. He set it before her and sat on the other side of the small cave, gesturing for her to eat her fill. "How do you feel?"

"Empty, but otherwise well, I think."

"It'll take some time for strength to return to your body. I'd advise you not to push yourself too hard, yet."

She chewed on the cut of beef, briefly wondering where it had come from, before asking him, "What comes next?"

"Your training, if you still wish it. To begin, I'd like you to recover the ability you had with adani before you attempted to ascend."

"To learn the void, you want me to study adani?"

"To begin. There are other methods, for those younger and less set in their ways, but your quickest route to the truth will be through what you already know."

Elyn looked around the cave. It was small, no more than four or five paces deep and about three wide, but the red sky outside made her certain she was still on the emissary's planet. "Will I even be able to work with adani here?"

"The adani in your body is still your own. You don't need any more."

"And after that?"

The emissary smiled as he stood to leave. "And then I'll teach you of the void, and you'll understand the truth."

18

Bael and Elian rode Arok well past the breaking of the dawn and into the new day, landing only once the sun had stretched high into the sky. The ride had been mostly silent, and Bael had spent half the time thinking that his life was as good as over and the other half cursing himself for allowing Elian's involvement. Bad enough that both Rydal and the clan wanted his head, but now he'd doomed the most legendary warrior the clans had known since Abram.

All because he'd been a fool and worse.

Elian hadn't chosen a friendly environment to hide in. Bael had recognized it from the sky, a stretch of deadlands still not healed by the efforts of the wandering clans. It wasn't as dead and lifeless as the stories told, but only because Samora and the other healers had spent decades bringing life to the barren wastes. Their work wasn't over, but at the pace the land recovered, the deadlands would fade into memory within the lifetime of the next generation.

Even someone as thickheaded as him understood why Elian had chosen this place. The web of adani was weak here, which would help hide them from the adanists who would send their adani across the land to find them. It wouldn't be enough to deter pursuit for long, but any help was better than none.

They dismounted, and Bael's feet sank into the sandy, loose soil. He hated the deadlands, hated how they numbed his own senses and disconnected him from the deep well of adani most lands possessed. He hated that they needed to be here. Elian clambered off of Arok like a spider and landed softly beside Bael. He couldn't bring himself to look up from his feet, though.

Elian clapped him on the shoulder so hard Bael was almost knocked out of his boots. Instinct drew his gaze up, prepared to meet a threat, only to find Elian grinning from ear to ear.

"You looked less glum when the council was sentencing you to death. Surely my company can't be that painful to endure?"

Bael stared, mouth slack. Where were the threats, the long lectures? The punishment he so richly deserved?

Was Elian *happy*?

His great-uncle's face fell, but even in Bael's stunned state, he recognized Elian's dramatics for what they were.

"It is my company, isn't it? Capricia told me you'd get bored with an old man."

Bael grunted, and then his composure broke. He chuckled and shook his head. "You're a strange one, uncle."

"Maybe so, but there's no point in losing your joy and your head in the same day."

Bael gestured to the deadlands surrounding them. "Hard to summon a smile after the past few days."

Elian's lips turned up in a half smile. "All the better reason to try, then."

Bael shook his head again. Of course, Elian was trying to cheer him up and keep his spirits high, but Elian also wasn't the kind of man to lie or put on an act for the benefit of others. Despite everything, Uncle wasn't actually bothered by being exiled by his clan and becoming one of the most wanted men in the land. Bael mourned what was no longer his, but how much more had Elian given up?

The thought would only send him spiraling downward again, so he forced himself to address more pertinent problems. "Did you have any plan after helping me escape the clans?"

"We train together and figure out how to defeat the emissary. Then we go and beat the emissary. Should solve most, if not all, of your problems."

"That...lacks a certain amount of specificity."

Elian's grin returned, as wide as ever. "Details were never my strength. That's why I always kept Samora and Capricia around."

"The clans will find us. All the strongest adanists can search the deadlands even with the weakness of the web."

"Which is why I know what technique I'll teach you first."

Instead of saying more, Elian began manipulating adani, first within his body, then around it. Bael jumped back and bit back a shout as his sense of Elian vanished. He needed a moment to reassure himself Elian was still standing in front of him, looking like a child showing off a new trick he'd just learned.

And it was quite a trick, for Elian in particular. The man's presence was equal to a squad of ascended adanists, and he pulled adani wherever he walked. Sensing him vanish from adani was like having the entire sky go dark in the middle of the day.

"How?" Bael asked.

"Figure it out for yourself. You're close enough to sense every detail."

He'd forgotten how challenging training with Elian could be. His uncle made his students fight for every scrap of knowledge, but once they'd won it, they possessed it for life. Bael calmed his racing heart, then stretched his adani toward Elian. He hadn't even reached his uncle when it started twisting away, caught in a current that circled gently around Elian.

Bael frowned and pushed, and the circle around Elian shrank, but his adani never reached Elian. He pulled back, then thrust hard, but again it simply flowed around.

"Your Grandmother taught me this trick. It's not perfect—an adanist who knows what they're looking for will sense this, too, but there aren't many who know it. Samora could find me, but she'll let us keep our distance while we train."

"You expect me to layer this technique on top of everything else I'll be trying as we train?"

It was the wrong question, and he knew it as soon as it left his lips, and he hung his head, so that Elian didn't have to answer.

"Samora and I developed the technique because we planned on fighting another war against the Debru, who are particularly sensitive to adani. We thought that if we could hide our movements from them, they'd have no chance against us. Turns out, it's useful for other purposes as well. But yes, it was always intended to complement combat techniques."

Elian left Bael to teach himself the technique while he spoke with Arok. Bael wasn't privy to the conversation, but it lasted a good while, after which, Arok flew north. Then Elian sat and waited for Bael to appropriately master the new technique. It didn't take long even though it required mastery of both internal and external adani. Bael had always been a quick learner.

They moved on to basic combat training, allowing Elian to test Bael's mastery of the new technique while they lightly sparred. Then he pushed harder, until Bael was doing everything he could simply to keep up.

Elian broke off his attack, not even winded.

Bael swore. He'd improved in leaps and bounds over the past few years, and he thought he'd closed the gap with Elian. It seemed, instead, as wide as ever. Elian seemed equally confused. "Are you nearing your limit?"

There was no point lying. Elian would know the truth soon enough, so Bael nodded. Elian frowned and scratched the side of his head. "And you came close to cutting the emissary's core?"

Elian's doubt pierced as deeply as a spear.

"I did catch it by surprise," Bael reminded Elian.

"Even so, if what you say is true, and I do believe you, the emissary is weaker than the Vada. At least in terms of combat ability."

Bael's disbelief must have shown, because Elian explained. "I was weaker than you are now when I fought the Vada. You need to remember that I had only ascended while in battle with it. If not for your grandmother's help, I wouldn't have won, and I had only a fraction of your current strength."

Bael knew the story, had listened to Grandmother repeat it upon request until she was tired of hearing her own voice, but he'd never dared consider himself equal to either of the heroes of the clans. And he wasn't. He hadn't come close to Elian while sparring.

"And now? Do you think you could cut the emissary down?"

Elian shrugged, and then he burned adani, so bright Bael's first instinct was to disconnect from his heart so his senses wouldn't be blinded. But the brightness was only for show, and before Bael could protect his senses, Elian's overwhelming presence retreated. Not extinguished or diminished but contained. Bael's hair stood on end, even though he couldn't sense Elian with his adani.

His great-uncle moved faster than Bael's ascended eyes could track. In the blink of an eye, he was well behind Bael, a razor-thin blade of adani in his hand.

Bael swore, shook his head, then swore again as Elian let go of the strength he'd contained. He still couldn't sense his great-uncle, but that strength and speed was beyond what he'd even imagined possible.

Hope bloomed, washing away the disbelief of what he'd just witnessed. With this much strength, the matter was as good as settled. "All we need to do is get you close. You can end this nightmare with one cut."

Elian frowned. "Perhaps. It might be why the emissary has never appeared near me. Or it might be that it is holding secrets we can only guess at. Its apparent weakness makes me uneasy, and if we're wrong, it's innocent civilians that will suffer for it."

Bael's throat went dry, and he swallowed hard. Only days had passed, and had he already forgotten his lesson? How many more would have to die to teach him wisdom?

Elian thought a moment longer. "Still, it might be our best plan. If the emissary is so weak and we can figure out a way to kill it, our troubles might soon be over."

BAEL TOSSED and turned under the stars that night, wishing that his troubles might soon be over, but suspecting otherwise. The sleepless nights, the travel, and the training with Elian should have worn him out, but his mind raced on, powered by dark thoughts he had no control over.

His body ached, but it was clear he'd get no sleep anytime soon, so he rolled as quietly as he could from his covers and away from Elian, who snored the peaceful slumber of the guiltless.

A sleep Bael wasn't sure he'd ever experience again.

He walked in no particular direction, steps slow and heavy. The stars were clear and bright, and he'd often found solace under their silent flickering gaze, but tonight they accused him and judged him guilty, weighing him down under their relentless stares.

He deserved no less. More, probably. He'd known the risks of visiting Rydal, but had dismissed them out of hand. He hadn't killed Rydal's citizens, but their blood stained his hands and spirit all the same. Perhaps it would be easier for everyone if he submitted to Rydal's justice.

For a time, he'd thought he might be the one strong enough to kill the emissary, but Elian had shown him otherwise. Elian was more than enough, meaning Bael had no reason to keep resisting. At best, he was in Elian's way.

He was just wondering if Arok might take him to Rydal when the emissary appeared before him.

At first, Bael thought he'd become so tired he was imagining his enemies, now, but the hairs on the back of his neck stood up, just as they had when Elian had contained so much adani within his flesh. The similarity made his knees weak.

"I come bearing greetings," the emissary said.

Bael glanced back the way he'd came. He wasn't more than a quarter mile away from where he'd left Elian, but the original ascended adanist was still snoring away. And why not? Bael couldn't sense the emissary that clearly, and he was standing three paces away. Even Elian's sharp senses wouldn't pick up this conversation. Though if Bael flared adani, Elian would wake in an instant.

"I wouldn't," the emissary warned.

Bael had never been that great a listener, unless he was listening to one of Grandmother's stories. He reached toward the heart in his core, but before he could flare his adani, the emissary's fist was in his stomach, and all the air in his lungs fled for a more hospitable home. He gasped and fell to his knees, and when he blinked, the emissary was standing a few paces away, as though it had never moved. If not for the undeniable lack of air in his lungs, he would have thought he was imagining things.

The emissary stretched its hand. "Apologies. I only came to talk, but you're a difficult young man to convince to listen. I bring greetings from your cousin Elyn. She's started training with me."

Bael was able to force just enough air in his lungs to say, "You lie."

"It's easy enough to check, and you'll know soon enough. Regardless, I do not lie, and I've come to extend my offer one last time."

Bael pushed himself back to his feet, but he didn't burn adani. "You want me to join you? Why?"

"I want powerful servants who understand the truth of the world. And you want more strength, the same as you always have. Together, we both get what we want."

"I won't ally myself with a killer like you."

"And yet you eagerly accept Elian's training? His actions doomed an entire world, you know."

Bael shook his head. Elian had never done anything except defend this world. "And if I don't?"

"Then perhaps it's time for Elian to die. I've left him alone thus far, but he is proving to be a nuisance."

Only one threat, at that moment, could have caused Bael to hesitate, and the emissary had found it. He stopped, and he thought, and for the first time, he truly considered the emissary's claim. Elyn, for all her bitterness, was a good woman. If this creature told the truth, she wouldn't have joined him without reason.

He couldn't follow that path of reason for long, for he'd never been one to tie himself up in knots. What was right was easy enough to know, and didn't require long, drawn-out arguments. The emissary had attacked first, without warning, killing people who couldn't have fought back even if they'd known they were in danger.

The emissary was nothing like Elian, and Bael attacked, though before Bael advanced more than a step, the emissary vanished faster than a bad dream.

Bael nearly twisted an ankle in the soft sand as he turned and ran back toward their camp, hoping he hadn't just killed Elian.

19

"And then it just...left?" Samora asked.

Even after years of having these types of conversations, she'd never quite gotten used to how vulnerable she felt speaking with her brother through their shared connection. Here, there was no place to hide, even when there was no need to hide.

"Seems that way," Elian answered. His voice was everything she would have expected. Even, steady, dismissive, and unconcerned. The voice of the hero of the clans, the man who had learned to fight a Vada and only grown stronger every day since.

Except she could feel everything he felt, could sense the pounding of his heart and the tingle of fear in his chest that hadn't yet faded.

Tera had asked them once, before old age had taken her from them, why they didn't form similar connections with their bonded partners. For Samora, the matter was straightforward. The connection required the strength of a heart, and Aldrick would never possess one. Elian, though, hadn't considered it for more than a moment. A strong relationship, he believed, wasn't about knowing everything his partner thought. Despite what a young lover might think, there was very much a danger in too much knowledge.

It only worked for Samora and Elian because they spent most of their lives physically apart, and because they made few demands of the other.

"How's Bael?"

"Shaken, but he'll be fine. Full of questions, but he's not the only one."

"Like why you are even alive?"

"To start with, but I don't think we'll understand that until we can ask the emissary. Did it speak true about Elyn?"

"I'll see."

She sent out her adani, dancing from heart to heart until she reached the fields Elyn called home. When she didn't find Elyn there, she extended her search, and it was a good while before she called her adani back. Thankfully, she didn't need to say anything because Elian's spirit had been beside her the entire time. She didn't think she could have given the news to him.

"It doesn't mean the emissary was telling the truth," Samora said, grasping for some sliver of comfort.

Elian grunted, and too late, Samora realized her mistake. "Only other option is she's dead, and I'd much prefer to have her alive and training under the emissary."

She almost said she couldn't believe Elyn would do such a thing, but those words would be empty, too. Of anyone in their families, Elyn would be the most susceptible, only because she'd lost so much. The right promise would tempt her, and likely had. Once again, the emissary knew them too well.

Elian didn't want to linger on the fate of his daughter. "Still, the emissary made a mistake. Bael sensed the way it manipulated adani, and it's not that dissimilar from the technique you and I developed to hide from the Debru. If you seek that pattern out, you might find its allies."

"I'll try. You still think that's the most reasonable explanation for its knowledge?"

"I think so. It knows us well, both as a society and as individuals. Can't say I see it happening without many years of close observation. Combined with the different feeling of the attack in Rydal, and I think we're dealing with two different types of enemies."

Samora nodded. "Anything else?"

"I can't figure out why it tried to recruit Bael instead of kill him." Elian paused, "Why it's recruiting from our families."

"Reminds me of when we first fought the Debru. We suspected there was more going on that we didn't understand, and it's no different now. The emissary doesn't want to simply destroy the world. It's looking for hearts and strong warriors, but why?"

"And why hasn't it tried to recruit us? If it's looking for strength, we're still the strongest in the world." Elian almost sounded hurt that he'd been passed over.

"Maybe it knows we're too stubborn? Or too set in our ways? I hate to say it, but Elyn would be open to any number of promises, and Bael's been so desperate for a fight, the emissary might have thought he'd be willing to abandon our world for one."

Elian mused on the thought, then said, "Perhaps. It still feels like there's something more, a purpose we haven't guessed at yet. I won't say this to Bael, though I think he'll figure it out soon enough, but I think the emissary deceived him the first time they met, reacted slowly so that Bael would think he was stronger than he is. Make him think he had a chance of beating it."

"Why?"

"Because it knows Bael. If I were going to train him, what would I do? I'd give him a challenge just a bit beyond his skill. He sinks into himself when the challenge is too great, but when he's sure he can triumph, he'll give it his all. If Bael followed the emissary, thinking he could beat it with a little bit of training, the emissary wins."

Samora didn't disagree with Elian's assessment, but still, "That's an incredible insight into Bael's spirit."

"Like I said, it knows us well. Maybe even better than we know ourselves. I never would have expected humanity to divide so cleanly and so quickly, but here we are."

A commotion stirred near the edges of Samora's awareness, near the edges of the camp. "Something's come up, and I need to go. I'll search for allies when I get the chance, but are you sure you're fine?"

"We're as well as can be. I'll talk to you soon."

"Love you."

"Love you, too."

SAMORA WALKED QUICKLY toward the disturbance on the south side of camp. Several adanists had gathered, their spirits active. As she came closer, muffled cries of pain carried her to the source.

Two adanists carried a third, Olin, between them. Olin was ascended, though had only passed the trials a couple of years before. Samora had overseen much of his training, although that was true for almost all the Wolves. She liked him, because he never fell into the trap of believing his strength put him above anyone else, a common curse among the more recently ascended adanists. He kept a grin on his face whether he was on a dragon patrolling the land or elbow deep in a deer's carcass, pulling out the organs for later use. He was rare among the Wolves, in that he hadn't bonded with another adanist, but a merchant's daughter from Nevan.

None of that mattered, now, though. Olin's face was pale, and blood leaked from the slack corner of his mouth. His eyes were distant, and he didn't respond to his name being called. He cried out as his friends dragged his feet over clump of thick grass, but Samora couldn't see anything visibly wrong with him.

They were already heading toward the healing tent, so Samora joined them, and though many of them had been glaring at her earlier in the day, they were grateful for her presence now. "What happened?" she asked.

No one knew, and the story only emerged in bits and pieces. Olin had been on close patrol tonight with another adanist. They had been on foot, walking the perimeter of the camp. One of the other patrols had sensed a brief flare of adani and heard a cry, and they'd run to help their friends. When they'd arrived, they found Olin on the ground, a pool of bloody vomit beside him, and nothing else. There was no sign of his partner, and Olin hadn't been able to tell them anything.

They all rushed into the healing tent together, and Olin cried out again as they placed him on one of the cots. Samora put her hand to his stomach and was surprised how thin he felt. To her knowledge, he hadn't lost any significant weight lately, nor had he been sick.

She sent out a pulse of adani, then inhaled sharply through her nose and took a step back.

The adanists who'd carried him in looked at her, questions in their eyes, but confident that whatever had happened, she could heal him. She was Samora, the greatest of the clan healers.

She gathered her wits and placed her hand on him again, although this time close to his shoulder, and she swore silently to herself.

Parts of him were simply missing, the same way parts of Rydal and Nevan were missing, consumed by a void that left nothing behind. Not just in his chest and stomach, but in his mind, too, smaller holes, no bigger than the size of a pea, but scattered around in as if a farmer had been careless with a bag of seed.

Samora's adani reacted to her emotions, burning the heart as though it were a star, but it did nothing but seep from her skin and bleed into the surrounding air. It was impossible to believe he'd lived as long as he had.

She cooled her adani and took a step away from him. The merciful course of action would be to kill him now, but she doubted any of his friends were thinking so clearly. "There's nothing I can do for him."

Their reactions were slow in coming, their belief in her so absolute they didn't realize there was only so much even she could heal. The death of that belief came hard, and anger filled in the gaps in their spirit. "Why not?" one demanded.

"It's the emissary's work, or someone allied with it. Too much of his body is missing. Organ, muscle, and bone. They even took from his head. I could flood him with adani, but it would only prolong his agony, and I can't heal what's been done to his mind."

She shouldn't have accused the emissary, true as it was. Another pointed at her. "This is your fault for letting Bael leave. It's a message to us."

Samora agreed, though she didn't think the message said what they thought it did.

Olin saved her, at least for the moment, by breathing his last. She sensed the moment his spirit returned to the world, weakened and tired from its final suffering. It sank down into the web of adani and unraveled, its final journey in life. He'd deserved much more from life than what he'd been given, but she took a small measure of comfort in knowing his spirit was at peace.

She wished she could say the same for her own. Elyn missing, Bael's attempted recruitment, the division of humanity, and now the death of another good man. Some weights were too heavy to carry within the sight of all, and she slipped out of the healing tent as Olin's friends paid their final respects. The walls of the tent squeezed at her as she slipped through, but the camp beyond was nothing more than a larger cage. The air seemed warm and heavy, and her heart pounded as it had when she was younger and had to face the council.

She hurried toward the edge of the camp, wanting to run but afraid that if she did it would arouse even greater suspicions, and her bid for a measure of freedom would be cut short by friends that would follow her. She still endured questioning looks, fleeing from Olin's death, but no one stopped her or followed her.

The air beyond the boundaries of the camp was cool, and she wiped the sweat that had beaded on her brow. She didn't stop until she was several hundred paces beyond the walls of the last tent, and she breathed heavily, as though she'd just run a long race. Slowly, so slowly, her heart's beat returned to normal, but she couldn't so much as glance back at the camp without it picking up speed again.

She wanted Mother, to collapse in her strong arms and ask her how she'd kept her and Elian together when they'd fought so much, because her clan, her family, was being torn apart. But Mother was long dead, and she hadn't been able to protect her, much as she wasn't able to protect her clan from the emissary's schemes.

She sat in a cross-legged position and placed her palms against the soil. Knowledge was her refuge and always had been, and she trickled adani into the web. At first, she looked for Olin, but his spirit was nowhere to be found, or more accurately, it was everywhere, just not a whole spirit. Death returned adani to the world and spread it far and wide, unraveling it until there was nothing identifiable left. Elian still claimed he had sensed Harald's spirit once, long after his death, but neither of them had experienced anything similar since.

And Harald had truly been a great spirit. For as much as she had loved Olin, he wasn't of a kind with Harald. Few, if any, were.

But her adani continued to spread, diffusing from her body, because within the web of adani that stretched across the world, all was as it should be. It welcomed her with open arms, promising eternal peace from all her human suffering. The more she wove adani, the more she became convinced that this was where she belonged, her true home, taken from her through the blessing of birth.

She wandered without reason until she came to the nearest village. It wasn't much. Smaller, even, than the one she'd grown up in. Less than a hundred people, but growing with every season, a home for those not quite willing to adopt the lifestyle and trials of the wandering clans, but quieter than the cities. Dozens of similar villages had grown over the last decade, the perfect compromise for many. As it was the middle of the night, the village was quiet. No watches were kept, as until a couple of weeks ago, there were no threats to fear.

Except there was movement. Nothing she noticed immediately, but only after her adani lingered among the silent homes. It bent and swirled in places where it should have traveled straight, and that slight whirlpool of adani moved.

If she hadn't known better, she would have wondered if Elian had chosen the village to hide in.

But he and Bael were in the deadlands, which meant she'd found two of the emissary's allies, making their home in the village closest to the Wolves' camp. Perhaps returning from Olin's murder?

She held onto the knowledge of their location, spreading her adani farther yet. To the next village, and the village beyond. To Rydal and Nevan, and every gathering of humans between. In every place, the same story, told a dozen different ways. In every group, an ally of the emissary, a slight swirling of adani no one would notice unless they were looking for it, and even then, hard to find.

The emissary's allies weren't just here.

They were everywhere. Dozens of them.

And one group was heading toward Elian and Bael.

20

E lian and Bael squatted around a rough map that Elian had sketched in the loose soil. Dawn threatened the horizon with bloody streaks of red, but the sun hadn't yet risen, leaving Elian's lines barely visible in the pre-dawn light. Elian poked his stick in the soil six times, just east of where he'd drawn their camp. He'd drawn a few features of the land in, too, but there wasn't much. The deadlands had been a relatively flat prairie before the Debru had decimated the land, and what groves of trees had once existed were long gone.

Elian tried to hide his eagerness from his nephew, but Bael was too sharp not to notice. Bael said nothing, though, as he shared the same sentiment. Here was a chance to fight back, to test themselves against the emissary's power.

"Six?" Bael asked.

"As near as Samora can tell. There may be more, but there won't be less."

"I can't decide if I'm hurt it sent so few, or honored it sent so many."

"Suppose we'll find out soon enough."

"Any strategy?"

Elian stared at his map and wondered why he'd even drawn it. The deadlands had no terrain to use to their advantage, and it was likely the emissary's allies could sense them, anyhow. "They'll likely try to keep us separated, so try to stay close to me. Otherwise, nothing you wouldn't have already thought of. External adani is probably useless here, too, although I'd ask you to throw a few spears, anyway, just so we can be sure."

"What about Arok?"

"He'll be close in case we need to escape, but he'll have no other role."

"Are you sure? It might not make any sense to drop adani on them from above, but those claws and teeth of his are plenty sharp."

Elian bit back his retort. Yes, Arok's teeth and claws might aid them, but the risk to his friend was too great for too little benefit. The dragons' capture by the Debru, decades past, burned bright in his memory, and the dragons hadn't kept pace with humanity's development. They possessed deep wells of adani, but any ascended could kill them with their greater strength and control. How much more dangerous were the emissary's allies?

"I'm sure," Elian said, and Bael, for once, didn't argue. Maybe there was hope for him yet.

They stood and stretched, facing east together.

"You don't need to worry about me," Bael said, and Elian wondered who he was trying to convince.

"How much I worry about you has very little to do with how strong you are."

Bael nodded. He shifted his weight from one foot to the other, bounced on the balls of his feet, and wiped the palms of his hands against his pants.

Elian kept his thoughts to himself, made himself as still as stone. He didn't doubt Bael's strength or skill, but the young man had never been tested. Bael had hunted and trained his entire life, but never faced an opponent that wanted to kill him. Even the emissary, it seemed, hadn't wanted him dead in their previous encounters.

Sending these warriors, though, sent another message. Bael would have no more chances.

Elian wondered if Bael had made a mistake in not accepting the emissary's offer. If nothing else, his nephew might have had a chance of finding Elyn and bringing her home.

He pushed the thought aside as the emissary's allies appeared on the horizon. They looked as human as him or Bael, and walked with a confident stride, hunters certain of their prey.

Elian stretched one last time. "I'm a bit ashamed to admit it, but I'm looking forward to this."

All Bael could summon was a grunt. Elian glanced over at his nephew, rooted like an ancient tree.

"Come on. No point making them walk all the way here."

He took a few steps forward, then glanced back. Bael stood, still rooted, but then he lurched forward, as though breaking chains that had kept him in place. The first step was the hardest. The second was difficult, but by the time he reached Elian's side, his steps were smooth. Elian kept a step ahead of his nephew, giving him someone to follow.

Though they'd started miles apart, it didn't take long for the two parties to close the distance. The emissary's allies never rushed, and though Elian itched to dart forward, he kept his own pace even to match theirs. The fight would come soon enough.

They were still hundreds of paces away when Elian said, "Throw a few spears their way. Enough to kill, but don't waste your adani."

It was a test, both for Bael and for the emissary's allies. Bael passed his trial, their slow advance giving him time to gather his courage. He bound adani, not into a spear as Elian had asked, but into the dart form his grandmother had used to such great effect against the Debru decades ago. He threw them, and they sped across the gap, faster and straighter than any arrow launched from a bow.

The one in the front of the advancing allies formed...nothing, and Elian sensed his first use of void techniques. It wasn't a shield, for a shield implied the creation of something. The ally instead took away, creating an emptiness before him that swallowed Bael's adani whole.

The adani didn't unravel, at least not in any way Elian could sense. It simply vanished, as though thrown into a hungry maw.

The lead ally dropped his defense and continued walking, undisturbed by the attempt. Elian's fingers danced alongside the side of his thigh, and he grinned. He couldn't count the years since he'd faced such a challenge.

"Would you mind sending out your adani?" he asked Bael.

Seeing the confusion on his nephew's face, he explained. "Do they have a core that moves, like the emissary?"

Bael nodded, a quick flush of red rushing to his cheeks, his unspoken assumptions laid bare.

Elian sensed the wave of adani, and what it lacked in subtlety it made up for in strength. A few steps closer to the emissary's allies and Bael said, "Not that I can sense, although it's difficult to tell. The emissary's spirit was easier to find. I think they die like we do."

A dark sphere, smaller than the leather-wrapped balls the children of the clan liked to play with, formed in front of the emissary's allies. At first glance, it looked like one of the shadow spheres the Debru had been so fond of, but Elian couldn't sense it, so it was likely void instead of shadow. It hung in the air for a moment, then raced toward Elian.

"Shield!" Elian called.

Bael obeyed, weaving a layered shield in an instant, a skill that had once taken Samora precious moments. Void met shield and the shield disappeared, as though it had been nothing more than an illusion. Bael cursed, surprised, like he'd already forgotten how adani and void reacted to one another.

An adani sword appeared in Elian's hand, an extension of the heart's strength, and he cut at the sphere. The edge of his blade struck true, and he felt a moment of resistance, but then he was through. The sphere vanished with a small pop, as though he'd burst a thick-skinned soap bubble and not a deadly technique.

A promising start, though the resistance from the sphere worried him. His sword would have carved through dragon scale as though it was warm butter.

The emissary's small war party stopped and sent more spheres after the first. Most came for Elian, but enough came for Bael that his nephew had to help himself. Elian cut through several and dodged two others. Instead of continuing past him, though, they stopped and attacked from behind, forcing him to turn and cut them down.

Bael grunted as he cut at the spheres aimed for him, but his sword cut through the attacks, too. At least they weren't helpless against the servants' attacks. Still, distance would kill them slowly, if he allowed it. He looped more adani in his legs and ran forward. An emptiness appeared before him, and he stabbed out with his sword.

The wall resisted the point of his blade and forced him to slow. Adani and void wrestled for control of a space not much larger than the head of a pin, but Elian possessed more adani. The tip of his sword cracked the void, and like the spheres, it vanished with a louder popping sound. His success earned him another wave of spheres, too dense for him to keep himself safe, either through speed or by sword. He looped extra adani across his skin the moment before the two spheres that snuck past his sword struck.

They were like no blow he'd taken before. The outer layer of skin vanished as void consumed it, but adani ran just below the surface, carried through countless channels big and small. Light battled void, and as it had every time previous, it won.

But not without cost. The void wanted to consume adani, as it wanted to consume everything it touched. It pulled from Elian and his heart, pulled even from the deadlands beneath Elian's feet. Adani burned as it ripped through his body to fill the void, came close to shredding both muscle and bone as his channels overflowed with the sudden demand. He kept his feet, but that was more stubbornness than strength.

As quickly as the pain tore through him, it ended, his limbs aching with the memory. Bael screamed as a sphere struck him in the side, his legs collapsing as if someone had stolen the bones holding him up. More spheres formed above the emissary's allies, and Elian decided he was honored the emissary had sent six. Two might have been sufficient.

He focused the adani in his body, matching its pulse to his breath, turning the loops in his limbs to a wave that crested with deadly purpose. A single step became a leap, and then he was bounding across the deadlands, the next wave of spheres already behind him as the emissary's precious servants aimed for where he had been.

One reacted fast enough to place another wall between them and him, but Elian swirled the focused adani around his chest before flinging it through his arm and sword. When golden adani struck the emptiness protecting the invaders, it broke through in an instant. The man in the lead only had time for his eyes to widen before Elian's blade separated his head from his shoulders. Another step took him to the next nearest invader, and she wasn't quick enough to stop his blade.

A void sphere struck him from the side, and again it felt as though someone had knocked the spiritual wind out of him. The hit interrupted the delicate dance of adani in his body, leaving him vulnerable.

The emissary's servants never gave him a chance to recover

his balance. Though down two, the remaining four lashed at him with the cold fury of warriors who'd just watched their friends die. He formed a second adani blade and cut through as many of the void spheres as he could, but even two blades could only be in so many places at once, and there were too many of the spheres. His left shoulder went numb as one struck him next to his shoulder blade, sucking adani from him like a thirsty bat. Another slammed into his right calf, just below the knee, and he stumbled, almost falling.

He swung both swords, cutting through another four spheres, but one glanced off his right forearm and yet another punched into his left thigh.

Each hit made it easier for the next sphere to penetrate his defenses, and like a boulder gaining speed as it crashed down the side of a mountain, any thoughts of victory raced farther and farther away. If they'd just give him a moment to recover, he'd be back on his feet and ready for them, but they weren't interested. Sphere after sphere slammed into him, bringing him to a standstill and then to his knees.

Where was Bael? If his nephew could break their coordination, even for a moment, it might be enough for them to change the tide of this battle, but Elian couldn't summon the focus to search for him.

Void spheres landed on him like hail, each of them biting into his flesh and tearing adani from the heart in his core. His adani fought a losing battle against the assault, and the spheres started digging deeper into his flesh, like a healer carving into him without numbing the pain. He screamed, but the battering continued.

Another scream joined his, and adani flashed brighter than the sun as Bael flew like a fiery comet into the midst of the enemy. Elian raised his eyes as he seized the opportunity Bael offered him, focusing his adani and looping it in powerful patterns.

Bael barely looked himself. Chunks of flesh were missing from his arms and face, and his dark clothes were stained darker from the loss of blood. He looked like a walking corpse, but his body blazed with adani, his core glowing like nothing Elian had seen before. Elian couldn't tell where the heart ended and Bael began.

Bael's charge pulled all their enemies' attention away from Elian. Two formed barriers of void that vanished as soon as Bael's sword cut through them, and the other two formed a handful of spheres to chase the threat away. They threw at Bael as the barriers fell, and Bael made no effort to stop them.

The spheres struck Bael's skin but didn't penetrate, the adani flowing too fiercely through his flesh. He roared, though, and Elian knew all too well the pain those spheres brought. Bael swung his sword, but his targets shifted away, faster than the blurred edge of Bael's blade. For all this newfound strength, Bael wasn't any faster than before.

Adani surged through Elian as he fought his way back to his feet. His flesh pulled and shifted around his wounds, sending a needle of fire up his spine and straight into his skull. He winced and squeezed his eyes shut, then looped adani tighter. When the strength crested, he launched himself back into the fight.

One pair turned to meet him, and after the first exchange, Elian already knew the future of the fight. His wounds slowed him too much, and he'd lost that razor-thin margin of speed he needed to cut them down. He kept his pair occupied, but it wasn't enough to save Bael.

The other pair kept hammering at Bael, gradually wearing down his adani, each strike making the next easier. And then the light surrounding Bael winked out and he screamed as the void spheres worked even deeper into his flesh.

Elian cried out, but the moment he turned to help, spheres struck him down, and both he and Bael crawled through the loose soil as void drilled into their backs. He struggled to reach his nephew, but his arms gave out before he'd crawled half the distance, and he fell face first into the soil.

The pounding upon his back ended, and Elian tried to summon adani, but his body was too battered, his channels too weak to sustain the heart's strength. He stretched out his hand toward Bael, but his nephew was beyond reach.

One of the emissary's allies squatted beside Bael. "One last chance to serve our master. Otherwise, you will die here."

Tears ran freely down Bael's cheeks, watering the soil so desperate for moisture. Bael looked at Elian, and all he could push out was a single word. "No."

"Very well."

The emissary's ally stood and extended his hand. Bael's eyes widened, and he screamed like an animal being staked alive to the ground. He clutched at his stomach, which rippled like water in a bucket, then his screams were silenced as he vomited blood. What little adani remained in his body withered as the void ravaged his insides. Only the heart remained, but it might as well have been sheltered within a corpse.

Elian reached for adani, tugged at the heart within him, but his body refused to obey. He could do nothing but watch as Bael was executed. He shouted, though the emissary's allies paid him no heed and Bael was in a place beyond hearing.

The last flicker of Bael's spirit dove for the heart, so faint, Elian could barely sense it. Void sought to stop it, but Bael's spirit was still at home in this body, and it found a way around void, and the last of Bael's energy made contact with the heart.

His nephew erupted in light and adani, but Elian's exhausted mind could make nothing of the maelstrom. Waves of force emanated from the place where Elian swore Bael had died, and for a moment, everything else was forgotten as he was half-rolled, half pushed away from the site, and all of his wounds screamed at once, reminding him he was almost as broken as Bael.

The force knocked the emissary's allies back as well, and Elian shielded his eyes against the glare to see them crouching over, as though ready to start a race, hands and feet scrambling for purchase in the loose soil. Whatever force they wrestled against, they were losing. They snarled like dogs, but Bael's technique, whatever it was, overpowered them.

The blinding light slowly faded, and with it, the force that had pressed so strongly against their enemies. In the light's place stood Bael, eyes closed and face upturned, as though basking in the warm light of the sun. His skin still glowed, golden as an adani spear, lit from within. His chin, chest, and clothes were caked in blood, but there was no sign of the wounds that had caused them.

Elian squinted, certain his imagination conjured illusions, but the sense he had of Bael was like nothing he'd sensed before. Before he'd questioned where adani ended and where Bael began, but he'd been premature. Now Bael was nothing but adani, burning as though he was pure spirit.

One pair of enemies attacked, and Bael didn't so much move as he shifted. Void spheres dove at him from all directions, but a wall of light sprang into existence around Bael, and the void didn't break it. The pair glanced at one another, questions in their gazes, as though they'd never seen their spheres so ineffective.

The wall of light became a sword in Bael's hand, but he didn't get a chance to use it. A tear in the world opened up behind the enemies, and they fled through it. The tear closed as soon as the last one was through, and the deadlands were once again at peace.

Elian tried to reach for Bael, but his arms were too weak. He called out, but his voice didn't even reach his own ears. He battled the darkness that encroached at the edges of his vision.

Bael's golden light flickered, and then he groaned and wrapped his arms around his stomach, doubling over as though he'd been punched. The light beneath his skin died, and whatever lived within Bael folded up, like a child folding a piece of paper over and over again until it fit in a small box. The force faded into Bael's core until Elian couldn't sense it, and then it was just Bael, the same as Elian had always known, standing before him, looking lost.

Bael turned and saw him, and his eyes went wide and his lips moved, but Elian heard nothing as he finally lost his fight against the darkness that stole his consciousness away.

21

Elyn twirled like a child a quarter her actual age, a smile painted permanently on her face. This world was devoid of both people and judgment, so her steps weren't weighed down by the fear of discovery. Her only visitor was the emissary, whose visits had become more frequent since her healing was complete.

She couldn't remember how long it had been since she'd felt such joy. Since she'd felt whole.

How many years had she survived by telling herself that she didn't need adani? That the ways of the wandering clans were outdated and useless in their new world? She'd taken comfort in knowing that she wasn't alone, that many who lived in the villages and cities agreed with her.

But this, this strength was why she'd never been able to believe, in the deepest corners of her spirit, those claims. The discipline and hardship inherent in the pursuit of ascending struck many as unnecessary, but only because they'd never understood what possessing such power meant.

It meant never having to labor for weeks, only to watch a field die. It meant never having to fear the predators that roamed at night, and it meant having choices when other people had none.

Adani was worth the suffering, and she'd always known that. It gave her the power to matter again, to be useful to others.

And it had been given back to her, not by Father or Samora, but by the emissary. She still wasn't sure if she'd sorted out all her feelings about that, but for now she simply took one small step forward at a time, feeling her way into a future she hadn't expected.

She sensed him now as he appeared, a dark mist that rapidly coalesced into the human form he used when they spoke. She bowed to him, and he returned the gesture.

"You seem well today," he observed.

"I am, thanks to your healing."

The pain of those days seemed a distant memory now, her body eager to forget the torture of the void working its way through her, limb by limb. In time, she'd probably look back fondly on the experience, knowing all the ways it had changed her life.

"I may have performed the healing, but it was you that endured it. There are few who could."

Elyn bowed again. "Tea?"

"Not today, although I thank you for the offer. I came to see how your lessons are progressing."

"Well, though I confess that mastering the void seems a distant goal."

"Perhaps, although I think you'll be surprised. Your training as an adanist, crude as it was, has given you almost all that you need. I suspect that once you truly understand the technique, mastery will follow soon after. Show me."

Elyn did, pulling the small heart that had once been within her out of a pocket and holding it in her hand. Once, she'd adored the hearts, but now she suppressed a shiver as she held it tight. The emissary had claimed there were other ways to master the void, and she'd begged him, at first, to teach her those other ways, but he'd been adamant in his refusal. Her body knew the heart, and he didn't have the time to teach her other paths.

She questioned his hurry, but hadn't dared ask him yet.

Elyn swallowed hard and connected with the heart, and its power flowed through her. She let out the breath she held every time, afraid it would worm its way under her skin again.

But it had to be welcomed, and never again would she allow that.

The vast river of adani revealed the sliver of void within her core, first discovered by Father and Samora in their desperate pursuit to destroy the Vada. Father had realized, first, that the void could be filled with a heart, filled with pure adani, and with that realization, became the first of many ascended adanists.

But the emissary had explained that at that moment, when one had gained enough strength to reveal the void, a choice revealed itself. One path, followed by ascended adanists, filled the void with adani and light. The other path, which she currently studied, was to allow the void to expand. An idea simple enough to understand, but the practice was difficult to master.

Once she found the void in her spirit, she pulled adani away, allowing the void to expand. This much, at least, she'd become competent at. It was doing anything else she struggled with.

The emissary picked up a loose stone and tossed it once in his hand. He nodded to her and threw it high.

One didn't weave void, as there was nothing to weave. Instead, one projected it. Elyn tried, and a small void sphere shot from above her hand toward the flying stone.

The void in her spirit collapsed as she lost focus, and the void sphere disappeared before it struck the stone. She stared at the ground. The emissary hadn't yet shown her any anger, but her continued failure must frustrate him.

His voice was gentle, though. "How often do you practice?"

She bowed her head at the question. "Several times a day."

"And how often did you practice when you were trying to master adani?"

"I'm not sure there was ever a moment when I wasn't practicing," Elyn admitted.

"I've given you the secrets to perfect freedom and complete control over worlds, but they mean nothing if you can't reach out and seize them."

Elyn nodded. The emissary spoke true, as he always did, but that didn't make his guidance any easier to follow.

He stepped closer. "The heart won't be able to harm you, not ever again. Your parents and clans were fools for letting you attempt to ascend in the first place."

That was the confirmation she'd waited so long to hear, and she stood silently for a moment, as though she'd been finally forgiven for a sin she hadn't committed. For decades, everyone she loved had silently accused her for failing, but finally, here was the emissary, more knowledgeable than anyone she'd met before, telling her that her parents and family were at fault. Confirming the truth she'd always known, but that only she had believed.

In that moment, she feared she would have followed the emissary anywhere.

He seemed to understand, as he always seemed to understand her, and he didn't take advantage of the moment. He wanted her to follow him, but only by her choice.

Which made that choice all the more appealing.

The emissary bowed and said, "Live with the void every moment of every day and see what strength you develop. After, you can decide if the path is for you."

With that, the emissary dropped off the supplies she'd need to live until his next visit, everything this dead land couldn't provide. Then he became mist and was gone, leaving her fate in her own hands.

TIME MOVED STRANGELY in Elyn's new world, and it didn't feel as though it passed in the same manner. The lack of proper days was part of it, but there was more, too. A moment here didn't feel the same as a moment on the world of her birth. She ate when she was hungry and slept when she was tired, though her sleep wasn't as restful as she was used to. In between, she trained as the emissary had asked, her mastery over the void growing slowly. At times, her attention slipped. With nothing to do but to train, eat, and sleep, her body lost touch with the daily rhythms of her farming life. She would catch herself staring off into the distance, unsure of how much time had passed.

As she trained, the slips became more common, her mind and thoughts empty. Once, the emissary must have appeared and left her more supplies, for when she came to, a filled sack sat beside her. She hadn't sensed him or seen him.

Or had she?

The longer she spent on the desolate world, the more she wondered if she was gradually losing her hold on reality. No day or night, no plants to tend and no animals to hunt, no people to endure. She imagined she was as alone as any human had ever been, and though the fact tasted slightly bitter on her tongue, she didn't complain, even to herself.

For her strength grew. Even when she slipped, when she returned, she felt stronger, more in command of the void. She could expand it within her core, use it to strike at anything she wished. Her adani continued to burn bright, but she found she appreciated the cold simplicity of the void. Her physical heart might always skip a beat when she wrapped her fingers around the gemstone heart she'd carried to this world, but she almost became eager for it, because through it, she could control the void. The longer she controlled the void, the better at it she became.

She didn't know how long she'd been on the world the first time she slipped while holding the heart. An eighthday? Maybe two? But she'd been training with the void, practicing forming spheres, throwing them, and bringing them back. She'd started with several, but as her focus had wavered, one after the other had winked out of existence until only one remained. She'd been content with only the one, and she'd been laying on her back, tossing it up and pulling it down, as though it were one of the leather-wrapped balls she'd played with as a child.

Then she lost the focus for even that, but didn't break her connection to the void. She sat within the emptiness, simply resting. She closed her eyes, and the void blossomed behind her closed eyelids. A sea of stars surrounded her, so many of them home to adani. She sensed an enormous passing of time, an age even by the standards of the dragons, and some of those lights winked out, but others bloomed among younger stars. Always a balance, though that balance shifted over time. There was a battle throughout the stars, but unlike any of the stories Father had told. At this scale, there were no dramatic victories, no heartbreaking losses. Just the winking of lights, in and out, as light fought back against the void.

She detested the light, for it was noise and chaos and judgment and love and lies and hate and death, for all that cries must one day die. The void was cold and uncaring, but it was honest, and it was peace, and it was order.

The void that surrounded her bent and snapped, thrumming like a bowstring the moment after it launched an arrow. She couldn't say how she knew, but she knew then that something had happened, and that the emissary would soon visit her.

Elyn blinked and opened her eyes to the red-shaded world, and she wondered what was more real—this daily existence or the vision the void had shown her?

As she'd guessed, it wasn't long before the emissary appeared again. She'd been walking, allowing her thoughts to wander, with no particular destination in mind. He walked beside her without interrupting her thoughts, and she wondered if there was enough of him left to still have preferences, and if so, if he liked it here, quiet as it was.

"Something happened," she said.

He glanced sharply at her, studied her face for a moment, and saw something there, though she couldn't guess what. "You've spoken with my master."

Her wandering stopped. "Your master?"

"The source, Void itself. The place you go, when your thoughts end and you find yourself nowhere in particular."

She wandered forward again, lips pressed tightly together.

"Are you disappointed?" he asked.

"I'd expected something more physical. More embodied."

The emissary went silent at that, and Elyn thought the look was one of a man who knew something and was deciding whether or not to share it. Eventually, he said, "I, too, had once envisioned it much different than it is. I'd thought it some giant human form, swallowing up entire worlds."

"It does swallow up worlds."

A hint of a smile played across the emissary's face. "But not as the monster I'd imagined. It's a force, and worthy of every bit of respect we pay it, but it isn't what you think."

At Elyn's frown, the emissary gave a brief smile, then said, "Such conversations are best left until one has more experience with the mysteries. For now, let us say I'm impressed you've come so far in so little time. I expected you would take to the void quickly, but even I didn't think you'd learn this fast. You are right, something has happened, back on your home world. Two of my servants have been killed."

"My father?"

"Yes, and though it is the death of my servants you felt, it isn't what concerns me and the other emissaries."

An interesting fact, that, the first time he'd referred to other emissaries. It wasn't a complete surprise, given that he was training her to join him, but a useful confirmation, anyway.

"What concerns you?" she asked.

"Your cousin. Bael. He tapped into a power he shouldn't have been able to, and in so doing, kept both him and Elian alive. It means that my plan for your world is up for debate."

She stopped again, trying to work through everything the emissary had just said.

Bael and Elian fighting the emissary didn't surprise her, because of course they would. And likely hurt as a result of their stubbornness.

Her love for Bael was a distant one, the love for a relative she liked but rarely saw, too young and headstrong for his own good. She would be sad to lose him, but not heartbroken, cold as she knew that made her sound.

But the thought of losing Father—that would take time to wrestle with. Time she didn't have. Easier instead to focus on what else the emissary had said, about the plan for her world.

"What does that mean?"

"It has always been my hope and my intent that your planet could become something new for my master. A garden, if you will. But now there are loud voices arguing that the world is too dangerous and the resistance too strong. If something isn't done, I fear more—direct—interventions will be considered."

Elyn eyed the emissary. She didn't believe for a moment that the emissary's truths had always been complete, a feeling reinforced by her encounter with Void itself. It wasn't benevolent, no matter how the emissary presented it or its actions. She couldn't guess at the larger game being played, but she watched the emissary closely for any clues. Unfortunately, a being that could shape itself into any form possessed a firm mastery of its expressions.

"Why are you telling me?"

"I've personally made several attempts to recruit Bael, much as I've recruited you. He's just proven his potential, which makes him all the more valuable to me as an apprentice."

Elyn's snorted. "You want me to convince him to join you?"

"I do. Far better the offer come from you than from me. It's no longer just about him, you understand. It's about the ultimate fate of your world. I can convince the other emissaries the world poses no threat if he's studying here, with you, but if he remains, I don't know that I'll be able to."

"I think you dramatically underestimate how stubborn Bael can be."

The emissary shook his head. "I think you underestimate yourself. You've accomplished incredible feats in the short time you've been here. I believe you'll accomplish even more back home. Will you?"

She'd rather have stuck a needle in her eye than gone back to face Father, but she believed the emissary's threats, if nothing else. She nodded, and her passage back to her home world was arranged.

⚜ 22 ⚜

Bael held his hands against Elian's shoulder and side, pouring adani into him as though dumping a bucket of water over a blazing fire. His great-uncle's body consumed the adani like a starving wolf, ripping it into shreds and transforming it into flesh, blood, and bone. The damage those void spheres caused was different than any wound Bael had encountered before. A normal wound might cut through an adani channel, or bend it, or even knot it, and as a child he'd learned how to heal each type of wound. He lacked Grandmother's skill, but he knew enough to save a life.

Where the void had struck Elian, the adani channels were simply gone, their ends cut off and cauterized as though sliced by a hot blade. A normal healing realigned the adani channels, stitched together what had been cut, but he'd never tried to grow new channels to replace ones that had been destroyed. He'd never even considered it necessary.

So he did what he could, though it felt like pitifully little. His heart, combined with Elian's, provided his channels enough adani not to collapse any further, but that was about it. The flesh that void consumed healed far too slowly, and it was far from certain whether or not Elian would live to see the sunrise.

Bael looked around, as though someone was standing nearby who might help him, but there was nothing for him to see, not even any trees to break the line of the horizon, here in the deadlands.

And if he looked too long, his thoughts started to turn toward the battle and his unblemished skin.

Whenever they started to escape, Bael locked them back in a chest and shoved the chest deep into the back of his mind. Those thoughts might kill him, might tear him up worse than Elian was now. Someday, maybe, he'd consider them, but maybe, if he had his way, he'd never have to.

Instead, he'd turn his attention back to his great-uncle and wonder how he was supposed to save him, or if he could even be saved.

If Grandmother were here, she would know what to do, but he didn't dare return to the camp, not because he was afraid of what they might do to him, but because he didn't dare move Elian in his condition. That his great-uncle held onto life at all was remarkable.

Round and round his thoughts went, until eventually he could take them no more. He would fall over from exhaustion before he healed Elian, so something needed to be done. He'd long since passed the point of doing all the meaningful good that he could.

Arok was nearby. Bael wouldn't have given the dragon a second thought, but as he fought to keep Elian alive, Elian's criticism of Bael's attitude toward the dragons echoed in his memories. Perhaps Arok would have an idea that hadn't occurred to him. Slowly, Bael withdrew his adani from Elian, then breathed a sigh of relief when Elian continued to draw a steady breath. He stood and hurried toward Elian's dragon.

The dragon was well-nested when Bael approached, but

cracked open an eye as Bael drew close. "May we connect?" Bael asked.

Arok's answer came in the form of a thread of adani, extended in offering. Bael accepted it, and a human form appeared before him, the only sign of its draconic origins the golden eyes with vertical pupils. His deep voice rumbled, "Will he survive?"

"I don't know, and I'm out of ideas that might help." A thought occurred to him then, something he hadn't considered before and was a fool for not thinking of. The dragons could help save Elian's life." "My grandmother might know how to heal him, but it's beyond my skill. Is there a way to let her know what has happened? Could you please speak with one of the other dragons at her camp?"

Arok snorted, the physical dragon and the mental illusion mirroring one another in a way that made Bael's head hurt. "You think she doesn't know? She's already on her way. All you have to do is keep Elian alive until she arrives."

SAMORA HAD no desire to relive the horror of battle, but separating herself from Elian during his fight with the emissary's allies was out of the question. Better they both be present, both so she could see how they fared and to lend a hand understanding the emissary's techniques. For all that the emissary had changed their lives, they still knew precious little about how his abilities worked.

Elian's pain had become her own, and she'd grit her teeth so hard she was sure they were going to crack trying not to scream. Aldrick was beside her, ready to help in whatever way he was needed, and she gripped his hand tightly as her brother and grandson fought this new threat.

So, she'd seen the end, and wondered with Elian what had happened to Bael, but none of that mattered when Elian lost consciousness and rendered their connection useless. No matter how she pleaded with him to wake, his mind had been overwhelmed by the pain and refused to cooperate. She knew he was still alive, could sense him even though Bael maintained the presence of mind to swirl adani around them as camouflage, but she couldn't reach him.

She broke away from him herself and turned to Aldrick. "I need to go to him."

"The council will flay you alive." Not an argument against going, just an observation, a reminder of what was at stake.

Samora knew that leaving now was as good as stepping into the same self-imposed exile Elian and Bael had adopted. Leaving now meant leaving the greater part of her family behind to save two bullheaded men. But she didn't have a choice, not really. The rest of her family was safe, and Aldrick was more than capable of looking over those that remained. Elian needed her, and perhaps so did Bael. She didn't know what to make of her grandson's new abilities.

She scooted closer to Aldrick, and he wrapped his arms around her. They sat in their tent together, and Samora took strength from his quiet acceptance. She nuzzled deeper into his chest. "Did you want to come?"

She listened to his heart beat faster. "I do, but my place is here, at least for now."

"I know. I'll miss you."

"And I you. But we'll see each other again."

As she left the tent a while later, she thought of those words again and hoped they were true.

BAEL LIFTED his hands to protect his eyes as Samora's dragon kicked up dust and soil in the process of landing. She was off the dragon a moment later, running to him. She grabbed him by the shoulders and looked him up and down as a surge of her adani went through him. Then she swept him into an embrace that he was all too happy to return. Even if she couldn't do anything, simply having her here made all the difference in the world, because he wasn't alone.

She sent another small wave of adani through him, and he pushed himself away. "We can talk later. Elian needs you."

She nodded, then walked over to where Bael had done all he could to make Elian comfortable. She didn't cry or weep at the sight of her brother's broken body but squatted beside him and buried something from one of her pockets in the loose soil. Bael sensed the heart as soon as it took root. Grandmother worked her way around Elian, burying four hearts in total, which provided more than enough adani to keep Elian's body alive.

The temporary gathering ground created, Samora began her healing by studying Elian. Bael waited for her questions, eager to share his knowledge with her, but she didn't ask him anything.

With nothing else to do, Bael settled in to watch. He'd never seen this side of her before. Grandmother was a storyteller and a healer, the kindest of her generation, in Bael's own experience. And while she'd often told of her involvement in the war against the Debru, there were times when he'd wondered if she'd emphasized her own achievements a bit much. He'd never been able to imagine her in battle.

This woman, though, was a stranger to him, and battle-hardened. When he'd been hit by the first void spheres, the pain had rendered him next to useless. She'd seen Elian's injuries and not even blinked.

He had a lot left to learn, if he ever hoped to become anything like her. He began by wandering over and kneeling on the other side of Elian. When she looked up at him, he asked, "Is there something I can do to help?"

"No, I don't think so. But you can watch, and if you can follow what I do, then maybe later. He's hurt worse than he was against the Vada."

So Bael watched, and the first lesson he learned was just how much he didn't know. He'd never heard of the technique Grandmother used, much less sensed it himself. She didn't heal so much as create. Bit by bit, she created a web of adani that came close to matching the missing channels, and when that web came into contact with the cauterized flesh, Elian's adani raced through, creating new flesh as though it were a normal healing.

A simple enough idea, but nearly impossible to perform, and Grandmother almost made it seem easy. Bael could weave a tiny dart of adani nearly a quarter-mile away, but this level of control was beyond him.

Grandmother's presence meant that Elian would live, but he wouldn't regain consciousness anytime soon. The healing was slow and demanded tremendous amounts of adani, and after a time, Bael couldn't pretend to be interested in observing any longer. He silently excused himself and left.

He tried to sleep, but racing thoughts made that destination as elusive as a city that welcomed wandering adanists. All of this was his fault, from their self-imposed exile to Elian's injuries. He tried to do right, but every choice he made took him farther from the futures he desired.

His racing mind meant he was still awake when he sensed the new arrival. He scrambled to his feet, because the arrival's appearance used the same technique the emissary's allies had used to escape earlier that day. Before he could form a sword, though, he sensed the arrival's adani, and it made him pause long enough to recognize Elyn, or at least, something that felt like Elyn, but powerful instead of weak.

He blinked at the sight, wondering if his tired mind had conjured her out of thin air. The woman standing before him didn't feel like the Elyn he'd grown up seeing occasionally, and the Elyn he knew didn't step through holes in the air.

But she called his name, and he was a child again, visiting his strange cousin who had once been a wanderer but had put down roots and started a farm. He remembered her mostly as someone kind enough, but distant and odd. Meeting her had been the first time he'd met someone who had left the clan, and he hadn't been able to understand why. It was only when he'd gotten older and neared his own ascension that he learned the full story of how her ascension had gone wrong.

"What are you doing here?" he asked.

"It's a long story, but is Father hurt?"

"He is, but Grandmother is with him now, and I think she knows how to heal him."

"Good." Elyn looked that way and extended her adani, confirming his answer. Her gaze lingered, and Bael took a step back.

She couldn't send out adani. She wasn't supposed to be able to do anything with adani.

"What are you doing here?" he repeated.

"I came here for you."

He embraced the strength of his heart as he shook his head. It couldn't be true. Not his own family.

But she had stepped from a portal with abilities she shouldn't have, trying to recruit him just like the emissary had. What other explanation was there?

"Tell me you aren't with it," he demanded, and her silence was answer enough.

He bound two adani spears and threw them, not to kill, but to wound her before she could attack him. A void barrier appeared between them and swallowed his spears whole. Bael cursed and formed a sword. He darted in at her, ready to cut through the void barrier and protect those in his family who hadn't turned traitor.

Elyn dropped the barrier, though, as she dropped her hands to her side.

He cut at her throat, but she made no effort to defend herself.

Bael stopped his blade just as it cut into the side of her neck. A trickle of blood ran down the edge, but she hadn't so much as flinched away. He growled and flexed his grip on the adani blade. She served the emissary, and the cut would be easy. But he also knew right from wrong, even if he couldn't always explain his reasons.

He allowed the adani in his hand to unravel. He couldn't kill Elian's daughter.

"Why?" he asked.

"Because I didn't come here to fight you."

"Why are you serving the emissary?"

"Ah." She looked like she might object, then reconsidered, and her face fell. "I went with him first because he promised to heal me, which he has. He's taught me some of his techniques and has taught me even more about adani and void."

Bile rose in his throat. "He might have killed hundreds of humans with a thought, but at least you don't have to farm anymore, is that it?"

She paled and trembled. "It's not that simple."

"Seems pretty simple from where I'm standing."

She clenched her fists, and Bael prepared for the fight to resume, but she didn't strike. "I came here because I thought it was best. The emissary is worried about you."

"Nice of it to care, but you can tell it I'm fine."

"He's worried about what you're becoming. He didn't share the details, but something you did in your last fight caught his attention. If you don't come with me, there will be consequences."

"Like what? Is it going to destroy another city? Ruin my life more than it already has?"

"I'm trying to save you! I'm trying to save as many as I can."

"Then teach us what you've learned. Show us how to beat it."

"You can't. No matter what success you think you've found, you don't understand his true strength, or the force behind him."

Bael didn't doubt that she believed every word. She didn't see the contradiction in her position, that if the emissary had sent her because it was worried about his strength, it could be defeated. "You give up on us too easily."

Her look hardened, but he didn't know why what he'd said was wrong.

"You're the ones who gave up on me too easily. And now I'm here, trying to save lives, and it still doesn't matter to you. He'll destroy the wandering clans unless you come with me."

If nothing else, Rydal had taught him the value of consideration, and so he didn't reject this final plea outright.

Despite Elyn's implied promise of safety, accepting the emissary's offer was the same as drawing a knife across his own throat. Of that, he also had no doubt. But, if he accepted, might the loss of his life protect the lives of those he cared about? Because if so, he should follow Elyn with his neck bared and a smile on his face.

The trouble was, he didn't share Elyn's belief in the emissary's intent. It may have healed Elyn, and for that, he'd offer it a bitter thanks, but it had done nothing to earn his trust. If he sacrificed his life, it would all be for nothing, for the void was death, no matter how it cloaked itself.

"I won't go, cousin."

Her hand clenched tight to something in her pocket, and adani flooded through her body.

Recovered as she was, her adani remained nothing more than flickering candle next to the bonfire that burned in him, so he made no move to defend himself, and because he remained relaxed, he sensed the delicate unfolding of the void within her core.

After a day full of surprises and questions, he made note of what he sensed, but he was exhausted, and his overwhelmed mind couldn't understand.

She reached not for adani, but for the void, and too late, Bael prepared to fight.

She didn't attack, though, as unable to strike Bael with void as he'd been unable to cut her with adani. Bael used the opportunity to prepare his defense, though he didn't know how useful it would be against the void in his current state.

Elyn formed a void sphere, and her body trembled as she gathered the courage to attack.

Then, with a small shake of her head, she let the void go. Her failure complete, the hole in the air opened behind her.

He thought she might have some final word for her father, wounded nearly fatally by the creature she now served, but she stepped back through the hole without another word, leaving behind a new void in Bael's spirit.

23

Samora was in what Aldrick called a "meditative state" when Elian finally awoke late the next day. There was nothing meditative about it, though. Her mind danced between this world and the world of dreams, never staying too long in either realm. She barely noticed when her brother turned over and opened his eyes, but the shift in his adani was strong enough to pull her from her near slumber.

He grunted and held up a hand, as though to confirm he still had one. He grunted again when he glanced over and saw her sitting next to him. "So that's why I'm still alive."

"Bael deserves some recognition. He kept you flooded with adani while I rushed here."

"How is he?"

"Physically? Fine. Otherwise, I'm not so sure. He wasn't in the mood to speak to me after I pulled you through the worst of your injuries."

Elian frowned but was too polite to ask the question.

Samora sighed. The truth had to come out sooner or later, and he'd want to know right away. "Elyn appeared while I was in the midst of healing you. She and Bael argued."

Elian said nothing, but his aura shifted, becoming a chaotic storm that made Samora's stomach queasy. His control over adani had improved over the years, but he still possessed a bottomless well most dragons were jealous of.

Samora sighed again. "Elyn, it appears, has been recruited by the emissary. It healed her. Bael said that the heart was no longer lodged in her core. But she's also learned how to use the void."

Elian closed his eyes and turned to his breath, making it slow and even. In time, the chaos of his aura calmed. A few moments more, and he asked. "Was she hurt?"

"No. She and Bael didn't fight, and Bael said she looked unharmed."

Again, Elian didn't respond, but his aura settled further. After a few moments of silence, he grunted. "I should be frustrated and afraid that she's with the emissary, but I'm mostly glad she's alive and finally healed."

"She betrayed us. Is betraying us. Bael tried to convince her to stay, but when she failed to recruit him, she left without another word. She didn't even come to check on you."

Her arguments failed to disturb his aura. "She'll find her way back to us, but I can't fault her for wandering. After what she's been through, it's the only way for her to discover what matters to her."

"She might as well have left you to die."

"And that hurts, but she's my daughter. I love her even when she doesn't act in the ways I wish she did. You'd feel the same if Killan or Bael were in her position."

Samora snorted. "If either of them even considered joining the emissary I'd tan their hides in an instant."

Elian chuckled and rolled out of the bed. "Thanks for healing me, again. I'm surprised you were able to."

"About that."

Elian squatted, twisted, then stood straight and bent over and touched his toes. His movements weren't as energetic as they had been four decades ago, but he still moved well. "What?"

"I was able to heal you, but I don't know how many others could have. Less than half a dozen, certainly. And it wasn't a healing one could complete behind a battlefield. It took me almost two days of intense focus, aided by all the hearts I carry with me. And for as many hits as you took, none of them reached too deep. If they'd gotten much further inside your body, I'm not sure I could have done anything."

Elian finished stretching and stared off at a distant horizon. "So, we can't heal the injuries from the emissary and its servants easily."

"If we fight them directly, even the healers won't be able to save many."

"Thanks for letting me know. Though you've been with the clans more recently than me. What are the odds I could even convince them to fight?"

"Slim and growing slimmer by the day. They don't view the emissary as a threat."

Elian sat with that for a while, then fixed her with a questioning stare. "Samora, are we wrong? Our families, our clans, everyone feels like they're against us. It makes me think they're seeing something I'm not."

"I think they'd rather feel safe and comfortable with a chain around their neck than risk everything for mere freedom."

"Only problem with living with a chain around your neck is that eventually, someone is going to pull it, and I get the sense the emissary isn't the most compassionate of masters."

Samora shrugged and nodded, to remind Elian there was no argument coming from her. The wandering clans seemed more than happy to believe the best about the emissary, conveniently forgetting it had announced its existence with the largest mass murder since the Vada had terrorized their world.

But it hadn't been their friends or family murdered, and so it was all too easy to reason away the emissary's sins.

None of that meant she had any idea what to do.

"Are you going to return to the Wolves now?" Elian asked.

"Don't know. I want to talk to Bael first, because there's more he's not telling us, and then I'll decide. Truthfully, though, I'm not sure I'll be welcomed back, or if I can make the sacrifices necessary to be welcomed back. Once they know how easy it is for me to find you, they'll lean on me to track you down."

"Sorry for putting you in such a position."

"It's been a while since you've made my life a living nightmare. I suppose it was time."

The words were sharp, but said with a smile, and Elian chuckled. "True. I have been remarkably well-behaved as of late."

"And yet somehow, I don't think the streak is going to last much longer."

Elian laughed out loud, and the sound warmed her spirit. She'd missed that blind optimism that shone so brightly on the darkest days and hadn't realized just how much.

"I think you're right, but this time, I think I'm recruiting your grandson to join in the fun. Let's go find him."

IF SAMORA HAD to choose one word that defined Bael, a single word to describe the entirety of his life, she would have chosen "vitality." As a child, he'd kept Killan and Kaeda running after him day in and day out. Killan had always been strong, but after a full day of parenting, he looked worn and haggard, as though he'd just finished running a deer down on his own without the help of adani.

Bael had carried that same spirit into his adolescence, though most of it became focused on his single goal of becoming the strongest adanist the world had ever seen. Killan no longer looked so haggard, and his eyes shone with pride at his son's achievements.

Some of that pride had soured in the past few years. Bael's progress had hit a plateau, and his strategy of simply throwing himself whole-heartedly into his training no longer rewarded him as handsomely as it had when he was younger. That vitality that had driven him to the top needed new targets, and some of those Bael had pursued were questionable at best.

Samora and Killan agreed that Bael needed a goal worthy of him, but neither had found one suitable. Samora had wondered if Bael shouldn't lead some sort of expedition to explore the farthest reaches of their world, but Killan hadn't been ready to let his boy wander that far.

Bael lived, and was unharmed, but as Samora and Elian approached the slight rise in the deadlands he'd claimed as his overlook, she wondered if the emissary had killed that formerly indomitable spirit. His shoulders were slumped, and his aura was weak and chaotic. She'd felt more adani emanating from children in the wandering clans who weren't anywhere close to ascending.

By unspoken agreement, Elian sat on one side of her grandson while she took the other, as though they were worried he might try to escape.

"Samora tells me you spoke to Elyn. What happened?" Elian asked.

Bael told the story, his voice sounding like it came from some-place far away, but sharing far more detail than he had in his brief conversation with Samora. They listened without interruption, and when it was done, Samora rubbed at her chin. "What happened to you when you were fighting the emissary's servants?"

"I'm not exactly sure," Bael said.

Elian shook his head, and Bael cast his gaze down, then sighed. After a few moments, he said, "It's difficult to describe, but at some point, I knew I was close to dying, but I still had all my adani and all the heart's adani running through me. I wanted to fight, but couldn't, and then the heart made me a promise."

Bael paused again, and Samora met Elian's gaze over the back of Bael's head.

"I know how silly it sounds, right? The heart can't make promises, but I don't know how else to describe it."

"It doesn't sound silly at all. Something similar happened to me back when we were fighting the Vada," Samora said.

"Really?"

"Not the same, but I've sensed adani whispering promises. You should talk to the dragons about it sometime. They take it incredibly seriously."

Normally, Bael would have openly scoffed at such a suggestion, but today he nodded and accepted the idea without question. Samora said nothing, but she took note of it. Bael was changing, and in more ways than one.

"What was the promise?" Elian asked.

"Peace. That if I surrendered to it, gave myself completely to it, I'd reach a level of strength no adanist had before. I accepted the deal, and that was when the emissary's allies ran."

Bael brought his knees to his chest, and his eyes were sunk deep into his skull. Both Samora and Elian sensed there was something more, but only Samora, having some idea of what Bael had gone through, could guess at the reason. "You broke the agreement, didn't you?"

Bael nodded. "Once I realized what it meant, yes. I pulled away. Reasserted myself and snapped back to this world. Uninjured, though I'm not entirely sure why."

Elian frowned; confusion written on every line of his face. Samora swallowed the lump in her throat, and she wanted to reach out and wrap her arms around her grandson, but he didn't want them there. He wanted to fight this battle alone and report to them when it was over.

"Why did you break the promise?" Elian asked.

Samora grunted to herself, wondering if there was ever a point in Elian's life when he would have understood. Maybe three or four decades ago, when he'd recently become a parent.

Maybe.

A slight shudder went through Bael's body. "I was scared."

Elian, still lost, asked, "Why?"

Bael wouldn't meet their gazes, his own stare locked on a point between his feet. "The only way to accept the heart's full strength, the only way to become something those warriors fear, is to give up everything of yourself, including your body."

Bael turned to look straight at Elian.

"To ascend to the next level, I have to die."

ELIAN AND SAMORA were walking by themselves, giving Bael the space he was too shattered and broken to ask for. The air felt heavy, like a storm was building just beyond the horizon and preparing to break over their little camp, but Samora didn't think it was a storm. It wasn't just the air. Her shoulders felt as though she'd carried a pack for days without rest, and her family had just added another broken dream to it for her to carry.

Elian's footsteps were ponderous, his feet barely lifting high enough to be called a proper step. If he moved any slower, he'd be shuffling like an elder from their childhood.

"Is he right?" Elian asked.

"No way for us to know for sure, but I don't see any reason to doubt him. It's similar enough to what I felt back in those days that it's more than possible. And it comes close to explaining what you saw."

Elian made a noise that was half grunt, half bitter chuckle. "Does it? Because I'm not sure I understand it at all."

Samora had forgotten that for all they shared through their connection, Elian couldn't actually read her thoughts, and she rarely spoke about her more esoteric ideas. She walked beside him for a few paces while she ordered her thoughts. "We've talked about the idea that adani and shadow are mirror forces."

Elian nodded. They'd discussed it often, and though they both agreed the statement felt true, they had no way of studying shadow after banishing the last of the Debru, and the sentiment itself meant little that mattered.

"Well, I've long wondered what it would mean if that statement was actually true. We know that at the highest level of shadow, a Vada had surrendered its original physical form. If the forces are mirrors of one another, it stands to reason that to ascend higher, we, too, would give up our bodies. I was certainly tempted, back then."

"So, all we have to do to reach the next level is die?"

"I don't think simply dying is enough, unfortunately."

Elian snorted. "Unfortunately?"

"You know what I mean. There's another part of the process, something we're missing. Bael stumbled across it, even if we don't know exactly what it is. I'm guessing he was well on the way to becoming something else but pulled back at nearly the last possible moment."

"And that's why he's healed?"

Samora shrugged. "We've all been shaped by adani, the ascended most of all. If you're asking me to guess, it's possible that when he pulled back it was to the body adani remembered, with all his old adani channels reconstructed."

Elian didn't look convinced, but she wasn't either. "It wouldn't have been that unlike how I healed you, just more dramatic."

Elian let the matter drop and slowed to a stop, and Samora stopped with him. Together they looked at Bael, who hadn't moved from the spot he'd claimed as his overlook.

"It should have been one of us," Elian said.

At first, Samora thought Elian was jealous of Bael's near-second ascension, that he wanted Bael's power as his own, but she was corrected when he said, "He's too young to be asked to sacrifice so much."

Samora's throat constricted, and she nodded quickly. "Then let's find out what he discovered, so he doesn't have to."

"I will," Elian promised. "But what of you? Are you returning to Aldrick?"

She wanted nothing more, but she could do no good with the Wolves. "No. We need to know more about what the emissary is planning and what the emissary can do. I'm going to travel to the cities and find out."

Elian raised an eyebrow. "That didn't go so well for Bael."

She wrapped adani in a circle around her, the same way Elian hid from those who sought him, just performed better. His eyebrow rose even higher as she completely disappeared from his senses.

"Ah," he said.

"Someone would have to bump into me to sense me, and even if the emissary's allies do sense me, I'll feel more like one of them than an adanist. We can't fight without knowing more."

Elian wrapped his arms around her and held her close. "Be careful, will you?"

Samora snorted. "That's rich, considering the stunt you just pulled."

When they separated, there was no humor in his eyes, and she held up a hand to stop him. "Fine. Fine. I'll be careful. But you should be, too. If the emissary is that worried about Bael, there's no telling what it might do next."

"I'll do everything I can to keep him safe," Elian said.

Samora bit her lip and nodded. She wasn't worried about that. Elian would always do everything he could to protect his family.

She just worried that it wouldn't be enough.

24

Elyn returned to the emissary's world with a single step, but it felt as though it had carried her a hundred miles. The doorway closed on Bael's disappointed look, as though she'd murdered his entire clan. She huffed as the doorway vanished.

Prideful fool. He was the same as all the rest of them. She'd known he would reject her, but she'd had no choice. Why couldn't he understand what she was trying to do?

At least the blood that was about to be spilled wouldn't be on her hands.

She huffed again and turned around, locating herself within the desolation. The doorway had returned her to almost exactly where she'd left from, which she appreciated. She turned in the direction of the cave which served as her shelter.

Two steps later her steps faltered. Father had almost been killed, and though she hadn't asked, something had been different about Bael, something not explained by time alone. And she'd left without even checking on Father.

When they met again, would they view her as an enemy?

Would they be wrong if they did?

She'd done nothing wrong, though. She'd sought healing, found it, and studied the void. What was there to judge?

Not that the wandering clans had ever been slow to jump to judgment, especially of her. She'd tried to save lives, hadn't she?

Elyn didn't fall, though her legs felt like waterlogged paper. She breathed deep, trying to circulate adani through her limbs, but her weakness had nothing to do with her health or physical strength.

For the first time since arriving here, she wished she had someone to speak to, someone to share her questions with. Alone, she'd get trapped in her own head, running in circles instead of moving forward, whatever direction that might be.

A longing for the world of her birth hit her, carving a hole in her spirit the same way she expanded the void in her core. Father and Bael had been in the deadlands, but compared to this planet, the deadlands were a never-ending parade of life. Her adani, active but quiet within her body these last few weeks, had churned and twisted and danced with the weak threads beneath her feet.

Some part of her had even enjoyed arguing with Bael, preferred it to the silence of her new life. She'd even hoped the emissary would be here waiting to express his displeasure. And maybe he was. When her cave came into view, it flickered with light, deep orange shadows bright against the fading red sky.

THE ONE WHO waited in her cave looked like a man, but Elyn didn't think he was. Lines of not-quite-adani ran through him, but the pattern they formed wasn't human. No one but an observant adanist would notice, though, and then only if they were looking.

The emissary's servant, then. One of many, she suspected,

which would explain how the emissary had known humanity so well.

He looked up when she approached, and his eyes were wrong, lacking the animating force she took for granted in her kind. Every detail of their appearance was perfect, but without spirit, eyes were nothing more than squishy spheres.

"You failed," he said, voice flat and expressionless.

Elyn brushed the dirt off her boots and stepped into her cave. "Rude, showing up at a stranger's home and tossing around accusations."

His face didn't so much as twitch, and if she hadn't seen his lips move a moment ago, she might have thought he was carved from stone. She considered stabbing at his eye with an adani dagger, just to see if that would inspire a reaction.

"As you guess, you'd be disappointed. And then you'd be in tremendous pain for simply attempting it."

For a moment she thought she'd spoken out loud, but she knew she hadn't. "You know my thoughts?"

"We are joined by the void. I can hear the thoughts of all my brothers and sisters, whenever I wish."

"I didn't give anyone permission to be in my head."

"You gave it when you accepted the emissary's training, but you seek to distract me with frivolities. You failed in the task our master set for you."

"I was always going to fail. It would have been easier to convince a mountain to dance than get Bael to leave behind everything he loves."

She didn't see him move, though he had to have moved. One moment he was sitting by the fire and the next he stood before her. "You think your failure is a laughing matter? The consequences may set our master's plans back decades, if not more."

"Because one adanist refused to return with me?"

"Because now your world is almost certain to be considered a threat, and our master's plans may be overruled by the other emissaries."

"You keep saying he's our master, but I've taken no oath."

The servant nodded once. "Which is why I'm here. Our master's kindness and generosity only extends so far, and he is displeased by your lack of effort. The boy should be here."

"I tried."

"Did you? Or did you just say a few words and then turn around, defeated by mere stubbornness? You have the greatest force in the universe at your command, and you listen to the self-righteous anger of a man who is barely older than a child?"

"The emissary asked me to convince Bael, not pull him back here kicking and screaming." The emissary's servant might not get angry, but Elyn did.

"Our master made it clear the boy needed to return, and you didn't bring him. Now it is time for you to decide where your loyalties lie. Who do you stand for?"

When she'd first spoken with the emissary, she'd formed half a plan where she grew strong enough to face him and defeat him. She still thought of it, and maybe considered it her goal, but it was a distant goal, requiring years of training at best, and curse it all, the emissary's servant could look into every thought of hers as though peering through an open window.

"Have no fear," the servant said, voice as expressionless as ever. "Our master tempts many with the prospect of someday defeating him. You are hardly the first and won't be the last."

"If you can read my thoughts, what's the point in answering your question?"

"The question isn't for me. It's for you, to force you to think and nudge you toward a decision. Though you should have put a knife to your cousin's throat, I won't put one to yours. You will join us willingly or not at all."

Her heart pounded loudly in her chest. There was no web of

adani here to accept her spirit if she died. What would happen if she was killed here?

She wanted to be home. Not here, in this cave, but back among her fields.

The emissary's servant made no move toward her and seemed willing to wait for as long as necessary for her to decide, even if it took days.

"Why, specifically, are you here?"

"To guide you to a choice."

"How?"

"Through your past. There is nothing to fear. I have done this many times with many hopefuls. You won't be in any danger, unless you are frightened of revelation."

"You can't teach me what I already know."

"You might be surprised."

What choice did she have? She couldn't well refuse him, and his smug confidence made her want to challenge him, to dare him to change her mind.

Which was likely exactly what he wanted, but who cared?

She sat down across the fire from him. "Then let's get started."

IF THE EMISSARY'S servant meant to mine her memories the way the adanists far to the north mined the mountains for their precious ore, there was no richer vein of despair than the fateful day she had attempted to ascend, the youngest ever to do so. As she followed his instructions and closed her eyes, she expected to find herself living that day again, as if she hadn't relived it in a thousand nightmares already.

Instead, she found herself outside her body, observing a scene she could barely summon to her conscious memory. She couldn't have been more than seven or eight, and what little she could remember of this day she remembered fondly.

A poor choice, if the emissary's servant hoped to prove that the void was preferable to the light and warmth of adani.

It had been a spring day, not that unlike the ones she'd so recently left behind. The fires of the sun overhead gently battled the northern breezes that carried air chilled as it passed over snow covered prairie. She welcomed the warmth of the sun as she rested between exercises and thanked the northern breezes as she pushed her small body to its limit.

The memory was far more vivid than she could recall in her mind's eye, yet she didn't believe it was some trick of the servant. Everything was true, a rightness she sensed with her spirit more than reasoned with her mind.

She and Father trained together, far away from the rest of the clan. Such days were rare, as he usually insisted she train with the rest of the clan's children to avoid any accusations of favor. She didn't know why he had changed his mind this day, but she'd known, even then, it was a gift she shouldn't take for granted.

They began as if it was any other training day, stretching their bodies and focusing their adani, and she feared that perhaps this day wouldn't be as special as she had hoped. Father asked her to demonstrate several of the techniques she'd learned with the others, and she did so competently, if without enthusiasm.

Present day Elyn cocked her head to the side as she watched. In the story she told herself, she'd always wanted to be first among her class, had always wanted to impress her parents, but that wasn't what she saw today. Her promise had been apparent, but she'd lacked the will to transform her possibility into strength. She did only what was necessary to avoid trouble and nothing more.

Father squatted so that their faces were level. "Do you want to become an ascended adanist?"

The hope in his voice cut like a cold knife, and if she'd been corporeal, Elyn would have stomped over and slapped him in the face.

"I don't know," young Elyn answered honestly.

"I think you do; you just don't realize it yet." Father reached into his pockets and pulled out a small gemstone. Young Elyn's eyes went wide, for every child in the clan would recognize a heart when they saw one, just as every child knew that there was no trouble like the trouble they'd bring down upon themselves if they attempted to touch one.

Father held it between them. "You know we don't normally let children close to the hearts, but I spoke with your mother, and we agree that you're ready. Focus on your breath before you touch it, because it will want to overwhelm you. It might even hurt a little, but if you can relax, its strength can be yours. Are you ready?"

Elyn nodded and did as Father said. This was why he'd brought her out here on Arok's back, far away from where any of the other children might see. Once her breath was even and her body was as relaxed as she could make it, she reached out and placed her hand on top of the heart.

There was no pain. Present Elyn remembered that, and remembered how ever since that moment, she'd believed that she was fated for this, that her and the heart were meant to become one.

Father made a sound in the back of his throat, as though he'd never had a doubt, even though present Elyn couldn't help but notice the flash of worry in his eyes as her childhood self reached for the stone. Instead of pain there was only strength like she'd never imagined. She had become, for the first time in her life, something special

They ran and jumped through the fields together as Elyn grew used to her new abilities. This was what she remembered most, not just the feeling of the wind in her air as she leaped over small trees, nor the satisfaction of chopping down thick branches with her bare hands, but the day she played with Father, not as a child plays with their parent, but as an equal.

Elyn cursed the servant, though he had shown her nothing but what was true. Even so, by bringing her here, he'd taken one of her warmest memories and covered it in cold dirt. This was the day she'd chosen to become an ascended adanist, but had the choice ever been hers?

The emissary's servant wasn't finished polluting her memory, though. "Look at how he looks at you now," he said.

She did, even though she remembered without help. Father's smile was wide and easy, his gaze nothing but pride.

"He loved you not for who you were, but for what you were capable of," the servant whispered, saying out loud everything she knew in her spirit to be true.

She had underestimated the servant, but the servant didn't gloat over his victory. He seemed to understand, and she wondered if once he'd had his own comfortable lies stripped from him.

"I've seen enough for now."

The servant shook his head, and though the vision faded, the darkness was heavy with anticipation, a new vision ready to replace the first.

"I'm sorry, my friend, but we're just getting started."

25

Samora spent an eighthday hiding in the foothills outside Nevan, probing the emissary's defenses around the city and preparing for her one-woman scouting expedition. Eight days of lurking, creeping, observing, and studying. They'd never studied any of the Debru encampments this thoroughly, but there'd been no need.

Sometimes the absurdity of it all made her chuckle bitterly. A season ago she could have walked into Nevan, asked for an audience with the council, and received it that day. The same was probably true now, except they'd all be sharpening their steel swords in preparation for her execution.

Nevan's betrayal cut Samora more deeply than most, for she still remembered its founding. The land they built on was land she had scouted with Aldrick in the very early days of their wandering, a land nearly ideal for a city. It was far to the west of where the wandering clans had once called home, nestled among the eastern foothills of the long mountain range that cut a jagged, north-south line through the continent. Clean water, lumber, and stone were plentiful, and the land just to the east of the city invited farmers to plant enormous fields.

She remembered describing the land to the villagers displaced by the war with the Debru, remembered most the hope in their eyes at starting afresh in a place far more welcoming than what they'd grown accustomed to.

Nevan wouldn't exist without her and the wandering clans. She'd found the land, and the dragons and the clans had transported the first settlers. Hundreds of flights, at least, had given the villagers everything they'd needed to start the new city. Wandering clans had hunted and fed the city while the farmers waited for the first harvests.

Some down below probably remembered, but not many, she suspected. Most had been born there and had never known anything else.

Whenever such thoughts arose, and they did several times a day, she pushed them away. She could wish for a better world a thousand times, or she could simply get to the work of making it better, which was why she was here.

Her precautions were possibly excessive, but after Bael's experience, her caution seemed justified. She stayed out of sight, although there was less movement in the foothills than she remembered, so it was rarely difficult. Most of her days she spent extending slim threads of adani towards the city to gather as much information as she could.

If she ignored the hole near the center of the city, her investigations revealed little of interest. The academies were busier than she'd ever sensed before, what with the youngest generation now compelled to develop their adani. Otherwise, the daily life of the city appeared much the same as she'd always known it.

Now that she knew what she was looking for, she also sensed the emissary's servants. Five of them lived in the city, and Samora focused a considerable amount of her time on learning all she could about them, which, unfortunately, was far less than she would have liked.

They didn't draw any attention to themselves. As they walked down the streets, people didn't scurry away or stop and bow or do anything that would indicate deference or obedience.

The five of them also seemed to keep a close eye on Nevan. Each had an area of the city they almost never left, and they were frequently on the move within that area. When she felt bold enough, she was able to sense their own adani, which they kept extended throughout their area.

No wonder Bael had caused the disaster he had. If Rydal's arrangement was anything similar, they would have known almost the moment he arrived. The real question, and the one she hadn't dared to answer yet, was whether or not they'd be alerted to her presence.

Someday soon, she'd have to find out for herself, because some answers couldn't be discovered with adani, and most of those had to deal with what was happening in the hole in the city the emissary had created. There, she had little idea what was happening, but everything in the city circled around it.

Adani gave her some clues, small as they were. Every day there was a constant stream of travel between the training grounds and the hole, and while they were there, the adanists did something, although her thin threads of adani couldn't penetrate any deeper into the mystery. She wasn't sure why. It wasn't like the old Debru circles, which had pulled adani in and shredded it, nor was it like the deadlands that lacked a strong web to send adani through. She should have been able to explore it without problem, but when her adani neared, it twisted and spun around the perimeter of the circle, unable to advance.

Knowing she'd have to go into Nevan to find out what happened, she tested the city's defenses. She wandered close at night, adani extended to see if any of the emissary's servants would react. As near as she could tell, none did, and no one destroyed any more of the city, which she took as a good sign.

She retreated back to the foothills as the sun threatened the horizon with its presence and made her preparations to enter the city the next night.

SAMORA CAME DOWN from the foothills once the last dying gasps of the sun's light had disappeared behind the distant horizon, a one-woman army invading an enemy stronghold, not to conquer, but to learn. The five she'd sensed before remained active, moving through their separate parts of Nevan. The movement of adanists between the training ground and the destroyed center of the city hadn't slowed either. For a city so dark and quiet, there was an incredible amount of adani on the move.

She paused in a small grove of trees a few hundred paces from the first homes that currently formed the city's boundary. How close could she approach before her discovery doomed some large portion of the city? Had she already come too close?

They needed to know what the emissary and its allies hoped to accomplish, and when she'd been with Elian, what she'd needed to do had been clear. Now she looked at all those houses filled with families, and nothing was certain. The emissary didn't mean them well, but those families had gone to sleep believing that their surrender had earned them a tenuous peace. Who was she, to risk taking that away from them?

She wrapped adani even more tightly around her, snugger than any cloak. Even she would barely be able to sense herself from more than a few paces away. If they had any hope of unveiling the emissary's true plan, it had to be her.

She snuck from the grove, walking on shaky feet toward the edge of Nevan. Her thin and wispy adani stretched out before her, keeping one eye always on the emissary's servants and one on her more immediate surroundings. Neither gave her cause for alarm as she reached the first homes.

This far out from Nevan's city center, the homes reminded her of the villages of her youth. Most were small, somewhat haphazard looking affairs. The wood to build them had been collected from the nearby forests, a service that also helped clear the land for the planting of fields. Their locations had been selected even more haphazardly, as new arrivals had simply claimed locations as their own and began building.

It shouldn't have been like this. The beginnings of Nevan had been carefully planned, but they'd all underestimated how quickly the cities would grow. The city council was supposed to parcel out land to new arrivals, but either through overwhelm or neglect, had clearly failed to fulfill their role.

That was a problem for another day. Or for another person. Even if they defeated the emissary, it had opened a division between the wandering clans and the cities Samora wasn't sure they would ever heal.

Her arrival didn't cause any parts of the city to disappear, though, and the emissary's servants maintained their normal routes, and so she continued deeper into the city. It was a trivial matter, with her adani scouting ahead of her, to avoid any of the few citizens out at this time of night.

She paused halfway through the city to give her extended adani more attention. As near as she could tell, she still hadn't been spotted, either by a curious citizen or the emissary's servants, but the ease of her infiltration made her want to check over her shoulder. Bael had thought he was unobserved, too, and his confidence had nearly destroyed everything he held dear.

She twisted the majority of her adani threads and sent the weave toward the center of the city in the hope her proximity would be enough to uncover what project the emissary had bent her fellow adanists to. She could penetrate the perimeter of the city's wound, but she couldn't push deeper. Every thread she sent got caught in a swirling web that locked adani close to the boundary. A strong surge might be enough to push past the boundary, but doing so would alert the emissary's servants to her presence.

She tried to break through with her slim threads for a bit, eager to be as far away from Nevan as her legs would carry her, but the boundary remained impenetrable.

Samora brought her adani back toward her and walked deeper into the sleeping city.

Walking the streets reminded her of walking through a healing tent after a battle. The citizens of Nevan put on brave faces, going about their daily tasks as if nothing had happened, as though the hole near the heart of the city was a wound one could just walk off. They were warriors, too, even if they didn't realize it, minimizing their hurt so their neighbors would take strength from their courage.

It was a shame it so often took disaster for humans to reveal their true characters.

Peace was a poison. One she'd gladly drink over and over, but still a poison that blighted the spirit. She'd seen it with her own clan. Against a challenge they would rise as one, fighting with a ferocity that sent their enemies fleeing. Against a long eighthday with nothing to do except eat and sleep, though, they would divide into camps and fight small wars of their own choosing, arguing over late-night noise or over which family got the choicest cuts of meat.

Unfortunately, by the time the emissary had revealed itself, the poison had already worked itself deep into their bones, and she wasn't sure she knew how to cure what ailed them.

She was getting close now, only a couple of turns away from the boundary that remained dark and cold to all her senses. She ignored her desire to pause and search with adani again, certain it was nothing but her fear speaking. Anything that waited to be discovered needed to be seen, so she slowly poked her head around the next corner before turning and continuing toward the darkness.

One last turn put her on a narrow street that led straight to the hole in the city. At first glance, it was less than she'd expected. Buildings stood tall on the other side of the hole, which couldn't have been more than a half mile in diameter. There wasn't even a hole. For all the strength the emissary had displayed, it had done nothing more than wipe the surface of the land clean, and Samora was reminded of Mother swiping her hand and clearing their dinner table of the dolls Samora had left there.

Except then, Mother had only been moving the dolls, not destroying them until not even ash remained.

Samora hurried down the quiet street and pressed herself deep into the shadow of one of the buildings that stood at the boundary. She observed the same fact Elian had told her about, how the shadow had carved such precise lines into the edges of the building, destroying part of it completely but leaving the rest pristine. From her hiding place, she looked into the center of the city, which, despite how it felt to her adani, was anything but empty.

No, far from empty indeed.

The hole in the center of the city was filled with adanists, if the title truly applied. Perhaps it would be better to say it was filled with people practicing with their adani, mostly older boys and girls. Samora's gaze wandered up to the night sky, as though to confirm that it was indeed the middle of the night, an unorthodox time for training. The boys and girls sat in the ashes of their friends and relatives and placed their hands on the ground, and though Samora couldn't sense what they did, she could guess, for she'd once done much the same. They were sending their adani into the land, but to what end? Whatever their purpose, it was local, as none of their adani escaped the boundary of the devastation.

The youth were supervised by a handful of instructors, some of them familiar faces. One or two had even spent some time training under Samora, though they'd chosen not to ascend and instead live a more comfortable life inside the city.

It could have been a training session, although it wasn't. Samora had sensed the constant flow of adanists in and out of the void, and suspected that what she observed was their greater purpose. But what was that purpose? Sight alone wasn't enough, and she was contemplating risking walking through the barrier when the scene changed.

The youth stood and stretched, their movements sluggish, as though they'd finished running a race while sitting in place. The instructors seemed pleased as they drifted to the center of the group, where they squatted down and dug their hands into the loose soil that reminded Samora of the deadlands. One of the instructors pulled something out of the ground, but it was too far and there were too many bodies in the way for Samora to see.

Then the instructor raised her hand over her head so all the youth could witness the fruits of their labors. She held something small between her forefinger and thumb, and Samora squinted, then swore. The something small glowed with a dull red, like a moon burning as it rose above the horizon.

Samora couldn't sense it, but it had to be a heart, although corrupted somehow. The only way to know would be to cross the barrier, but there was no place to hide if she tried. Was the knowledge worth the lives it would cost?

The instructor took the corrupted heart to another woman, who'd been standing still since Samora arrived. The instructor bowed to the woman and handed her the heart. As soon as the woman touched it, the heart disappeared like a bad dream in the morning light.

A sixth servant. It had to be, and Samora didn't want a fight. She'd seen enough for now, and she retreated, careful to remain unobserved as she fled the city.

26

Elian's bound sword slipped through Bael's guard, and there was nothing Bael could do against it. The sword unraveled before it cut through his flesh, but Bael had no problem imagining the sharp edge neatly taking his head from his shoulders.

Elian sighed and took a step back. "Care to talk about it?"

Bael swept his hand in a small motion by his side, encompassing the deadlands, their little camp, Elian, and their training, all in one gesture. Elian had noticed Bael's distraction, because one couldn't hide anything when swords clashed, and he'd asked before, but Bael had never wanted to share. He couldn't say for sure what was different about today. Perhaps he'd sat alone with his thoughts long enough, or perhaps he'd just grown too dissatisfied with the choices he'd made. Regardless, he spoke his mind. "This isn't the way."

He didn't mean for it to be a condemnation. Elian had likely saved his life, and because of that, Bael had discovered a new ability he still wasn't ready to embrace, much less think about.

To his credit, Elian didn't shrink from the accusation like a lesser man would have. Instead, he stood tall and asked Bael to verbally strike him again. "How so?"

"All of it. There's no training that will help us defeat the emissary, so all our sparring means nothing. And while we spend all our time hiding, with no real plan, the emissary is using other adanists to harvest whatever it's harvesting."

Grandmother's discovery of the "corrupted hearts" as she was calling them, though Elian made it clear the title came with a long list of caveats and doubts, worried him. Not only had Grandmother found the harvest happening in Nevan, a similar process was happening in Rydal. As near as Grandmother had been able to tell, nowhere else, though. Two places were bad enough, though, and learning of the emissary's success only stoked Bael's desire to do more.

"What would you have us do? If we return to the clans, it's likely you'll be captured and sentenced to death. If we try to fight on our own, well, we've seen how well that worked for us. What other plan do you have?" Elian asked.

"Not a plan so much, but it's time for us to return to the clans. We can't fight this alone."

"And you're willing to fight the friends you grew up with?"

"I'm willing to argue with them, and if they still want to condemn me to death, at least now I know a way to avoid that, don't I?"

Elian's answering look made it clear he saw straight through Bael's false bravado. "It's smarter for us to stay here."

"Safer, you mean. For now. You're making the same mistake the clans are, but you can convince yourself you aren't because you're making it in a way no one else likes."

That hit Elian hard, and for a long moment he stared at Bael. "Is that what you truly believe?"

Bael nodded.

Elian took a deep breath. "If we go back, I'm not sure I'll be able to protect you."

"And although I appreciate everything you've done for me, I

never asked for protection. Maybe it's a mistake, but it's one I'm willing to make."

Elian needed another moment to accept the decision and all the consequences that came with it, but Bael knew the battle was won. Finally, Elian agreed. "Let's leave, then."

"Right now?" Bael hadn't expected it to be so quick.

"No point in waiting, right?"

Bael couldn't suppress his grin. If nothing else, Elian was still one of the most decisive people he'd ever met. "I suppose not. I'll help you pack up our supplies."

<hr />

ELIAN HAD Bael connect with Arok on the ride back, claiming that he needed the time to think. Bael was more than happy to oblige, and as they flew, he spoke to the dragon through their connection.

Could you teach me to speak across distances, the way you and the other dragons do? he asked.

I could, though it would be better if you were taught by a dragon you were closer to. The connections are easier to learn at first.

It wasn't a denial, exactly, but Bael's sense of Arok's spirit was that the dragon would prefer not to teach him. Still, it could be taught. Perhaps it was time to select a dragon to partner with. When Bael said as much to Arok, the dragon gave a great, rumbling laugh.

We've long wondered when you would come to your senses on this matter.

Bael felt as though he was coming to his senses on a great number of matters, but didn't say as much to the dragon. The threat of imminent death cleared his vision, as though cleaning dirty glass.

The flight that returned them to the camp was even longer than the one that had taken them away, the miles that passed so rapidly beneath them interminable. Bael knew he should be thinking about what he would say and do once he returned to the clan, but Shayna consumed his every thought. Leaving the clans when he did hadn't been a mistake, but leaving her behind had been.

They flew through the rest of the day, rested for a portion of the night, then returned to Arok's broad back as he carried them the rest of the way, the Wolves' camp coming into view just before midday.

At Bael's request, they circled once before landing, a last chance to check with his gut and confirm this was exactly what he wanted. Then he told Arok to land, and the dragon obeyed.

His approach and arrival had not gone unremarked, and already a group of warriors gathered at the edge of the camp closest to where the dragons nested. Elian hopped off Arok as though he'd just returned from a hunting trip, a smile on his face and his hand raised high in the air to greet the others.

Had anyone else tried the same, Bael would have called them a liar, but Elian didn't have a deceptive bone in his body. And why should he? What could he gain by deception that he hadn't already earned with strength? Elian was almost certainly happy to be back.

Bael could only give a small shake of his head while he remained on Arok, because as long as he did, he wasn't committed.

And that was yet another difference between him and Elian, made manifest in this moment.

Bael had watched Elian and listened to stories about Elian for as long as he could remember, seeking the clue that would explain not just his great-uncle's strength, but his courage. How did he walk so bravely into the literal den of the Wolves, bearing a smile instead of a shield?

If Bael could just know that, maybe he would be able to complete the transformation the heart had begun within him.

Maybe he wouldn't pull back at the last moment, desperate to cling to life.

Elian's cheerful approach did nothing to melt the stony expressions on the Wolves' faces. Lieran emerged from the camp and took a position at the head of the warriors, and he looked ready to murder whoever argued with him first.

Bael cursed softly, first at the situation he'd led them into, and then again at himself. He'd led Elian here, and now he sat upon Arok, wondering if it wasn't best if he took to the skies again. Far away, when the conflict had only been in his imagination, his courage had bloomed, but here it withered.

He wouldn't let Elian go on alone, and he wouldn't let the clans continue to hide behind easy decisions.

He thanked Arok for the ride, then leaped off the dragon's back. His sudden movement caught everyone's attention, and Bael realized they'd been expecting Elian to plead for mercy or understanding. Bael snarled at himself. Even the warriors he was supposed to lead one day expected him to hide in Elian's shadow.

Time for them to learn a new day had dawned.

Bael strode forward, rapidly overtaking Elian's easy stride and advancing before him. Elian made no move to stop or slow him, and perhaps Bael was imagining what he wanted, but he thought Elian approved.

Lieran gestured with his left hand, a sign Bael was plenty familiar with, a sign to prepare for battle. The adanists behind Lieran hesitated, casting glances back and forth as though silently asking who would be the first to obey. A bound spear appeared in Lieran's right hand, and as though driven by instinct, the others followed.

Bael resisted the temptation to connect with his heart. He hadn't come to fight. At least, not with adani.

"Have you come to surrender?" Lieran asked.

"No. I came to speak with the council."

"You're not welcome around the council fire."

"Maybe not, but I will speak with the council all the same."

Lieran shifted his stance, spreading his feet wider and drawing the spear back, ready to thrust its point into Bael's chest. "Surrender, Bael. If you care at all about the Wolves, surrender now."

Bael had always been a little taller than Lieran, and now that Lieran was crouched and ready to fight, Bael stood even taller. How many times had the two of them sparred, and how many times had Lieran won? There was no doubting his strength, but Bael could count the number of times the other man had bested him over the years on his fingers. Now, after Bael had been training with Elian?

The thought snapped a string that had slowly been wrapping itself tighter and tighter around his spirit, and it almost made Bael laugh.

He didn't care anymore, not about this petty struggle for power and control. Life had thrown them in a small boat rushing toward a fatal waterfall, and Lieran was arguing over who got to sit in front. Bael's shoulders relaxed, and a smile spread across his face, and he knew, without looking, that it matched Elian's.

He spoke, not to Lieran, but to the adanists behind him, holding their spears gingerly, as though the bound adani might be coated in the leaves of poisoned elderberry bushes. "Brothers and sisters, we're better than this. Our enemy's brilliant master stroke was convincing us to turn on each other instead of uniting against it. I have fought the emissary, and Elian and I have fought its servants, and there is no doubt it's an enemy stronger than any we've faced before. That's why I'm here, because I can't fight it alone."

Lieran jabbed the spear at Bael's chest, stopping his blow just short of piercing the skin. "There is no fighting that creature. The combined councils have already decided. You've been sentenced by your own people, so surrender now, before more people are hurt."

Bael ignored Lieran. "I don't deny the danger we face, but

neither will I lie to myself. The emissary doesn't attack us now because there is no need. But this passive surrender isn't some sort of compromise or treaty. It's only pushing our deaths back to a later day. I do not know about you, but I'm a Wolf, and I've trained my entire life to fight. I won't surrender, not to another Wolf, nor to the emissary."

Words would never be enough, and Bael knew that. The adanists behind Lieran wavered, but not so much they would turn against a council order. Tradition held them too strongly. His words were nothing more than seed of doubt, scattered in the fertile soil of their spirits. For them to grow, they'd need to be watered with blood.

"If you won't surrender, then fight!" Lieran shouted. In a blur, he drew the spear back and thrust it at Bael's heart.

Bael saw the blow approaching and sensed the killing intent behind it. His body, trained to fight and react to any surprise, screamed and reached for the heart burning bright in his core, but he kept an iron grip on his adani, and kept it far from the heart. He made no move to defend himself.

A lesser opponent would have killed him, but Lieran, thankfully, was among the best the Wolves had raised. The tip of his spear pierced Bael's chest, but only deep enough to draw blood. Bael let it trickle down his sternum. He stepped forward, and Lieran was forced to let the adani unravel as he stumbled backward. Bael didn't so much as give him a glance as he passed through the line. The other adanists let their spears go and parted to make way for him.

"Come back here!" Lieran shouted.

Bael kept walking, and a spear of bound adani sped over his shoulder, cutting another bloody line in his flesh. The spear unraveled before it struck anyone else, but Bael didn't turn back to face Lieran.

Shayna was ahead, not in the usual place she set up her tent, but somewhere closer to the center of the camp. Her adani felt weaker than it should have been. Bael weaved his way through the tents, drawing stares as he went. No one challenged him directly, but few seemed glad to see him.

He found Shayna in the healing tent, one of two adanists within. He froze at the sight of her.

She lay on a cot, but her hands were shackled behind her with the iron manacles the clan had received from the mountain smiths. Another pair of manacles bound her ankles. Her face was bruised, with one eye swollen shut. She rolled over to face him as he stood there, and from the way she moved, the bruises on her face weren't the only ones she endured.

Still, she smiled when she saw him, and she was as beautiful as ever. "I knew you'd come back."

He swore, in that moment, that he'd never leave her again. "Who?"

"Lieran might whine like a child, but he hits like a giant."

The other adanist in the room, a young man named Oren, stood to block Bael from coming in farther. Before he'd made it two steps, Bael fixed him with a murderous glare. "If you value your life, you won't come one step closer to me."

Oren hadn't ascended yet, which made his choice a simple one. He swallowed hard and nodded, and Bael swept into the healing tent. A thin knife of adani appeared in his hand, and with quick, careful cuts, he removed the manacles. "Anything serious?"

She held onto his arm and pulled herself to a sitting position. "Nothing an actual healing won't cure, but Lieran denied me one."

"He'll die for this."

Shayna's hand tightened on his arm, and her presence drew his gaze toward her. She looked into his eyes, as though looking for confirmation of something she already suspected, then gave a little nod. Somehow, Bael had the feeling that she already knew what had brought him back, even though he hadn't told her anything. She knew him that well, and even injured, was ready to guide him through the uncertain paths ahead.

She'd always seen the future more clearly than him. "No," she said.

"There's no honor in this." Bael's voice was flat and cold. Not even the emissary stoked the same depth of emotion. The emissary was an enemy, one whose purposes were different than Bael's. Such behavior was to be expected. But not from one of his own clan. Not from someone who was supposed to fight by his side.

"There's a better way," she said. "If you attack him, now, even if you beat him, it will be a loss. But there's a way to use this."

He clenched his fists. There was a time for taking advantage of the situations life presented him and a time for justice, and this was very much the latter.

But the memory of Rydal, and of his and Elian's failed plan to fight the emissary, made his judgment less reliable than he'd believed, and so he forced himself to take deep breaths and to listen. As she told him, the fire in his spirit cooled, hardening into a whetstone that would serve to sharpen the fangs and claws of his precious Wolves.

27

Elyn woke from her latest nightmare and groaned at the dim red light that constantly worked its way into the cave, mixing with the dark stone to surround her with blood-red walls. She dug her heels into the ground and feebly shoved herself back until her head struck the wall. From there, she shifted onto her elbows, then pushed herself to a sitting position.

A lifetime ago and a world away, she'd rolled her eyes as she'd listened to Samora explain how closely the human body and spirit were connected, how diseases of the spirit affected the body, and how a weak body caused the spirit to deteriorate. A pointless lesson, or so she'd thought at the time, because everyone knew the stronger your physical body, the more your spirit was capable of.

The truth of that lesson was written upon her muscles now. She moved every day, from long walks when time allowed, to climbing cliff walls she'd found higher in the mountains. She should be as strong as ever, but she felt weaker than when the heart had twisted her body into a broken, chaotic mess.

Because of the servant? He'd be easy to blame, for he was the one that brought the memories. And yet, she couldn't blame him, because he never lied. He showed her only what was true, the suffering she'd lived with for so long. She'd never seen so clearly, but the truth was a bitter brew to swallow.

In her moments of weakness, she wished she could forget. She'd cursed her poor memory when she'd been younger, but now considered it a gift. Forgetting was the only way humans could make their way through the world they'd broken. It was the only way they let go of all the pain and suffering they'd endured, the only way they could live with those who'd hurt them so many times.

Aunt Samora had always talked about forgiveness, but forgiveness was a lie. There was only forgetting.

Insulted by your brother? Only once the words are forgotten could you move on.

Betrayed by a lover? It was no wonder so many turned to the liquor that flowed out of the city, for only the liquor allowed them to forget.

She'd forgotten, too. Or pushed the memories so deep into her spirit that they never should have risen again, like a body buried so far below the surface even the worms couldn't find it. Forgetting had allowed her the illusion of peace, had let her pretend she had a life as useful and normal as anyone else. It hadn't been much, but it had been something, even if it was a lie.

The servant didn't let her forget. In this cave and on this world, now there was only memory. She couldn't think of adani without remembering Father and the hundreds of ways he'd pushed her too far, too fast, laying the foundation for the disaster that would eventually befall her. Only now did she realize how he'd manipulated her, in ways both dramatic and subtle, onto a path from which her younger self had felt there was no escape. And then, when she'd failed, he'd blamed her and left her behind.

Elyn sensed the servant when the portal open and it stepped through. The emissary's head servant, the one who had tortured her with so many memories, appeared at the mouth of the cave and looked in, his face the very mask of concern. "You look ill."

"You poison me and then ask why I'm ill? I thought you more committed to the truth than that."

The servant came in, even though he hadn't been invited. He strode forward as though he owned the cave and she was nothing but a guest. He squatted before her. "What you call poison I call healing. The truths I show may not be pleasant, but they are true."

"There's no need to show me anymore. I've seen plenty."

She expected a quick rejection from the servant, for that was all she'd received before. Instead, he studied her closely, then nodded. "Perhaps you are finally ready. You haven't seen the truth quite yet, but you're close. Maybe close enough."

"Ready for what?"

"For me to offer you the most important choice you've ever faced. You've lived through every memory, and you see clearly now the stain upon the world that humanity represents. But that doesn't mean that humanity is useless. As we speak, a new breed of farmers is being raised, and their first harvests have proved very…desirable…to the emissaries. There are those, though, that resist the inevitable. The same ones who harmed you. Those like your father."

She tired of the way he danced around his request, as though she couldn't guess the thrust of his demand. "Speak clearly. What do you want me to do?"

A memory, though thankfully not one of her own, bloomed in the broken wasteland of her thoughts. "There are a pair of ascended adanists on your home world, not of your former clan, who seek to attack one of our farmlands. They've told no one of their plans, and think themselves sly, but their intent is as clear as day to our master."

The servant paused, and Elyn waited for it to finish, too exhausted for his flair for the dramatic.

"Kill them."

Her stomach rebelled at the thought. "You've reminded me, time and time again, of my father's failures, which are many. But do you think me a child? That I would lash out at all adanists, simply because of how I feel about one?"

The head servant shook his head. "You misunderstand my purpose still. Your greatest suffering revolves around your father and your own failure to ascend, and so those are the memories I return to you. But your suffering is not unique. All who live suffer. It is the curse of life, and the curse Void means to lift across all the worlds."

"You have not persuaded me life has no value."

She hoped to goad him with his failure, but he simply nodded, his expression fixed as ever. "Nor did I think I would. Not yet. It is still in your best interest to kill the two."

"Why?"

"Because deep in your spirit, you still want to be useful, and this is the way to be so."

Elyn scoffed, but the servant's confidence rattled her. He knew her well. His access to her memories and thoughts guaranteed that. And he was no fool, so he came fully expecting her to accept.

What did that make her, if he was so certain she would kill adanists who'd done her no harm? "Explain," she demanded.

"The adanists know they cannot hurt the servants who watch your world. So they will attack the adanists in the cities, thinking that in so doing, they'll stop what I've already put in motion. They view those adanists as the weakest link, the only place where they can strike back against me and cause me harm. They'll kill hundreds in the mistaken belief they'll be doing their world a favor."

"Won't they be?"

"All they'll accomplish, at most, is introduce a slight delay into our master's plan. Hardly worth the trade of so many lives.

At worst, though, they'll doom your world. Void doesn't have the emissaries or the servants necessary to subdue worlds, for it has never had to before. Your world only lives because it is useful. These adanists threaten that usefulness. Other emissaries may insist it would be better if we simply destroyed your world."

Elyn swore at herself as her hands trembled.

Mere words, and yet the truths within them were enough to question everything she'd believed of herself. Her voice trembled like her hands when she said, "So, at worst, I save hundreds of lives, and at best, I save the world?"

The servant nodded.

"If I do kill them, then what?"

"Then take the hearts from their bodies, wrap them in a sphere of void, and press them into your core."

Elyn sat up straighter. That sounded suspiciously like an ascension ritual, and the first time she'd attempted that, it hadn't gone well. "Why? What will happen to me?"

"So long as your desire is pure, there is no risk of harm, and I speak not as your ignorant father, but as a servant who has shepherded countless others through this process. The heart of a dead ascended adanist and the void will make for a powerful combination, and your body will accept the new strength. You'll still be able to use adani, but you'll become a true servant of the emissary, in body and in spirit."

Elyn swallowed hard. She'd hoped for more time, but the time had come to choose.

"And if I refuse?"

"Then our time together is at an end. Our master has been lenient with you, as he believes you have much to offer Void, but one condition of our order is that your faith must be absolute. You've been given enough time, and more importantly, you've been given access to the mysteries. You're too dangerous, now, to be allowed to live freely. Either join us now or be returned to the adani from whence you came."

Elyn closed her eyes. Her memories assaulted her, reminding her of all she'd endured. Some part of her had always known that this was where the emissary's influence would lead, but the final step wasn't so hard to take. She didn't want to kill adanists she didn't know and had no grudge against, but if it allowed her to save the world? To finally make a difference? She hated how obvious the choice seemed.

She nodded, and the deal was made.

ELYN STEPPED through the portal and back onto the world of her birth, but her arrival didn't engender any of the feelings of relief or return that she'd expected. Her time on the emissary's world, short as it was, had cleanly cut through any of the strings that had tied her here. Given that she hadn't even noticed they were cut, perhaps they hadn't been that strong to begin with.

The portal closed behind her, and Elyn turned, surprised the servant hadn't followed. He'd been beside her the entire way, so close it was as if he worried she might collapse from the mere act of walking. But now that she was home, she was alone, the message as clear as if it had been written in blood. This was her test to either pass or fail, and she had no doubt of the stakes involved.

The portal had opened up in the midst of an expansive forest, one Elyn didn't think she'd ever visited before. Chipmunks scurried up trees as though they were roads, and the tall oaks shaded her from the glaring sun overhead. Even so, she squinted as she looked around, her eyes watering from the sudden abundance of light.

According to the servant, the adanists would be passing through the woods later that day, on a path less than a mile east from where the portal had left her. Elyn hadn't asked how the servant knew so much about the adanists' plans, nor had she questioned the servant's accuracy. Part of it was obvious enough. The emissary's servants could pass as human, even to an adanist standing a couple of paces away. They'd been upon this world for a time, watching and learning about their opponents, if humans even deserved the title.

She made her way east and tried not to think about what she was about to do, a task made easier by the memories that continued to fill her thoughts, that made it difficult to focus on anything but the myriad ways she'd been wronged by so many.

Was she really going to go through with this? In the caves the answer had seemed so obvious, and even now, she thought that she would, but under the bright light of a different sun, she wasn't so sure. She kept putting one foot in front of another, though, and soon she found herself on the path, though she had only the vaguest memory of wandering through the woods.

Elyn turned south, the direction the adanists would come from, and kept walking, a slow pace that would barely cover a few miles over the course of a day, but movement, nevertheless. Better to keep moving than to stop, because she wasn't sure she'd move again if she rested.

Time and distance meant nothing, but eventually, she sensed them up ahead, and she knew without seeing them, that at some point in their lives they'd trained under Father. Not only had they ascended, but they pulled adani toward them as they walked, a result of Father teaching them adani manipulation in his particular ways. And of course, it would be adanists trained by Father who would be so foolish as to attempt to attack the emissaries and their servants.

By the time they came into view, following the path around an enormous oak, Elyn had coerced a smile onto her face, and she forced herself to bow in greeting. If they were concerned about meeting a stranger in the forest, they didn't show it, but why should they be concerned? They were ascended, up until a few months ago the most powerful beings anywhere in the world.

They might know better now, but a lifetime of becoming used to deference and safety was hard to overcome.

Both were vaguely familiar, which wasn't a surprise, if Father had trained them. She'd probably trained beside them when they were children.

A flash of recognition on the face of the man meant he'd remembered, too.

Elyn reacted without thought. She squeezed the heart stronger still and embraced its power, not because of the adani it granted, but because of the small void it opened up within her, the part of her spirit that was most true.

The spheres came naturally to her now, and she sent two at each, aimed at the center of their chests. The adanists were slow to react, the one who'd recognized her slower than the other, as his mind had to make an extra leap to realize it was in danger. Both had been trained well, worthy of the wandering clan they represented, and both bound a shield before the void struck them.

The shields were an instinct, trained into them over years, and against another adanist or the Debru, the shields would have served them well. Against the void, though, not so much.

Both hunkered down behind their shields, expecting protection, but when the first spheres struck the shields, both spheres and shields vanished, leaving the adanists exposed. Before they could react, the second spheres, stronger than the first, struck flesh and buried deep into their chests.

A properly trained adanist could survive an incredible amount of damage, but fatal was fatal, and the body needed a physical heart to go on. Her voids destroyed those hearts, pumping furiously the moment before they vanished, as though effort alone would be enough to save them. Both adanists collapsed, and she took pride in the fact their deaths had been quick, the same way she took pride in the swift and painless deaths she gave the deer she hunted.

It shouldn't have been so easy, but they were dead, and her decision was made. Thoughts swarmed her, but she kept her mind blank and focused only on the next task ahead of her.

She formed two more spheres and sent them into the adanists' cores. They dug holes through flesh, viscera, and blood, and when they came into contact with the hearts, now made solid in death, the voids allowed the hearts in, but nothing else.

Elyn called the voids back and they returned like obedient dogs, floating before her with their dangerous burdens. She leaned forward to inspect the hearts more closely. They were no longer clear, but stained red. She couldn't guess at the meaning, but she dismissed the spheres and let the stones fall into her hand.

A sudden tremor ran through her body.

She'd been here once before, but that time, she'd been surrounded by friends and family, or at least by people who'd given themselves that title. Accepting the heart into her body had stolen decades from her life and was easily the greatest mistake she'd ever made.

Now the emissary's servant asked her to accept two.

She closed her hand around them so she couldn't see them, though the gesture did nothing to stop her from feeling the power that wanted to rush through her hand and into her body.

There was no deep thought that pushed her over the edge, no decisive logic. Step by step, she'd been pushed down this path, first by Father and then by the cruel but honest manipulations of the emissary. Momentum had a force all its own, just as she'd been taught as she'd been learning how to fight, and she didn't have the strength or the desire to change her course. The red hearts would end the pain adani had brought her, and that was more than enough.

The servant had left her no specific instructions, but her body knew what to do, and the void, once introduced, was simpler than adani. She held onto the heart that had nearly destroyed her entire life and opened the void. She tossed the two red hearts into the air and wrapped them in spheres and directed them to her core.

She braced for pain but there was none. The spheres slid into her core, less painful than a knife sharpened to a razor's edge. Two became one, and that one became part of her, the way she'd always imagined it would be if she ascended. Their union didn't flood her with strength, the way adani once had, but she sensed the vast emptiness now at her control. She didn't need to connect to it the way she had to adani, it simply existed in her core, fully a part of her.

Clan lore taught that adani was natural, but maybe they were wrong, for this felt as natural the breeze against her skin or the sun on her face.

Strange, that though she had welcomed the void into her core, she'd never felt more whole.

She held her old heart in her hand, the stone silent but full of strength she no longer needed or wanted. She bent down, used a void sphere to dig a small tunnel into the soil of the woods, then dropped the heart in and covered it up. She didn't look back once as another portal opened and she stepped through, leaving her old world behind.

28

Shayna stood, but the effort cost her, and she almost fell back into her cot. Her wrists and ankles were chafed red and raw from where the manacles had scraped constantly again her skin. Bael reached out and steadied her, and she took a deep breath as her legs quivered. "You haven't just been beaten, have you?" he asked.

"Lieran told me that if I wasn't going to help the clan, there was no need for the clan to help me. Said I could get my own food, which was complicated by the fact I wasn't allowed to move."

"And Grandfather allowed this?"

Shayna coughed. "I'm not sure how much Aldrick knows. I haven't seen him since they confined me, and everyone who guarded me was Lieran's."

Bael frowned, but he could work out the implications on his own. "Lieran's looking to take over the clan."

"He lost it after Samora left. Claimed that half the clan was planning an attack the unified council had already decided was foolish. It's been tense around here."

"Aldrick should have been able to control Lieran."

"Yeah, well, he's had other problems on his mind."

"Such as?"

"We're losing adanists."

Bael's frown deepened. "They're being murdered."

"Maybe. We don't know, but no small number of warriors have left and not returned, and our best adanists can't find them. Samora might be able to, but she's gone, too. Aldrick and Killan have been pushing themselves to find out what's happening, but they haven't had any luck."

Bael cursed. "I shouldn't have left."

Shayna nestled her head against his shoulder. "I'm glad you did. You would have died if you surrendered to Rydal."

"Anything else I need to know before we leave this tent?"

"I love you. No matter what happens, you can always believe in that."

Bael leaned down and kissed her. "I always have. It's one of the reasons I kept fighting."

It was also one of the reasons he hadn't completed the transformation the heart asked of him, even now. Perhaps some part of him would come back, but all of him wanted Shayna, and he'd never take the risk.

The light outside the tent was bright, and he squinted for a moment while his eyes adjusted. When he opened them fully, he saw his arrival had attracted a crowd, most of whom didn't look pleased to see him. Only a few weeks ago, he would have wilted under that judgment. A leader couldn't lead adanists who looked at him like that.

Bael stood up tall, giving Shayna his arm to hold onto for support. He met every angry gaze, letting them see him and more importantly, see Shayna.

What he wanted was to cast a cloak over her and hide her injuries and weakness from sight, to preserve the fierce pride that had always been hers. But this was her choice, hers more than his.

And he was wrong anyway. He knew that when he glanced down at her. Beaten and starved, but she was the only one standing here who still held onto her pride.

One by one, the gazes turned away, until only a few remained. Lieran's most faithful, Bael assumed, and he noted each one.

He didn't need to speak loudly, for the space around the healing tent was silent except for the slight breeze that twisted and meandered through the tents. "You're cowards, all of you, for letting this happen."

No one answered, though Bael sensed Lieran's closest allies preparing adani.

He walked forward, Shayna at his side, and the crowd separated before them. Only one, Flyn, stood his ground, his adani ready for a fight. "You both deserve this and worse," Flyn said.

"Are you going to stop me?"

Flyn's eyes flicked over to his friends, but they waited in the crowd to see how Bael would react to the challenge. The sight of them gave him courage, and Flyn set his feet and bound a sword in his right hand. "I am."

Shayna let go of Bael's arm without being asked, and the moment she did, Bael summoned all his adani and breathed it forward, cycling it through his body the same way Elian had taught him. He was back at Shayna's side before the pain of the blow had even reached Flyn's face.

Flyn's sword unraveled as he wrapped his arms around his stomach and crumpled to the ground. He tried to suck in air to replace what Bael had punched out of him, but he couldn't summon the strength.

Bael stepped over him, guiding Shayna so she wouldn't trip. "Good thing the healing tent is close. It's about time it gets used as it was intended."

A voice called out from behind him, one of Flyn's friends, though Bael wasn't sure which. "You can't do this!"

Bael paid them no attention and kept walking toward the

council circle. He hadn't bothered to summon them, but he was sure they'd be there, all the same, like deer herding together when they knew they were being hunted, hoping the Wolf would only take the weakest of them.

"Training with Elian made you stronger," Shayna observed.

Bael nodded. "Yes, but this battle won't be won because I can punch harder than I used to."

"Good thing you have me, then."

Bael smiled, the first time he had since Arok had landed on the outskirts of the camp. "I was just thinking the same thing."

FATHER FOUND them before Bael reached the Council circle. He paused when he saw Shayna, but his momentum carried him forward and he threw his massive arms around his son and held him close.

Then he stepped back and looked closely at his son, not quite able to look at Shayna again. "I'm sorry."

"Good. But my fight isn't with you. Shayna tells me you've been busy, and that Lieran kept you in the dark."

"It's no excuse."

"No, but it's a reason. Are you going to try to stop me, too?"

Father didn't answer for a moment, then shook his head. "Are you sure about this?"

Bael looked into his father's eyes, searching for any sign of doubt. There was none—just the fear of a father for his son as his son marched into battle. "As sure as I can be."

Father nodded, then took a single step back and studied Bael. "You're stronger?"

Then Father snorted. "Of course you are. That much training with my uncle? I've no desire to pick a fight with you now, that's for sure."

"Thanks."

Father offered him a short bow, then went ahead to the council circle.

Bael and Shayna arrived not long after, and as Bael had guessed, most of the council was present. Father and Grandfather sat together, but they sat alone, the others splitting into smaller groups, leaving gaps in a circle that should have none.

Bael set aside his heavy spirit. He led Shayna into the center of the circle, where all could see her. She stood as tall as she could, though the bruises along her side eventually forced her to hunch over again.

Lieran started to speak, but Bael snapped his head and fixed the council member with a glare that caused him to clamp his jaw shut and take half a step back. Too late, he realized he'd shown his fear, and he gathered his courage to speak, but Bael stole the opportunity from him.

"Is this what we've become?" he asked.

A long silence answered his question. When Lieran started to speak, Bael interrupted him again. "I returned to tell the council of what I've learned, and to discuss again the future of this clan, but when I arrived, I find Shayna bound, beaten, and starved in the healing tent. Is this how we treat one another now?"

Lieran started to speak again, but Bael once again turned to him. "Don't you dare speak in her presence!"

Lieran stepped back again, his mouth moving, but his arguments were stuck in his throat.

Bael knew better than to give him a moment to regain what he'd already lost. He spoke again. "Besides, what do your words matter, when we can see so clearly the type of man you are?"

He punctuated his question by gesturing at Shayna.

The leaders of this clan cast their eyes down. Some drowned in guilt, while others were only dirtied by association, but none were innocent. In another world, one that wasn't threatened by the emissary, he wouldn't have settled until his need for vengeance was sated, but in this world he had to starve that desire. They were all called to something greater. He let them flop about in their guilt for several long moments, then lifted their chins.

"I didn't return because of Shayna, though what's happened to her is indicative of the rot that threatens the spirit of this clan. I've come to remind you of who you really are. Our world is once again in danger, and we stand meekly by. No longer."

Bael expected challenges, and he expected Lieran to lead them, but the council member hadn't recovered from the violent exposure of his sins to the light of day. Instead, they came from his own father.

"You question decisions that have already been made, my son. This council made its judgment, a judgment you yourself accepted," Father said.

How could his own father stand against him, and now, of all times? Bael almost lashed out, then bit back his retort.

He studied Father for a moment, but there was no hatred, jealousy, or envy in the steady gaze that met his. Bael grunted to himself. With that question, Father had presented himself as the neutral party, the impartial judge. The others would be more prone to trust Father now.

But at the same time, he opened the council circle to Bael, allowed him to present his arguments. It was as fair a hearing as Bael could expect, given all that had come before.

If the situation had allowed, he would have bowed deeply to his father, but Father would understand why he couldn't.

He took a slow breath to calm his heart, forcing his thoughts into order. Then he spoke, just loud enough for the council to hear. "Like you, I'm not without guilt. As Killan has said, the council decided, and at the time, I accepted it. I was wrong to flee the council's verdict, and once the emissary is beaten, I'll accept whatever judgment the council proposes. But in fleeing, I learned much."

He paused, though not long enough for anyone to interrupt.

"For one, I learned that the emissary is scared of us. Three times now it has tried to recruit me, and three times I've turned it down. Because it failed, it sent its servants after me and Elian. They were stronger than any opponent I've trained against, but they do die. Elian proved that decisively."

Bael glanced around the circle, wishing Elian was there to support him, but his great-uncle was nowhere to be found. He wasn't a member of the Wolves' council, but he was Elian, and so he was allowed anywhere.

Bael continued. "I also know that the emissary is using the adanists in the cities to harvest corrupted hearts, which only make it stronger. We balance on the edge of a blade. If we fight together, I believe we have a chance to drive the servants from our lands. But that moment won't last long, and the more we sit here and hope the threat will pass us by, the less a chance of success we have."

Father waited to make sure he was done, then said. "You've told us little we didn't already know. It's no surprise the servants can be killed, but you yourself admit they're tougher enemies than you've ever faced. As it stands, the clans remain safe and the cities, though wounded, are no longer under attack. Why should we act?"

"Because you know that no matter what you tell yourself, none of this will last long. And you're not as safe as you believe. Shayna told me of your missing adanists that no one can find. As long as we leave our throat bared to the emissary, we're helpless. Better to fight now than die later."

Father looked disappointed. "These are the same arguments you made earlier, and we didn't find them compelling then. Say we agreed with you. How would you have us attack such a powerful foe?"

Bael hadn't figured that out yet, but he was saved by a new arrival to the circle.

"That's a problem Samora and I have been working on, and I think we have a solution," Elian said.

All eyes turned to him, and though there were several who hated the sight of him at their fire, most looked grateful.

Elian's smile was knowing, as if he possessed a secret they'd all be eager to hear, and Bael hoped he did.

"We're going to assassinate all the emissary's servants," Elian said.

❧ 29 ❧

Samora walked farther than she needed to, but she didn't mind. At first, she'd told herself that the caution was necessary, that if she approached Sanza too closely with a dragon the emissary's servants would know her as an adanist. She left herself more than ten miles to cover on foot, but now she was thinking she would have been safe at half the distance.

Caution wasn't why she'd landed so early, though she hadn't realized it until she started walking.

She needed time to think, and long experience had taught her the best time to think was while she was on foot. Something about walking loosened her thoughts and allowed her mind to jump to conclusions it wouldn't reach otherwise, and she needed that now more than ever.

Though she'd witnessed no violence in Nevan, the sights had stuck to her memories, like a burr that couldn't be removed. The emissary's servants had turned adanists into farmers and forced them to cultivate a land that should have been consecrated as sacred. It sickened her.

She and Elian had fought the Debru not just to survive, but to create a world where their children didn't have to live in fear. The emissary and its servants had taken that away, and though they didn't spill blood as freely as the Debru had, the fear was the same.

But how did they fight back? Her expedition to Navan had given her vague ideas, but it wasn't until she'd walked a few miles that they took definite form.

Sanza would tell her if her plans had any merit.

It was too large to properly be called a village, but too small to be a city. It was one of several Scorpion villages that had grown rapidly after the end of the war. Sanza nestled in the foothills of the mountains, a convenient location that gave it easy access to quarried stone, fresh lumber, and wide fields. While the Scorpions had rebuilt their fortress up in the mountains, they maintained the tradition of only allowing a certain number of citizens to live within its walls, which meant the villages in the foothills had exploded as the population recovered.

She'd visited the village once before and had been impressed by its leadership then. They weren't content merely to grow in size. They'd wanted their village to be beautiful, and to last long after they were gone. Buildings were made of stone, instead of the wood used by most other villages. Decorative flourishes were added to doorways and windows, graceful lines that bent and curved.

As she finally neared the outskirts of the village, near the middle of the day, she saw the following generation of leadership had embraced the same ideals. The buildings near the edge of the village were also stone and were even more beautiful than she remembered. No two were the same, a far cry from the basic layout used by settlers to build their homes almost everywhere else across the land.

Sanza greeted her arrival with the sounds of growth. Stonemasons worked on the east side of town, closest to the mountains and the quarries, and they chipped and chiseled stone with an intensity that would have put most craftspeople to shame. A few used adani, weaving the force into unique shapes that carved out otherwise nearly impossible patterns into the stone.

If she lived through all this, she would have to make a point to return. She'd never sensed weaves like theirs before, and she wanted to study them.

Unfortunately, she'd come into town not as an adanist, but a mere settler. She kept her hood up and was grateful the cool wind blowing down from the mountains today gave her a reasonable excuse. Few, if any, here knew her, but there was no point taking a chance. Adani was wrapped around her tighter than her cloak, and she doubted anyone could sense any of the strength she possessed.

Sanza wasn't unique only because of its construction. It was also one of the only places where the emissary had placed exactly one servant, which was why Samora had chosen it as her destination.

Like any good hunter, she began with a careful study of the hunting ground and her prey. Sanza was as busy as a city, the streets crowded and loud, which provided her with all the cover she needed and more. Besides the stonemasons, the village smiths labored over the ore that came from the mountains. Sanza and the other Scorpion villages couldn't keep up with the demand for steel items, but the sound of constant clanging through the east side of the village proved it wasn't for lack of effort.

The central part of the village was quieter, but no less busy. This was the center of trade, and intrepid individuals from across the land had come to Sanza to trade for steel and stone. The other reason why Samora had chosen Sanza. A few other villages also contained only one of the emissary's servants, but in none of the others would a stranger blend in so easily.

She crossed paths with the servant several times, though

wasn't so bold as to attempt to follow it. The servant took the form of a short and stocky woman, who always looked like she had a specific destination in mind and wouldn't welcome any interruptions.

The servant took no particular interest in her, though she seemed to take an interest in most everything else. Her eyes roamed constantly, and when Samora paid attention, she could sense the woman using adani to scout the area. She was skilled, though not more so than any of the ascended adanists Samora had trained.

The emissary might seem like it was everywhere, but now that the secret behind its trick was revealed, Samora wasn't impressed.

She still didn't want to fight a servant directly, but she didn't think she'd have to.

She fought the temptation to rush. Her presence put the lives of everyone in Sanza in danger, and the last thing she wanted was to fall prey to the same overconfidence that had led to the disaster in Rydal. But the more she studied the city and her opponent, the more certain she was of her ability to hide from the emissary's gaze.

Only one question bothered her. Why Sanza? For all she appreciated about the village, she couldn't understand why the emissary would be interested in it. It was large enough to have one training ground for adanists, but the grounds were just about the emptiest part of the village. The location of the village meant that it was a hub for trade, both between different villages and between the villages and the wandering clans. Though within the bounds of Scorpion territory, Sanza was close enough to the border with the Coyotes' territory that they were often visited by their neighbors to the south and west. Was that why the emissary seemed so interested?

Nothing in the servant's wandering provided any meaningful clue. She wandered from the markets to the masons and smiths, then over to the far western side where most of the homes were, never spending much time anywhere specific. Then she'd run her route again, an endless loop that Samora guessed she'd been walking for as long as she'd been here.

Eventually, it seemed as though there was nothing left to be learned, and she had to make her choice.

It didn't take her long, for there were no other ways forward she or Elian could see. They had the seed of an idea, but they didn't dare risk all their strength until they were certain their idea had merit. Which was why she'd come today.

Could they assassinate a servant?

She checked to ensure that adani was wrapped tightly around her, that her presence wouldn't be noticed by any of the adanists in the village, and then she walked to where she knew the servant would eventually be.

The servant didn't follow the same path as it wandered through the village, but it followed close enough Samora could predict where it would be with relative ease. She took up position near a group of villagers talking with one another, not so close they thought she sought to join them, but close enough a passerby wouldn't pay her any particular attention.

The servant came around a corner, and Samora caught sight of it in the edge of her vision. The older woman didn't seem to notice her as she walked purposefully across the market. Samora turned, not to follow, but to cross directly behind the woman.

As she came close, the woman took note of her, but it was a nothing more than a glance that slid off her. Weak threads of adani reached in her direction, but Samora sent the adani circling around, so gently it would be almost impossible to notice unless one was searching for it, particularly in the crowd. The woman's eyes looked away and Samora stepped behind her.

Samora chose the sword, as she feared she might miss whatever vital point this creature had with her preferred darts. She weaved the blade as she swung her arm across, and the servant never reacted. Her head came free of her body and Samora let the blade go as soon as it finished passing through flesh. She stepped into the shadows of a narrow opening between two buildings and had already turned a corner by the time the screams in the market began.

SAMORA SAT in the shade of a tree, safely away from the village, and connected with Elian.

"It worked."

"Any trouble?"

"None at all. I was even outside the village before word of the killing spread."

Her brother was silent, though she sensed the slow movement of his thoughts in the quiet moments before his reply. "What do you think?"

"It's a devastating blow, if we can land it properly. There's no telling what comes after, though."

Another silence, the weight of so many lives pressing upon both of them. Unfair, really, as neither of them had asked for the responsibility. Yet she'd taught her children and her grandchildren that life wasn't fair, that it couldn't be fair no matter how hard they wished otherwise.

Elian was no more eager to decide than her. He asked questions, probing for weaknesses, for an excuse not to move forward. She recognized the hesitation, but indulged in it, because she wanted the same delay. "Can we land it properly?"

"Seventy-two servants. Well, seventy-one, now. If we figure one per servant and some more to identify and serve as reinforcement, we'd probably want a hundred skilled adanists. Even then, it's anyone's guess."

Elian sat silent on the other side, forcing her to commit.

She *tsked* but answered. "Assuming they take to the training, yes, we can land the blow."

"So, do we do it?"

The crux of the question, which they lacked the knowledge to make properly, because how the emissary would react was a matter of pure speculation. They couldn't even guess at the range of responses it might make.

"It was always going to come down to this," Samora said. "Either we take the risk and fight, or we surrender and see what future the emissary has in mind for us. But if we want to fight, this is the way."

They were closely linked, and Samora couldn't separate what doubt was his and what was hers, but their doubts fed on one another and grew bigger.

Elian snorted. "It's a damned clever enemy, isn't it? Hurts us in just the right ways, and just enough, to know how small our odds of beating it are. Then it harnesses our adanists, but not so tightly they want to fight. Even I'm sitting here, wondering if the council is right and we should accept this new rule."

"But?"

"But living under the thumb of another was never what we fought for, and it announced its presence by murdering hundreds without warning. I think Bael has the right of it. Any truce with a monster makes us as guilty as it."

Samora's throat tightened at the mention of her grandson's name. He'd been on her mind more often than not, ever since they'd parted ways again. She'd wanted a much different future for him. She still did, but that was another part of life being unfair. It wasn't up to her. But she could still fight for him.

She didn't feel any more doubt between them, and she searched Elian's feelings deeply. She made a harsh sound in the back of her throat and felt Elian's grin, and it reminded her of being much younger, because it was the grin he gave before he went off and did something reckless. The decision was made, with no need to say more.

"How is Bael?" she asked.

Pride warmed the connection, more than she'd felt from Elian in some time. "He's still torn about what he's discovered, but he's found his path. I think he's arguing with the council now. You'd be proud of him."

"I always was. Will he sway them?"

"Hard to say, but I think so. He's got that fire in him now. Reminds me of Harald, back then."

The grief that echoed in the empty space between them buffeted her, but she had enough grief of her own and didn't need any of Elian's. She gently shoved it aside. "Good. The clans need him, then."

She'd hoped that burden would have fallen to Killan, her strong and brave boy, who'd seemed born for the role when he'd been young. He was still her strong and brave boy, though he'd become a man many years past, but he'd never found that deeper well of spirit that drew people to him the way light had attracted otsoa back in the day.

There was nothing to be done about it, though. Life moved as it wanted, and it had chosen Bael, and she was proud, though she wished it had chosen another. He was finally growing into the leader she'd always known he could be.

She sensed Elian's desire to leave, so wasn't prepared when he asked, "Has adani spoken to you at all?"

"No, not since the attack," she replied, and didn't say that it hadn't spoken to her often for many years prior. Because of the arrival of the servants? Or for another reason she couldn't guess at?

Elian, pragmatist that he was, grunted and moved on. "Where to, next?"

"I'll wait to hear from you. For now, I'll rest for a few days."

"Take care of yourself."

"You, too. And Elian?"

"Yes?"

"Where are we going to find a hundred adanists willing to try our plan?"

He laughed. "I've got an idea for that, too. But for now, get some rest. I think it's time for me to help Bael and speak with the council."

❧ 30 ❧

Twice more Elyn traveled back to the world of her birth, and twice more she had been persuaded to kill ascended adanists. The first time it had been another pair, but such was her success that for her third trip, the servant had sent her to ambush four ascended adanists by herself. All three times, surprise and the void guided her to easy victory. Their adani returned to the land, and the blood-red hearts came to her. With every heart she brought into her body and offered to the void, her ties to the void grew stronger.

Now, on the world the emissary had brought her to, the one she had started to think of as home, she explored with the void the way she once had with adani.

In many ways, it was a simpler force. Life was intricate, complex, and varied, while the void was—universal. The emissary's servant only taught her a few basic techniques, from the spheres which had come so naturally to her at first to the barrier most used for defense. The only other technique was that of a bound sword, though the servant claimed she'd have little need for it. At times, it seemed that her own study of the void was nearly complete.

Her explorations with the void weren't pointless, though, for the closer she tied herself to it, the more of it she sensed. Not just on this world, but on interconnected worlds. Though she sat in a cave by herself, she was far from alone. She need never be alone again.

Because of that connection to the void, she sensed the emissary before he even came to her. Finding him had been one of the first challenges she had given herself, and it had taken two sets of kills and days of searching before she declared her hunt a success. He moved often, and she gathered his responsibilities extended far beyond her world. He had no need to open a portal, because when he misted, he became one with the void, then reappeared in another place a moment later. She tracked him through her newfound senses, felt the slight alterations in the void as he directed his will, and soon understood she could sense where he planned to go. So she knew, before he had even dissolved on the world he'd been on, that she was due a visitor.

Elyn put on tea. She had little need for sustenance any longer, the void now supplying almost all she needed, but she liked the taste of tea and appreciated the feeling it created in a place. Sharing tea was a mark of civilization. By the time the emissary arrived, she already had the water boiling.

He understood in a moment the importance of her preparation. "Your senses have improved considerably."

She bowed her head. "Thank you."

"It is I who should thank you. Your service has been a great help and has given me time I wasn't sure I'd receive."

She wished he would explain further, but he went silent, and she gathered that his thoughts were not for her. Unwilling to let the opportunity go to waste, she asked, "How is it that you and the other emissaries are able to become one with the void, but the other servants and I are not?"

His eyebrow rose a bit at the question, and he sipped his tea before answering. "Your senses have improved considerably. What do you think?"

She had a guess already; one she'd thought long and hard about. "I think your servants, including me, are roughly equivalent to an ascended adanist for the light. We possess knowledge and power of the force we're loyal to, but there's something more, another level that we must pass. You and the other emissaries have done so," and here she paused, worried of the judgment she might earn if she continued, but the emissary had never demanded less than perfect honesty, and so she said, "and Bael, I think, is close to passing to that level on behalf of adani."

The emissary allowed no reaction to reach his face, but she felt the stirring of void within him and knew she was right, or close enough, anyway.

"You're right, and before you ask your next question, no, you are nowhere close to becoming an emissary, although one day, if you continue as you have, you might."

She should have been too old for such promises, but what she discovered about herself on that day was that she wasn't at all. She was no better than she had been as a child, desperately waiting for the day when Father told her that she was good enough.

"What does it take?"

"For now, our traditions dictate that you must not know. But it is a sacrifice, and one you shouldn't be in a hurry to make."

In the back of her mind, she'd always known that the emissary was old. He was a being that traveled between worlds faster than she used to travel between villages, but it was only when he uttered that last line that she wondered just how old he was, because he spoke with a weariness the elders in the clan could only aspire to.

"May I ask why not?"

"Of course."

For a moment, she thought he wasn't going to answer, but he was only gathering his thoughts and putting them in order.

"Hard as it may be to believe, I once lived as a mortal being on a world far from here and long lost to history. Like you, I was dissatisfied with life, though my reasons seem foolish now. I was a quiet being in an unbearably noisy world. I was surrounded by endless, vapid conversation. My obsession was the structure and purpose of the universe, but I was forced to listen to endless drivel. All I wanted was silence and the space to think and study. My investigations into the nature of my world introduced me to what you think of as the void, and I embraced it wholeheartedly."

The emissary paused, and Elyn sensed an entire epic tale contained within that brief moment of silence. He had destroyed his world and become the void's emissary. Somehow, she knew there could be no other story that explained the being before her.

"I became a believer, and I gave everything to the void."

"You regret it?" Elyn asked.

"No, not regret. Just a more measured perspective than I had when I was younger. The life of an emissary is not an easy one. There are few of us, for few are worthy of the void's greatest gifts, and the void's demands are many. It is why your world is so important. The hearts we harvest there will give the void the strength to win this war and earn us all our rest."

Void tugged at her, then, but she was too focused on the emissary to pay much attention. "You plan to make my world into a farm that produces those blood-red hearts."

The emissary nodded. "This is how the void wins, and though I don't know how much it matters to you, it means that those you care for have an opportunity to live out the rest of their days in peace."

"Why do the other emissaries oppose your plans?"

"Most believe the risk isn't worth the reward. It is always easier to kill a person than to enslave them. Better, many think, to simply wipe the world clean and focus on our next victory."

"My father and the others will fight."

"I expect that they will, but it will be of no use. I've placed almost all my personal servants on your world, and they guard our first harvests well. Strong as your adanists have become, you know as well as anyone that they aren't strong enough."

She did know. She'd witnessed their shortcomings plenty as she killed them. "What would you have of me?"

A steel blade appeared in his hand, though she couldn't say where it had come from. "You've now heard more about me and my goals than most. Only Void itself understands me better. Pledge your oath to me, now, and together we can heal this broken universe."

Never before had a knife held such promise, but Elyn had lived too long to be so easily swayed by another's promises. "What oath?"

"An oath of blood. The same all my other servants have taken. It will grant me greater access to your thoughts and senses, and I'll exert some will over your own, though I can assure you I won't be able to force you to do anything you wouldn't want to do already."

"To what end?"

Elyn already knew the answer, but needed a moment to think and needed the emissary to say it out loud. He seemed to understand that, though, and when he answered, his voice was gentle. "You've communed with the void and understand its purpose. Life is suffering, and we seek an end to all suffering. You might call it destruction, and while the word itself is accurate, it doesn't capture our intent, which is mercy. Not a mercy recognized by those we deliver it to, but a mercy nevertheless."

She couldn't lie, not to him. "I'm not sure that I'm ready to believe that."

The emissary nodded. "I know, and in better days, I would give you more time to realize the truth, but there is little available to us. For now, I promise you that by accepting this oath, you'll be helping to keep your world alive, for it will last until the void's purpose is complete. You'll save more lives than any adanist ever has. And you'll finally show your family what you were always capable of."

Elyn still wavered.

"If there were time, I'd let you see, with your own eyes, why the void deserves to win. I'd show you the suffering across so many worlds, and you'd know I spoke true. But for now, I ask only for your trust, just as I've trusted you."

She didn't ask, but her confusion must have shown on her face.

"The void is a dangerous force. Allowing you the training I have already, without collecting your oath, is unheard of among the emissaries. But I believed you were worth it. Now all I ask is some measure of the trust I've shown you."

She almost asked why she should trust him but caught herself before asking such a foolish question. What most called trust was nothing more than believing in a pattern of behavior. So-and-so hadn't hurt me before, so they won't hurt me now. Real trust, though, could have no reason. That was why it was trust. As near as she could tell, though, he had never lied to her.

Nor did she ask what would happen if she refused, because that, too, was obvious.

And she'd already been walking down this path for some time. Still, it wouldn't hurt to be enticed just a little more. "And what do I get for this oath?"

"A share of my strength, a share of my experience, and in time, the ability to become an emissary. Not all are worthy, but you, Elyn, have been worthy from the day you were born."

Like so many of her recent choices, it didn't feel nearly as difficult as it should have, and Elyn held out her hand. The emissary nicked himself first, and liquid void, so dark she felt she could get lost within it, dripped from his palm. He cut her palm next, and they shook hands. The void leaped into her blood, and it was like accepting one of the hearts into her body except so much better. The void was vast and all-encompassing, and Elyn was sure that for the first time in her life, she'd never be alone again.

⚜ 31 ⚜

Elian stood as Arok swooped low and landed with a grace that should have been impossible for a creature of his size. He carried four adanists upon his back, but Elian cared only for the one sitting up front. Capricia waited until the others dismounted, then followed. Elian greeted her with an embrace, took her pack and slung it over his shoulder, then led her to where he'd set up their tent.

"Bigger camp than I expected. Are his gatherings always this large?" she asked.

"No. Bael told me that when he usually calls for a hunt, maybe fifty or sixty adanists appear. He figures there are maybe seventy or so that he considers part of his little clan. But when he sent out the invite, he stressed that anyone his friends thought was worthy was welcome. They heeded his call. We have more than we need, but that's a good thing, because not everyone will pass the training."

"How's that been going?"

"There's been good and bad. My techniques benefit everyone who studies them, but few have grasped how far they can push their bodies. But honestly, if it all goes according to plan, my training should be largely unnecessary. Samora's training is the more important, and she's having a more difficult time. For them to get close, they need to master her technique, and that's no small ask. Even I struggle with the control necessary for this mission. Fortunately, all these kids seem to be quicker learners than I am."

Capricia tugged on his hand halfway through the camp, and he stopped beside her. The camp was busier than any they'd been in for many years. Even those sitting around and helping with the food worked with an urgency rarely seen in larger camps. "Feels like I stepped back in time and we're facing the Vada again."

"Sure, except now all the adanists are looking at us like we're old."

"We are old."

"Doesn't mean they need to remind us every time we walk by."

She let him take her to the tent, where he let her pack down. "Care to take a walk?"

"After all that flying? Of course."

He led her through the camp and beyond its outskirts, wandering until he found a rise in the land that would allow them to rest, stretch, and look out over the campground. The training grounds were filled with Bael's friends training under Samora, resulting in a strange effect where Elian could watch them train, but could barely sense them with his adani. It reminded him of when he was younger and hadn't been able to extend his adani at all and reminded him that no matter how much he complained about his age, he wouldn't trade where he was now for anything.

Capricia knew him well enough to know something was on his mind, and her guess was intended to get him to open up. "How's Bael?"

The mere mention of Bael's name brought a smile to his lips. The cost had been far, far too high, but in this crisis he'd found the steel in his spirit. Elian was proud of him like Bael was his own, even though Samora and Aldrick deserved almost all the credit for raising him. "He's done well. It was a fight to convince the Wolves' council to let him go, but they weren't prepared for our defiance. Since we've left, though, he's become a leader in his own right. Some of those adanists might have come because they heard Samora and I wanted to fight, but most of them are there because of him."

"It's Elyn, then."

Elian's throat tightened, and he nodded. "I don't know how we bring her back."

Capricia's hand settled on his leg and tightened. "She might be our child, but she's no longer a child. She's made her own decisions for a long time, now."

"It can't be that easy for you," Elian snapped, knowing it wasn't, but unable to keep the edge off his voice.

Capricia's look of warning was enough to quench his temper. "It kills me, the same as it kills you, and if there was anything I could do to bring her back, you know I would. But she's beyond our reach and was even before the emissary whisked her away."

"I should have done more. Brought her back to the clan, somehow."

"Maybe we both should have, but we always did what we thought was right. We held her tight when we thought that was what she needed, and we gave her space when she wanted."

There was a stone in Elian's chest, heavier than any mountain, and he blinked back tears. "I can't lose her."

"Then don't. I don't know how, but I know she'll be back, and you'll have another chance."

He swallowed, and the stone in his chest grew lighter, but just barely. "Which brings me to the other problem. I can't fight the emissary. At least, I can't fight it and win."

"Hopefully you won't have to."

He gestured to the camp below. "All this? I believe in it, and there's little I can do here beyond what I've already done. I've been thinking about what comes after, because I doubt the emissary will let this world go without a fight, and once it comes, I don't know how I beat it."

"What have you tried?"

Elian snorted. "I've been trying to uncover the transformation that Bael discovered, but Bael doesn't understand it well enough. He describes it as breaking down all the barriers between the heart in our cores and our body, but even when I try, the result is nothing more than flooding my body with adani. What he's done is something different, and I can't find it."

Capricia started at his word choice. "What he's done? Not what he did?"

"He's not simply ascended anymore. He's straddled the transformation ever since it happened, and it's only because he's kept it locked tight that he hasn't surrendered to it. It's his to grasp whenever, but he doesn't dare even look in that direction."

"Which is why you'd rather take it on. You want to make the sacrifice instead of him."

Elian nodded. "We don't know for sure what happens through the transition, but it seems likely that the body is sacrificed in the process. If the Vada is any indication, it means that if I survive, I'd be able to take any shape I'd like. Or, it might just mean death. Either way, though, better me than him. I've already lived more years than I ever expected, and he's too young."

Capricia leaned up against him. "I don't suppose you were ever going to ask me what I thought about all of this?"

Elian hung his head, then grinned. "Sorry. I've been meaning to, but a lot has happened. I figured you'd be glad to be rid of me so you could find someone younger and more interesting."

Her glare silenced him, but only for a moment. "I figured you'd understand. That if you were in my place, you'd do the same."

She wrapped her arms around his arm and held him close.

"Doesn't mean I want to lose you, even if it's just your physical form."

The weight in his chest became a little lighter, just light enough that he could convince himself he could carry on. "I couldn't have done any of what I've accomplished without you."

"I know. It's important to remind you sometimes, though."

She snuggled up against his arm, and he wondered if just maybe there was hope for them once all this was over.

BAEL HAD LOST track of the number of times that either Grandmother or Elian had warned him to stay close to the camp, but what was the point of leading this small rebellion if he was going to listen to the rules others made for him? The camp was too close, and though every face was friendly, he sometimes felt as though it was difficult to breathe. For this, he needed space, where all true wandering adanists thrived.

Shayna was at his side and a step behind, following him into the unknown without question. When they'd first met, Bael had thought she was too eager to follow, as though she didn't have enough confidence to simply be herself.

Time had taught him a different truth, though. Shayna would never lead a clan, but she'd never wanted that. She was strong in her own right, as competent an ascended adanist as one was likely to find, but she wanted to use that strength not to lead, but to support, and in him, she claimed she'd finally found someone worthy of lending her support to.

She'd changed his life, and he wondered if sometimes she knew how much. Her constant, quiet presence beside him gave him courage he never would have had otherwise, for if he'd earned her trust, that meant he was worthy of trust from others.

They found a place away from the camp where if they laid down together it was as though they were the last two in the world. Their clothes formed an impromptu blanket, and he tried to say with his lips and hands all that he hadn't found the right words to express. After, she rested her head on his shoulder, and they looked up at the stars together.

No amount of debate would resolve the conflict tearing his spirit in two, and his time with Shayna failed to bring the clarity he'd hoped for.

"Would you think less of me if I said we should run away and find someplace to hide out the rest of our days?" he asked.

"I would."

He breathed in deep, the scent of her sweat mixed with the late spring blooming of the prairie flowers. It was moments like these, perfect moments embedded within the storm of daily life, that he couldn't let go. All of what made life worth living was contained in these moments, and to surrender them would be a crime.

Her right hand played idly with the hair on his chest. "Whatever happens, I'll be fine."

"Doesn't mean that I want to lose you."

"But you don't know what will happen. If it works, and you figure everything out, I'll join you."

He didn't deserve her. The ache in his chest throbbed whenever he thought about losing her, and the more he thought about it, the more certain he was that if he obeyed the heart's summons, he would lose her for good. But she wouldn't let him run from his duty, either.

They'd spoken plenty of his dilemma, and Shayna had never been anything except encouraging, but her encouragement wasn't enough. Especially because she said one set of things but meant another. She told him she would be fine, but her lie wouldn't have convinced a child.

She rolled on top of him, sitting on his lower abdomen and straddling him between her legs. Lit by the soft glow of the moon and with the stars behind her, there had never been a more beautiful sight in all the history of the world. She fixed him with a stare, drawing his own gaze toward hers. Whatever she meant to say, it took her a long moment to summon the necessary courage.

"I want you to ascend," she said.

His heart raced faster in his chest, and he couldn't pull his eyes away from her stare. No trace of doubt flickered in her dark pupils.

"I don't want to lose you, but if you don't ascend, I'll lose you anyway. Merely being strong can't be enough for you. It never has been, and I've known that from the first day I met you."

He nodded, not to make a promise, but to acknowledge that she had been heard.

She held his gaze for one moment more, and then the seriousness of the moment faded, and she ran her fingers up his chest with an entirely different purpose in mind. He grinned and gently pulled her face closer to his, and for a time, he was able to forget the rest of the world.

B ael looked over the city of Nevan, unknowingly standing in almost the exact same place his grandmother had weeks ago. Ten adanists stood behind him, and Shayna stood by his side. They waited for the sun to drop so that they could approach the city without fear of being seen. Shayna extended thin tendrils of adani toward Nevan, confirming what Samora had told them before they left, at least as well as she was able. She nodded to no one in particular. "Five servants still in the city, and probably another in the circle of destruction, but my adani won't reach there."

Bael reviewed the plan once again, more for the sake of keeping his mind busy rather than uncovering some weakness they hadn't already thought of. It was far from perfect, but it was the culmination of many nights of shared imagination and debate. Grandmother and Elian had put forth the seed of the idea, but all had been welcome to challenge its weaknesses and improve upon it.

In the end, they'd had enough volunteers so that each of the emissary's servants merited a pair of ascended adanists. One trained to locate the servant, the other trained to strike a lethal blow. Of course, the training had overlapped, so if something were to happen to either half of a team, the other should be sufficient to finish the work.

The sun dipped below the horizon, and Bael turned to the adanists gathered behind him. They'd already been assigned to different parts of the city, and Shayna had sketched out roughly where each of the servants was. They may or may not be in the same place when the adanists arrived, but they had planned in enough time to find their target before the call was sounded.

"Any questions?" he asked.

Looks passed between the adanists, but no one spoke.

Bael looked each of the adanists square in the eye, proud to know each of them. In ones and twos they'd sought him out over the years, seeing in him a way to put the skills they'd struggled to develop to use. After a wait that was far too lengthy, the time had finally come. He silently hoped they would all return by sunrise. "Good luck. I hope to see you all soon with the blood of the emissary's servants on your hands."

They started down the path that led to the city, and Shayna was the last to go. He kissed her, and then she, too, was gone, leaving him alone for the moment.

Of all their targets tonight, two of the emissary's servants posed a particular difficulty. Each supervised the destruction where the city adanists harvested the red hearts. Because the supervisors stood in the middle of a barren wasteland of destruction, there would be no sneaking up on them, which made more creative ideas necessary.

He and his uncle had risen to the challenge. Bael would strike the servant in Nevan, and Elian would attack the one in Rydal. With luck, they would end this tonight, and Bael could turn his focus to other matters.

The heart in his core grew more insistent, and it took more of Bael's will to keep the transformation from taking over his body. He'd thought, after that last attack, that he'd pulled back from the edge, but once adani's invitation was accepted, it kept pulling him deeper. He realized he couldn't sit on the edge forever, but for now, he could delay the decision. With luck, he'd kill the servant before it realized the danger it was in, and if that failed, he hoped he killed the servant before he was required to draw forth his full strength. The more adani he used, the closer he came to jumping off a cliff from which there was no return.

Shayna's encouragement had helped, and he wasn't quite as torn tonight as he had been over the past few weeks. He had to take part in the attack, and so there was only so much he could control. He would fight, and if the transformation seized him, then so it would be. If it didn't, so much the better.

He waited until he was reasonably certain his friends had entered the city before summoning the dragon. He didn't dare extend his own adani, afraid he would warn the servants wandering the streets below, but his friends moved quickly, and no sound of trouble had risen toward him. They were likely close to being in position.

The dragon came in low, out of sight of the city, and landed in a depression behind Bael. He was a younger dragon, eager to test its agility against Bael's unique demands. Bael had asked Arok for a recommendation, and the almost-elder had suggested him. They hadn't reached the point of exchanging names yet, for such honor was not lightly given by the dragons, but Bael hoped that someday soon, they would. He liked the dragon.

"Ready?" Bael asked.

A powerful confirmation came through the bond, and Bael grinned. The dragons hated the emissary and the servants and were ready to do battle as soon as their human allies found their spines. The purity of their purpose cast all the debates around the council campfire in a less friendly light. For the dragons, the emissary was the enemy of adani, and it was as simple as that. Maybe humans had more to learn from the creatures than Bael had thought.

He climbed onto the dragon, and the dragon barely gave him time to settle before it launched into the sky and above the clouds that would keep it out of sight from any alert eyes below. He held loosely to the dragon's scales, closed his eyes, and basked in the feeling of flight. The moon's silver light reflected off the top of the clouds, and for a moment, the whole world was his.

The dragons had also provided the answer to the question of how the adanists would coordinate their attack, for the adanists weren't sure how the servants communicated with one another, but they suspected it was quickly, perhaps through a connection similar to the one Grandmother and Elian shared. A connection similar to the one the dragons also possessed, a connection the adanists would make full use of tonight.

The time is drawing close, the dragon spoke into Bael's mind.

"You be the judge. I do not think it will take more than a few moments to identify the servant within the destruction."

Agreement passed through their connection, and Bael prepared himself for the fight to come. He cautiously opened the connection with his heart wider, allowing more adani to fill his body. The dragon dropped through the clouds, and Bael closed his eyes as mist dampened his face and hair. It dried quickly enough in the wind, and the dragon lost altitude quickly.

The hole in the center of Nevan was easy to spot, and from above he could see it was a perfect circle, darker than the rest of the city. The dragon plunged straight for it, choosing speed over stealth.

Connected to the dragon, he had some sense of the signal that was carried between the dragons. Most adanists couldn't communicate over vast distances, but the dragons could, and so it was the adani passing between the dragons that coordinated the attack. Across the land, as soon as the dragons felt the signal, they roared, passing the message onto the adanists waiting below. The signal brushed past his own adani, and his spirit caught fire. He roared with the dragon, so loud they must have been heard around the world. Below, as the emissary's servants looked to the sky, swords of adani would come for their heads from the shadows.

Bael focused his attention on the movement below, the adanists in the circle scrambling for protection. Only one figure stood still, eyes raised to the sky, and Bael pointed him out to the dragon. Their angle shifted slightly, and Bael dug into the dragon's scales with his toes. The dragon pushed out one last burst of speed, wings and adani working in unison to speed Bael toward his target.

He leapt as he filled his body with as much adani as he dared.

The air before the emissary's servant swirled as it formed a wall of void. Bael answered the shield with a long spear, aimed straight at the servant's chest. Spear met void, and such was Bael's speed and adani, the void shattered upon contact. He thrust his spear, but the servant twisted with reactions maybe even faster than Elian's. The point of the spear cut across the servant's chest and left arm, but not deep enough to be fatal.

Bael flew past. He tucked in his legs and arms while bracing his body with adani, and he bounced and skipped along the ground like a stone across a smooth lake. Three, then four impacts did little to slow him, but he'd covered too much distance, and he thrust out his legs, which did nothing but transform his bouncing body into a tumbling one. He tucked again; thankful his mistake hadn't cost him a broken bone.

He stopped tumbling a hundred paces away and wasted a precious moment finding his feet. By the time he did, half a dozen void spheres came at him from several different directions. Swords appeared in his hands, and he spun and cut, burning more adani than he'd intended. He kept ahead of the first attack, but the second was already on its way.

Bael ran at the servant, disrupting the spacing of the servant's attack. He cut through a handful of spheres, then turned and cut through the ones that had passed him and now chased him.

He swore as the servant formed another set of spheres. It was the same problem he'd encountered on the fields with Elian. Given enough time, the spheres would wear him down, and once they started devouring his flesh, it was as good as over.

The heart in his core demanded his attention, but Bael ignored it. He hadn't exhausted all his options yet. He kept after the servant but was forced to cut through another wall of void and then retreat under the assault of another wave of spheres.

Bael couldn't afford to wait. If the servants had a way of communicating quickly over vast distances, all it would take was a free moment for the servant to summon the emissary, and then the battle would be over for good.

The heart's promise was front and center in his mind, but he didn't need it. He pushed it aside and strode forward, forcing the servant to focus on him. The servant answered with another wave of spheres, and one gouged a shallow hole in his chest before he cut through it.

He breathed deeply as adani roared through his body. Contact with the void had affected the heart, and it tossed and turned like a leaf caught in a strong wind, like frightened prey trying to escape a predator. The adani that he'd kept under such close control started controlling him.

It was a flaw in his plan that he'd never considered. When he'd been a young man, he'd sat at his grandmother's feet and listened to her talk about adani, and one impression that stuck with him, though she'd never said it explicitly, was that adani had a will of its own, a voice that, if one listened closely enough, demanded to be heard.

Bael had never heard that voice, but today he understood his grandmother was right. Adani panicked like a drowning child, stretching into every corner of his body, seeking control where cooperation had once been enough. For the briefest of moments, he fought both void and adani.

He won the battle against both, but the time and effort cost him his fight against the emissary's servant. It had gathered more void spheres than before, a cloud of them hanging above its head, and Bael was in no condition to run.

A powerful wave of adani lit the night sky and crashed into the emissary's servant from above. The blast forced Bael to cover his eyes with his arms and brace his feet. After the wave of destruction passed over him, he cracked open one eye and saw the emissary's servant looking straight up, more annoyed than injured.

The dragon twisted in the air and formed a new weave, which Bael recognized from his own training. He grunted softly. Grandmother must have taught the dragons the weave, as it was one she had mastered. But he didn't know the dragons were capable of it. A shower of darts fell from the sky, each powerful enough to have wiped out any of the city's tallest buildings. The emissary's servant sent its spheres into the sky to intercept the darts, and as they impacted, the void proved its dominance over adani by swallowing the darts whole.

But there were more spheres than darts, and those that remained unused were directed upward. It seemed foolish to believe such small spheres would have any impact on a dragon, but the dragon couldn't evade, and Bael lost count of the track of spheres that struck the creature. Even the dragon's armored scales were no protection against the attack. The animating spirit which kept the dragon in the air, which inspired awe in whoever felt it, vanished, snuffed out like a candle between two fingers.

The dragon dropped like a stone, and the emissary's servant watched.

As ineffective as the dragon's attack was, it served the useful purpose of distracting the emissary's servant. Bael was on his feet before the spheres struck the dragon, and by the time the servant's gaze returned to the broken ground his master had destroyed, Bael was beside it. A sword flashed to life in his grip, and he cut across with all the adani he dared summon. The servant's inhuman reactions gave it time to form a wall, but Bael's sword was too close and his cut too strong. Adani and void contacted, and Bael's sword sliced clean through the emissary's neck.

He fell beside the emissary's servant, cutting himself off from the strength of the heart as quickly as he could. It struggled against the sudden confinement, but like a swaddled child, it soon settled and grew even in his core once again. He took a deep, shuddering breath and looked around. The dragon's roar would never be heard again, and the silence that followed the battle felt absolute.

That silence frightened him until he realized it meant the others had likely succeeded. He'd heard and sensed no other explosions of power, and so it seemed likely their attempt had succeeded.

Either way, tonight they had officially declared war.

And it hadn't been without casualties. Bael took a brief moment to grieve the dragon whose name he'd never had the honor of learning, mourning what might have been.

He forced himself to his feet and ignored the stares of the onlookers who hid near the outskirts of the destruction. He took off at a run through the city streets, intending to meet up with the others back in the hills that overlooked the city.

He left the city as quiet as a ghost, knowing only that the echoes of their actions would be heard around the world.

❧ 33 ❧

If adani had been as simple to master as void, Elyn believed that her world would have become one of the most powerful and destructive forces in the universe. She'd wasted an entire childhood mastering the nuances of adani, and even then, hadn't been able to ascend. Mastering the basic uses of void only took her a few weeks.

Granted, she'd already learned all the skills necessary to shape the primal forces of the universe to her will, and the only reason she'd contacted the void so easily was because she'd already developed her use of adani to a high level. Still, it all seemed too easy, but that was mostly due to the nature of the force she called void.

Void possessed little complexity. It destroyed. Adanists had learned to shape spears, swords, darts, and more. They learned to heal and to nurture life. The emissaries and their servants knew only spheres, the natural shape of the void. There was no point focusing the force, as even the smallest amount destroyed absolutely. For defense, they'd learned how to surround themselves with walls of void, and that was all most needed.

Nor was there any point in attempting to cultivate a greater amount of void, for such matters were largely beyond their reach. Adanists had long known that a healthy body and mind could summon and control more adani, as life begat more life. Void wasn't earned through training, though. It was granted by the force itself, according to one's need and ability.

All of which meant Elyn's training progressed rapidly. Once she learned the wall and the sphere, there was little more to do but practice under different circumstances, preparing for the battles she might someday face. She did learn she had a greater affinity than most servants for the sphere, as she'd grown used to forming adani spheres in her youth. She could hold a dozen spheres of void with little difficulty, a feat most servants wouldn't dare.

The emissary's head servant also taught her the portal technique the servants used, though it was less complex than she'd initially believed. All the servant did was create a door and asked the void for it to open at the desired destination. The technique was simple, once one knew the trick, but only useful to a degree, as it required the void's cooperation. She couldn't travel with her will alone.

She kept learning, though, even after the emissary's servant had run out of techniques to teach her. She studied the servants, and though the emissary rarely appeared, she sensed what she could of him and the others through her connection to the void. Her study was fruitful.

She would have guessed, given how simple the use of void was, that it would promote equality throughout the ranks of the void's servants and emissaries. She quickly learned that was untrue.

Void was straightforward, but to reach it in the first place required a considerable amount of training, and Elyn suspected the nature of that training determined how high one could rise.

The servant that taught her had incredible speed and reflexes, but not because of his mastery of void. That had come from whatever he had been before. That skill made his use of the void more effective, and thus, made him the emissary's most trusted and useful servant.

She noticed a similar pattern among the emissaries, as there were some that were constantly on the move through the void, while others seemed to be stuck in place, like a misbehaving child sent away from the camp until they could calm down.

She noted everything, but found none of it was more interesting than the void itself. The longer she spent on this empty world, the more time she spent listening to its silences, for if she listened long enough, she was sure that it wasn't as silent as she believed. The void spoke to all who were quiet enough to listen.

It didn't speak in words or images, but in feeling and intent, emotions that didn't quite match up to her human ones. The longer Elyn listened, the closer she grew to the void, and in return, it offered up more of itself. After a lifetime of being unable to please Father, to light his eyes the way she once had as a child, the simple nature of the exchange was an almost sensual pleasure. All she had to do was listen and be filled with the strength of the void.

She began to think that she was closer to the void than she'd originally thought. The darkness emanated from somewhere close, or at least it felt that way. She listened, hoping to find it, whenever she wasn't training.

She was listening when her world's adanists struck back. All servants remained connected to the void, their presences like lighter shadows on a dark night, and all at once, many of them disappeared. Their loss shook the void, a silent scream uttered by dozens of voices that echoed long after the source of those voices was dead. Void answered with a shout, and her emissary rushed to heed the summons.

As much as she wanted to remain, to press one ear to the door of the audience about to happen, self-preservation demanded she remove herself. She returned her focus to her body and opened her eyes upon the cave and the dark red sky beyond. It had become night, or whatever passed for night in this place, since she'd closed her eyes, and she didn't know if she'd only been gone a day or more.

She sensed the presence of an emissary, though its considerable strength marked it as different, not hers. It appeared outside her cave and stepped forward with the confidence of one who had bent far stronger wills than Elyn's. The emissary took the appearance of a woman, and Elyn bowed as she entered the cave.

"I don't care about your pretenses, girl. Void knows you, and you are not humble."

Her voice was ice and steel, honed sharp enough to cut the wing off a fly, and devoid of emotion. A far different emissary than the one she knew, then, who possessed almost enough feelings to be human, and susceptible to plays on his pride.

"What will happen to him?" she asked.

"Whatever Void wills. It has been an age since we've suffered such a blow. He lost more than fifty servants in one night. You're from the world. How did it happen?"

"I couldn't guess as to how. But I know who. My father and cousin. No one else would be so bold."

"They may have started a war they aren't prepared to fight. My brothers and sisters gather, ready for the order."

Her eyes never left Elyn's, searching for any reaction. She would have to leave disappointed. "If it is to be, it is to be."

A second emissary appeared in her cave, this one familiar and welcome. He looked at the new arrival. "What are you doing here?"

"I wasn't sure if your head would still be attached to your shoulders after your summons, so I came to care for your prized pupil."

Elyn hadn't realized she was prized, but she couldn't help but compare the two emissaries standing side by side in her cave. For the first time, she realized that her emissary was lacking. Not in any obvious way, but in how the void had blessed him. His strength was incredible, enough to reduce a large part of a city to dust with little more than a thought, but compared to this new emissary, it was nothing.

"I appreciate your concern," replied her emissary, his voice so dry it would have caught fire at the slightest of sparks.

Fortunately, the other emissary remained as cold as ever. "So, what's become of your precious experiment?"

"It continues," he answered.

If she was surprised by this, she didn't show it, but she looked at Elyn as if to ask if she believed.

Elyn didn't know. This acrimony between the emissaries was new to her, an idea she hadn't had enough time to wrap her thoughts around and make sense of. But she trusted the emissary who'd brought her here. He hadn't lied yet.

Sensing her failure to drive a wedge between master and student, the second emissary took her leave, vanishing without another word.

"What was that about?" Elyn asked.

Such questions rarely received answers, but the emissary was distracted, his thoughts not fully here. "My idea is not a popular one, and many have expressed skepticism about the resources it has consumed. Unfortunately, the actions of your family have proven many of them correct. We are weaker than we've ever been before, and the fault is my own. I underestimated the skills of the warriors on your world."

"You know what happened?"

"Not exactly, but I can guess the shape of it. They found a way to sniff out my servants and ambush them."

He went silent, but Elyn had the sense not to interrupt his thoughts. "It wasn't just that I underestimated them, though. I misjudged them. After so many years of peace, I didn't think they had any fight left in them."

"Will you destroy the cities?"

The emissary's laugh was bitter. "No, that was a bluff, though they didn't know it. I can't destroy the cities, at least not in the way their transgressions would demand."

She didn't dare ask why not, but he answered her anyway. "The red hearts are formed at the intersection of life and death. Not only do I need living souls to create and harvest the hearts for me, but if I destroy too much life, there will be fewer hearts."

He clenched his fists, then shook them out. "No, the appropriate punishment here is a more direct one. The attacks all came from a new camp of wandering adanists, and I suspect they pulled all the willing warriors from the other clans. In a way, they've done my work for me, by gathering themselves all in one place. I plan on summoning my remaining servants, and when night falls upon their camp, we shall show them the full power of the void."

He turned to her. "I had hoped to give you more time, or to avoid this choice altogether, but our master has spoken. He's noticed your attentions and returned them in kind, and now orders you to join me. What will you do?"

What could she do? As much as the memories of her childhood scarred her present, she hadn't reached the point where she wanted her family to die. But it wouldn't matter what she wanted. Bael and Father had sentenced themselves to death when they'd organized the attack, and their fate was sealed whether or not she participated. "Will I have to kill them?"

The emissary shook his head. "That duty is mine, and one I'll shoulder gladly. The fight, if it is even a fight, will be quick. You must only be there to protect me from whatever harm they intend."

That he wanted protection was an unsettling revelation, but she barely worried about it, so relieved was she that she wouldn't have to be the one that killed her family.

It wouldn't even be hard. She wanted to protect him. It was the least she could do after all he'd done for her.

"You have my word," she said. "I'll protect you from all who wish you harm."

34

Samora laid her hands on her grandson's shoulders as he rested in a patch of grass outside the tent. Physically, he appeared fine, and while she could guess at the rough shape of his thoughts, she couldn't say how deeply they cut into his spirit. He closed his eyes as she leaned over him, because he wanted to be alone, and if he closed his eyes, he could pretend he was.

The attack had been a success, but not without cost. Fourteen adanists had lost their lives, discovered by the emissary's servants before they could attack. Six servants remained unharmed, and Bael had agreed with Samora and Elian that they should be left alone. They'd spent their surprise, and any further aggression would cost far more than they were willing to pay.

She wondered, as she looked at her grandson, if the years had made her too cold. The skin around his eyes was puffy and red, and he sometimes sniffed through a runny nose. She could heal his physical symptoms, but there was little she could do to take away the new emptiness that threatened to consume him.

Would she put herself in his place, if she could? Grief was no stranger in her spirit, and she could argue she'd lost much more than Bael ever had. Mother and Father, Karla, Harald, Brittany. A child that had never made it from her womb. So many more, more than she could count, taken by violence, by sickness, and lately, by the simple and inevitable advancement of age. Each a scar that had never fully healed.

No, she decided. She wouldn't trade places with him. She'd earned the acceptance that sat in the core of her spirit. A part of her wanted to tell him that it would fade and pass, the same as all memory, but it was a cold comfort, and one he'd discover for himself once he'd lived long enough.

They were his friends. Warriors he'd drawn to himself over the years who'd believed in him. He needed to find his own way to accept their loss and accept his responsibility for their deaths.

She was more concerned with the adani tearing through his body. He'd returned on the back of a different dragon than the one that had carried him to Nevan, burning like a bonfire against her senses. Even the dragon looked sick having him so close, and as soon as he'd dismounted, had hurried away. The adanists that had ridden with him had thrown up once they touched ground, and poor Shayna had to be carried to the healing tent so someone could help smooth out the turbulent flow of adani within her.

Even Samora, who'd wrapped adani around herself to protect her spirit from the worst of his strength, felt her stomach churn.

She'd never felt anything like what was happening in his body, and after all she'd explored and seen, that statement of fact carried a weight most wouldn't understand. It wasn't just the amount of adani, which was greater than even she or Elian could summon, it was how it rushed through his body.

Boundaries. It was all about boundaries, and how she couldn't sense any within him.

Like blood, adani typically ran smoothly through channels in the human body. Not physical vessels, like the bloodlines that ran from the beating heart in one's chest, but more like lines of force that could only be sensed with adani. The channels, with training, could grow and accommodate more adani, or they could wither and weaken if exposed to poisons or wounds. Elian's channels were almost as expansive as his physical body. If the adani in most humans was like a tree, with the human core serving as the trunk and the fingers and toes serving as the twigs and leaves, Elian was all trunk.

And yet, and yet, he still possessed channels, a clear separation between his physical body and the world and strength of adani. He had boundaries.

Samora couldn't find Bael's, couldn't make sense of what was happening in his body at all. She felt his flesh under her fingertips, as solid and real as the grass or the bushes hiding them from the sight of the rest of the camp, but to her senses, his skin was part adani and part flesh, at times one and at other times another, and sometimes both.

She forced herself to keep her eyes on him. He was Bael, but he was also something else, something she didn't understand. The logical part of her wanted to put a fraction to him, to claim he was two thirds human and one third adani, but a fraction implied a separateness, and there was no separateness. He'd reached a place where logic didn't dare tread, and every time she sought an explanation, her mind threatened to tear itself asunder.

She let her adani return to her body and scooted a little farther away to give him space. Her throat was tight, and her thoughts were as slippery as a fish fighting to escape from her grip. She hadn't lost her grandson. He was right there, opening his eyes, and though he tried to hide his fear she saw him again as a child, afraid of the mysteries of this world. She grieved as though she'd lost him, even as she wondered what he was becoming.

He cleared his throat. "Well?"

There was nothing she could tell him he didn't already know. He'd always been sensitive, and the changes worked upon his body weren't subtle. She couldn't answer his questions, as he'd gone further than any of them. "I don't know, but whatever is happening to you will reach its conclusion soon. I'm not sure how you've lasted as long as you have."

He took the news as though she'd told him of his imminent death. "Soon as in…?"

"Today. Tonight, at the very latest."

He flinched. He'd expected longer. But he set his jaw and nodded. "Would you spread the word to gather? I'd like to share a meal with them."

Samora nodded, and her grandson closed her eyes, seeking an inner peace that had long been denied to him. She stood and left, nodding to Shayna, who'd been waiting a safe distance away, as she passed. Shayna returned the gesture and took her place, and Samora's heart broke for both of them.

SHE FOUND Elian outside the camp, sitting cross-legged with his eyes closed. She sat down next to him.

"He won't last the day as he is," she announced.

Elian didn't open his eyes, and Samora suspected it was because if he did, a tear or two would trickle down his cheek. "Do you have any idea what will happen to him?"

They'd already speculated endlessly, and so there was nothing more to be added. "No."

"I still wish I could take this burden from him."

"I would, too, if I could."

They sat together in silence, and though nothing was said, Samora's churning emotions gradually subsided. Elian wouldn't like the comparison, but he had something of the same effect on her as Aldrick. Both men were the rocks that formed her foundation and allowed her to reach for the heights that she had. If not for their quiet support, their silent belief in her, she would have given up long ago.

"Do you ever regret any of it?" she asked.

Elian gave that little grunt he gave when he found something funny, a sound that fell just short of a chuckle. "When the young ones ask me that, I always tell them no, because all the hard times have brought me the gifts I treasure most, like my clan and my family. And that's true, but the real answer is that it depends on the day. Today I wish I'd found another way that allows our families to thrive without risk, even though I don't think you can have one without the other."

She didn't respond, and after a few moments he asked, "You?"

"Right now, I regret that I ever heard of adani, and that I ever wanted to learn more about it."

She was grateful he didn't remind her that without adani they'd likely all be long dead, because of course she knew that. He'd always understood her, even when they'd been so young.

After another moment he said, "I choose to believe he'll find his way through. That he'll be stronger than us and better than us."

"But even if that's true, will he still be himself?"

Elian released a long, slow exhale. "I certainly hope so."

THEY GATHERED as Bael had requested, and it felt painfully obvious to Samora that too many had gone missing the night before. Any laughter around the circle felt forced and died quickly. Most kept looking to Bael, whose transformation was such that almost all had some sense of what was happening in his body, but he made his way around the circle, talking with his friends in small groups as everyone filled empty stomachs, celebrated their success, and mourned their losses.

Samora felt as though someone had hidden a number of needles in the grass where she and Elian were sitting, and she kept shifting her weight in a futile attempt to get comfortable. She'd expected some speech from Bael, some farewell in case the transformation meant the end of him. Instead, he acted like nothing was wrong. Some of his conversations were short, and others were lengthy, but his step grew lighter as he moved from one small group to the next.

Eventually he reached Samora, who sat with Elian and Capricia, the oldest group of adanists in the circle, and it wasn't even close. He sat down among them, a bowl of stew in his hands that was almost untouched. His first question was directed to Elian. "Will you lead them, if I'm gone?"

Elian nodded once.

"Thank you. And thank you for all you've done for me over the years. You've always been my favorite great-uncle."

Elian snorted. "I'm your only great-uncle."

"And you still only barely won the title."

Elian snorted again and shook his head but cast his eyes down. Capricia's hand went to his knee and squeezed.

Bael turned to Samora, and her heart felt as though it weighed as much as a dragon. It wasn't right, that his adani would rejoin the world's before hers. Parents were supposed to die before their children, and long before their grandchildren, and the fact that adani had both granted her long life and stolen Bael's was a bitter, bitter medicine.

Bael seemed to see into her thoughts. "Don't make this another burden you force yourself to carry, grandmother. It's not for you."

"Easier said than done."

"I've always found my greatest comfort in your stories, and that's as true today as always."

She didn't understand, for what story had she told that could guide him through this?

"You told me about the journey your adani went on before the battle with the Vada, about how you felt you were one with adani, and how comfortable and at home you felt."

Samora didn't remember ever telling Bael that story. She

thought only Elian and Aldrick knew it, but apparently Bael's ceaseless questioning had forced it out of her long enough ago she couldn't remember.

"There are times, now, when I feel it, too. When I let go of myself, just for a bit, and it's warm, comfortable, and right. I don't know how to explain it, but I'm ready, now. I think it will be all right."

She didn't bother trying to hide the tears that rolled down her cheeks, and he rose to his knees, knee-walked over to her, and wrapped her in an embrace. "I love you, Grandmother. I love all of you. Will you let Mother and Father know, if I don't return?"

Samora swallowed hard and nodded. "I love you, too, and I'm proud of you. Always have been."

Bael's eyes were rimmed with red when he let her go, and he bowed to the group and went to the next. The older adanists ate their stew, grieving alone but together.

Eventually Bael spoke to the last of the groups, stood, and took one step into the circle, which was already quiet but went perfectly silent as he looked around and smiled.

Samora thought he almost looked sheepish, standing around and being the center of attention. He was a leader, but not one naturally born to attention. He was a leader who attracted, rather than pulled along.

Bael scratched at the back of his neck, then said, "I keep thinking there's more that needs to be done or said, but you all can sense what's happening to me, and I think I've said everything that needs to be said to each of you. I'm not sure what's going to happen, but if I'm gone, I'd ask that you listen to Elian. He's guided me well, and I trust him to do the same for all of you. Otherwise, I just wanted to let you know that I love you all, and I'm so, so proud of what we've done here. You all are the future of the clans and the future of this world, no matter what happens to me. So take good care of yourselves, and don't be too stupid."

Beside Samora, Elian snorted yet again, and they shook their heads in unison, but the words had done their work and then some. The adanists here had already been willing to die for Bael, and some of their friends already had, but now he'd won their spirits, too.

The meal continued for a while after, and it was as though Bael had singlehandedly lifted the gloom that hung over them all. No longer was the laughter forced, and it often spread like wildfire around the circle. Samora didn't think she'd ever felt so many hearts beating as one, and it wasn't just a metaphor. The hearts in their cores kept the same time, pulsing together with a strength that raised her spirits.

Eventually they returned to their tents and the camp found a new rhythm. Samora tended to the injured while Elian led another training session for those who hadn't had enough fighting today.

That night, Samora sensed the moment Bael began the transformation, and sat up straight in her bed as his adani disappeared and dispersed through the land. Not long after, Shayna found her, tears in her eyes but her back straight and her voice proud as she announced that Bael's body had vanished in an instant.

Samora nodded, not knowing what else to do.

✦ 35 ✦

Bael's strange disappearance saved their lives. After the meal the makeshift clan had expected Bael's death, but the vanishing of his body left them wondering what came next. If he'd merely died, they might have found their way to sleep and then been surprised by the emissary's rude arrival, but his disappearance kept them on edge, kept them awake, kept them searching beyond the camp for signs of his return.

Elian was no different than the rest. He sat in a small circle with Capricia, Samora, and Aldrick, and threw another log on the fire to keep it burning. Tired as he was, there would be no sleep tonight. Not when it seemed possible that Bael might return at any moment. Other campfires burned around the camp, other adanists sat around their own fires, frequently sending out their adani for any sign that Bael had reappeared.

Because they weren't asleep, and because they had their adani extended, they sensed the arrival of the emissary's servants as soon as they appeared. Warning bursts of adani exploded across the camp, and Elian was on his feet in a moment.

Their fortune seemed too perfect to be coincidence. If they hadn't spent the last few weeks training to sense the emissary's servants, they wouldn't have sensed their quiet arrival. If Bael hadn't left in such a way that left them searching, they would have slept through the opening wave of the attack. So many ifs, all aligned to keep them alive as the emissary tried to deliver the fatal blow. It was the sort of coincidence that made Elian wonder if adani still guided them in its subtle and opaque ways.

The first wave of void spheres arrived moments after the emissary's servants, but the adanists were already out of their tents, golden swords, spears, and knives in hand. They slashed, stabbed, and clubbed the spheres, and though a few adanists suffered wounds, not a single spirit rejoined the great web of adani in that first attack. The dragons, sensing the danger, took off into the sky, and Elian hoped they had the wisdom to stay far away. There was nothing they could do here, and there was no need for any of them to lose their lives to the emissary.

Capricia strode through the battlefield beside Elian, throwing out her senses so he could keep his adani close. "There are six surrounding the camp," she announced.

He didn't know why there were so few, after this camp had brought down nearly ten times that number the night before, but he didn't question Capricia. If she claimed there were six, there were six. "Where's the closest?"

She pointed north.

"Then we kill it," Elian said.

They were both connected to their hearts, and Elian slowed a bit so they could run at the same pace. Void spheres came at them, but not as many as Elian expected. His sword flashed in the dark, relying on adani more than sight to guide his blade. Adani bit through the void, rushed through the world, across his body, and into his blade, overwhelming the void and slicing it in two.

The sky turned a warm gold as dozens, then hundreds, of adani spears took to the air, the combined might of a clan mourning the loss of their leader. The light allowed Elian to see the next two spheres he cut down and explained the lack of resistance to his charge.

He sensed Samora's hand behind their tactics, a better battlefield commander than him though she hated fighting. She'd gathered many in the camp and coordinated their attack.

The spears by themselves weren't dangerous. The emissary's servants could simply cast their walls of void between them and the falling spears, and the void would consume them. But they tore the servants' attention in two, and that was all Elian and the others needed. The spears landed, only a few at first, but then more, expending their incredible energies against the void, which swallowed it all without so much as cracking. The blasts rumbled the ground beneath his feet and turned the night sky as bright as day, but he maintained his charge, reaching the void wall just as the light faded from the last impact of the spears. He swung his sword, and adani and the void battled, but once again, his constant adani overwhelmed the void.

Half a dozen spheres greeted him as he passed through where the void wall had stood, but then Capricia was in front him with both her daggers carving bright lines through the attack. She didn't try to stop them all but cut down four and left the last two for him, confident he would cut through them without trouble. She threw her daggers at the servant, not to hurt it, but to force it to defend once again.

It blocked the daggers with spheres, but then Elian was there and cutting with his blades, and there wasn't a servant in any world that could have avoided him. His sword went clean through the servant once, twice, and then a third strike took off the servant's head. Easy, but he and Capricia had fought enough battles together over the years that they moved as one, and Samora's coordination from the camp had given them an incredible opportunity.

Strong as the servants were, six weren't enough to threaten the camp, and the emissary was no fool, so why send them?

His answer came sooner than he cared for, as the emissary arrived with another two servants. It announced its arrival with a surge of strength, the same push and pull he'd felt the day that the center of Nevan was destroyed.

Here, though, it didn't attack a defenseless city, but a camp that had just lost the reason they'd all come together, and they were angry. Not only that, but they had Samora, who'd studied under Karla. A bolt of lightning shot down from the star-filled sky, writhing like a serpent caught in a trap as it carved its way across the emissary's position.

Walls of void rose to greet the lightning, and the emissary finished preparing its attack. Elian sprinted in its direction, not needing Capricia's direction to feel its strength. He left her behind, his steps rapidly outpacing her own. He wouldn't be fast enough, though, and he knew it.

Another bolt of lightning stuck at the new arrivals, but this one came from below, summoned from the land like a mighty tree that grew in an instant. The servants, still holding the wall above them, weren't prepared, and the emissary was forced to drop its attack to defend itself. It formed a wall below its feet, and lightning lit the air as it crawled across the wall, searching for a gap to exploit.

Elian hadn't known Samora could do that.

Karla had only been able to summon lightning a handful of times before burning herself out, but Samora had the heart, and her assault was relentless. Many in the camp joined the attack, flinging hundreds of spears in the direction of the new arrival. They sped low, burning through tall stalks of grass as they sought a gap between void above and below.

The emissary raised its hand, and a new wall flickered into existence, but this one took the shape of a sphere. Samora's lightning played across the outside as spears thundered helplessly against it, and every moment it was up was one Elian came closer.

The frontal assault never broke, no doubt thanks to Samora's leadership. A constant stream of spears hammered against the wall and Elian angled for the backside so he wouldn't get caught in the deadly bombardment. He shouted as he drove his sword into the sphere.

It wasn't like the ones he'd attacked before. This void wasn't just hungry. It starved, and he gulped as a vortex of adani opened in his core. His body responded instinctively, pulling an enormous amount of adani from the ground below, so much that he felt as though his feet were on fire. The adani rushed through him, stretching his enormous adani channels to their limit. His shout became a scream as more and more adani rushed through him, more than his body had ever channeled before. He was being poured out into the void. The whole world was being poured into the void, which gobbled it up faster than children at supper after a long day in the fields.

When the void vanished, he stumbled forward, and for the briefest of moments, he feared the flood of adani through his body would be the end of him. His body continued to pull adani through his feet, but now it had no outlet, and his spirit and flesh bulged with excess.

A deep breath, and then something else, subtle but unmistakable. An invitation, extended by adani, a certainty that if he simply surrendered, he'd become more than he ever had before. An offer to shoulder the burden he'd hoped to take from his nephew, half an evening too late.

But the emissary was right there, its two servants, one man and one woman, standing before it, holding walls of void to protect it from the onslaught of spears, and Elian controlled more adani than ever before. He couldn't surrender anything, not now.

He breathed out and shot forward, breath, body, and adani moving in unison. The distance between him and the emissary disappeared in less than the blink of an eye, but then the male servant was there, impossibly fast, and Elian cut, but his sword met a sword of void. The forces warred as Elian kept his blade pressed against the other's. The void blade shattered, but the emissary's servant retreated fast enough to avoid a fatal blow. Elian's sword cut across the servant's shoulder and down his chest, but not much deeper than a scratch.

No matter. He'd broken the servant's defense and adani clamored for release. He stabbed out, only to find his blow deflected by the second servant.

Not a servant, though, as he realized as he cut at her exposed neck.

His daughter.

The blade of adani winked out of his hand as though it had never been more than a figment of his imagination.

Half a dozen spheres of void surrounded her, and she launched them without hesitation. Elian's body responded on his behalf, thrusting adani forward and absorbing the worst of the blows, but they still felt as though a giant was landing powerful body blows. He staggered and stumbled back. He grasped for adani, but his focus was shattered, and it slipped through his fingers like water.

It was his daughter. He recognized every line on her face, and knew, without her saying a word, that she was furious at him.

She'd been furious at him for a long time, though, and nothing he said or did seemed to make it any better.

The battle that surrounded him continued as he stared. The other servant had returned to the defense of the emissary, who was once again summoning that terrible power to lay waste to the camp. Elian could still reach it, but Elyn stood between them, and another set of spheres danced above her head.

She wouldn't. Even at her most furious, she'd never wished him dead.

But how much of his daughter remained? In the light of another pointless wave of adani, he saw that flecks of black void floated in her eyes. He took a hesitant step forward and held out his hand.

Elyn launched the spheres.

The threat sharpened his focus, returning adani to his will. A sword appeared in one hand and a dagger in the next, and he cut his way through the spheres, which didn't race at him the same way the others had. A lack of control, or a lack of desire?

He didn't know, and the question was meaningless. The emissary's attack was almost ready, and Elian was the only one close enough to stop it. He summoned all the strength his heart would give and sprinted for the emissary, giving Elyn a wide berth.

She shifted, though, keeping herself between him and the emissary.

"It's going to kill them!" Elian shouted.

"Yes," she said, and the voice was his daughter's, but the words couldn't have been.

"I don't want to hurt you!"

Elyn snarled. "Hasn't stopped you yet."

The words drove him back a step and disconnected him from his heart. What had he done to her? How had he failed her, to allow her to become...whatever this was before him?

He still thought of her as his little girl. He'd barely seen her enough as an adult to form new memories of her. She'd been so convinced she'd be stronger than him one day, and she'd worked so hard, and he'd been so proud. Did any of the girl he'd loved still exist?

He didn't have time for the questions. He'd waited too long to ask.

The emissary completed its preparations and flung a single sphere forward. Elian sensed it without difficulty, but there was nothing he could do. It sped toward the camp, far more powerful than the blast that had destroyed so much of Nevan.

❧ 36 ❧

Samora had done everything she could think of. She knew, as soon as the emissary's servants had arrived, that those who attacked them needed aid, and so she shouted for anyone who could hear her to attack the servants with spears. The servants, overwhelmed by the adani falling on them from above, weren't prepared for the adanists below. They'd fallen quicker than Samora had expected, and she'd wondered why they'd attacked at all.

Somewhere in the back of her mind, she'd known the emissary would appear. It had lost too many servants not to respond, and the only question had been what form that response would take. As soon as the servants had appeared, that question had been answered.

She'd directed adani at the emissary, knowing it would be nothing more than a distraction at best, but what else was there to do? Elian was close, burning with as much adani as she'd ever felt from him, and if anyone had the slimmest of chances against the emissary, it was him. She could trust him completely. She always had.

She'd done what she could, throwing her own darts at the

emissary's shields, content with being a distraction that allowed Elian to strike.

He'd failed.

The servants had stopped him. She couldn't sense why, exactly, but he'd been bested, or at least delayed long enough for the emissary to launch the sphere.

Time slowed as the sphere sped across the land. Had it been shadow it would have killed the grass beneath it, but void was more contained. She sensed the destruction about to be unleashed, the amount of void within the sphere somehow much greater than the size of sphere.

And what could she do? Attacking it with adani was pointless. Once it cracked open, it would unleash its destruction, and its power was such it didn't matter if the sphere was in their midst or still in the hand of the emissary. It only threw the sphere to protect itself. Her strongest shield wouldn't do much more than slow it down, but with nothing else to try, that was what she did.

She didn't sense Arok's arrival until she caught a blur of enormous color in the corner of her vision. By the time she focused on him, the almost elder, and one of Elian's closest companions, had flown straight into the sphere.

Samora swore and wove more layers of shield on top of those she'd already completed. There wasn't time to tell the others to take cover. The sphere of void dug deep into the dragon's flesh, and Arok roared loudly enough to shake the land. One adanist behind Samora dropped to his knees, but still had the presence of mind to throw a spear in the emissary's direction.

The void stuck Arok's core, which held a reservoir of adani only slightly less than a heart, and it cracked as adani fought against it.

Samora weaved one last layer of her shield, then closed her eyes and braced herself. There was nothing she could do for the adanists who left the camp to attack the servants, but maybe, just maybe, she could save those who remained beside her.

The void unleashed all its pent-up potential, expanding in a sphere that greedily devoured everything it touched. It started with Arok's adani, which absorbed an incredible amount of the void's expansive force, dampening the blast even as it spread through his body. His enormous bones, ancient long before Samora had been born, contained more of the blast, and the scales that had protected him from generations of threats contained a little more.

Samora sensed it all, the void spending nearly half its potential energy within the dragon's body.

Unfortunately, that left a whole lot untouched.

Arok's body didn't explode, for which Samora was grateful. As powerful as his death was, it was at least quick. The void worked its way outward, devouring adani, bone, scale, and muscle, and then raced outward as it finally broke free of Arok's sacrifice. Samora pulled all the adani she could from her heart and reinforced her shield with all the strength available to her. Adani rushed through her feet, cycled through the heart, and raced to the shield.

The blast struck, and the void and adani did battle once again.

Had Samora not been connected to the land and connected to her shield, it would have blasted through without problem, but she was, and adani and void warred for dominance. She felt as though she was trying to hold back a rockslide by herself. She groaned as the weight of the blast settled across her body, but she did hold back the rockslide, and the void spent itself long before her will or body broke. After the roar of the dragon and the blast of the void had faded from her ringing ears, Samora sent out her adani to see if Elian was still alive.

He was, though his battle with the emissary's servants had reached some sort of impasse. She sensed that he had a few new injuries, but nothing that would slow him in any meaningful way. Capricia was the only other adanist who'd charged the emissary to survive, most likely because she'd followed Elian and had been roughly behind the emissary when the void erupted, but she wasn't moving, and from her position, Samora guessed she'd gotten caught near the edge of the emissary's protection. Safe enough to survive but wounded enough that she wasn't going to help in the battle to come. All the other adanists who'd struck down the servants were gone, leaving only those who had remained behind in the camp with Samora. The emissary and its two closest servants were untouched, but everything else beyond her shield was gone, at least on the ground. Up high, most of the dragons had flown beyond the reach of the blast.

The blast left the ground leveled for hundreds of paces in all directions, making it seem like Samora and the adanists she'd protected stood on the tip of a peninsula. The only sound was that of clumps of dirt raining softly from the sky, no small amount of it dropping on the tents behind Samora.

Did they retreat? She glanced back, and what she saw didn't reassure her. Bael's friends and allies had trained to fight servants, but the power of the emissary was something else altogether. Unfortunately, it was too late for them to turn their backs and run. They couldn't outrun either the spheres or the emissary, and it wouldn't be satisfied until they were dead.

With no other options, she raised her hand and chopped it down as though it were a sword, and when it stopped, her finger pointed in the emissary's direction. The adanists were slow to obey, but they obeyed, and it wasn't long before another wave of spears arced up and toward the emissary, who was already summoning another of those dreadful spheres.

Elian had grown brighter against her senses, but he still wasn't attacking the emissary's second servant, much less the emissary that threatened to destroy them all.

She glanced back again at the adanists, and in their eyes she saw the truth reflected. She could form another shield, but unless a dragon or two came down to sacrifice themselves for every sphere, her shield wouldn't hold.

Elian still hadn't attacked, and it was only then Samora realized that Elyn served the emissary now, and she stood between Elian and the emissary.

The revelation added another stone to her burdens, and she didn't think she could carry any more. They were lost, then. Elian would never attack Elyn, no matter what tortures she forced him to endure, and she couldn't say the same about Elyn.

She called to the dragons, then turned one last time to the adanists behind her. They'd accomplished much, but it would be good for them to live to fight another day. Especially if Bael found a way to return. He'd want them by his side. "Retreat on the dragons," she shouted, and then walked alone toward the emissary.

Even if she couldn't win, she could do her best to protect them.

She smiled the way Elian did before a battle. A quick handful of void spheres came at her from the emissary's servant, but she batted those away with a sword with ease.

Her spirit dove into her heart, and then through her feet into the web of adani below, and for a moment, she felt everything everywhere, and everything was in her, and it was good. Warmth flooded up through her toes, around her calves, and embraced her legs and torso before traveling down her arms. She was almost home for good, now.

She spared a thought for Aldrick, and their ever-growing number of grandchildren, for she'd miss their companionship. Many might not understand, but Aldrick would, and it wouldn't be that many years before his adani joined hers in the heart of the world. Maybe it was nothing but a pleasant dream, but she liked to imagine their spirits, entwined together as they traveled the web of adani for the rest of time.

And who knew? Perhaps it was even true. If her time upon the world had taught her anything, it was that the world and life was full of more mysteries than knowledge. She was no dragon but connected to the heart, she figured she could absorb more than enough of the emissary's next blast to protect the adanists behind her.

Samora took another step forward and spread her arms out wide, gathering as much adani in each hand as she could. She shaped the power into the familiar weave of a dart, the tip of which was powerful enough to have destroyed the village she grew up in. She hurled the darts at the emissary and waited for its inevitable response.

The first answer to her efforts, though, came from an unexpected direction. A familiar voice she hadn't heard in many years. Adani spoke to her again, a language beyond words and images and yet perfectly clear in its intent. It was an invitation, an open hand waiting to be taken. And all she had to do was follow.

Once before, she'd been offered such an opportunity. And though her logical mind believed she had chosen well, her spirit sometimes wondered if it wouldn't have been better to accept that first invitation. She had feared, though she wouldn't admit it even to Aldrick, that the invitation would never come again.

So tonight, she had no hesitation as she reached out and took adani's hand and let it erase the thin boundary that still remained between her and the force. It consumed the boundary with a startling intensity, reminding her almost of the void in the way it destroyed the gossamer threads that made her Samora.

And yet, she surrendered easily because a part of her had been waiting for this moment for over forty years. Light seeped from her skin, bright enough that when she turned back, she saw the adanists who were rushing to their dragons casting shadows.

She offered them a final farewell and then turned to the emissary that had already taken so much.

But before adani consumed her completely, Elian unleashed an attack that caught even her by surprise.

37

E lyn stood before her father, holding half a dozen spheres of void above her head and hoping that this battle would end before either of them had to strike at the other. It had been easy to support the emissary's plan on a distant world, where all she had to rely on was logic and the countless memories of the wrongs that had been done to her. But now that she faced her father, she wasn't sure she could truly hurt him, wasn't sure she could recklessly attack him with sphere after sphere.

But why not?

Father had done nothing but hurt her for her entire life. He was responsible for everything, both before and after her failed ascension. He deserved each one of these spheres and more. He might not see it, but his resistance to the emissary would kill thousands, if not more.

She knew both what was required of her and what Father deserved, and yet the spheres remained, hovering above her head.

Father had a bound sword in one hand and a golden dagger in the other, but they unraveled as he took a tentative step toward her. He opened his arms and invited her closer, despite the fact she held her spheres as tight as ever.

Maybe she wouldn't have to attack. There was no denying her master's dominance over the battlefield. A single sphere from the tip of his finger had sent the clan adanists scurrying to their dragons and back to their respective clans. He probably didn't even need to kill them anymore. The one blast had scared them into obedience for the rest of their lives.

A new golden glow began to emanate in the direction of the camp, and Elyn quested with her adani to understand it.

She would recognize that aura anywhere. That was Aunt Samora, and she'd grown more powerful than Elyn remembered. Much more powerful.

Still, the display was pointless. Whatever strength her aunt had discovered, it was too late to change the course of the battle. She turned her attention back to Father, then froze as she witnessed the expression on his face.

He'd forgotten about his daughter completely. If she threw her spheres now, they were certain to strike true and end this battle with one decisive stroke. But she hadn't been able to bring herself to kill him when he had his blades bared, and she was even less capable killing him without him fighting back.

Elian stared at his sister, his mouth moving, repeating a silent "no" over and over. Eventually, he found his voice, and though the battlefield had gone quiet, she only barely heard him say, "Not her, anyone but her."

Elyn turned back to Samora and sought whatever Father noticed that she did not. But whether she quested with sight or adani, she sensed nothing of concern. Samora's power grew, but not fast enough to make any meaningful difference, and yet Father looked as though Samora was about to die. He was more terrified of whatever was happening to her than he'd ever been of what happened to Elyn, his own daughter.

She snarled at the thought, but before she could do anything with her anger, Father's adani surged as though he'd swallowed two dragons in one bite, and he exploded forward. Caught with her head and her senses turned towards Samora, Elyn couldn't react in time to stop Father's backhanded blow across her cheek.

It snapped her head around, lifted her off her feet, and sent her twisting to the ground. The surprise of being hit by her father overwhelmed the pain, and she brought her hand up to her cheek to confirm what had happened. She'd never before felt the full force of his strength.

Father darted past her, and she was forgotten as his focus shifted entirely upon the emissary, who himself seemed distracted by Samora's sudden growth in power.

She cursed herself. She'd failed to protect her master.

Thankfully, without the constant wave of adani from the camp threatening them, she no longer protected him alone. The head servant blurred in her sight as he intercepted Elian, and the two exchanged a series of cuts too fast for Elyn's eyes or senses to follow.

For all Elian's strength, he couldn't surpass the speed and precision of her master's most favored servant. The two fought to a draw, and there was nothing more to be done. The emissary had seen enough of whatever it was that had interested him, and he lifted his finger to end it all.

Except she didn't want it to be over. Not yet.

Father's hit would do no more than sting her cheek for a time, but it had broken the last thin string that had bound her to her past morals. The string that had no amount of terrible memories had been able to cut.

She rose like a shadowy wraith and turned her full fury upon her father's fighting figure. She'd lost the spheres from before, but it was nothing at all to make more. Adani still flowed through her, but it was like a distant creek she could barely hear off in the distance. All she felt was the void, and she welcomed its cold, constant embrace.

Father cut once, then twice, and most of her spheres vanished, but one struck true. A flash of adani protected him from the sphere penetrating too deeply, but the blow still rocked him backward. He continued retreating as the head servant chased him.

She didn't launch the next sphere until she knew her shot was perfect, and as it sped towards its target, she knew her aim was true, and that Father had no idea about the danger that approached.

The sphere caught him in the side, and Elyn sent another small sphere at him as soon as the servant was out of danger.

It caught him in the side of the head and hit Father harder than she'd expected. He stumbled to the side, and her heart pounded in a bitter, vengeful celebration that was every bit as fulfilling as completing a year's harvest.

She launched another swarm of spheres before Father could recover and before the head servant could interfere. Adani still protected Father's body, but not like it had before. Her spheres cut deeper and deeper, each an act of revenge for a memory that she'd been forced to endure during her training with the emissary's servant.

One sphere caught him under the chin and burrowed into his jaw, a suitable punishment for all the times he'd encouraged her to push herself farther than she should have gone. Another sphere dug into the side of his hip, and it was for the night she had overheard Father reassuring another child in the clan that they wouldn't end up like her, that the child had done everything right and there was nothing to fear when they attempted their ascension.

A final sphere drilled straight through his calf, and that was for the way he'd looked at her when she'd announced she was leaving the clan. A look that made her feel like she was the one in the wrong for leaving.

The spheres kept landing long after Elian stopped resisting, and each dug deeper and deeper. He screamed, but it was a distant sound that hardly reached her ears, and when it did, it sounded more like music than agony.

She didn't stop until a light in the direction of the now-empty camp exploded in the darkness.

38

B*ael.*
The name echoed in his spirit, but he couldn't remember why it carried so much weight. Who was Bael?

Once, the question had been easy to answer. A body that separated spirit from the web of adani that surrounded it. Memories, friends, and family that each contributed a small piece of identity. A story that he'd created by weaving those fragments into a narrative, a tale of a person.

He'd lived every day of his life believing the story was real, that all those fragments he had collected and painstakingly organized mattered. That they were as real as the grass he walked upon and the meat he ate at the evening meals.

Adani had gathered up those fragments and whisked them away, then burnt them in fire. His body was gone, and he was no longer a lover, a fighter, not even part of a wandering clan.

And yet the name remained. The spirit remained, which had always been woven into the body. He remained, though he was none of the things he'd thought he was.

Adani surrounded him, and he knew not what to do. Though it surrounded him, it lacked the shape and definition of his spirit.

He had a sense of motion, though it was indistinct, as there was no clear separation between his spirit and the river of adani he was caught in. It felt fast, though, and his physical surroundings felt heavy.

The current dumped his spirit into a sea of endless adani and the sense of movement faded. He tried to move and found it a simple matter. He could race along any line of adani with barely a thought, though when his effort was expended, he always returned to sea at the heart of it all. It was more than he'd ever known existed, sitting at the center of all adani. A heart of hearts, more powerful than anything he'd sensed before.

Time passed, though he couldn't say if it was the blink of an eye or the passing of a generation. The sea, which had been perfectly still, thrummed, and though it spoke without words, he recognized the invitation. To return to the surface and become...something. Bael, perhaps, though the question of what Bael was remained unanswered.

It was warm here, though, and comfortable, and if he refused, it would be no trouble to him at all. He'd never known true peace, and it was difficult to surrender. Here, he'd be content forever.

The sea thrummed again, reminding him that forever wasn't as long as he thought, if void conquered the world. Adani was eternal, right up until it met the void and wasn't.

He burned hot, hotter than the adani that surrounded him, and that fire was a barrier of sorts, a separation between him and the welcoming arms of pure adani. His snort was derisive. He'd had plenty of peace over his years, and he'd been raised for war.

Now that the war was here, he was missing out.

Quick as thought, he rose to the surface. Bael rose to the surface, his awareness growing stronger with every pace he approached the night sky. He understood adani better than he ever had, and it carried messages about the battle on the surface. It spoke of Grandmother, about to begin the same transformation he'd undergone. He listened to Elian's screams as Elyn tortured her father.

More than anything, though, he sensed the emissary and the incredible amount of void it was prepared to unleash upon the world.

Reforming the body he'd once known was a simple process, now that he understood the underlying structure and understood so much better how adani could create. He'd gone through most of it once already, when he'd come back from the wounds the emissary's servants had gifted him. They'd be disappointed to know their attacks had served as something of a trial run for his transformation.

He looked down at his hands as though he'd never seen them before, and though it was true, the hands were as familiar as every other sensation flooding through his limbs. A slight breeze tugged at his hair, and the cool air of the night sky sent a shiver down his spine.

It wasn't his body, but it was everything his body had been and more, and it was glorious. Why embrace the everlasting peace of adani when one could have the rich sensation of being embodied?

He looked up, and his eyes saw both levels of existence at once, the physical world he'd been first born in and the world of adani that he'd grown into. The emissary and its servants stood out among the brightness of the world. Both servants were a mixture of light and void, but the emissary was pure void, the opposite of his own rebirth.

The servant he didn't recognize came for him first, leading his assault with a dozen hastily formed and thrown spheres of void. Bael let them strike, and they carved out holes in his new flesh. Pain was yet another wonderful sensation but was easy to over-come. With no more than a thought his flesh was restored, a feat which earned him the emissary's full attention.

"Get back!" the emissary shouted to his servant, but it was

too late. Bael didn't move so much as shift his position, a process as quick as thought and will could make it, and the servant's eyes went wide as a blade of adani jutted through his throat. Bael flattened the blade and made it wider, and the surprised head rolled from its previous perch on the servant's neck, down his sword, and onto the ground.

The emissary had already prepared the void sphere and threw it the moment the servant died.

Bael held out his arm and the void sphere struck him in the center of the palm. It began consuming adani as soon as it made contact, enough that even a dragon's deep reserve wouldn't have lasted longer than the beat of a heart. Nothing else on the world would have survived, but he was no longer a creature separate from adani, but an expression of it. The void consumed its fill, unravelling his arm as though it were a bound sword more than flesh and bone, but in the end, it spent itself, and with a thought, his arm was restored.

He was pleased by his success until he saw the emissary create three more spheres, each as powerful as the first.

ELIAN FELT as though he'd been lying down as a line of dragons had taken turns walking over him. The spheres had broken or destroyed most of him, and he feared that even Samora's best healing wouldn't restore what had once been his. All he could do was stretch his neck, and he was grateful for that much.

Samora still burned with the power of potential transformation, and when Elian wasn't fearing for his own body, he worried about his sister. She'd discovered the secret that had eluded them both, and now he was close to losing both a sister and a nephew on the same day.

Then Bael arrived, or at least, a presence that felt like Bael. He glowed like a second sun and moved faster than Elian's eyes could track.

Elian stared, mouth agape, at this new transformation, the direction adani had pointed them in.

It was beyond amazing. The speed, strength, and sheer power of the form was beyond Elian's imagining. The servant that had matched swords with him fell to a single cut of Bael's blade, and the emissary's attack, powerful enough to destroy Arok completely and still wipe out most of the surrounding land, barely slowed him for a moment.

Humanity was in Bael's hands now, and Elian believed in his nephew. He had no choice, for he was out of the fight for good.

As Bael and the emissary battled, Elian reached out to Samora, the connection more difficult to establish than it had been since they'd first discovered how. She was there, but the rush of adani flooding through her body formed a barrier. He thought he was connected, but he felt nothing from her in return.

"Don't do it," he said.

She didn't respond, but the adani that had been constantly growing in her slowed. Whether it was because she was questioning her decision or because she was already reaching her limit, he couldn't guess.

"Don't do it," he repeated, "I can't lose you."

He felt the weight of her attention fall on him, and finally she spoke. "I'm not sure it can be stopped."

His head fell and the back of his skull hit the ground hard enough to jar what remained of his teeth. He could still watch the unfolding battle between the emissary and Bael, though, and could soon predict the course it would take.

In terms of raw ability, they were close to equal, though it was hard for Elian to tell, vast as their powers were. But the emissary had lived with its powers for countless years, and Bael had just woken to his own. Experience would make all the difference.

"Please, don't leave. Bael needs everyone's help, including yours."

"Which is why I need to go."

"There's no promise you'll return in time. Please, summon the others. It all has to end here."

That, finally, made her stop and consider. Then she broke her connection and launched a wave of golden adani high into the sky, visible for miles and miles. Before the light had faded from the darkness, she'd bound a handful of darts and flung them at the emissary.

Elyn sensed the attack, and with the other servant dead, had no choice but to abandon his broken body and defend the emissary.

Elian watched her go, her departure a dagger into his heart that not even Samora could heal.

BAEL RECOGNIZED THE SECOND SERVANT, the one who had beaten Elian to a bloody pulp on the other side of the battlefield. Elyn now served the emissary, and if she'd fallen so far that she would strike down her own father, she deserved no mercy from him. Her wall of void consumed Grandmother's darts without problem, freeing the emissary to focus exclusively on destroying Bael. Spheres darker than the surrounding night sped toward him, and he didn't dodge, so much as shift around them. They still struck close, and he threw up a shield of solid adani as the force of the blasts battered his defenses.

The blasts had barely faded when another set of spheres struck his shields, shattering them and barely slowing as they did. The first sphere took his left arm, and the second struck him in the chest, coming close to destroying his core.

He jumped, like a frightened rabbit, back into the web of adani beneath his feet as the spheres exploded.

SAMORA SWORE as the distant blasts forced her to shield herself from the destruction the spheres unleashed. Adani filled her body from toe to crown, and its invitation to join her was more persistent than the one she'd encountered so many decades ago. It was forceful, attempting to dissolve the barriers that kept her spirit separate from the web that flowed through all living things.

She didn't give it the opportunity. She broke her connection with the heart in her core, which cut off the pathways adani used to force itself deeper into her body. Breaking the connection had never been painful before, but it felt as though someone had reached deep within her core and pulled the organs out. She doubled over and gritted her teeth.

Thankfully, the emissary was no longer interested in her. She'd felt its attention as adani invited her into union, but it had slid from her as Bael had arrived.

And now Bael had...fled? The news adani returned to her senses confused her. For her entire life, her sense of a person's adani equated to where they were, and at the moment, adani told her that Bael had dove deep underground to hide from the spheres that destroyed the land above.

In a flash of insight brighter than one of her darts exploding, she understood the nature of Bael's transformation. Like the Vada, he could take whatever shape he desired, including no physical shape at all. His core, his spirit, remained intact even as it dove deeper into the ground than any human had dug with a shovel.

The maneuver had kept him safe from the spheres, but Elian had convinced her to summon the others, and even now the dragons returned with their riders. If Bael wasn't on the surface fighting the emissary, she'd doomed them all.

She tried to reach for him with her adani, but his spirit danced along the webs of life faster than she could follow.

Thankfully, he returned to the surface on his own, only a few paces from where he'd disappeared. His body looked whole and healthy, and his stance told Samora everything she needed to know about his conviction. A white sword appeared in his right hand, and he leaped toward Elyn and the emissary just as the dragons arrived with his makeshift clan.

AN UNLIKELY CALM had fallen over Bael after he'd hidden deep within adani's web, born of a confidence he couldn't justify but accepted anyway.

The dragons, loyal guardians of adani since long before humans had made their appearance, carried Bael's clan toward the battle, and only one obstacle prevented them from turning the tide of this fight.

Bael fixed his eyes on Elyn, silently apologizing to her.

Some additional sense must have warned her about his attention, because she turned to him as he shifted toward her. She threw up a wall of void, and the emissary threw a sphere to intercept where Bael would have run, but he shifted around the sphere easily, and her shield shattered as soon as his sword made contact. Then he stood before her, and her eyes went wide.

He'd intended to cut her down, but at the last moment he twisted his wrist and struck her across the top of the head with the pommel of his weapon. Her gaze went blank as her body twisted and tumbled into the grass.

The emissary's retaliation struck barely a moment later, a rain-cloud of small spheres Bael's physical body would have never escaped. Instead, he ducked into the web of adani and reappeared to the emissary's side.

He couldn't match the emissary's skill at distant attacks, but he'd trained his whole life with a bound sword in his hand, and he shifted closer to the emissary. Once, he'd believed he was almost as strong as the creature, and now he was certain he could kill it with his blade.

He understood its speed better now, for it was a mirrored image of his own, and as the emissary tried to evade, Bael kept beside it, looking for a devastating opening.

He still took the emissary too lightly. It kept ahead of him without problem, dropping spheres as it retreated that threatened to shred Bael's core into ribbons. Try as he might to keep up with the emissary, he eventually had no choice but to pause his pursuit while he sought a better way.

His answer came from above. Dragons and adanists, flying high enough to avoid the greatest of the emissary's dangers, dropped powerful darts. The emissary formed a wall of void above itself, but it frowned when Bael seized the moment and charged again. It looked up, then back at him, then came to a decision.

The creature's limbs began to fade, and Bael swore.

He shifted again, snapping along the weakened lines of adani until he was behind the emissary, white sword in hand. The emissary's head whipped around as its limbs regained solidity, and Bael cut at its core as it released a sphere of void directly into his.

He sensed his sword cut through the emissary's core, a clean strike even as the emissary tried to shift the core's position within its body. His sword passed through flesh and core, and then empty air.

But though the emissary was gone, its last attack remained, and it burrowed straight toward his core before releasing its incredible latent energy.

🪬 39 🪬

Elyn woke and immediately regretted it. Every beat of her heart sent a fresh wave of agony ripping across her skull, and when she moved, a sharp pain shot down her neck. Her limbs were sluggish, as though her muscles had been replaced with water.

Nothing compared, though, with the reverberating void that threatened to crack her bones and split her skull in two. It reminded her of when the emissary had lost so many of his servants, except this was so much worse. Void was angry, and its servants bore the brunt of its rage.

The emissary had been killed, then. Bael was the only one who could have done that, so there was no further explanation needed. Her spirit threatened to break in two, as though she'd lost not just one but two fathers today.

Once again, she'd failed, just as she'd failed at everything else she'd tried. She couldn't be an ascended adanist, and now she'd lost her only hope at becoming someone useful. She couldn't even revenge her master. Against whatever Bael had become, she was nothing.

She gritted her teeth together and pushed herself into a

kneeling position where she could look around. Dust billowed to the north of her, where the emissary had been killed. She thought, perhaps, that the emissary had taken Bael with him, but as the dust cleared, she saw Bael on his knees, an enormous hole in his chest.

Except he was somehow breathing without lungs, and when she blinked, he was whole again, and she wondered if she'd imagined the injury.

Without the emissary, what was left for her? Dragons and adanists flew in the skies above, their shouts falling from the sky like bitter rain. They'd land, soon, and she was in no condition to fight. These were the warriors that had trained to kill servants, and her vision still went blurry every time she moved her head.

They'd kill her, especially once they discovered what she'd done to Father.

She turned to find him but couldn't see him beneath all the dirt that had settled in the aftermath of the fight. She could sense him, though, his adani weaker than she'd ever felt before. A child could have beaten him up.

Either she'd spent her anger or Bael had knocked it out of her, because even the thought of him did nothing to spark a fire in her spirit. She'd woken up hollow. Not filled with the emptiness of the void, which was its own comfort, but just...numb. She thought about her farm, about transporting herself back there and trying to live as a simple farmer again. It would take the clans time to recover, and maybe, once their tempers had cooled, she could beg to be spared so long as she remained on her land.

Except, no, the farm had never been for her. It had been a role to play, a way to fill her time, but it had never grown roots in her spirit. She'd always wanted something more for herself, and the emissary had recognized as much.

She stumbled to her feet, and there was still enough dust in the air she didn't think she attracted any special attention. Her freedom wouldn't last long, but it would be enough.

She did the same as all children did when faced with tragedy: she ran home, which wasn't the farm or a wandering camp, but a cave on another world. She formed the portal, as the head servant had shown her, and the void allowed the connection, so she stepped through without a glance behind her.

***

BAEL PAUSED outside the healing tent and swallowed hard. Shayna squeezed his hand, and the gesture was like a bucket of cool water dumped over him on a hot day. It reminded him that they were both here, even though he wasn't exactly sure what "being here" meant for him anymore. She didn't care, though. She remained by his side, the same as she always had.

No thanks in the world were sufficient repayment, but fortunately, none were required.

"I'd rather fight a pair of emissaries," he confessed quietly.

She squeezed his hand again, and the simple physicality of it grounded him. One of the problems with being able to be anyplace with little more than a thought was that it was hard to be wherever he was. Adani constantly flooded him with information, and he'd soon found the hardest thing in the world to pay attention to were the people and events right in front of him. Shayna's touch kept him here, kept his attention where it needed to be.

"I know, but he's been asking for you."

He'd promised to visit, but now wasn't sure he could keep his word. Elian was a giant. The man who had defeated a Vada and guided the wandering clans through the longest peace in their recorded history. He was strength personified.

Not this.

Bael nodded and stepped into the tent before he could convince himself otherwise. His eyes adjusted instantly to the darker rooms, and they were greeted by Grandmother, who'd hardly left the tent for the last three days. She'd lost too much weight, her skin was pale, and loose skin hung from her arms. He'd heard about and sensed the amount of adani she'd used simply to keep Elian alive, and he'd guided more her way, but as all healers knew, sometimes no amount of adani was enough. Some wounds couldn't be healed. Despite it all, she smiled when she saw him. "He'll be so happy to see you."

Bael spoke lowly, so his voice wouldn't carry. "How is he?"

Grandmother looked as though she might cry, but she took a deep breath, stood straight, and composed herself. "He'll live, though I'm not sure what that will look like. The void took more out of him than just muscle and bone, and adani doesn't respond within him the way it should."

"Do you know why?"

Grandmother shook her head. "If you discover anything, as you're close to him, let me know."

Bael swallowed the stone that had appeared in his throat and wiped his eyes, then nodded. He and Shayna followed Grandmother to the back of the tent, where Capricia sat next to a cot. His great-aunt's eyes were sunk into her skull, but she still looked better than Grandmother.

He stopped when he caught his first clear view of Elian. He'd heard, of course. Everyone had. But seeing it in person was a different form of torture. Grandmother's healing had restored some of his flesh, but the void had taken too much. He had holes in his body where muscles had once been, and the bottom of his jaw was a misshapen mess.

Bael imagined that even eating would be a challenge for Elian now, and there was no question that he'd never fight again.

That, somehow, was the worst of it. Elian was nothing if not a fighter, and if their positions had been reversed, Bael knew he would have wished for death. Of course, Elian still had gifts to offer and wisdom to share, but it wouldn't be enough, not for a man who'd lived and trained his entire life to protect those he loved.

He forced himself to look, no matter how he wanted to turn away. Elian had given everything for the clans and for humanity, and this was his reward, betrayed by his own daughter.

Difficult as the injuries were to look at, seeing the light gone from Elian's eyes was even worse. As long as he'd known his great-uncle, Elian had always been looking forward to something. Even when he'd joined Bael in exile, he'd looked forward to the future. That lively gaze was no more, buried forever underneath a mountain of betrayal.

Bael searched for the words, but anything he'd normally say to the injured sounded hollow here. Elian would live, but never get much better. He'd never lead a charge again, nor hunt to feed his family. What comfort could Bael offer?

Elian reached up with his left hand, the one closest to Bael, and Bael instinctively took it. He'd felt the power of Elian's fist before, and little of that strength remained, but Elian squeezed his hand tight.

"Good...to see you." Elian stopped here, though Bael had the sense he wasn't done. Elian turned his gaze to Shayna and said, "Together."

Bael understood. "It's good to be back, and together."

Elian shifted his head, a small gesture that Bael took to be a nod.

"The clan...yours," Elian said.

Bael wiped his eyes with his free hand, then clasped Elian's hand between both of his. He bowed deeply. "I won't let you down. I promise it."

Elian shifted his head as he had before, then looked away, tears welling up in his own eyes. Capricia shifted uncomfortably on her stool and shot a nervous glance at Bael, who understood this, too.

Bael bowed again, and though he knew Capricia wanted him

gone, knew that his presence only hurt Elian and reminded him of what he'd lost, he couldn't bring himself to just leave.

Except there was nothing he could do. He saw Elian not just with the eyes of his birth, but through the eyes of adani as well, and Elian's core was broken, his adani ravaged by the twin burdens of overuse and void. Elyn had struck him at the worst possible time. Bael could direct adani into Samora for an eighth-day, and still there was little more she could do.

He bowed one last time, then left without a word.

If he couldn't promise healing, he could at least promise revenge. Elyn had disappeared after the fight, which meant that someday, more servants or more emissaries would come for his world.

But when they did, they'd find at least one wandering clan ready for them, and they'd be angry.

ALSO BY RYAN KIRK

The Legend of Adani
Born of Light and Shadow

From Shadow to Flame

The Ascension of Light

Children of Light and Shadow

Legacy of Light and Shadow

A War of Light and Shadow
Waterstone

The Rise of Shadow

The Shadows Beyond

The Last Sword of the West
Last Sword in the West

Eyes of the Hidden World

A Sword Named Vengeance

Wraith's Revenge

Frontier's End

Song of the Sagani

Legend of the Sword in the West

Nightblade
Nightblade

World's Edge

The Wind and the Void

Blades of the Fallen

Nightblade's Vengeance

Nightblade's Honor

Nightblade's End

Saga of the Broken Gods

Band of Broken Gods

Fall of Forgotten Gods

Rise of the Resurrected God

Oblivion's Gate

The Gate Beyond Oblivion

The Gates of Memory

The Gate to Redemption

Relentless

Relentless Souls

Heart of Defiance

Their Spirit Unbroken

The Sentinels Saga (with Taylor Crook)

Path of the Eternal Sun

A Path Divided

A Path Reforged

Primal

Primal Dawn

Primal Darkness

Primal Destiny

Song of the Fallen Swords

These Fallen Swords

Standalone Novels

The Last Fang of God

Blades of Shadow: A Nightblade Story

ABOUT THE AUTHOR

Ryan Kirk is the award-winning and internationally bestselling author of over thirty fantasy novels spanning nearly a dozen worlds. He lives in Minnesota with his family, where he enjoys long, meandering walks outside even when the snow is high enough to cover his legs. When he isn't glued to his keyboard, he's usually in the woods, either on foot or on bike.

facebook.com/waterstonemedia
instagram.com/authorryankirk
bookbub.com/authors/ryan-kirk

.